EMPIRE STATE

Also by Henry Porter

A Spy's Life
Remembrance Day

EMPIRE STATE

Henry Porter

ORION

First published in Great Britain in 2003 by Orion,
an imprint of the Orion Publishing Group Ltd.

A CIP catalogue record for this book is available
from the British Library.

ISBN 0 75285 683 9 (hardback)
0 75285 684 7 (trade paperback)

Set in Minion

Printed in Great Britain by
Clays Ltd, St Ives plc

All the characters in this book are fictitious,
and any resemblance to actual persons living or dead
is purely coincidental.

The Orion Publishing Group Ltd
Orion House
5 Upper Saint Martin's Lane
London, WC2H 9EA

For Graydon Carter

Acknowledgements

Thanks are due first to my agent, Georgina Capel, who showed great faith in this book from the start, and also to Jane Wood, my editor, who tirelessly made suggestions and gave me encouragement during its writing. She was helped by Sophie Hutton-Squire. It would be difficult to overestimate their contribution, or that of Puffer Merritt, who read and corrected the first draft with her usual enthusiasm and generosity.

The idea for *Empire State* came to me on a fishing trip organised by Mark Clarfelt in June 2002. So I thank him for the happy accident that set off a train of thought, and also Stephen Lewis, Matthew Fort, Tom Fort, Jeremy Paxman and Padraic Fallon who unwittingly nurtured the plot during the course of a very idle afternoon by the river. My friend David Rose introduced me to Hadith literature, Roger Alton made many clever suggestions, Lucy Nichols helped with occasional research and Aimee Bell gave me the 1949 first edition of E.B. White's hymn to New York, *Here is New York*, which contains some inspirational thoughts used here.

During the research of a book of this nature there are many who help but cannot be thanked by name. I was particularly grateful to a man who, at some risk to himself, arranged a tour of the Egyptian prison system, and then found the island where part of this book is set. My contact in Albania was also invaluable. He shed light on his mysterious homeland and gave me insights into the history and workings of the intelligence service.

Empire State is a work of fiction – no secrets are betrayed here – but there is some authentic detail which has been gathered from numerous sources. Without them I would flounder. In parts of the book I drew from actual incidents. There *was* an al-Qaeda cell in Albania. Five suspects were arrested in a CIA-backed operation and flown to Egypt where they were tortured before being tried. Two were subsequently executed. I have also used part of a story of a group of migrant workers who were gunned down by the Macedonian security forces on March 2, 2002. At the time, it was alleged they were terrorists, planning an attack on the US and UK embassies in the Macedonian capital, Skopje, a claim which the United States government was unusually forthright in rejecting.

Finally, I would like to thank my wife, Liz Elliot. Throughout the writing of this book, as with the others, she has been the source of much support and good judgement.

PART ONE

CHAPTER ONE

The passenger known as Cazuto arrived in the Immigration Hall of Terminal Three, Heathrow, in the early afternoon, carrying a raincoat and a small shoulder bag. He joined one of the lines in the non-European Union section. Looking mildly about him, the American registered the two uniformed policemen with Heckler and Koch machine guns on the far side of the immigration desk, and then a group of men who were clearly searching the lines of travellers about to enter the United Kingdom on that stupefyingly cold day in May.

Larry Cazuto, in reality Vice-Admiral Ralph Norquist, guessed they were looking for him and noted the urgency on their faces. This interested him because they could not have known which flight he was on. His schedule was kept secret even from his wife and secretary, who knew only that he would be in Europe for a time, not on what day he was travelling or that he would be seeing the British Prime Minister and his intelligence chiefs.

The President's special counsel on security matters decided that he would not at that moment make himself known. Instead he did what comes easily to a middle-aged man with a paunch and a slight academic stoop – he merged with the crowd and turned his benevolent gaze to the line forming behind him. He glanced upwards to the security cameras but none was trained on him and it was clear they weren't sweeping the surge of travellers in the Immigration Hall. In front of him, a woman in her late forties – rich-looking and attractive in a brash way – was struggling to change her phone from an American to a European service while keeping hold of several pieces of hand luggage. He leaned into her vision to ask if he could be of assistance, and as she replied she dropped the open passport clamped in her teeth. He picked it up and returned it to her, noticing the semi-circular impression of lipstick on one of its pages. 'You've given yourself a visa stamp,' he said pleasantly.

The woman smiled. As she took the passport, one of the bamboo handles of a large tapestry bag escaped her grip and the contents tumbled to the floor. He crouched down and helped her again. As she swept everything back into the bag with the speed of a croupier, he examined her and wondered whether he imagined the intent that pulsed briefly in her eye. She got up, thanking him profusely and they went together to the desk, where he made a point of looking over her shoulder to see if the name in her passport matched the initials on the silver cigarette lighter that he'd retrieved from the floor. This was second nature to him and it struck him as odd, and almost certainly significant, that they did not tally, not even the first name and initial.

By now the men on the other side of the barrier had spotted him. Norquist recognised one of them; the knobbly faced Peter Chambers, a senior bureaucrat from MI5 whom he'd met eighteen months before.

'I'm afraid we've got an emergency, Admiral,' said Chambers. 'We're going to escort you into London.' He gestured to a man who had come up behind him. 'This is Sergeant Llewellyn from the Metropolitan Police Special Branch. He will…'

Before Chambers could say any more, Norquist held two fingers to his chest then jabbed them in the direction of the woman, who was now headed down the escalator to the Baggage Hall, her bags hooked over her shoulders and the little gold-coloured mobile raised to her ear. 'Can you check her out? Her passport says her name is Raffaella Klein but she has the initials E.R. on her cigarette lighter. She seemed to be making a point by dropping everything. This may help,' he said, slipping Chambers a chip of plastic the woman had failed to pick up and which he'd palmed as a matter of course. It was the SIM card for her US phone service and it would tell them everything they needed to know.

'We'll get right on to it,' said Chambers. He beckoned to a lean, casually dressed man who had been hanging behind the two armed police officers and gave him the card. 'Get Customs to search her and then keep her under observation.' He turned back. 'Now, if you don't mind, sir, we're in a bit of a hurry. Your luggage has been taken directly to the car. I'll explain everything once we're on our way. We really *must* go, sir.'

'If you've got the baggage it means you know the name I was travelling under.'

'That's rather the point, sir. Your security has been compromised.'

They made for a door at the side of the hall, which opened from the inside as they approached, and passed along a corridor of mostly empty offices. Here two policemen in anoraks and fatigue trousers joined them, so a party of more than a dozen descended three flights of a metal stairway, causing it to vibrate with a dull ring. At the bottom the corridor turned right and led to a fire exit where a security officer was on hand with a swipe card. He signalled to a surveillance camera above and operated the lock, throwing both doors outwards. The fumes of aviation fuel and the noise of taxiing aircraft filled the corridor. Rain slanted through the door. Norquist began to put on his raincoat, but Llewellyn took it from him and passed it, together with Norquist's bag, to one of the policemen behind. He waved the two uniformed police out to a line of four cars just visible off to the right.

'We're having to make this up as we go along,' said Chambers. 'We've had very little notice.'

Norquist shrugged. 'Right,' he said.

They waited a few more moments until a voice came over Llewellyn's radio. The rest of the men bunched round Norquist and they spilled from the door in a security rush, holding his head down until he was in the back of a black Jaguar. Chambers climbed in beside him; Llewellyn got in the front. The rest of the men divided between a dark green Range Rover, a Ford saloon and a BMW which brought up the rear.

'What's going on?' asked Norquist.

'We understand they are going to make an attempt in or around the terminal. I'm afraid this arrangement is far from ideal. We'd have preferred to use a helicopter to get you into town. We may yet have you picked up on the way, but the main thing is to get you away from public areas of the airport now.'

Norquist nodded patiently as if being told of some further minor delay in his schedule. The plane had already stopped for two hours at Reykjavik with a computer fault.

'We think it's a big operation. No details though,' continued Chambers, giving him a significant look which was to say that he couldn't talk in front of the driver and Llewellyn.

The cars moved off, weaving under the piers of Terminal Three. They had to slow for aircraft manoeuvring in and out of the gates and occasional service vehicles that blocked the route across the concrete apron. The squall that had blown in from the south-west didn't help their progress either, and several times the Jaguar hesitated, either from poor visibility or disorientation in the sprawling tentacles of the airport. After a few minutes they cleared Terminal Two and set off at speed over the open ground between the take-off and landing runways, towards the vast hangars on the east side of the airport. They were held up once by a yellow airport car to allow a 747 to be towed across their path from the service hangars. Instead of taking the exit by the British Midland hangar off to their right, they moved towards the head of the runway a few hundred yards away, close to the eight aircraft waiting to take off. Rain and exhaust from the engines blurred the landscape and they had to slow to look for the exit. Someone spotted a policeman on a motorbike waving in the distance.

Llewellyn yelled into his radio over the noise of the engines. 'Route Three. Is that understood? Route Three.' He sat back as the cars started forward and said under his breath, 'Let's hope this works.'

A little over a mile away a man held a Bresse Optic telescope to his right eye and scrutinised the procession of vehicles with twenty times magnification. The few plane spotters that had remained with him through the rain and poor light on the observation terrace of Terminal Two also trained their binoculars and telescopes to the head of the southern runway – or, as they referred to it, Runway 27 right. But when the four cars veered off through the grass margins of the airfield towards the emergency gate in the perimeter fence, their interest returned to the line of Boeings, followed by two Russian-made aircraft – a Tupolev Tu-154 and a Yakovlev Yak-42 – which by chance landed seventy seconds apart on the northern runway – or 27 left.

The men on the observation terrace mostly carried telephones. Some even held hand-radios with which they chatted to fellow enthusiasts around the airport. So it was perfectly natural for the man with the Bresse Optic to turn away from the noise of a taxiing Tunisair flight, to gaze across Heathrow's roofscape of air-conditioning ducts and radio masts and dial a pre-set number on his phone. Muffled in their anorak hoods, absorbed in the comings and goings of the jets, fiddling with their Thermos flasks and packets of sandwiches, the plane spotters paid scant attention to what he said about the cars leaving the airport and turning right towards the A30.

A surveillance operation of an entirely different kind had just ended in the Terminal Three Departure Lounge when a mixed team consisting of an Arabic speaker from MI6 named Isis Herrick, three officers from MI5 and four members of the police Special Branch were pulled off the observation of Youssef Rahe, an Arab bookseller. They were told by New Scotland Yard and MI5 headquarters at Thames House that an important American had just arrived in the terminal and that the highest possible priority was being accorded to moving him from the airport to Whitehall. The Prime Minister's armoured Jaguar, being driven back from Cardiff to London without its usual passenger, had been diverted to Heathrow. Through her earpiece Herrick then heard that the four undercover policemen with her were being summarily removed from the mixed surveillance team and would be armed with handguns in a room near the Immigration Hall.

Herrick and her three slightly dour colleagues from MI5 – Campbell, Beck and Fisher – went off to have coffee, Beck caustically remarking that the Special Branch officers had taken with them the keys and parking receipts for two of the three cars. As they sat, they were informed that the few Special Branch officers permanently stationed at Heathrow had also reported to the Immigration Hall. She realised this meant that Youssef Rahe would leave Britain unobserved, except by the security cameras. It was no great disaster. As an anonymous voice pointed out from MI5 headquarters, Rahe, a minor intellectual figure in London's North African Community, represented no threat to the aircraft whatsoever. He and his baggage had already been thoroughly searched and he was, after all, travelling on

7

an Arab airline to an Arab country. Once he got to Kuwait, the cooperative members of the local intelligence service, al-Mukhabarat, would watch him and log any contacts he made.

Still, Rahe's hasty departure from the Pan Arab Library in Bayswater had interested Herrick because there was no warning of his trip. He travelled little, spending most of his days seated at the desk in the front of the store, glasses dangling on a chain, testily answering customers' questions or consulting his computer. He was not a key figure by any means: they weren't even sure if he had connections with Islamist groups. However, during the sweep of Arab communities in Britain the name of the bookshop had come up, and it had been learned from the FBI that a suspect arrested in Canada had visited it while in London.

Herrick had been assigned to the operation for a few days. She had taken the first appointment at the hairdresser that lay diagonally across from the Pan Arab Library. She arrived just before it opened at 9.45 a.m. and by ten she was in position at the seat nearest the window where the mirror allowed her a clear view of 119 Forsythe Street, an unusual nineteenth-century building, Italianate, a cut above its neighbours.

Rahe usually appeared in the shop just after ten, having left his family in the flat above, and unlocked the door from the inside to a sluggish morning trade. The plan was for her to drop into the bookshop in this slack period, look around for a while and engage Rahe in conversation on the pretext of needing to practise her Arabic. Despite Rahe's unfriendly manner, she'd learned that he appeared to have an eye for English women. The watchers monitoring his visitors from the street and from a room in a flat opposite had noticed he stared longingly at the fair women passing his shop and that he became more helpful on the rare occasions they went in.

'You never know,' said the officer running the surveillance, 'he might take you to dinner. There are one or two very good Leb restaurants in the area where you can order in Arabic and then you can charm him.'

Herrick watched for signs of Rahe in the mirror, but nothing happened until 10.35 a.m. when she saw him step out into the street with a small suitcase and what looked like a folder of travel documents. He was dressed nattily – bright tie, dark grey flannel trousers, olive green

8

jacket and shoes with a showy buckle at the side. A few moments later a minicab pulled up and, after patting his right breast pocket to check his passport in the gesture of nervous travellers the world over, Rahe climbed into the back.

Herrick got up, removed her gown and shook out her almost-dry hair. She reached for her black leather jacket, and announced she'd just remembered she had a meeting. By the time she was outside and calling the other members of the team on her mobile, they had already phoned the cab company and learned that Rahe was on his way to Heathrow. A search for his name on the airline computers began.

Three surveillance vehicles followed the cab along Goldhawk Road and the M4 to the drop-off point for Terminal Three departures. Rahe got out, entered the building then walked out. This he did a total of three times without checking the notice boards for the 2.15 p.m. flight to Kuwait on which they had now established he was booked. At length he seemed to settle something for himself and walked purposefully to the Heathrow chapel near Terminal Two, where he sat in the Garden of Remembrance reading a newspaper and occasionally checking his watch. Herrick thought he seemed unsure rather than nervous, and wondered whether he was expecting to meet someone. But after half an hour he suddenly got up and hurried over to the check-in area, where he waited behind about half a dozen passengers. He did not speak to anyone or, as far as they could tell, use his phone.

Still, his behaviour was considered suspicious and when he got to the security checks he was asked to step into a room and submit to a thorough search involving sensors being run over his clothes and shoes. His suitcase was examined intensively and scrapings of plastic were taken from the handle and sides and tested for explosives. Everything was found to be in order and Rahe was sent on his way. It was at this moment, as he wandered off towards the duty free shops, his dignity visibly ruffled, that the order came from New Scotland Yard that Special Branch officers watching Rahe should instantly drop what they were doing and report to Peter Chambers in the Immigration Hall.

Herrick had grown slightly impatient listening to Campbell, Beck and Fisher discuss the events of the morning in the usual oblique code. Thames House had made the connection between

Rahe's presence in Heathrow and the arrival of the American but had concluded that it was nothing more than coincidence. Besides, a few minutes before the American had been located in Immigration, Rahe's distinctive olive green jacket was seen on the security cameras, making its way to the gate where he duly presented his passport again and boarded the Kuwaiti airliner.

As she was about to suggest they all return to London, Campbell, Beck and Fisher were summoned to the Baggage Hall to observe a woman named Raffaella Klein and follow her from the airport. They left immediately, now intrigued by the flow of commands from London.

Herrick, alone with her coffee and free of the in-house banter of her MI5 colleagues, began to think about Rahe's behaviour. It just didn't seem right that this unimpressive North African had suddenly departed for the Middle East. She wondered if he had a rendezvous on the plane – the best possible place for a long, unobserved talk, as long as you fixed the seating. She drained the coffee and experienced a random flash of memory: fishing with her father in Scotland, making the last cast of the day without hope of a pull on the line. What the hell, she had nothing else to do. She'd go to the security room and see what she could find out about the people on the Kuwait flight with Youssef Rahe.

Fifteen minutes later she was sitting at a desk with the passenger manifest of Kuwaiti Airlines KU102 on a screen and noting down the names of the people seated in Rahe's immediate vicinity at the back of the plane. Around her were three men from Heathrow security who had kept tabs on Rahe by the airport CCTV system as he moved through the terminal to his departure gate. She asked them to print off the complete manifest from the computer, then let her eyes drift to the screen immediately in front of the supervisor, who had compiled a medley of clips showing Rahe as he progressed through the airport. He appeared in the check-in area at 12.30 p.m., a few minutes after the flight opened. At no stage did he talk to anyone or make any sign to a fellow passenger. The cameras then picked him up just after he had been searched and followed him to the duty free shop where he paid for two bottles of Johnny Walker Black Label whisky with cash. Ten minutes later he was seen buying a newspaper, then he crossed the field of another camera and entered a coffee bar. After this he vanished for a period of about twenty minutes, although the supervisor insisted that with a few hours they could piece together his movements for the whole period. As things were, they could be sure that Rahe had got on the plane. He ran the final film and Herrick watched Rahe approach the desk, swap the duty free bag and his little suitcase from his left to his right hand and show his boarding card and passport.

She put her hands to her mouth, aware that her mind was tripping over something. 'That's not the same man,' she said, without consciously understanding what had produced such certainty. 'That's not bloody Rahe!' Vehemence made her voice rise.

'Right gate,' said the controller, yawning. 'And the jacket – I doubt there're two jackets like that on the planet, let alone in this airport.'

'It's the same jacket,' she snapped, banging the desk with her hand. 'But it's not him. Rahe is right-handed. When he gave his passport to the woman at check-in he took it from the left breast pocket with his right hand. Here he's using his left hand to take the boarding card out of his right pocket,' she said, jabbing at the screen. 'Look! He changed the bags over so he could do that. Even from behind you can see they're different – this man's got a narrower head, a longer neck. He's thinning at the crown.'

The supervisor leaned into the screen. 'Maybe you're right. But the angle's not too clever up there. We had to shift our cameras because of work on the cabling ducts for the visual recognition system. It's a shame we don't have a head-on shot of him there.' He knew she was right.

'I've been following Youssef Rahe all bloody morning and that's not him.'

They went back over the footage of Rahe in duty free, and noted how he walked away from the camera with short paces in which his feet veered outwards as they came down. The man who had just boarded KU102 walked with a definite roll and his arms worked more as he went along. There was a further, clinching anomaly. As Rahe waited in duty free he looked at his watch several times, thrusting his wrist out of his sleeve and revolving the gold strap which hung loose like a bracelet on his wrist. The man at the boarding gate appeared not to be wearing a watch, at least not one that could be seen below the sleeve of his jacket, nor as his left hand reached up and plucked the passport and boarding card from his inside pocket. Admittedly, they were seeing him from above and behind, but there was no doubt that while Herrick caught a flash of shirt cuff in this movement she could not see a watch.

She didn't need any further confirmation. She dialled the direct line to the operations room at the Security Services. 'Youssef Rahe didn't get on his plane. There was a stand-in. Rahe may be your problem.'

Route Three took the convoy of cars from the north perimeter road westwards towards Terminal Four along a canyon formed by tall leylandii bushes and noise barriers at the edge of the airport. They travelled at 80 mph with the Range Rover sitting within a few feet of the Jaguar's offside rear bumper. One false move by the Prime Minister's driver, Jim Needpath, and there would certainly be an accident, but he had worked with the protection officer in the Range Rover before. Out in front, five police outriders leapfrogged each other and raced past the convoy of cars to hold up traffic at every intersection. As they came to the roundabout near Terminal Four, they turned left and doubled back along the A30 towards London, the plan being to cross over to the M4 motorway by a dual carriageway and make their way to central London using the fast lane reserved for buses and taxis.

Inside the Jaguar, Chambers was on the radio, demanding to know why there was no sign of the police helicopter that was going to act as a pathfinder into central London. The sardonic reply came back that it was generally considered poor aviation practice to place a surveillance aircraft in the main flight path into Heathrow. At this Norquist smiled and looked out at the dismal housing estate rushing by – people walking with their heads bowed to the rain, a pair of cyclists struggling along in cagoules and an Indian woman sheltering her kid in the folds of her sari. He wondered briefly how the Brits managed to keep their sense of humour in this climate.

The outriders shepherded the motorcade smoothly through the roundabout under the M4 before the four cars rose on a slip road to join the motorway. Two motorcyclists stayed just in front of the Jaguar while the other three formed a chevron to snowplough the traffic out of the fast lane with their sirens and lights. At this point the helicopter appeared and hovered for a second or two at about 1,000 feet before spinning round to join the flow of traffic eastwards. Llewellyn was patched through to the pilot and told him that he needed an exact description of the traffic conditions ahead, and a warning about vehicles parked on the hard shoulder and on or under bridges.

The road was unusually clear and they covered the four-mile stretch quickly, with the pilot giving regular snatches of laconic commentary. Suddenly an interested note entered his voice and he told them he was going to take a look at a white lorry that had pulled up about a mile in front of them at the beginning of the elevated section. As they rounded a bend they saw the truck with the helicopter positioned above it. Llewellyn told the drivers to reduce their speed and then sent the three motorcycles on to investigate.

'What do you see?' he asked the pilot.

'There's just one man in there,' came the reply. 'I'm taking her down a bit. He looks Asian, but I can't be sure. He's not responding to anything we do. He looks a bit freaked.'

They saw the helicopter descend on the left of the motorway.

'Hold on,' said the pilot, 'the lorry's moving. No. He's stopped again. He's put the vehicle across both lanes. You might just squeeze behind him or in front of him, as the cars are doing, but there's not much room either way.'

'That's not an option,' said Llewellyn. It was fast occurring to him that there were very few options. If they tried to pass the lorry and a device was detonated inside, it would certainly blow them all into the next world. And they could not cross the central reservation to the westbound carriageway or mount the bank to their left, which was fringed with dense hawthorn trees. Reversing up the hard shoulder to the service station a mile or so back was the only way left to them, unless the lorry moved of its own accord.

By now the Jaguar and its escort had slowed to 35 mph. The traffic that had been held up behind the lorry had all slipped through the gap and a stretch of about 800 yards of open road lay ahead of them. The two remaining police outriders had dropped back to prevent anyone overtaking the convoy.

'Shit,' said Llewellyn. 'This is a fucking mess.'

'If you can keep this part of the motorway clear,' said Chambers, 'you could bring the chopper down and we can hitch a ride.'

'Let's do that,' said Norquist, his voice moving from compliance to command.

The pilot heard this in the cacophony that was now reaching him from central control, but he had other things on his mind. 'You've got two vans approaching from behind – a red Transit and a dark blue Toyota. They're about half a mile along the bus lane and closing fast. I'll come down and get you, but the wind isn't good for this kind of thing and you've got to do something about those vehicles.'

Llewellyn told the drivers of the two unmarked escort vehicles to fall back and prepare to block the vans, forcing them off the road if necessary. He knew the conversation was being heard in New Scotland Yard and he told them very deliberately to open fire if they judged it to be the only way of stopping the two vans. He was now convinced that an attempt on Norquist's life was in progress and he said as much to New Scotland Yard, adding that it wasn't effing well going to happen on his watch.

The Jaguar and Range Rover shot forward over the next seventy yards then coasted along the hard shoulder, reducing their speed to almost walking pace. Jim Needpath's eyes moved from his wing mirror to the lorry, every part of his being jangling with the imperative to take flight, to bolt from the situation and save his passengers. In front of them they saw the driver of the truck jump down from the cab, run the few yards to the side of the deserted carriageway and scramble up a bank towards the breaking wave of hawthorn blossom. Two of the three police motorcyclists brought their machines to a halt just before a narrow rail bridge over the motorway, kicked them back on their stands and set off in pursuit of the driver. The third drove up to the truck, circled it and accelerated away shouting in his helmet microphone that a liquid was seeping onto the road from the side of the truck. The vehicle was an Iveco diesel but the liquid smelled like petrol.

The helicopter pilot took matters into his own hands and decided to land on the motorway. The aircraft swooped over the rail bridge and flew at a height of a hundred feet towards the Jaguar, throwing up a storm of spray in its wake. At the exact moment that he lifted his nose and settled the aircraft onto the tarmac, the red Transit burst along the hard shoulder followed by the police BMW. The driver of the Range Rover saw what was happening, slammed his vehicle into reverse and went to meet the van, colliding with it a second or two later.

Needpath didn't wait any longer. He shot the Jaguar forward to the helicopter, pulling the car round with a handbrake turn so that Norquist's side was protected from whatever was going on behind them, which was not at all clear because of the roar of the engine and the swirling clouds of spindrift. Llewellyn and Chambers got out, dragged Norquist from his seat and pushed him towards the helicopter, ducking under the rotor blades. They were halfway there when the Toyota van appeared through the mist and hit the Jaguar on its flank, just behind Jim Needpath's seat, and caused it to spin round. The Ford saloon carrying four Special Branch police officers was not far behind, but it slewed to a halt without hitting either car and disgorged at least three of the policemen, who began to shoot at the van. The same thing had occurred on the hard shoulder after the Range Rover launched itself backwards into the red Transit van.

Llewellyn and Chambers didn't wait to witness the battle on the motorway. As they lifted Norquist through the door of the helicopter, a shot glanced off the hard perspex in front of the pilot. Chambers had just scrambled in behind Norquist when the helicopter rose, tipped forward and roared away.

They climbed to 1,000 feet before the co-pilot turned round to check that his passengers were strapped in and saw blood was coming from a wound in Norquist's neck.

He was already unconscious.

CHAPTER TWO

On a grassy bank running down to a swollen stream about ten miles from the Albanian border, a man dozed in the morning light. The sun had not yet risen above the hill in front of him so the ground and his bedding were still wet. For some time he had been aware of his travelling companions moving around him, packing and rolling up the sheets which they'd hung between the bushes to give shelter. They coughed and grumbled to each other, mostly in languages he didn't understand. But the sounds of the camp breaking in the early morning were familiar – men stiff from a night in the open, wondering how they found themselves without bed, food or a good woman.

Someone was prodding the campfire into life. At first he didn't understand why: they'd eaten the last of the food the night before – dried lamb and a broth made from chicken bones – and he knew there was no coffee or tea. Then he smelled the mint and remembered they'd gathered it in a ditch the night before. They'd made mint tea and now one of them was beside him, nudging the back of his hand with a warm tin cup. He opened an eye to see a grin of chipped teeth, spreading in an unwashed, slightly pock-marked face: the youngest of the three Kurds, an amiable character who was always jollying the others on. He said in English, 'Drink, mister, for your health.'

The party began to move off down the bank towards the track, but he still couldn't bring himself to jump up and follow. The delicious memory of his dream was still fresh and part of him didn't want to leave it behind. He watched shafts of light moving over the hill to catch the top of a tree nearby. A tiny bird, one that he had never seen before, was flitting to and from a vine that had become detached from

16

the tree. Each time it arrived to perch on the twig, it bobbed up and down, checking the area for predators before diving into the shade of the vine to feed its young. He realised the bird must have been there all night, within a few yards of the fire and the men under the shelters, and he marvelled at its nerve and discretion.

At length the sunlight fell on the ground above him and he shook himself from his reverie, stood up and stretched. He had only a few possessions and it didn't take long for him to bundle them up and tie them together with the belt that he'd kept with him these past six years. As he made his way down the bank, slipping on the damp grass, the men's voices were brought to him on a soft, warm wind. It would be a good day, he thought. Yes, they were due some luck after all that had happened to them. Maybe they would find a way of crossing the border into Greece without being arrested and treated like dirt.

In the past he might have prayed to Allah. Now it did not even occur to him. After so long in the holy war the Western part of him was reasserting itself. He was leaving the wilderness and the barbarity behind and he was taking back his old name – Karim Khan – and with it the hope of finding the young medical student, who drank alcohol and loved and charmed but who was no less in awe of the Prophet because of these activities. Belief had not deserted him, but faith in sacrifice had gone, along with the *nomme de guerre* – Mujahad, or soldier of Islam – and just now he would rely on himself and not God's will.

He climbed down on to the track and noticed the bunches of twigs that had collected in the ruts along the road, borne there by the rain-water of the day before. Beetles were feeding on insects drowned in the storm. The pulverised rock in the road's surface sparkled with chips of quartz. Everything seemed beautiful and in its place that morning, and he felt a surge of optimism. He shuddered at the words that had taken him to war: 'Allah has conferred on those who fight with their wealth and their lives a higher rank than those who stay at home.'

No more of that. No more slaughter. No more chaos.

But whatever he thought, he was still the veteran campaigner and his ability to march on an empty stomach was undiminished. Soon the stragglers of the group ahead came into view. As always it was his two fellow Pakistanis at the rear. Both were very thin and clearly at the end of their resources. Nine months the two had been on the road. Having started from a mountain village in Northern Pakistan they had crossed to Iran and walked to the Turkish border. Most of their money had gone when a con man promised them flights and a visa to Greece, but they kept enough to get them to Bulgaria. Ahead of them went the Turk, Mehmet, and the Arabs, a Jordanian called Mumim, and a Palestinian from Lebanon who gave his name as Jasur. Out in front were the three Kurds – the young man who had given him mint tea, his uncle and a friend from his uncle's village. They had the promise of work in Athens and had only been travelling for a matter of weeks. They were the freshest of the party and it was clear they felt themselves out of place in this group of migrants, harried from one country to another and sometimes reduced to eating leaves and grubs to survive.

High in the pastures above them Khan noticed one or two locals moving about with their beasts. Cow-bells sounded with an unmusical clank across the valley. He was glad his party was not walking bunched up together because that always made people suspicious. In this country, where Muslims were so feared, they had to keep their wits about them. The men with dark skin – the two Pakistanis and the Jordanian, who had African blood in him – had to be especially careful. Not for the first time, he was grateful for his own light colouring, which family tradition held came from Alexander the Great's soldiers. Some part of him registered that he should feel at home here in Macedonia.

As he was having these thoughts he noticed the Kurds hesitate. He stopped and put his hand up to the sun and tried to see through the shimmer of heat already coming off the road. They had seen something in front of them. One had dropped his bed-roll and knapsack and spread his arms in surrender. He was showing that they weren't carrying weapons. His companions turned round to consult the others, or maybe to warn them.

Khan saw a figure moving in the clump of bushes on the left of the road. He was wearing a uniform that was exactly the same colour and tone as the shaded vegetation. A wisp of smoke came from behind him – a campfire – and beyond that tarpaulins had been stretched across the lower boughs of the trees. On the other side of the road, parked up in a cutting, were a truck and two covered jeeps.

The Kurds didn't seem to know what to do. One of them began to retrace his steps. He was gesticulating, shooing the rest of the party back up the way they had come. More soldiers moved from the shade onto the yellow strip of road; they swaggered and almost dragged their weapons along the ground. Khan recognised the type – soft, untested, conscript bullies. He had seen them before in the Balkans and he knew exactly what was going to happen next.

One of the soldiers, probably the first man to move from cover, raised his gun waist high, fired and brought down the retreating man. The other two Kurds turned back in disbelief to the soldiers, raising their hands. They dropped to their knees to beg for their lives but were killed the instant they touched the ground. One slumped forward; the other keeled over in slow motion.

With the first shot the remainder of the party had taken to their heels. The two Arabs and the Turk ran straight up towards Khan, but the Pakistanis had thrown away their possessions and dived for the bushes. The soldiers were galvanised. They ran across the road, climbed into their jeeps and, with great swirls of dust, turned the vehicles and tore up the valley towards the three men still on the road. Unlike the first shots that had killed the Kurds, the fusillade of gunfire that came from the lead jeep echoed around the hills. The Turk was hit in the leg but limped on. One of the Arabs stopped and tried to drag him to safety, but the soldiers were upon them in a second and both men were mown down. Khan moved to the side of the road into shade. He watched the jeep pull up and the soldiers unleash a volley of shots into the corpses. The other jeep had stopped a little further back so that the Pakistanis could be hunted down. Shortly afterwards Khan heard another crackle of shots. A man cried out. Then a lone shot – the *coup de grâce* – snapped through the woods.

Khan shouted at the Palestinian who was now about a hundred yards away. He knew their only chance was to head off into the trees above them. He yelled and yelled at the man as if willing him to win a race. Khan had been in such situations before and, judging by the way Jasur was bent double and zigzagging the final few yards towards him, it wasn't the first time he'd been under fire either. Together they slipped through a gap in the bushes and began to climb. The undergrowth was still wet from the storm and the soil gave way easily under their feet, but in a few minutes they got above the road and saw that both jeeps had pulled up below them. They heard shouting and a few shots were loosed off into the trees, but it was obvious the soldiers were unwilling to go in after them just yet. A truck arrived and they saw a man get out, an officer shouting at the top of his voice. He was clearly organising a sweep of the hillside.

Khan watched for a few seconds longer, steadying Jasur by holding his shoulder. He looked up the slope and decided that rather than crashing on through the wood and giving away their position, they should stay where they were. He explained in a mixture of Arabic and English, then pushed his still uncomprehending companion into the undergrowth and covered him with saplings wrenched from the loose soil. He went to find his own hiding spot about twenty paces up the hill and dug himself in, efficiently covering his legs with dirt and pulling boughs across him to hide the disturbance. Once in place, he hissed a few words of encouragement down to Jasur just as he had done a few years before when waiting in an ambush with a group of novice Mujahadin, all of them quaking in their boots.

For about fifteen minutes he heard no noise from either the road or the woods around them, but gradually the sound reached him of the soldiers slashing at the undergrowth and calling out to each other. He fastened his gaze on the bushes where Jasur was hidden, hoping that the Palestinian's nerve would hold when the soldiers passed by. He wriggled a little and felt in his back pocket for the knife he'd picked up in Turkey. He placed it in his mouth then swept the dirt back over his chest and arms and sank into the forest floor.

The soldiers were close to them now. He estimated that one was about thirty yards above him while another, who was moving much more slowly, would eventually pass between him and Jasur. He held his breath and waited. Suddenly the uniform appeared a few yards from him. The man stopped, unzipped himself, thrust his pelvis forward and started pissing. The stream of urine glittered in the light filtering through the trees. As he neared the end he shouted up the hill to his friend, a crude joke bellowed to the forest.

Khan decided to launch himself the moment the soldier turned away. Just then, the saplings which had so artfully concealed Jasur erupted, and his head and torso appeared. The soldier was caught unawares. He turned and yelled out a single syllable of surprise. But instead of firing he struggled to zip himself up and seemed to have difficulty getting hold of the automatic which he had swung round on his back while he urinated.

He must have heard Khan behind him, the movement of earth and rush of air, but he showed no sign of it as the weight of his body was pulled back onto the knife. His shaven head came back and his eyes met Khan's with a strange awkwardness, an embarrassment at the sudden intimacy with the man covered in dirt, not understanding that the first blow of the knife had neither punctured his heart nor severed his spinal cord, and that there would be no second blow. Khan let him sag to the ground and in an instant removed his water bottle, gun, and ammunition clips. He wagged his finger at the soldier and put it to his own lips. The soldier looked up terrified, but managed a nod.

Jasur came to his side and crouched down. They were hidden from the soldier above them who had started to call out to his companions, repeating one name. Alarm rang in his voice, which communicated itself up and down the line of soldiers and they all started calling out. Khan darted another look at the soldier and jabbed the gun at him in a way that couldn't be misunderstood. They turned and began to climb, moving around the main thickets so as to make as little noise as possible.

A minute or two passed then all hell broke loose. The soldiers discovered their wounded companion and started up the hill, firing shots into the trees above them. The old maxim of mountain warfare came back to Khan – flight is always better than fight. Long-practised at fleeing into the mountains, he quickened his pace and blocked his mind to the pain that would come with the exertion. They went straight up for a hundred and fifty yards but soon Jasur was begging him to slow down. He had given his all in the sprint up the road. Khan put an arm round him and felt his skinny frame heaving and his heart racing. There was virtually no muscle or fat on him. He tucked his hand under Jasur's armpit and started to haul him up the hill, the Palestinian's breath wheezing in his ear. They went another fifty yards and scrambled over some rocks. Ahead of them the trees thinned out to the pastures where he had seen the cattle herds. Beyond these he remembered the rocky crags that he'd noticed in shadow when he was lying in the field. It meant they were steep, but it didn't follow they were impassable.

He turned round. Jasur, who had fallen to his knees, was silently coughing phlegm onto the rock. His eyes and nose were streaming and his skin had become grey. The medic in Khan guessed these were not tears but some kind of allergic reaction, probably caused by pollen or the leaves he'd been covered with, but when he took hold of his head and looked into his eyes, his diagnosis changed. Jasur was having an asthma attack and showed every sign of heart strain. Khan rolled him onto his back and started to give him mouth to mouth resuscitation, then pressed down rhythmically on his chest a dozen times. The Palestinian coughed again and began to breathe more easily, but his eyes showed that he knew exactly what was happening and Khan thought he'd probably experienced an attack like this before. He put his hand to the man's pulse – more regular now – and lifted his head to give him some water from the soldier's bottle. At that moment they heard the soldiers making their way up the hill. He dragged Jasur back across the rocks so he was out of view and then snaked forward on his stomach to look over the edge. There were four of them and further down the slope came another trio, but they had no appetite for the climb and were stopping every few feet to mop their brows and curse.

He tried the safety catch of the AK47, made sure that the magazine would come away when he needed it to, then lay flat on the rocks with his face resting on the polished wooden stock. As he waited his thoughts slipped back to the first moment of the day and he realised dully that whatever his dreams and hopes for the future, this was the way his life was cast. His fate was to be covered in grime and sweat, waiting in ambush with a murderous old gun in his hand.

Behind him Jasur uttered a dramatic series of gurgles and retches. Khan was worried for his companion but could not risk turning now. He nudged him gently on the shoulder with his boot and that seemed to quieten him. For one moment he thought the change in direction of the soldiers' voices meant they had given up, or taken a path off to the left, but suddenly he heard them directly below him. He pulled himself forward and raised his arms so that the gun was angled downwards over the edge of the rock. After the initial burst he bobbed up and saw that he'd hit some of the first group in the legs. They fell backwards without even knowing where he was. One recovered and fired in the direction of the rocks, a long way wide of the mark. Khan sneaked another look and squeezed the trigger. This sent them tumbling from their cover down the slope. They don't mind killing unarmed men in the open, he thought, but they've got no taste for real battle. He fired, changed clips and fired some more. Now there was no sign of them, although he heard one yelping like a lost puppy in the woods.

He turned and wriggled back to Jasur, lying against the rock, facing away from him. He touched him on the shoulder and said they ought to be going. Could he make it? He shook him and, feeling no life, rolled the Palestinian over.

His skin was ashen, saliva foamed at his mouth and his eyes stared without meaning at the tiny red spiders that circled on the rock surface in front of him. Khan was shocked. Bewildered. He pushed himself to his knees and shrugged, thinking that he should – no, he must – find out who this man was and one day let his family know what had become of him. He felt all over the body and eventually located a little pouch hanging from a string inside Jasur's trousers. He flipped it open and saw some folded documents, one or two pictures, a printed prayer and an identity card. He would look at them properly later. Now he had to leave and hope that the Macedonians would bury the Palestinian.

He got up, and without looking down the hill, jogged off into the next clump of trees and made for the crags above.

CHAPTER THREE

Herrick put down the evening paper. It reported that Vice Admiral Norquist had not recovered consciousness before expiring at 5.30 a.m. this morning, May 15. He had died from heart failure during an operation to remove the bullet that had lodged in his spine. The President of the United States issued a statement saying that the assassination of his friend and mentor was a deep personal blow to him and his family, but more than this, it was another strike against America and all good Americans should mourn his sacrifice.

Thinking that the report was less than complete, Herrick turned to her desk and the FBI watch list, a summary of essential information on every known Muslim terrorist. She found this easier to use than the British version because of its layout and concision. From left to right appear the first names of the suspect or wanted felon, followed by his aliases, date of birth, US social security number (if any), place of birth, address, phone number and email. The far right column gives a unique identity number for the suspect and, in the middle of the page, there is a column headed Function. This column is left blank in the version of the list circulated daily at 8.00 a.m. EST to banks and airlines, and copied into their computer systems so that any transaction made by one of the individuals triggers an alert. But in the thirty-four-page document lying in front of her, the FBI logged trades against the names of some of the 524 men – computer expert (trained engineer), weapons and explosive expert, strategist/trainer, banker, facilitator and communications specialist. Most were guesses and the addresses and email accounts had long been abandoned, but the list fixed the last known position of suspects and in one or two cases hinted that they were anchored to a cover, like Youssef Rahe, although his name did not appear.

She flipped through the list once more, making notes and adding to a chart she'd begun on a large sheet of drawing paper bought from a shop in Victoria that afternoon. A series of names plus lines and arrows and several brief sentences were written in her neat hand. She knew the diagram didn't add up to much, but she found it a useful way of working through a problem, putting a thought down, discarding it and moving on. On her desk were two packets of sandwiches, a piece of fruit cake wrapped in cellophane, a bottle of water, a banana and a bar of chocolate – not a feast considering the quantities of food she put away during periods of concentration. She ate one of the sandwiches distractedly and turned to the papers propped against her computer screen and on the floor around her feet. These were printouts of web pages showing the landing and take-off times for planes that passed through Terminal Three the day before – a timetable that varied considerably from the published schedules, she noted.

She didn't expect to prove anything conclusively; it would be enough to show that Rahe's disappearance was important, though he clearly had no role in the shooting of Norquist. She now knew for certain that he had not got off KU102 in Kuwait. Half an hour before, a clear head-shot had arrived of the man travelling on Rahe's passport, taken in Kuwait City airport before the individual flew on to the United Arab Emirates. By this time he had disposed of Rahe's clothes and adopted the local white jellabah. However, the Kuwaiti Intelligence service, al-Mukhabarat, were certain it was the stand-in.

She emailed the picture to Heathrow security and asked them to go through CCTV film to see if he'd come from London or arrived on another flight. Her belief was that he'd flown into Heathrow that morning, which was why she was trying to match possible suspects' names with passengers who had ended up in Terminal Three, a forlorn task if ever there was one. Still, she liked the solitary purpose of working late and was buoyed by the idea that while the rest of the Secret Intelligence Service was absorbed by muffled agony over the killing of Norquist, she was at least making some positive steps to unravel the events at the airport.

As she talked on the phone to a security officer named George, she looked out of the window and into the streams of traffic moving along the north bank of the Thames. Her focus drew nearer, to her reflection in the window, which she examined without reproof or anxiety. She looked good for thirty-two, although the lights made her appear haggard and – God – she *had* to get some new clothes!

George still had nothing for her. She put the phone down and went back to the watch list, thinking that Manila was the perfect place for the stand-in to embark. Just then she noticed a movement behind the glass panel in the office wall and saw Richard Spelling, deputy head of MI6, and his sidekick, Harry Cecil.

Before she had time to compose herself or her desk, Spelling was inside the door. 'Mr Cecil here says you've got something good.'

'That would be a bit premature of Mr Cecil,' she said, smiling at Cecil without affection.

'Well, you must have something if you've been asking favours of our friends in Kuwait City.'

'I was checking on the man who took Rahe's place on the Kuwait flight. As you know, I told Thames House yesterday afternoon, but I think they're rather tied up at the moment and nobody has got back to me about it. So I thought I'd do some ground work.' This was weak. She knew she was going way beyond her role of walk-on part in the surveillance of Rahe.

Spelling sat down on the other side of her desk and indicated to Cecil that he was dismissed. 'I'll say the Security Services are tied up!' he said.

Herrick cautioned herself not to say too much. She nodded.

'It doesn't get much worse than the President's special envoy being killed before his meeting with the Prime Minister. I mean, how bad does that make us look?' He gave her a despairing look and then exhaled heavily, which caused his lips to vibrate. She didn't like Spelling, his punchy name-dropping manner or the managerial style that someone had described as exultant decisiveness. Around the building it was said that his intelligence was sharp rather than deep and that he had none of the incorruptibility, shrewdness or ease of the outgoing Chief, Sir Robin Teckman. Spelling had won the appointment as a moderniser. There was much talk of horizontal management structures and the flow of ideas between different levels, but the evidence pointed to the opposite leaning. He was a hierarchical bureaucrat pretending to be a general.

'What do you make of it?' he asked. 'The shooting, I mean.'

'Well, I've been pretty busy today. I haven't had time to catch up with the people I was working with yesterday.'

'Yes, yes, but you have a view. You must wonder.'

'Yes, I wonder why Admiral Norquist was on a scheduled flight and there was no security prepared and ready to meet him. It all seems a bit slapdash.'

'And further down the time line…?'

Time line was a typical Spelling phrase. 'You mean later on – when the shooting occurred?' She put it as neutrally as possible. 'It looks pretty confused.'

'Yes, it was certainly that.'

She remained silent. It was still his call.

'And you don't have any theories about where that bullet came from?'

'Nothing apart from what I've read. I imagine they'll know if they retrieved it from his body.'

'Oh, I don't think that will happen.'

'So there *was* an exit wound. I didn't notice that mentioned in the papers. They said it was lodged in his spine.'

'They tend not to publish too much of that sort of thing – it's distressing for the family.'

'I see,' she said, understanding that there would be no official revision of the story. Norquist had been 'assassinated' in an operation involving a pair of young men, traced by the registration of one of the vans to the Pakistani communities in the Midlands, and the truck driver, who was also believed to be of Asian origin. With the two men dead and the driver still missing after an escape through the undergrowth along the railway embankment, the British media happily accepted the theory of a carefully coordinated plan. The enthusiasm for this account had not been dampened by the fact that no detonator had been found attached to the drums of petrol on the lorry.

His eyes scanned her desk. He reached forward and turned one of the Terminal Three schedules towards him. 'Now, tell me what you're doing here, Isis.'

'I'm trying to see what Rahe's likely destination was yesterday.'

'Any ID on the man who took his place?'

'Not yet.'

'Could you write a side of theory backed up by a few facts? The Chief's very interested in what happened out at Heathrow.'

She hesitated. 'You want a report on this? It's all very preliminary…'

'By tomorrow then. If you need help, Sarre and Dolph are around. Tell them this is for me and the Chief.' He made for the door, but before he reached it, stopped. 'And in your report, leave out all mention of the shooting. Just focus on the contemporaneous events at Heathrow. That's what interests us.'

Herrick went back to the airline schedules. Out of seventy-two flights to land between 5.55 a.m. and 1.45 p.m., fifty-one had come from the United States or Canada, which she excluded for the moment because of the heightened airport security and emigration watches in North America. The remaining twenty-one flights came from places such as Abu Dhabi, Dhaka, Johannesburg, Beirut and Tehran, cities where controls were far less stringent. She guessed that most of the aircraft were wide-bodied jets, carrying an average of two hundred passengers, which meant that around four thousand people had landed at Heathrow that morning. It would be an enormous task to search all the flights for a man matching the picture, and to establish what had happened to Rahe.

She founded Philip Sarre in the library, leafing through some material on Uzbekistan, which he informed her was now his speciality. 'If you go to Langley, you find whole rooms of Uzbek specialists; here it's me in my coffee break.'

Sarre always maintained that he had been brainwashed by MI6 and was actually meant to be in Cambridge watching particle acceleration experiments. His friend Andy Dolph was equally improbable. The son of an independent bookie, he had come to MI6 via the City of London and a banking job in the Gulf States where he had allowed himself to be recruited to relieve the boredom. Sarre reported that Dolph was across the river in a pub waiting for him and an Africa specialist named Joe Lapping. Sarre said he'd extract both men and bring them to Heathrow.

*

An hour later Herrick and the three men were crowded into the security room at Terminal Three having arranged for two of the technical people to stay as long as they were needed. Their first break came after 1.00 a.m. Dolph had been going over the film from the gates of two flights that landed consecutively from Bangkok at 9.15 and 9.40 a.m. when he saw the man who had taken Rahe's place walk off the second flight. Wearing a dark red jacket, a bright tie with hibiscus motif, grey trousers and black shoes, he was among the last passengers to leave the plane. This told them that he had probably been seated at the back of the Thai International Airways 747. The airline's records showed that one of the rearmost seats had been occupied by an Indonesian national named Nabil Hamzi, who they later found was travelling on to Copenhagen at 11.40 a.m. from Terminal Three.

Herrick gasped. 'Rahe didn't check in until past midday,' she said.

'So?' said Sarre.

'Don't be a fucking idiot,' said Dolph. 'It means that Rahe couldn't have made the Copenhagen flight. And that means there wasn't a straight swap between Rahe and Hamzi.'

'There had to be a third man, at least,' said Sarre.

'By George, he's got it,' said Dolph, pinching Sarre's cheek.

'And the third man must have arrived in the airport before eleven to give him time to change clothes, tickets and passports with Hamzi and get himself to the Copenhagen departure gate.'

They crowded round a screen to watch film of flight SK 502 to Copenhagen boarding and with little surprise saw a man in a red jacket, hibiscus tie and grey trousers waiting to present his boarding card and passport. It was neither Rahe nor Hamzi but another individual who was the same height and build and who was also in his mid-to-late thirties. After a couple of hours they found this man on footage from one of the long corridors leading to the departure gates. Then, working back through recordings made by a series of cameras, they traced him to a flight from Vancouver. This worried Herrick – it had implications for the other North American airlines. Still, there was no way of pairing the face with a seat number and therefore a name, because they couldn't work out at what stage he'd left the aircraft. However, Dolph realised that there was probably a pattern.

'Look,' he said. 'These guys aren't going to be travelling with baggage in the hold. And they are all likely to be booked on connecting flights out of Heathrow on the afternoon of the fourteenth. So all we have to do is go through the manifest of the Vancouver flight and match the two criteria.'

This produced the name Manis Subhi, who was travelling on a Philippine passport and had left London for Beirut four hours after landing.

Herrick wondered out loud whether she should let Spelling know the provisional results.

'No, let's tie this thing up, darling,' said Dolph. 'Present them with a fucking bunch of roses in the morning. Let's follow the trail until it ends.'

Sarre reminded them that they hadn't yet discovered the eventual destination of Rahe.

'Maybe it's not so important,' said Herrick. 'Perhaps he was just one element in a serial identity switch involving many people.'

'A daisy chain,' said Dolph.

'Yes, just because we spotted that Rahe didn't get on the right plane, it doesn't mean he's the crucial figure. He unwittingly let us in on the secret – that's all.'

'He loaned out his identity?' said Dolph.

'Could be. The whole point must be to shuffle a lot of key figures at once, and they can do that here in Terminal Three.'

'Because it's like the General Assembly of the United Nations,' said Dolph.

'No, because departing and arriving passengers mingle on their way to and from the gates. Also, passports are barely inspected when passengers are boarding – the airline just matches the name on the passport with the name on the boarding card.'

They watched film of the Middle Eastern airlines flight to Beirut, recorded by a camera close to the desk, and duly noted that Manis Subhi had been replaced by another, obviously taller man who, other than wearing the red jacket, hardly bothered to impersonate him. He also carried a bag that Subhi had not had with him. Then by chance, when the technician made an error and fast-forwarded the film instead of rewinding it, they spotted Rahe in a dark suit carrying a camera bag. This meant that Rahe had left for Beirut with another man involved in the operation.

It was now 5.00 a.m. and Herrick had seen all she needed. She asked the technicians to splice together the film of each man onto a single videotape. Then she borrowed a security pass and a radio and walked into the terminal building. There was a surprising amount of activity in the public areas – maintenance men fiddling with cable ducts, gangs of cleaners moving slowly with their machines like ruminants, and one or two passengers waiting for the first flights out. After half an hour, having tramped the best part of a couple of miles, she found what she was looking for.

Discreetly tucked into a bend was a men's lavatory, the entrance completely hidden from CCTV cameras. She went in and found a cleaner wiping down the basins. The name on his identity tag read Omar Ahsanullah and by the look of him she guessed he was Bangladeshi. The washroom was relatively small and consisted of six cubicles, a row of urinals, four basins and a locked storeroom.

She nodded to the man, then went out and radioed Dolph in the security room. She wanted him to watch as she walked down the corridor so that he'd see the exact moment she disappeared from view on the cameras. They found there was a blind spot of about fifty feet either side of the entrance. Although they were unable to watch the washroom's entrance, she realised they would be able to go back over the film for the two nearest cameras and get all they needed: anyone making their way to the men's toilet would have to pass under them. Dolph said he would try to verify her theory by checking the film for these two cameras from 12.30 until 2.00 p.m. to see if Rahe showed.

The sight of the cleaners reminded her that there must have been a man on duty in the lavatory when the men were swapping their clothes and possessions. She went back in. The cleaner explained that there were two shifts, one that started at 5.30 a.m. and finished at 2.30 p.m., another that ended at 11.30 p.m. It was possible to do a double shift, and those with many relatives back home often needed the extra money. As he spoke, she suddenly saw the drudgery and fatigue in his eyes and she remarked that it must be a hard life.

He stopped polishing the mirror and replied that yes, it was tiring, but he was in the West and his children would get a good education.

He was lucky. He paused, then told her if he was looking unduly sad that day it was because a friend, a fellow Bangladeshi, had died in a fire. His wife, two children and his mother had also died. Herrick remembered hearing about the blaze in Heston on the radio news the day before. It was being investigated as a hate crime. She said how sorry she was.

The man continued to talk about his friend in a distracted way and then as an after-thought mentioned that he had been a cleaner at Heathrow too. He had been working there on the day he died, the fourteenth.

'Here?' asked Herrick, now very alert. 'In this washroom?'

The man said that he was on this floor on Tuesday because they had both worked double shifts that day. But he couldn't be sure that he was working in this exact toilet.

'I am sorry about your loss,' she said. 'Is it possible for you to give me his name?'

'Ahmad Ahktar,' said the man.

She said goodbye. As she was about to leave the washroom she noticed a sign propped under the basins. She bent down and turned it, almost knowing that it would read 'Out of service'.

By the time she got back to the control room, they had found Rahe on the film taken near the lavatory. More important, they had got him in both sets of clothing and were able to see which man he had changed with. Dolph and Lapping had started cross-referencing the information they had gathered with names on the FBI and British watch lists. It was an inexact process but they had seven faces to play with. Dolph made an impressive case that two of them belonged to an Indonesian cell. He told them he'd lay odds on it.

Herrick had other things on her mind. It was obvious that the timing of this operation was subject to flights arriving late or being diverted. They must have built flexibility into the schedule so that if one man was delayed, there was still someone for him to switch identities with. That probably meant there were one or two floaters, men who at the beginning of the day were prepared to be sent anywhere. These would have to be European citizens with clean passports who could board a plane bound for Barcelona or Copenhagen and enter the country without raising suspicion. She thought of Rahe, a British citizen, sitting in the Garden of Remembrance. Although they hadn't seen him use his phone, he must have received a text message or phone call to tell him when he was due to swap.

Some of the detail could wait, but they were getting a picture of an impressive operation. To put as many as a dozen people into Heathrow from all over the world, with passports that were stamped with the correct visas, and then to achieve what was in effect a relay switch, required miraculous scheduling skills. Whoever was controlling the switches would need to speak to each man the moment he arrived, which was why, she now realised, three suspects had been filmed talking on their mobiles just after disembarkation. The controller would also have to ensure that the men didn't all arrive in the washroom at the same time. An early flight might leave a man loitering in the corridors, drawing attention to himself, so a premature arrival would have to be taken out of circulation, perhaps hidden in the locked storage cupboard, until the moment his pair arrived and he could be sent on his way.

There was one more question she needed to answer before returning to London and writing the report for Spelling, which she now rather relished.

She went down to Arrivals, bought a cup of coffee and stationed herself under the flight displays. Heathrow was now open for business. Four flights were expected in the next quarter of an hour and already the roped-off exit from Customs was fringed with small welcoming parties.

She noticed that the chauffeurs and company drivers seemed to know instinctively when planes had landed and the passengers would start to clear Customs. Often the drivers appeared from the car park exit with just a few seconds to spare. She asked a lugubrious man clutching a sign and sipping coffee how they managed it. 'Trick of the trade,' he said, blowing across the cup. 'The top deck of the car park for this terminal has the best view of the airport. When you see your aircraft landing you drive down to the lower floor and then you know you've got another half hour or so to wait. It makes a difference if you're doing this three times a week.'

'What about when it's busy?' she asked.

'At peak you've got about forty to fifty minutes,' he replied.

Herrick could have gone back to the control room, satisfied that she'd tied up all the loose ends of the operation, but the obsessive part of her nature told her there was always more to be had by seeing something for yourself. A few minutes later she was standing in the open on the top level of the car park with a little huddle of plane spotters. She watched for a while, briefly marvelling that men stirred so early in the day to jot down the details of very ordinary-looking Jumbo jets, then caught the eye of a man with an untidy growth of beard and asked him if this was always the best place to see the aircraft.

'Not always,' he replied without removing his eyes from a jet taxiing in to the terminal. 'They change the runways at three in the afternoon on the dot. Whichever one is being used for take-off becomes the landing runway. Then we go across to Terminal Two and watch from the proper viewing terrace.'

She was about to ask him whether he had seen anyone acting unusually the day before last, but thought better of it. That was a detail. Special Branch could deal with it later.

She walked out of earshot of the plane spotters towards the centre of the near-empty car park and dialled the duty officer at Vauxhall Cross.

It was 6. 45 a.m. Isis noticed she was very hungry.

CHAPTER FOUR

Silence. No word from the Chief's office; not the merest hint that her report had been discussed at the Joint Intelligence Committee, which Herrick knew was meeting four times a day in the wake of the death of Norquist. Even the people in anti-terrorism, who had been known to make the odd, oblique compliment, said nothing. Dolph, Sarre and Lapping shrugged and went back to their work. Dolph said, 'Fuck 'em, Isis. Next time we'll stay in the pub.' Sarre pondered the behaviour and came up with the phrase 'institutional autism', then went off to look at a map of Uzbekistan.

Herrick was not as easily resigned. She didn't understand why there was not an immediate operation to trace the men who had darted into the glare of Heathrow's security system and dispersed into the dark. Anyone could see these men had been imported into Europe for a specific purpose, a particular act of terrorism. But the trail was growing colder by the minute.

This just confirmed her belief that the parts of the Secret Intelligence Service were more decent and reasonable than its sum. She trusted colleagues individually, but rarely the collective, which she regarded by turns as needlessly calculating, merciless and plain stupid.

This had been her view since the Intelligence Officers' New Entry Course when, like the others in her class of a dozen, she was sent abroad on what was presented as an actual mission. A cover story was provided, fake credentials, a task and a deadline. Everything seemed straightforward, but during the trip the trainees were arrested by the local counter intelligence service, held and questioned, the object being to test their powers of resistance and resourcefulness.

The test is never pleasant but Herrick knew that, like most female entrants, she had received especially severe treatment. She was detained by the German police and members of the BFD for a week, during which she was questioned for long stretches at night, roughed up and deprived of sleep, food and water. The particular harshness perhaps had something further to do with the fact that she had followed her father into MI6. No daddy's girls in the Service, not unless they could stand having a chair broken over their back by a borderline psychopath.

Every reason to take the Cairo posting offered to her a couple of weeks earlier and get out of Vauxhall Cross. Egypt was one of the few Arab countries where she could use her language, and work without having to remember at every step she was a woman. Besides, the cover job in the embassy as political counsellor would not be too difficult to master alongside the business of spying.

She shook herself – she had work to do – and returned with little enthusiasm to the investigation of Liechtenstein trusts being used to move Saudi money to extremist clerics and mosques around Europe – a worthwhile job perhaps, although it seemed pedestrian after her night at Heathrow.

Khan had kept going through the first day and, having taken care to memorise the shape of the landscape ahead of him, walked through the night, too. By the following morning he reckoned he had put a good distance between himself and the security forces. He decided to rest up in the shade. But down in the valleys he saw much more activity than would be normally expected in the pursuit of one fugitive. He realised they couldn't let him leave the country with his knowledge of the massacre of innocent men. He lay low until the early evening and set off again in the warm twilight, eventually coming across a village in the mountains where some kind of celebration was in full swing. A small dance floor had been erected; strings of lights had been hung between its four corners and a band was playing. He guessed it was some kind of religious feast or a wedding.

He had gone for two days without food, sucking leaves and grass and eking out the water in the soldier's canteen. But he made himself wait a good half-hour, watching a group of houses that could be approached under cover of a wall that ran down from a ridge not far from where he lay. He set off, moving cautiously, at every step of the way looking back to see his best escape route. He entered two houses but in the dark couldn't find anything to eat. He came to a third and felt his way to the kitchen, where he found a loaf of bread, half a jar of nuts, some dried beef, cheese and olives. He wrapped them in a piece of damp cloth that had covered the bread.

An ancient voice croaked from the room next door, making him freeze. He put his head round the door-frame and saw an old woman sitting in a chair, bathed in red light from an illuminated religious icon. Her head moved from side to side and she was slashing at the air with a stick. He realised that she must be blind. He crept over to her, gently laid his hand on hers and with the other stroked her brow to reassure her. Her skin was very wrinkled and cool to the touch and momentarily he had the impression that she had woken from the dead. He caught sight of a bottle of Metaxa brandy and a glass, which had been placed out of her reach. He poured an inch or so, put the glass in her hand and helped her lift it to her lips. Her wailing suddenly stopped and she murmured something which sounded like a blessing. Placing the bottle in his piece of cloth, he left the house by the front door.

A couple of dogs pursued him along the wall and he was forced to sacrifice some of the meat which he hacked off with his knife and chucked at them. Then he melted into the rocks and scrub, making for the place where he had left his belongings. He ate a little of the cheese and bread to give him energy, but it was another hour before he found some rocks where he could make a fire that wouldn't be seen from below, or indeed from any other direction. He prepared a sandwich, eating it slowly so as not to give himself indigestion, and washed it down with some brandy mixed with a little water. It was his first alcohol in seven years and he knew himself well enough to watch his consumption.

He did not stamp out the fire straight away, but moved some flat stones into the flames then settled down near the light to look through the Palestinian's pouch of documents. There were a number of identity cards with different names. The most frequent name used was Jasur al-Jahez and all the cards included pictures of the dead

Palestinian. He noticed that many were out of date, but felt sure that somewhere among the mostly Arabic documentation an address would be found. When he'd had them translated he would write to Jasur's relatives and tell them what had happened. The death of the man who'd fought so hard to live had stayed with him all day and, as with his men in Afghanistan, he felt a keen responsibility to the relatives who had been left behind.

Some time later, he pulled the stones from the fire and placed them in a line, digging them in so their tops were flush with the surface of the ground. Then he swept the embers away, buried them and laid his bed-roll where the fire had been and along the line of warm stones. It was a trick he'd learned during his first winter in Afghanistan. Going to sleep by a fire was less efficient than lying on ground that had been heated for several hours. With rocks placed in a line under your body you stayed warm all night, or at least warm enough to go to sleep.

Next day he woke at dawn and packed his things quickly. He was about 700 feet above the village and a good mile away as the crow flies. A slight haze hung over the mountains. When he moved to look down he noticed that an army truck had pulled up in the main square of the village and a knot of figures were gathered round it. It could mean nothing; on the other hand, there was every possibility that the old lady had reported him and the missing food had lent credibility to her story. He moved off without a second glance and decided on the tactics he'd used the first day, of marching further than anyone thought possible. But it was already quite hot and the one thing he hadn't thought to do while in the village was replenish his water supply. He would have to save the cup or two that remained in the canister.

Half an hour later a helicopter appeared and circled the ground immediately above the village. He saw troops moving up the mountainside. They were much fitter and faster than the soldiers who had hunted him two days before and he estimated that if he stayed where he was they would reach him in under an hour. However, it would be suicide not to pick his route carefully while the helicopter was so close.

He waited under some bushes, remembering what a Stinger missile launched from a man's shoulder could do to a chopper. As soon as it shifted, he sprinted into a plantation of pines and moved rapidly up the slope, running with the gun in one hand and the sack of possessions tied round his back with the gun strap. He reached some open ground and decided to make for a long shelf of rock about a hundred yards ahead.

Something must have attracted the pilot's attention. The machine dipped and slewed across the mountainside towards him. Khan dived under a clump of bushes to his right, rolled onto his back and pushed the muzzle of the gun through the foliage, briefly aiming it at the tail rotor as it came into view. Instead of settling over the bushes the helicopter passed him. He wiped the sweat that was trickling from his brow and took a sip of water from the canister. He could see very little, but from the rhythmic thud he judged the helicopter was in a steady hover high over a position about a thousand yards to the north of him.

He pulled the shirt-sleeve across his face again, dabbed his eyes and took in the pinpoint clarity of the day. The sun had burned away the haze and was heating the ground so that the air was filled with the smell of herbs.

His eyes returned to the skyline above the shelf. One or two scrawny mountain sheep had appeared and were looking over the ten-foot drop. They were joined by the rest of the flock, obviously scared by the helicopter. With one sudden movement they cascaded over the edge, many of them landing legs akimbo or on their sides. They struggled up and stampeded past him like a river in spate, down towards the pine trees. They were followed by a pair of dogs and a shepherd boy who stood on the edge of the shelf, waved a stick and shouted. Khan noticed that he had a blanket tied across his chest and was carrying a good many pans and bottles that made almost as much din as the sheep bells. As the boy scrambled down, a corner of the sack-cloth came loose and neat bunches of herbs tumbled out. He dropped the sack and ran on after the sheep without noticing Khan's boots protruding from beneath the bushes.

The helicopter's engine was producing a more laboured note. He saw it pop into view above, climb rapidly and drop away to his left. He caught another noise – the unmistakable sound of automatic weapons firing and a heavy machine gun, or even a cannon.

He scrambled up to the rock and put his head above the parapet.

About two hundred yards away he saw a group of men moving into the open from an old stone shelter. They didn't seem to be in the least concerned about the presence of the helicopter sitting above a cliff some distance away, and were moving without haste up the scree towards a cleft in the mountains. Several packhorses or mules followed them.

He realised these must be the insurgents he'd heard about from the Bulgarian truck driver who had brought them all the way from Eastern Turkey and left them near the town of Tetovo, West of Skopje. It was a long way from the agreed drop-off point and they had missed their connection, so the driver had got out a road map and showed them that they were south of the place where the borders of Macedonia, Kosovo and Albania meet. He told them there was a lot of trouble because the men from the north crossed into Macedonian territory and stirred up trouble with the local Albanian population. He had been forced to change his route countless times by the Macedonian patrols. Khan had only half-believed him, but here were the men he had spoken about and they might well provide a means of getting over the border.

Shading his eyes from the light, he peered down the mountain to look for the soldiers. At first there was no sign of them but then he noticed that the sheep which had scattered into the pine plantation were now bolting from cover. He saw a figure flash across a patch of light and realised that the soldiers were nearly in range. They would reach him in minutes. He had a choice. He could try to conceal himself but risk being discovered, or he could warn the men above him about the size of the approaching force. He opted for the latter, and jumped up, letting off a burst in the air to gain their attention, then loosed a full magazine into the trees without hope or desire of hitting the soldiers. They rose to the bait and returned his fire and so announced their presence. He turned and raced across the plateau towards the men, shouting and waving, praying they understood he was one of them; at least that he had earned an audience.

This performance brought them to a halt and even now they seemed to have time to exchange looks and rest their hands on each other's shoulders and point at the man tearing across the bare plateau. He reached them almost incapable of speech, but gestured down the mountain and said the word soldier in as many languages as came to mind. The men stared back at him. They were all quite short with dusty hair and faces. Beneath the grime was two or three days of stubble and without exception a look of undisguised suspicion. One of them gestured he should fall in behind the column and then they moved off again. A hundred feet up, Khan saw why they were so confident. Hidden behind a wall of boulders was a heavy six-barrelled American machine gun, known as a Six-pak. As soon as they passed the gun, a young man of no more than eighteen years, with eyebrows that met in the middle of his face and the solemn concentration of the truly insane, opened fire, strafing the ground immediately in front of the rock shelf and kicking up an impressive spray of pebbles and dust. Still firing, he swung the weapon in an arc towards the helicopter and pumped rounds in its direction, causing the pilot to rise and feint to the left. He kept up intermittent bursts until the men and mules passed through the opening of the rock, at which point he gathered up the gun and ammunition belts and ran to join them.

'Albania,' said the man who was evidently their leader. 'This Albania. Albania is shit. And you? Who you are?'

'Mujahadin,' replied Khan, thinking that this was his only recognisable credential, but at the same time regretting that he had resorted to his past. His name was Karim Khan now.

'Mujahadin is shit also,' said the man.

CHAPTER FIVE

It seemed to Herrick that life continued with bright, feverish simplicity. The Saturday papers learned that Norquist had been travelling in the Prime Minister's car and concluded that the events of May 14 could only be read as an attempt on the Prime Minister's life. No one seemed to take any notice of the reports in the *International Herald Tribune* that asked how the terrorists knew Norquist's travel plans when his own secretary hadn't been told. It also questioned the nature of the information that the British had been acting on. Was it a tip-off or the result of secret surveillance? The most important issue, said a columnist from the *Herald Tribune*, was how the Pakistani assassins mistook the President's old ally for the British Prime Minister. The two men could not be more dissimilar, even in the reportedly wild conditions on the M4 that day.

After finishing the papers, Herrick did a couple of hours impatient shopping, which produced two new suits, a pair of blue jeans and a white shirt. She dumped the clothes without looking at them again at her house in West Kensington and returned to Heathrow, this time on an entirely unofficial basis. What had hardened in her mind was the absolute need to link the identity switch with the operation against Norquist. But the contrast between the care and timing of the switch and the haphazard nature of the hit, which had apparently only succeeded because of a stray police bullet, suggested that different minds were behind them – unless the disparity had been planned.

At Heathrow, she went to the viewing terrace and began asking the plane spotters tucked away in a shelter whether they had seen anyone acting unusually in the last week or so. They were unsurprised by the question because the police, for which she read Special Branch, had already been to talk to them and they had provided a description of a man in his late thirties. He had Mediterranean looks, was overweight by twenty or so pounds and spoke fluent English with an Arab accent. His knowledge of aircraft was good but he seemed a lot more interested in the carriers than their planes. Referring to their notes from May 14, one or two were able to place him in the context of planes arriving and leaving and claimed to remember him making a remark about two Russian planes. No one could remember seeing him after that day.

She took the description to the incident room at Hounslow police station, where she had arranged to meet a Chief Superintendent Lovett who was leading the investigation into the fire at the home of the washroom attendant. The policeman was cagey but eventually agreed that the washroom attendant Ahmad Ahktar had associated with a man who more or less fitted this description. He had made contact at the mosque in central London which Ahmad had attended when his work allowed him. They were treating the case as multiple murder because the injuries on Ahmad's head and back could not have been sustained by the roof collapsing. There was another, more telling clue: the youngest child was found to have high levels of Tamazepam in her body. The remains of the other members of the family were being tested and there was some hope of retrieving enough tissue for analysis.

Herrick had all she needed. The Ahktar family had been murdered to stop Ahmad talking about the identity switch and it was possible that the man who had watched the planes come in was responsible for this. But the important fact was that her line of inquiry had already been followed by Special Branch. They had made the connection between the man on the viewing terrace and the fire in Heston. In other words, someone was acting on the memo and the medley of CCTV clips she had sent.

Late that afternoon, she called Dolph and arranged dinner in a room above a pub in Notting Hill. Dolph arrived late and for a time they talked about 'the office' in neutral terms and drank some cocktails of Dolph's invention.

'They're holding their breath, Isis,' he said, 'waiting for something to happen – or not to happen. The whole bloody place's on edge. You can feel it.'

Herrick murmured that she thought something was already happening, but that they were being kept out of it. Dolph didn't pick up on this.

'They're constipated,' he said, 'bent double with it. They need a fucking good dump.'

Herrick grimaced. 'You're a barbarian.'

'You can't deny there's something weird about it.' He paused and looked across the room of mostly young diners. 'Look at this lot,' he said. 'There's not a person in this room who earns less than we do – and that's including the waiters. What we do it for?'

'Vanity?' she offered.

Dolph turned back. 'That's why I like you Isis. You get it all. Do you think this weird mood in the office has anything to do with Chief going?'

'Might have.'

'Oh come off it. Talk, for Christ's sake. I want to know what you think.'

She smiled. 'I am talking, but this isn't the best place for it.'

Dolph eyed the waitress and then let his gaze fall on Herrick. 'Okay, tell me about you. What happened to the man in your life – the academic?'

She shrugged. Daniel Brewer, outwardly a soft-hearted academic, had turned out to be an incipient drunk, a clever Cornish working-class boy prone to bouts of despair and unreason. 'He found someone who listened better than I did. And he didn't like our business – the vanishing act, the secrecy. He felt excluded.'

'You told him what you did?'

'No, but he guessed. That was part of the original attraction, I think.'

'What about your father? Did he like him?'

'Didn't say.'

Dolph ordered some wine. 'Did you know I went to your father's lectures? My intake was the last to get the Munroe Herrick treatment. He was very impressive. Believe me, I'd never have survived all that crap in the Balkans if it hadn't been for him.'

'Yes – he had stopped by the time I was taken on.'

Dolph regarded her sympathetically with his handsome, dissolute face. As he was choosing the wine she had noticed his expression suddenly betray the very sharp intelligence which lay behind the façade of effortlessness. 'I often think about you,' he said. 'I wonder what's going on with you.'

She shrugged. 'Nothing Dolph, just bloody work. I'm considering taking the Cairo job.'

'You should have some fun.'

She revolved her eyes in an arc, knowing what was coming next. 'Yes, I should,' she said. 'Which is why I'm going to take Cairo.' She smiled a full stop.

He laid his hand on hers. 'Look, this is embarrassing. But I'm really fond of you, Isis. Really, I mean, I think you're the one.'

'And I'm fond of you too. But I am not going to sleep with you.' She let his hand remain for a while then gently removed it.

'Pity,' he said morosely. 'Are you sure?'

She nodded.

'You'll miss the pillow talk that keeps the girls coming back.'

She shrugged. 'It's hardly an inviting prospect, Dolph – the idea that I would be one in a bus queue of women listening to your ravings.'

'God, you're so fucking prim. Perhaps we should do it now – I mean the pillow talk.'

'If you can do it discreetly.'

'Loosen up, Isis. That's the point of pillow talk.' He drank a glass of wine and smiled at the restaurant. 'Your friend, the man in the bookshop, was doing interesting things with his PC.'

Herrick set down her glass and looked at Dolph's black eyes dancing. 'Can you talk about this *now*?'

'Of course. He has a novel line in screensavers. Actually it's one screensaver – an aquarium with fish swimming across it. You know the kind of thing.'

She nodded.

'Only, his aquarium is different, you see. It's got a little timer in it that ticks away and then releases information.'

'There was a message hidden in the image?'

'Not quite. What happens is this. He logs on in the morning and automatically downloads the same screensaver – same bloody guppies, same bloody eels, same bloody octopus with the smiley face. Then half an hour later, maybe an hour, maybe two hours later – the interval changes according to the day of the week – he clicks on one of the guppies and a message is sent from the screensaver to a pre-prepared file on his hard drive. You only have a few minutes to read it before it disintegrates.'

'Where'd you get this?'

'Friend of mine – a bloke I play poker with in the office. Good guy. Crap at cards though.'

'Why'd he give it to you?' She lowered her voice. 'This is sensitive stuff.'

'He owed me a couple of bob from a game. I told him he had to tell me something interesting to stop me breaking his legs.' He saw Herrick's brow furrow. 'Look, I'm joking. Don't be so fucking serious.'

'What else did you find out?'

'This and that.'

She gave him a look of exasperation.

'Try me,' he said.

'Okay, so why was Norquist here?'

'Cabling – they're going to lay high capacity cables under the Atlantic so the Americans can get more of the stuff they already don't have time to read. It's as simple as that.'

'But why was the Prime Minister involved? That's all a bit nuts and bolts for him, isn't it?'

'Strategic matters also, I hear. That is to say, what are we going to do about the Europeans?' Dolph lit a cigarette and offered her a drag which she declined. 'We'd be good together, Isis. Really, we'd be fucking wonderful because we get each other.'

She shook her head. 'So this screensaver works like a virus?'

'Not quite. It's more targeted than a virus. For one thing it doesn't reproduce itself, and for another it's got a very short life span. If the correct procedure isn't followed at the right moment the message disappears. And here's the beauty of it. If the screensaver is intercepted, all you get is fish. Nothing else. It doesn't work unless you've got the software that goes with it – the male plug and the female socket, if you see what I mean.'

'Yes.'

'Good pillow talk, no?'

She nodded. 'What do you think it means?'

'That Rahe was a shit-load more important than we thought he was.' Dolph looked out on the muddy evening sky. 'The men at the airport, why do you think they were all dressed like Senegalese lottery winners? What was that about?'

'Reverse camouflage,' said Herrick quietly. 'The more noticeable your clothes, the less people look at your face. It's the opposite effect to the one you achieve, Dolph.'

He ignored the remark. 'Like having a parrot on your shoulder?'

'Yes. Can I ask something else?'

'You have my full attention.' He began to fold his napkin.

'Do you think the two things were connected at Heathrow?'

'Of course they were. I quote you the product law of probabilities. "When two independent events occur simultaneously their combined probability is equal to the product of their individual probabilities of occurrence." That means it was bloody unlikely that the two events were unconnected. They were *syzygial* – yoked, paired, conjoined, coupled – like we should be.'

He finished the origami with the napkin and balanced it on his shoulder.

'What's that?' she asked.

'A parrot – so you won't notice what I look like.'

CHAPTER SIX

The silence ended with a single dramatic sentence. 'Youssef Rahe was ours.' Richard Spelling said it with studied understatement. 'He was our man.' He folded his arms and looked at her over a pair of slender reading glasses.

Herrick was not totally surprised. She had been at the point of articulating Rahe's double role for herself, but hadn't gone the whole way because of the surveillance operation. Why had they put all that effort into watching a man who was already working for them?

'Was?' she said.

'Yes. His body was found in the boot of a car near the Lebanese border with Syria. He had been very badly treated and finished off with a shot to the head which, without going into detail, made him practically unrecognisable. As well as this, the car had been set alight. However, we are absolutely certain it is Rahe.'

'I see,' she said. 'Was he killed by the second man on the Beirut flight?'

'We're not sure. We suspect he had something to do with it but there were others involved.'

She asked herself why they were telling her this. Not out of any sense of obligation, that was for sure. She had been summoned to the high table and was being told an intimate secret for a reason. She looked around the room and wondered what they wanted from her, apart from silence. The constituent parts of this late night gathering were altogether odd. Colin Guthrie, head of the joint MI5-MI6 Anti-Terrorism controllerate, well, you would expect him to be there, but not Skeoch Cummings and Keith Manners from the Joint Intelligence Committee. The JIC provided intelligence assessments for the Prime

Minister and the Cabinet and wasn't responsible for making or imple-
menting policy, yet here they were, comfortably ensconced in the
inner sanctum of the intelligence executive. And why Christine
Selvey, the deputy director of Security and Public Affairs? What the
fuck was she doing there, with her powdery skin and brittle, bouffant
hair which Dolph had described as 'South coast landlady with a
passion for china dogs and young actresses'?

There was one other man there and his presence baffled her most.
As she entered he had risen, turned and offered her a soft, cool hand
and asked after her father, a pleasantry which seemed out of place and
was calculated, she thought, to wrong-foot her in some way. Walter
Vigo, the former Head of Security and Public Affairs. Isis knew perfectly well that her father would have nothing to do with him. Why
was Vigo there and not the Chief? What did Vigo's presence mean six
weeks before the handover from Sir Robin Teckman to Spelling? Vigo
was the outcast, the defrocked prelate who'd been exposed by a
former SIS man, Robert Harland, for his connections with a gun
runner and war criminal named Lipnik. She'd got some of the story
from her father, who had trained both Vigo and Harland at different
times during the Intelligence Officers' New Entry Course. Vigo had
escaped prosecution because he was in a position to make life seriously unpleasant for the entire Service. Instead he had been declared a
pariah, with Teckman forbidding all contact with him and the
members of Mercator, the security consultancy he ran in tandem with
an antique book dealing business called Incunabula Inc.

There was silence. She was expected to ask a question. 'If he was
ours, why was he under surveillance?'

'Our relationship was a very, very secret matter,' Spelling replied.
'We shared his product, but not his identity with anyone. Only four
people knew that he worked for us. Those were his conditions when
Walter Vigo came across him two years ago and we abided by them.'

Vigo stirred to give Spelling a nod of gratitude.

'The surveillance was to give him credibility?' persisted Herrick.
'Was that why we laid it in on with a trowel?'

Spelling whipped off his glasses and folded them in his left hand.
There was something unpractised and self-conscious in the gesture.
'Yes, he was worried he'd been tumbled.'

'Can I ask whether you knew about the operation at Terminal Three in advance?'

He shook his head. 'No. No, we don't think even he knew what was happening, though he had told us in the morning that he was going to a meeting with some important people. We were hoping for big game. But we had no notion of the switch you spotted and that means he didn't have any idea what was to happen at Terminal Three. We now think he believed he was being observed by them at Heathrow and was worried about making a call to us. No doubt he hoped we were there watching him too and we were, which is how you noticed what had happened. We realised he was in trouble when you called in, but by this time things were unravelling, and it's fair to say we lost sight of what was important. A few hours later he contacted us from a room in the Playlands Hotel in Beirut. They said the meeting would take place in the next few days and that he should stay put until they got in touch with him. Very shortly after making that call he vanished. We didn't have time to get anyone over to the hotel.'

Guthrie coughed and said, 'All of which underlines the thesis implied in your report on the events of May the fourteenth, that the alert over the President's man was a…'

'A strategic diversion,' offered Vigo, with his eyes closed.

'To achieve several things,' said Guthrie, 'among which was enticement of Rahe out of the country.'

'Can I ask you if the information about the hit on Norquist came from Rahe's computer?'

Vigo shot her a look of interest.

'What do you know about Rahe's computer?' asked Spelling sharply.

'I assumed that if he was working for us you must have had access to any information that came to him via his PC. After all, he barely left that shop and we had his phone covered so I imagined it was simply a matter of interception somewhere along the line.' This was feeble but she had to protect Andy Dolph. 'I'm simply asking if the information about the possible hit on Norquist came from Rahe, by whatever means. From the outside that seems to be the important point.'

'There was an oblique reference to it amongst the usual blazing rhetoric,' said Guthrie. 'But this was released after he left for

Heathrow. Another source confirmed in some detail what was to happen.'

Spelling moved to take control. 'We believe he was unmasked during WAYFARER. As most of you are aware, this was the operation to track a hundred-odd kilos of sulphur and two hundred of acetone from Rotterdam to Harwich and then on to a factory in Birmingham. They must have examined their security arrangements after that and come up with Rahe's name. He was involved in some of the shipping arrangements.

'The important thing is that Rahe was tortured very badly indeed. He will have told them everything he knew about us before he died, which owing to Walter's deft handling was kept to a minimum. Still, he wouldn't have failed to learn quite a bit during the course of the twenty-odd months he was working for us, if only from the questions we asked him. And we must assume certain techniques are now in the hands of the terrorists.'

There was a pause. Vigo had listened to this expectantly, as though waiting to make a bid at an auction, but he said nothing. Christine Selvey seemed to be readying herself for something – a straightening of the back, a pluck at the front of her Sunday blouse.

'We heard you were out at Heathrow yesterday,' said Guthrie in what was clearly a planned intervention. 'What were you doing there?'

'Trying to tie up some loose ends for my own satisfaction. I wondered if the murder of the lavatory attendant and his family had anything to do with the man who was seen watching aircraft landing from the public viewing terrace. You see I hadn't heard from—'

'Yes, well, no more blundering around like that,' said Spelling fiercely. 'This is a very delicate situation and we can't afford the local police or anyone else putting it all together and feeding the theory to the media. Nobody – I repeat *nobody* – must know that we appreciate the real significance of the events at Heathrow.'

Given that she'd spotted what was really significant that day, Herrick didn't much feel like the gesture of submission that was called for, but she apologised nonetheless, saying that it was often difficult for someone at her level to see the whole picture.

'There is one thing,' she said, levelling her gaze at Spelling. 'Won't our discovery of Rahe's body in Beirut mean they expect us to go back over his movements at Heathrow? After all, he was meant to be in Kuwait or the Gulf States, not the Lebanon, and that might very well lead us to check which plane he boarded and so go over the film.'

'It's a good point,' said Vigo. 'I'd like to know the answer to that one.'

Spelling shook his head. 'We didn't move the body. His wife doesn't know he's dead and I'm afraid we're going to leave things that way. She must believe he's alive in order for our operation to go ahead. And they must believe we've lost him. It will be essential to the safety of the people we're going to put in the field over the next few days.' He cleared his throat. 'As you know, the Chief has asked me to oversee the setting up of RAPTOR, the name of our response to the events of May the fourteenth. You will hear in the next few days what your part will be – the arrangements are being finalised at the moment – but I wanted to speak to you this evening because everyone involved must understand that this is an exclusively transatlantic operation. We are going to work very closely with the Americans on this, but not with the Europeans.

'International cooperation in the war against terrorism is still at a very early stage of development. Everyone pitches in and there have been some notable achievements in the sharing of information, but we're a long way from full cooperation. You'll remember Djamel Beghal, one of the men who was planning to blow up the US Embassy in Paris. He was arrested on his way back from Afghanistan and began to talk, providing valuable names and addresses, top grade material in fact. The counter-intelligence services of France, Spain, Belgium and Holland ran a joint surveillance operation in their individual territories to watch the cell at work. But then details were leaked to the French press, with the result that most of the network escaped. One or two were arrested, but there wasn't enough evidence to put them away for any length of time. In our opinion it was a serious loss not to be able to observe and watch these people's MO, the way they moved their money, communicated, planned, provided themselves with false papers and the supplies necessary for the large-scale attacks that they need to keep their movement alive. That's something we're not going to allow to happen again. Owing to your excellent work at Heathrow – a superb piece of intelligence gathering – we are now in a position to watch eleven individuals who are currently under surveillance as they merge into their new covers. We and the Americans plan to observe these men and get a fix on the person running the European networks. We know next to nothing about him, but believe him to be in Europe.'

'The same man who planned May fourteen,' she said. It now seemed more like fact than opinion.

'Possibly – certainly a very ambitious mind was deployed that day, someone who sees an operation as a means of achieving several things at once. It was daring and well thought-out to pull off an assassination of that order while shuffling his men around Europe.'

'But surely—' she began.

'If you wouldn't mind.' Spelling gave a tight smile that indicated he wouldn't suffer the interruption. 'I should have mentioned that tests have been carried out and there's no doubt that the bullet came from the machine pistol in the first van. Abdul Muid was the assassin. I gather that will be the finding of the inquest that opens tomorrow. It will also make plain the pattern that the two men – Muid and Jamil Siddiqi – were pulled from our midst to perform these acts of terrorism. Neither of their backgrounds suggests training by al-Qaeda in any formal sense, which I think is an interesting aspect that the Security Services will want to explore. There is still no trace of the lorry driver, which perhaps indicates that he was an integral part of the plot, rather than someone who was caught up in the incident.'

Skeoch Cummings nodded. Guthrie brushed the end of his nose twice while Vigo looked into the distance with an expression that suggested he had not even heard what was being said.

Fine, she thought, they're running with that fiction. The possibility that a British bullet had killed Norquist was not going to be contemplated, which obviously suited both sides. The Americans knew what had happened, but when it came to their closest allies they were capable of miraculous forbearance. After all, they had absorbed the blow of Israeli warplanes attacking and sinking the USS *Liberty* spy ship in the Six Day War without any public comment whatsoever. Norquist had already been buried at the Arlington National Cemetery with full military honours. His widow had received the folded Stars and Stripes from the President himself and not a word of official complaint had been made. Not in public, at any rate.

But it was another matter in private, she thought. The White House must have used Norquist's death to maximise the US position. They would have received something in exchange and it was likely to be the contents of her report passed up to Number Ten through the Joint Intelligence Committee. She imagined a telephone conversation between the White House and Number Ten during which the President insisted that the US be involved as an equal partner in the pursuit of the live cell. That meant the continental intelligence services would be kept in the dark.

Now she understood why Teckman was not there. The chief had either lost the battle to keep the Europeans involved, or was standing back waiting for his successor to make a hash of things while he was still in control. Whatever the tactic, it was his absence that gave the meeting its furtive air. This, and Vigo. Spelling may have been in the chair but it was Vigo's return that established a new era of transatlantic exclusivity.

Spelling put on his glasses again and read something from the paper in front of him. Then he looked up, as if to address the whole room, and began to outline RAPTOR. Each of the eleven men so far identified and tracked would be allotted an entire team that would remain permanently on that individual's case. In effect the teams would mimic the classic cell structure of terrorist organisations, shadowing the suspects and bedding in around them with an equal regard for cover and security. Herrick would be in one of those teams, and those involved would be expected to drop everything for the operation. That requirement had had some influence on the personnel being chosen: men and women with families would take roles where they could be inserted and removed without rippling the surface. Both the CIA and MI6 would call on the services of retired intelligence officers used to long-term surveillance operations, who would bring the field skills that were perhaps lacking in some of the younger generation.

'This is about close surveillance of an exceptionally discreet order,' he said, splaying his fingers on the table. 'It may go on for months, even years, because that is the timescale the terrorists work with. We will have to match their stamina and patience. Every step of the way will be monitored by us here and the Americans at Langley and Fort Mead. The risk assessment for the entire operation will be provided by the staff of the Joint Intelligence Committee, which will report three times a week. The Americans have agreed to abide by their recommendations though I stress that these reports will not define policy. The JIC will simply gauge the degree of menace presented by these men at any given moment. The Americans will naturally take their own view of how things are progressing and have insisted that each surveillance team has access to armed back-up. That means they can move against a target and arrest him if the situation requires. And so can we.'

Spelling's confident presentation of the battle plan didn't fool anyone. If the Americans and British, already welded together in an exclusive eavesdropping treaty known as Echelon, were to start killing or seizing suspects on European soil, untold damage would be done to an already shaky Western alliance. The resentment would last for years. This was to say nothing of the risk – or in Herrick's mind, the certainty – of one or other European agency catching on and, out of justified concern or sheer bloodymindedness, pre-empting the situation by arresting the suspect and causing the others to flee. She also knew that the terrorists were nothing if not close students of Western intelligence tradecraft, and that the mastermind who had planned the switch at Heathrow would be the kind of man who had set up trip-wires to give early warning of just such an operation. Sooner or later, someone would stumble across one.

Everyone got this. Equally, they understood they were just at the start of RAPTOR. As time went on, the situation would change; the grand scheme would be buffeted by chance and circumstance. They were going along with it because during an operation the policy makers – in this case a none too bright President and a Prime Minister with attention deficit problems – would become dependent on those who implemented their plan. All of which meant there were great opportunities for the secret servants: advancement, increase in influence and, in Vigo's case, rehabilitation.

But why show *her* the secret mechanism? The answer, of course, was that she had made the breakthrough, put it all together, so

Spelling had been forced to include her. But why not Dolph, Sarre and Lapping? Simple. She had written the two-page report and then followed it up with her own inquiries at Heathrow. She understood the total operation on May 14 but had not spoken about it to them. That's what distinguished her and that's why Spelling had to get her on-side.

Spelling moved his papers together and looked around the table. 'I think we've just about covered everything. Isis, have you any questions? You will of course be briefed over the coming week. In the meantime, I suggest you take some leave, say two days. We'll see you on Wednesday. You'll receive instructions tomorrow about time and place.'

'There's one thing,' she said. 'I want to get clear in my mind why we're excluding the European agencies as a matter of course.'

'Because that's what our political masters have decided,' replied Spelling crisply. 'And that is what the Chief agreed with the Prime Minister and Foreign Secretary this morning at Chequers.'

The invocation of all these authorities seemed weak, apparently even to Vigo, whom she was now sure owed his place in the secret deliberations to something more than his recruitment of Youssef Rahe. He shut his eyes with a hint of exasperation, and Herrick had the odd sensation that it didn't matter whether they were open or closed, Vigo still watched.

She was dismissed a few minutes later and left convinced that she'd already blown it by raising the business about the Europeans. It was crass of her, especially as she now understood that the sole point of the meeting had been to test her reliability, to see if she was fit for the game only the adults played.

She went to her desk, picked up her bag and left a note saying she would be out for a couple of days and if there were any problems to call Guthrie or Spelling. She saw a few people – the shades that always haunted Vauxhall Cross at night – but there was no sign of Dolph, Sarre or Lapping, whom she knew would be regarded somehow as her co-conspirators. They would be seen too, but she didn't think they'd get the full treatment with Madame Selvey, Walter Vigo and the inscrutable pair from the JIC.

She left the building, collecting the cell phone that always had to be checked in at the front entrance. As she walked out into the dreary no man's land of the Albert Embankment she noticed that she had a text message. 'Drnk tonite any time – Dolph.'

She replied. 'No thanx. Dead tired.'

CHAPTER SEVEN

Khan expected the Albanians to descend into the valley once they crossed over from Macedonia, but they marched on into the mountains taking increasingly untravelled, treacherous paths that caused the six mules to stop every so often, snort and shake themselves as if to adjust their loads. After the first exchange with the head man who had given his name as Vajgelis, they said little to Khan and seemed bent on covering as much ground as possible before the middle of the day. A couple of the youths tagged along behind, apparently speculating about him and his bundle of possessions, which they occasionally poked with their sticks. He turned round and grinned at them, but the only response was a surly lift of the chin to tell him to keep his eyes on the way ahead.

When the sun was at its highest they stopped in the shade of some pine trees and squatted to eat a little cold meat and onion stew, produced from tall canteens. They offered it to him saying, 'Conlek, eat Conlek.' In return he offered them food stolen from the Macedonian kitchen, and then asked for water. They gave it to him gracelessly and now seemed to be making jokes at his expense. He smiled, nodded and thanked them. He remembered what they had said in Bosnia, the tales of savagery and endless slaughter amongst their Muslim cousins in Albania. For nearly thirty years the country had been the world's only official atheist state and under Enver Hoxha the people had happily pulled down their mosques or turned them into cinemas and warehouses. The civilised Bosnians shuddered at the godless barbarity of what had happened under the Marxists. But there again, he thought, he'd seen plenty of that kind of thing in Afghanistan without doing anything: the destruction of monuments; the execution of a whimpering boy who'd been caught listening to a music tape. He'd seen it and, willingly or not, he'd been part of it.

After eating, the Albanians dispersed through the woods to sleep, leaving a couple of men to guard the mules. Khan lay back where he had been sitting on a carpet of pine needles and, hugging his gun and pack into his stomach, told himself that he must snatch the rest while he could. He closed his eyes in the songless, dry forest and fell asleep thinking that he would now have to make his way to Italy rather than Greece. They were a more tolerant people.

In what seemed a very short time he was woken by someone tugging at his gun. The muzzle of a pistol was drawn across his cheek. He looked up. The two young men who'd trailed him during the morning were crouching either side of him.

'Come Mujahadin. Good. Come.' Standing above them was Zek, one of the mule guards, who placed his boot on the AK47 while one of the younger men pulled it gently from Khan's grasp. The third, who had been holding the pistol to his face, withdrew it.

'Okay. Mujahadin. Come.' Zek, who was a wiry man of about twenty-five, motioned for them to hurry. Khan got up and shook himself free of their grasp. He didn't know what they wanted, but since they had tossed his gun away he had to go with them. They walked to a hollow, about fifty yards from where the others were sleeping, and he was prodded roughly down the slope. Khan thought he knew what they were going to do. What they planned to do afterwards was anyone's guess – shoot him and say he had started the fight, or simply throw him down the ravine they had skirted a few minutes before entering the forest? He raised both hands and made as if to welcome the idea by reaching out to touch Zek's shoulder.

Zek told the two younger men to hold Khan over the tree, and started unbuckling himself to reveal a rank pair of undershorts. With an interested glance Khan again tried to show that he was more than happy about the situation and indeed enjoyed the prospect of indulging them. He even made to undo his own trousers. But they turned him and forced his head down violently on the tree trunk. The smell of resin and forest mould reached his nostrils. He glanced under the young man's arm and saw the guard behind readying himself. Lust

59

had drained all meaning from his expression and he hissed for his two accomplices to hurry. Khan placed his feet squarely apart, to appear cooperative, and wiggled with a little coo of excitement. The young man holding the gun to his head sniggered, relaxed his grip and swapped hands to free himself to help yank Khan's trousers down. This was the opening Khan had waited for. He slipped from under his captor's arm and jabbed his left elbow back twice into his face, grabbing the barrel of the pistol and sending him to the ground. The completion of the movement brought him face to face with Zek, whose expression flooded with consternation. He smiled awkwardly just before Khan butted him once in the forehead, then knocked him cold with a second blow from his forehead delivered as he grabbed the man's shoulders and held him.

He spun round, but there was no need to attack the third boy, who had jumped away, raising his hands with a sly smile as if to say the whole thing had been a bit of harmless horseplay. Khan arranged his clothing and walked to the top of the hollow where he found Vajgelis contemplating the scene. He held Khan's AK47 under his arm and his hands tucked into the waistband of his chocolate brown corduroys.

'These men shit,' he said, his chin jutting with contempt. 'These men, they fuck pigs. I sorry for these hospitality. These men...' Words failed him, he shook his head and held out the machine gun for Khan, at the same time reaching for the pistol that Khan had taken from the young man. As Vajgelis took hold of it, he snatched the machine gun back from Khan's grasp. 'You walk with me now, Mujahadin.'

A minute or two later the two injured men staggered up from the hollow with blood over their faces. Zek's nose was split and ballooning. They went to Vajgelis and Khan understood they were pleading to be allowed to kill him, but the request met with a tirade of abuse from Vajgelis, who tweaked Zek's ear and cuffed the younger man around the head.

A few minutes later they set off, Vajgelis at the head of the column and Khan just behind him with two older men now appointed as his minders. For four or five hours they walked along the parched tracks. As the sun sank behind the mountains they came to a lumber road littered with bark. The mules were tethered to the trees where they hung their heads and steamed and stamped their hooves. The men stood around smoking and glancing down the mountain.

Shortly, Khan saw truck lights slash through the trees and heard it grinding up towards them with many changes of gear. The men began to loosen the straps on the mules, but were told to stop by Vajgelis. He ordered them into the middle of the track with their guns showing. The truck appeared a few minutes later and pulled up. About a dozen men, all armed to the teeth, scrambled down from the back and flashed torches across the faces of the men in the road. Vajgelis moved forward. Recognising the driver of the truck, he signalled for the mules to be brought up and unloaded.

Long before this moment Khan had suspected that Vajgelis's band was involved in drug smuggling, not insurgency, and as the first tightly filled sacks were deposited at the tailgate of the truck, he wasn't in the least surprised to see the driver slit one open with a knife and taste the contents. Each time a mule was unloaded he sampled at random.

The time came for departure and the men from both sides lined up to face each other. Vajgelis pointed to a man in the line opposite and beckoned him across the track. Khan realised they were exchanging hostages. Now it was the driver's turn. Vajgelis moved closer to Khan, laid an arm round his shoulder and moved him back out of range of the truck lights. The trick worked perfectly. The driver walked over to them, placed his hand on Khan's other shoulder and steered him to the truck. Vajgelis laughed and murmured, 'Mujahadin is shit also.'

Khan was thrown in the back and nobody took much notice of him as the truck made its way down the mountain and then bumped across a flat plain to the coast. A couple of hours later, the truck suddenly turned off the road, careered down a rutted track and juddered to a halt. The men tumbled out, unloaded the sacks and bore them off to a jetty where a powerboat was tethered. Khan could make out its shape in the dark and he heard the engine's exhaust spluttering in the gentle swell.

They set off back up the mountains and after a couple more hours came to a small, almost derelict village. They pulled up in some kind of farmyard or compound. Cats darted from the lights of the truck and some dogs barked. Here the remnants of an old agricultural living were jumbled with the trophies of drug trafficking. There were animal stalls, a collapsed cart and a hay-rick, but also a large satellite dish and a pair of identical black SUVs chained by the fenders to a metal post. Khan was stiff from the ride and moved gingerly into the light. When the men saw his face for the first time there was a sudden uproar, and he was pulled from one man to another, spat upon, kicked and rifle-butted. There was no doubt in Khan's mind that these were his last moments on earth. But their anger subsided and the driver who had picked him from Vajgelis' group walked up and looked him over, muttering imprecations under his breath and asking questions. All Khan could do was smile idiotically and shake his head saying, 'English? I speak English only.'

'No ingleesh,' said the driver. 'No ingleesh.'

He was taken to one of the stalls and tied to a beam, while they made a cursory search of his possessions. At length someone was fetched from a neighbouring village to interpret. He was a mild, emaciated man in middle age, wearing mittens and a scarf wrapped around his head though the night was warm. He introduced himself to Khan as Mr Skender. He had once been a waiter in London, he said, but returned to his village after developing tuberculosis. To Khan he looked very sick indeed.

'I have to hear some things from you,' said Skender, rubbing the circulation into his hands and wiping a runny nose. He gestured to the driver. 'Mr Berisha wants to know why you are working with Vajgelis. Tell Mr Berisha who you are.'

Khan gave his name and said that he had come overland from Pakistan, looking for work in the West. All the time looking directly at Berisha, he said he was from a high-born family but that he was without money. He had rich friends in the United States – one who was like a brother to him. This man would reward handsomely anyone who helped him now, in a way that was beyond Mr Berisha's dreams. He added that they should take no notice of his present appearance.

Skender gave a brief translation to the driver, who called for a table and chairs. More lights were brought. Berisha sat down and poured some *konjak* for Skender and himself.

'Mr Berisha thinks you are terrorist,' said Skender.

'Then tell Mr Berisha that I'm not a terrorist,' said Khan. 'All I want is to find work and continue my medical studies.'

'You are a doctor?' asked Skender doubtfully.

'I studied medicine in London and I plan to return there to continue.'

At the end of the translation Berisha stroked his chin and growled a few sentences.

'Mr Berisha wants to know why a doctor, an *educated* man, is in the mountains with Vajgelis? He is a very dangerous man, this Vajgelis. You are fortunate to be alive. He trusts only his own people.'

Khan told him about the killings on the road, his flight from the Macedonian security forces and how he'd met Vajgelis' group on the border. Berisha sat with his lower lip hanging and his foxy little eyes darting around Khan, as if this would somehow prise out his secret. Skender explained that Berisha was a very clever man: Khan's presence there was like a philosophical problem to him. He might be a Muslim terrorist, or he could be a Macedonian agent who'd been sent to infiltrate the network and report back to the authorities. Maybe he was a plant from the Vajgelis clan to see if his part of the network could be taken over. The very thought of this prompted Berisha to get up and prowl around the stable stabbing at his imagined foes in the dark.

'Mr Berisha wishes you to know that he is strong and will not tolerate a challenge to his authority in this part of the mountains from Vajgelis. He will cut Mr Vajgelis' testicles and feed them to his dogs. He wishes you to tell this to Vajgelis if you are allowed to live long enough to see him again.'

To emphasise this point, Berisha opened a door and allowed two fighting dogs to bound into the stable and sniff around Khan's feet.

Skender went rigid. 'Mr Berisha will discover the truth of your mission if he has to rip your testicles off with his own teeth.'

'I can see that Mr Berisha is a man of standing,' said Khan, making sure that he did not give the dogs the slightest provocation. 'But tell him I could not be a plant because he chose me. Mr Berisha walked to the line and chose me himself. Vajgelis could not have engineered that.'

'Mr Berisha believes he was tricked by Vajgelis to think you are important to him,' said Skender with a note of sympathy entering his voice. 'He says you are worthless. Now he is having to pay money for his cousin who is with Vajgelis and that makes Mr Berisha very angry. He says he may kill you now because you are a worthless piece of shit. Forgive me, Mr Khan, this is Mr Berisha's words, not mine.'

'But it is obvious that I am worth more alive than dead.'

Skender tried to translate this but was suddenly silenced by a dusty cough that rose from the depths of his lungs and convulsed his whole body. At one point Khan thought he'd pass out from lack of oxygen but Skender eventually managed to recover and drank a little of the *konjak*. Then he wiped his eyes and nose with the shirt-sleeve, throwing Khan a glance of terrible resignation.

'You should see a doctor.'

Skender shook his head and inhaled gently so as not to aggravate his lungs again.

'Tell Mr Berisha that I will only talk to him if he pays for your medical help.'

'I cannot tell him this,' Skender looked shocked. 'You do not bargain with Mr Berisha. Mr Berisha is the boss here.'

The driver made them go back over the ground they'd covered while he finished the bottle. Then his head began to droop. He got up, ejected the dogs and announced that he would decide what to do in the morning. In the meantime both Khan and Skender would sleep in the stable under guard. Skender seemed to have expected this and, without complaint, lay down on a rough blanket and wrapped the free side around him. Khan was cut down and his possessions thrown at his feet. He pulled them into some order but instead of laying out his bed-roll, he propped himself up and tried to block out the smell of drains that seeped from under the wall. Any fears he had about falling into too deep a sleep soon vanished with the sounds that came from the house, the unmistakable noise of a woman being beaten and taken by force.

Khan looked over to Skender who raised his hands above him hopelessly. 'In what neighbourhood in London you were living?' he asked by way of distracting them from the murderous noises next door.

Khan replied that he had shared an apartment in Camden Town with some students.

'I am living in Hoxton,' Skender said. ' There was I happy.' His cough began again, with a more rasping note.

Khan listened for a while then reached down to the bottom of his trousers and silently made a little opening in the seam. From the cavity in the material he withdrew a roll of money slightly thicker than a cigarette. He got up, crab-walked over to Skender and placed the four twenty dollar bills – half of what he had left – in the palm of his hand. 'This will buy you a visit to a doctor and some medication. It seems that I may not need it now.'

Skender shook his head but his hand closed around the money. 'Thank you, Mister Khan.'

'I want you to do something for me in exchange. Do you have a pen?'

He produced a stub of pencil from his pocket and handed it to Khan, who quickly wrote a message on one of the three remaining postcards.

'I want you to send this to America by airmail. If I am killed, please write separately to the address and tell them how and where I died. You understand? Tell him what is happening to me.'

Skender took the postcard and slipped it into his clothing. Khan scuttled back to his bundle to await his chance to escape, reflecting that he had never been in as wretched and menacing a place. Berisha was, he thought, probably mad. He felt that anything could happen to a human being who came into Berisha's orbit. For a time he listened to a young woman's voice alternately wailing and remonstrating until the volume of the TV was turned up and a soccer game drowned her words.

Next thing he knew it was daylight. He woke to see Berisha sitting not far from him, holding a cup. He was dressed in sports kit – trainers with a gold Nike flash and an outlandish American football jacket with a dragon emblazoned up one side. Beside him stood Skender and two men in uniform.

'Mr Berisha has made decision,' said Skender apologetically. 'You must go with these men from police.'

Isis Herrick was met at Newcastle station by her father, who had bought himself a new car, a replacement for the dark blue Humber

Super Snipe that had met with an unspecified end a month before. The Armstrong Siddeley Sapphire was older and less sedate. Herrick eyed it with little enthusiasm, but the journey to Hopelaw village fifteen miles over the Scottish border passed without incident and the car did seem to make her father happy. As they climbed through the moorland, upholstered in the soft green of new bracken, her spirits lifted and she told him that she was coming round to the Siddeley.

They didn't talk properly until after lunch, when they took a walk up to Hopelaw Camp, an iron-age fort above the house. They reached a flat rock pitted with ancient cup and ring carvings and sat down. The discussion was new for them: they had never spoken about her job, let alone discussed individual operations, and she thought they would find it awkward. But he listened to her acutely, gazing south, his eyes watering slightly in the breeze, occasionally pressing her for detail.

'When your mother died,' he said, 'I thought the best thing I could do was to keep you out of this business. But it wasn't my choice, was it? You did what you wanted and you never asked my advice.' He searched her face. 'But at least you're doing so now.'

He picked up a field snail's striped shell and examined it carefully. She knew it might appear in one of the paintings her father had been producing on and off since he was required to find himself a convincing cover during World War II in the Pyrenees. Herricks were now more sought after than ever; they fetched thousands of dollars in America and on the continent, although his work was generally disdained by art critics for the simple reason that they missed the point of minutely recorded still lifes. One said that they were just 'quotations' from nature.

He peered at the shell again. 'It's the surface of things that's usually important. Most people don't understand that everything is staring them in the face. They just have to look a little harder than they are accustomed to. Here, have a squint at this.' He handed her the shell and a magnifying glass. 'You'll see that there's a yellowish varnish that's been worn away in some parts by the sun, and beneath that there are little ripples made as the snail secretes the substances that make the shell. From the top you can see the black stripe achieves a more or less perfect spiral, yet there are flaws in the design that remind you of the miracle of its creation. Here you have all you need to know about the snail, but it's remarkable how few people are willing to spend time looking closely at anything.'

She had heard the lecture before. She handed the shell back to him. 'It's lovely. But what do you think about this operation?'

The old man looked across the hills, and she wondered whether she should be bothering him with it. 'Intelligence work contradicts my view about the surface of things,' he said, 'I think your operation is probably destined to failure because of that.'

'How?'

'Because you can't get an idea what these people are planning from simply watching them. Before the attacks on America in 2001, I understand various security agencies had those characters in their sights. The cell in Germany was under surveillance and I believe someone in the FBI had noticed that they were taking flying lessons. They were looking but they didn't see.'

'That was a failure of the system – people not putting it together with other data.'

'Data! How I do hate that word.'

'You know what I mean, Dad – intelligence. They weren't analysing it properly.'

'The only way to deal with these bastards is to penetrate their organisation and that's going to take a long time, unless you're lucky enough to have one of them drop into your lap. None of it's going to mean much until you've got the man on the inside telling you what's going to happen.'

She told him about the murder of Youssef Rahe.

'That's a bad sign,' he said. 'It means they know you tried and are now aware of the process which led him to become your man, the recruitment and so on.'

'Yes, he was tortured.'

'But not by the characters who have flown into Europe for their big party. Some other part of their organisation determined that he was working for you and got hold of him.' He coughed and felt for a pipe that wasn't in his pocket. He had given up tobacco four months before. 'In that case I think this is a very dangerous affair. These people have already proved exceptionally adept at carrying on their business while being observed. I'd take the view that there's very little useful intelligence to be had from watching them. Arrest the whole lot and throw them into jail on whatever charges keep them in there longest – or worse.'

'You mean kill them?'

'Yes, these men have no fear of suicide. They've moved to a certain level. You can't reason with men like that or seduce them from the cause because self-interest in the normal sense has been rejected.' He paused and raised his eyebrows. 'And Teckman is apparently out of the picture?'

She nodded.

'And that bloody little tick Vigo is back – astonishing!'

'Yes.'

'Well, I doubt the Chief is really out of it. Just lying doggo, waiting to make his move.'

'Against his successor?'

'Let's hope so. Spelling is all mouth and no trousers. Complete phoney.'

She smiled. Her father's forceful opinions meant that he had never stood a chance of rising in the Service, although the operations he conducted against the KGB along the Iron Curtain for twenty-five years were textbook studies, celebrated for their panache and cunning. He had once summarised it thus: 'They relied on my judgement to keep myself and others alive in the field, but when I got back to London I was expected to let others think for me. I couldn't get used to it.'

'What about the operation itself,' she asked. 'Any advice for me?'

'You know it all, Isis. Probably more than I do. The first thing you must realise is that these men know they're in enemy territory. They're like we were during the war. We couldn't trust anybody in France and these holy warriors will suspect everyone they come in contact with. They will have had training in anti-surveillance techniques, so don't fall into any dry cleaning traps. If they're taking a particular route every day they'll get used to the sights along that route and will know what is normal. They will also build in a couple of observation spots along the way so they'll be able to tell when they're being followed. Apply all the same rules if cars are involved, only more strictly.'

She nodded. She knew most of it but there was no stopping him now.

'What you need to do is to learn the place thoroughly before you start the watch. There wasn't a street I didn't know in Stockholm or Vienna during the Fifties. I could have been a tour guide in Istanbul. This is very important: you can't just go to a foreign town and blend into scenery without knowing the place like the back of your hand. Take care with your clothes, too. Study what the women wear locally. There're always slight variations of fashion between towns on the continent. A particular shop may be popular and you will need to get one or two items from there. If you need cover, a job to help you get close to your target, choose this very, very carefully. It's important to keep your flexibility, so don't rush into his local café and get yourself work as a waitress on the grounds that he visits the place twice a week. You won't learn anything that way and you'll tie yourself up. Other opportunities will present themselves.'

He stopped and examined her with fierce compassion. 'Isis, you know these men aren't playing things the way we used to. If we were spotted it often didn't matter. It was part of the game of cat and mouse. But these men are utterly ruthless – they butcher air stewardesses without the slightest qualm; they think nothing of killing thousands of people one fine morning. They're different from what we had to face – much, much more dangerous. But remember, you're different too. You're one of the few people who know the full extent of the operation against them. If you fall into their hands, they may work out that you have a lot to tell them and that is not an enviable position to be in.' He put up his hand to stop her interrupting. ' Of course I know there will be others with you, but from what I gather your people are nothing like as good at field craft as we were. Not interested in the detail, no preparation. You'll have to watch your colleagues as closely as you do your own behaviour. I don't want some berk from Vauxhall Cross on the phone telling me you've been killed, do you hear? You've got to use your own judgement.'

He slapped his hand against his thigh and then rubbed his knee. 'It's not much fun, this business of getting old. I've lost the feeling in my legs sitting here. I'm going to have to move.'

She helped him up. They stood on the Cup and Ring Rock and he looked at her, his rigid grey hair standing up in the wind, his eyes misted by limitless affection. 'You know I can't help seeing your mother in you. It's twenty-four years since she died, but there hasn't been a day I didn't think about her. And now I see you so close to the age she was when she died, well... I fear for you, Isis.' He stopped and looked apologetically down at her. 'It's an old fellow's panic, I know. But I think I've reason enough to be worried.'

'Come on, Dad. I may look like Mum but inside I'm all you – hard and practical.'

'You're going to have to be very hard and very practical,' he said, almost angrily. 'Don't lose your concentration for a moment.'

They took the longer route back to Hopelaw House, stopping along the way for her father to pluck things from the hedgerows and scrape pieces of moss from the trees. 'I mean to go on to some studies of lichen,' he said, 'and the moths that pretend to be lichen. They're getting rarer and that's because their camouflage is only good for one set of circumstances. The lichen disappears with all this pollution and the moth is left sticking out like a sore thumb. So, end of moth. It's a point to remember. Your cover should be adaptable.'

'Dad! I've been trained.'

'Yes, you have,' he said as though to scold.

They tramped back to Hopelaw House and her father disappeared into his study where the bits and pieces he had collected on the walk were interred in cotton wool. Then he emerged clutching a felt envelope.

'Found this the other day,' he said. 'Thought you ought to have it. Mislaid it for years.'

She undid the package and found inside a photograph frame and a small black and white picture of herself and her mother, bent double with laughter in the sunlight of an afternoon long-ago.

CHAPTER EIGHT

Khan was beaten casually and inexpertly as a natural part of deten-
tion. Perversely the treatment gave him hope. As he sat, shackled to a
chair in the first-floor interview room, hearing the sound of children
playing in a sunny courtyard below, he reasoned that if the police had
thought him important, they'd have made sure that they could hand
him over to higher authorities without a cut lip, swollen eye and
bruised ribs.

The police captain, a man named Nemim, had departed. Khan sat
respectfully and passively, hoping to look cowed. The hot afternoon
passed slowly. A lone policeman sat in a chair tilted against the
wall. An old 303 rifle lay in his lap. Khan thought that he might be
able to overpower him, if he could persuade them to remove his
manacles – perhaps for prayer – and climb down from the window
into the courtyard. But where to after that? He didn't have the
strength to run. He had caught sight of his reflection in the police
van's mirror on the way in and hardly recognised the haggard face
staring back. He looked condemned, just like the two poor Pakistanis
on the road. It would be better to sit this out; get some food in him,
sleep, make a plan.

This discussion with himself ended when Captain Nemim came
back with a sheaf of papers and an open notebook. A look of animated curiosity had entered his expression. Khan realised that
Nemim now saw him as an opportunity, a gift to an officer who could
speak English and harboured ambitions way above his present tenure
as the chief in a mountain station.

'So, Mister Khan, or is it Mr Jasur? What do we call you?'

'Khan – Mister Khan.'

'Then why you are carrying these documentations belonging to Mr Jasur?'

'Mister Jasur died when we were chased by Macedonian security forces. I took his possessions so I could tell his family when I reached safety.'

'Ah yes, the terrorist party executed by the Macedonians. You were with them?'

'Yes, and so was Jasur. But we were not terrorists. You have to believe me. He was a Palestinian. A refugee. He died of a heart attack while we were escaping.'

'Of course we Albanians are used to these stories about terrorists. To the Macedonians and Greeks we are all terrorists and we do not believe what they tell us. But the Macedonian army say there were eight terrorists on the road.'

'That's right. We were just looking for work. We wanted to go to Greece. Those men with me were all innocent. None of them was carrying a weapon.'

'But, Mister Khan, you are not understanding what I am saying to you. Maybe you do this on purpose – not understanding me?'

'No, no. I am trying to understand what you want.'

'They say there were seven terrorists and one other who escaped after he was cutting the Macedonian with knife.'

'Yes, that's right. That was me. I stabbed him and took his gun.'

'Look at these photographs. Mister Khan.' Captain Nemim flourished a newspaper and showed him a photograph of a mortuary in Skopje. Seven bodies were lined up and at their feet lay an assortment of automatic weapons, pistols and grenade launchers. Khan recognised the men – the Kurdish trio, the Pakistanis and the rest of them, laid out like trophies with their killers standing behind them.

'They weren't carrying these weapons,' he said.

'We know that,' said Nemim. 'This weapons used by the Macedonian security forces. But you make not to understand me again. I am not stupid man, Mister Khan. You see? Which is the Palestinian gentleman please?'

Khan peered at the picture. 'He's not here. They must have left him on the hill. Maybe they didn't find him.'

'But you say seven men were killed. There are seven bodies here but where is Mister Jasur?'

'Hold on,' said Khan, adding up the members of the party again.

'Maybe he was ghost. Maybe this Jasur has flown away.' Nemim seemed pleased with his sarcasm and looked to the junior officer who had come into the room, as if to say this is how it is done; you are watching a master at work, a man who is going far.

'But the soldier I injured with the knife knew there were two of us who escaped. He would have reported this to his senior officer. There were nine people in our group.'

'No, this is what they say. The Macedonians like to boast about this murders so there is no reason for them to lie. They say seven men were killed and one escaped. That is you. There is no other man.'

'But they saw the other man…'

Nemim shook his head. 'There was no other man.'

There followed a hurried exchange with the junior officer during which Nemim's eyes never strayed from Khan's. Then the junior left and Nemim folded his hands on the table with a look of satisfaction.

'You know we weren't terrorists,' said Khan. 'You said yourself that these weapons belong to the Macedonians. So why are you holding me here?'

'It is necessary for us to know who you are. I have spoken to Mr Vajgelis.' He nodded several times to signal that this was the first of many trump cards. 'Mr Vajgelis says you are fighter. He saw you attack the security forces with a machine gun and then you were wounding his men with your head and arm like this.' He threw his elbow backwards and did a head butting action. 'He say you are professional Mujahadin. And you tell him you are Mujahadin. You are saying this to Mr Vajgelis. That is why he gives you to Mr Berisha and Mr Berisha gives you to me. They are good men.'

Khan's shoulders sagged, as much out of fatigue as frustration. 'Good men?' he said. 'What are they taking to the coast – peanuts and Coca Cola? These are good men in your country, Captain Nemim? No, they are drug smugglers. If these are good Albanians, I pity your country.'

Nemim leaned forward and hit him hard with the back of his hand on both sides of his face. 'Who are you?' he shouted. 'What are you doing here in our country?'

A rotten taste spread in Khan's mouth, which at first he imagined was some physical manifestation of his fear, but then he realised that the blow on the left side of his face must have burst an abscess. It was months since he'd cleaned his teeth properly and he had been aware of a swelling on his gum. In Afghanistan he had periodically developed these infections, lancing them himself and treating them by washing his mouth out frequently with salt water. He supposed the bacteria had never cleared properly and in time built up to form another abscess. But this gush of decay in his mouth was something else entirely and he was disgusted – by this taste and also, now he came to think about it, the stench that rose from every part of his body and seemed to fill the room.

'I will tell you about myself, Captain, but I must wash. I need to do this, sir. You can hit me as much as you like, but I will talk better if I am allowed to do this. For our religion I should wash before I pray this evening.'

The Captain considered this for a few seconds then gave some instructions to a policeman standing outside the door. Khan was taken to a tiny chipped basin at the back of the building under which was a large container of water. He took the block of soap and for ten minutes washed all over his body. He cleaned his mouth once again and then dried himself with part of his shirt.

He sat down now opposite Nemim determined to bring some reason to the interview. 'I told Vajgelis I was a Mujahadin fighter because I wanted him to accept me,' he began. 'I wanted to escape and I needed his help so I shouted out the first thing that came into my head. The reason I hurt his men was because three of them tried to assault me. You know what I mean. Any honourable man would have done the same.'

'Before this, where you come from?'

'Bulgaria, Turkey, Iran.'

'With all these men?'

'No, we came together in Turkey. Then we went by truck to Bulgaria, but were cheated many times. Our money was stolen by men who promised to take us to Greece by boat. There was no boat.'

'You say you are Karim Khan – not Jasur…' he checked the notes and the identity card he had in front of him. 'Not Jasur al-Jahez. Or

Jasur Faisal or Jasur Bahaji. The man with many names. You are not him.'

'No, I am Karim Khan.'

'How can I believe this?'

'Because it is the truth. Look at the picture of him. He is younger than I am and he is different. Look at him. Jasur has curly hair. I have straight hair.' He touched his damp head.

Nemim shrugged, then moved on to examine the photograph in Khan's passport. 'Why you are not black like Pakistani man? You are like an Arab man, I think. You are Palestinian terrorist, no? You are Mister Jasur?' He held one or two of the passport's pages to the bulb above them, which had attracted a swirl of small black flies. His brow furrowed. Then he brought it down on the table and began to scrape at the page that included Khan's details and photograph.

'This passport is changed – here.' He held it out to reveal the spot where the expiry date had been altered. 'And here the paper. Where is the paper? Why no paper here?'

The page had been razored out by the man in Quetta who'd suggested that an entry stamp for Afghanistan at the tail end of 1996 was enough to put him in jail. The same man had changed the date, quite expertly, Khan had thought, but he had to admit that the passport was barely tested. He had crossed from Pakistan to Iran along the Siahan range without being stopped by a border patrol, and the man on the Turkish border with Iran had not looked beyond the twenty dollar note folded in the front.

Nemim flipped through the passport again and came to a page containing a British visa.

'So you go to London City in nineteen ninety-one?'

'Yes, that was my second visa. I was studying to be a doctor. I was at school in London before then.'

The policeman looked at him sceptically. Khan had the odd thought that perhaps he had dreamed his past; everything before Bosnia and Afghanistan had been a kind of fantasy to protect him from things he had done and seen. Nemim was talking but he didn't hear properly and asked the policeman to repeat himself.

'This British visa is dated. This makes your passport thirteen years old,' he said. 'No passport can be that old. This passport is dead.'

He closed it and swept the notebook and Jasur's documents up from the table. 'We understand you. We know who you are. You are international terrorist,' he said. He got up abruptly and marched from the room.

Two hours later Khan was shaken awake. He saw the bread, cheese and water that had been set in front of him while he slept. He snatched at it but managed to eat only a little before being taken from the room. Outside the police station quite a crowd was waiting, in the middle of which was a TV crew. Khan stood in the glare of the lights, feeling shrunken and exposed. Nemim was enjoying the moment, although he did not seem to know whether to present his captive as the heroic survivor of Macedonian brutality or a dangerous terrorist, and allowed for both options in his manner.

The media opportunity ended, but instead of being taken back into the police station, Khan was placed in a van and borne off into the night.

CHAPTER NINE

At 7.00 a.m. Isis Herrick arrived with her bag at the gentrified mews house – French shutters, geraniums, carriage lamps – not far from the American Embassy in Grosvenor Square. The door was opened by an American carrying a machine pistol. He explained – a little apologetically – that the house was part of the embassy and she was now on US soil. Then he showed her to a room where two men stood listening to Walter Vigo, installed in a revolving leather chair with a cup of coffee and the *Wall Street Journal* draped like a napkin over his lap. Vigo was in his element – the nexus of the 'special relationship'.

'Ah,' he exclaimed, tipping the paper to the floor. 'Here's the brains responsible for RAPTOR.' He introduced her to the two men. 'This is Jim Collins and Nathan Lyne from the CIA's Directorate of Intelligence. Both these gentlemen were with the Directorate of Operations and have experience in the field so they know the problems and pitfalls of an operation as complicated and wide-ranging as this. Jim is one of the people in charge of things out at Northolt and Nathan is running your desk.' He stopped for the Americans to murmur hello and give Isis firm handshakes.

'Northolt?' she said.

'Yes, we've moved the operation out there. I think you'll be very impressed with what you're going to see. We expect you to spend a week or two there before a transfer to the field but, as you'll appreciate, things are and will remain very fluid. I hope, by the way, you won't mind the accommodation, but it seems simpler and more secure if we're not all being ferried to and from the Bunker in minibuses.'

'The Bunker,' she said, surprised. 'Are we confined to barracks?'

'No,' interjected Collins, a stout man with a pinkish complexion and a brush of fine blond hair. 'But we're trying to keep this as tight as possible, at least for the time being. There are not too many great restaurants in the area, but you're welcome to leave for R&R when you need. It's more a question of not having large numbers of American spook-types filling up the trattoria in Mayfair. Besides, the facility under Northolt has a great deal of space and there's plenty of room for solitude. There's even a restaurant and a gym.'

Collins nodded to Nathan Lyne, who rose and moved to sit on the sofa beside her. Tall, with a slow, understated manner, Nathan Lyne haemorrhaged high caste Yankee confidence, which she later learned was the result of Harvard law school and a short period with a Washington law firm.

'You're the only person we've brought on the team who doesn't need the introduction so I'll cut to the chase,' he said. 'We now have eleven suspects under surveillance. All of them passed through Heathrow on May fourteen and as far as we know at the present time, they are all lilywhites. No record of any misdemeanour and only tenuous Islamist affiliations. Certainly no training in Afghanistan. We're making some progress on who they are and we have names for some of them.'

'We've split the suspects into three groupings – Parana, Northern and Southern. The Parana group has a homogeneity of its own and it's the one we've had most success with. Your work at the airport allowed us to trace three of the eleven suspects to the Shi'ite community in the tri-border region of Brazil, Argentina and Paraguay. The river that flows through the area is named the Parana. There's a strong Lebanese contingent in the area that has links to the Hizbollah organisation and its many business interests in Lebanon. The three men appeared to have been sheltered rather than trained in the towns and ranches, sitting out the worldwide hunt for terrorists and establishing unblemished credentials for themselves. A successful operation to penetrate the community by us put names to the stills from the Heathrow security film. These guys had the smell of North Africa about them, though no one was certain about their exact nationalities. Anyway, eventually the trail led to a man named Lasenne Hadaya, a former officer in the Algerian security forces who was reported to have undergone a religious conversion after seeing a sign written in a desert rock.

'Hadaya led to a man named Furquan, with whom he had had contact in Rome. Finally we nailed the identity of the third man, a Moroccan engineer and part-time college professor named Ramzi Zaman. By the way, we had help with all this from the North African intell' services but they have no idea exactly what we're doing. Anyway, these three guys vanished in the late nineties, having lived quietly in Italy's large North African community and worked in various menial jobs that were way below each man's capabilities.'

Without asking Herrick, Collins placed a cup of coffee in her hand. She nodded gratefully.

'So, these men wind up in Western Europe. Hadaya is in Paris, Furquan in Stuttgart and the Moroccan, Zaman, is in Toulouse. Each was received by a bunch of North African helpers, who prepared for their arrival by arranging work, accommodation, cars and all kinds of local permits and passes.'

Lyne continued for another half-hour talking without pause. The Northern group consisted of five men, two in Copenhagen, one in Stockholm and two who had come to rest in Britain after flitting around Europe on May 14 and 15. They were working on the suspects in Scandinavia and were now sure that they included an Indonesian national called Badi'al Hamzi who had once been a science teacher in Jakarta. The Syrian in Denmark and the Egyptian in Sweden were unknown quantities. The two suspects in Britain were a Pakistani and a Turk. Lyne said neither of these gentlemen could break wind without MI5 and Special Branch watchers knowing about it.

'In fact they had an astonishing piece of good fortune yesterday. The Turkish fellow, Mafouz Esmet, was taken ill on the street, outside a tube station in East London. One of the female officers with the Security Services called for help and then went with the guy to hospital. He was suffering from appendicitis and had an operation last evening. She's going to visit with him tomorrow, and you know what, this could be a very important break for us.'

'Okay, so now we come to my specialty – the Southern group. These three men landed in Rome, Sarajevo and Budapest. For a time we lost one of the guys in Budapest but then we got another lucky break. An agent with the FBI's outfit in Budapest, which is mostly devoted to the Russian Mafia's activities, was travelling on a bus and just happened to see the very man whose picture he was carrying in his breast pocket. He trailed him to a poor part of town where the guy is living with a couple of Yemenis. This rang bells and again we had all three members of the Southern group checked out against descriptions of men who served in Afghanistan. But Pakistan's Inter-Service Intelligence couldn't find a match for any of them. Besides, these men don't really look the part. They're out of condition and spend a lot of time eating, drinking and smoking. They're not clean-living Muslims, that's for sure.' Lyne put his hands together and turned to look at her with radiant American purpose. 'So, basically, your job will be to chase up everything you can on these three guys. You speak Arabic, I hear. There's going to be a lot of reading to be done. You'll live and breathe these men for as long as you're with us.'

'Questions, Isis?' said Vigo, in a tone that implied he didn't expect any.

'Yes, do we have any idea about their plans? I know it's early. But are there any suspicious shipments being made? Have they been observed looking at potential targets? Do we have any communications intercepts?'

'As yet we don't have the vaguest notion what they plan,' said Collins. 'They haven't been talking to each other and there's no movement of anything like your WAYFARER. Chemicals and stuff – nothing like that. There's a general feeling among the surveillance teams that the suspects are in period of stasis, a kind of hibernation.'

'Aestivation,' said Herrick.

'Come again?' said Lyne.

'The summer equivalent of hibernation,' said Vigo, not disguising his irritation.

'Perhaps I should say something about how RAPTOR is set up,' said Collins. 'We've split the operation between surveillance and investigation. The surveillance teams on the ground – there are about thirty officers in each team – report to a desk dedicated to each suspect, which is manned twenty-four seven. Once the subject is moving, his route is plotted on an electronic map so everyone knows where he is. The field officer in charge of each surveillance consults the desk on questions of strategy and security. When there's a problem with implications for the entire operation the issue is settled by RAPTOR control, which consists of myself, Walter here and a representative of the National Security Agency. Beyond that there is a level of analysis and risk assessment reporting to our respective governments.' Collins smiled weakly, as if he had made a poor joke.

'There should be a lot of interaction between the two sides so anyone working on the investigation desks, like you, will have real-time access to surveillance, all the communication traffic between the watchers, photographs and film, when they are available. Equally, we want to feed the material you're finding out to the surveillance teams as soon as you get it.'

'Can I ask a little about the surveillance? How many of our people are involved?'

'You know a few of them,' said Vigo. 'Andy Dolph, Philip Sarre and Joe Lapping are all involved on the ground, as you would expect. You will know many others too, but as we've made clear, this is a very closed and secret order. We've had to chose personnel who do not have past associations with the cities we're covering, except in the case of Sarajevo where we felt it would be better to have people who've got Balkan experience. That's why Dolph is there.'

Herrick could feel herself bridling and hoped it wasn't showing. Dolph deserved a place in any surveillance operation: he was sharp and versatile. Sarre was at best mediocre and Lapping downright feeble. She remembered what Dolph said about Lapping after they'd been on a job together. 'He needs help crossing the road, that Lapping. You've got a better chance of going undercover with Liberace.'

Vigo saw what she was thinking. 'There's no room for personal competition on this team,' he said firmly. 'It's all for one and one for all right from the top. Believe me, those people in the field will need to be rotated and your turn will come. But we thought you would appreciate a period experiencing the whole operation beforehand. After all, it's your baby, Isis. None of us would be here were it not for you.'

She made appreciative noises.

On the way to the car that would take them to the outskirts of West London, she saw Collins murmur to Lyne, 'Brittle, but cute.'

'And a fair lip-reader too,' she said, before climbing into the Chevrolet. 'Though not in Arabic.'

The Bunker was part of the Nato command centre at Hillingdon and sat directly under an airfield where there were one or two military and private aircraft. At first glance she thought of a trading floor built for decades of nuclear winter. Two constellations of circular desks spread out across the vast space, almost like molecular diagrams. RAPTOR's full complement was never seen because of the shift system but at present she reckoned there were about 130 officers from three US agencies, the FBI, CIA and NSA, and the British counterparts, MI5, MI6 and GCHQ. Lyne explained that the surveillance operations were handled to the right of central aisle. To the left were the investigation and intelligence desks, three modules per terrorist group. They walked towards a vast notice board which featured the faces of the eleven suspects. Every known detail had been summarised and added next to the name. Lyne said the board was more reassuring than helpful. He was equally dry about the tracking operation in which the suspects' positions were marked at any time of the day or night on one of the electronic city maps. A touch of a key would give an officer a record of an individual's movements over the entire course of the operation and, if desired, the program would helpfully point out his favourite routes, where he met contacts, even the bars where he took coffee in the morning. All of this had been subject to furious but so far fruitless scrutiny, he said.

RAPTOR was still experiencing teething problems. Technicians were crawling about the floor, adjusting screens or hooking cables across the ceiling. NSA programmers struggled with two large mainframes that lived in their own special environment way off in the distance. There was a good deal of noise above, and someone from a surveillance desk would occasionally call out that one of suspects was on the move. 'Number Two going walkabout, number Six in transit.'

Raised from this activity was a control box with glass sides where Vigo, Collins and the man from the NSA, a Colonel John Franklin Plume, worked. Vigo had already taken his seat and removed his jacket to reveal a pair of vermilion braces. In front of him was a large screen, split to accept several different feeds at once from secret surveillance cameras. Above the aisle was a much larger screen that could be seen by everyone. The screen was being tested and flashes of blue TV lightning probed the recesses of the cavernous space above them.

They went over to the investigation and intelligence desks. Lyne introduced her to his group, then to the 'Wallflowers', a team of twenty eager young American research assistants whose work stations were ranged along the concrete wall of the Bunker. 'These are the slaves of the investigation desks,' he said, giving a managerial shoulder rub to one of them. 'Our Stakhanovites.'

She looked down at the desk. Each Wallflower was on the internet. Their work stations were choked with boxes of files and copies of every conceivable reference book. Herrick read some of the titles – *Gulf Maritime Conventions*, *Ancestry and the Tribes of Saudi Arabia*, *The Dictionary of Muslim Names*.

'That's about it,' said Lyne. 'Coffee, food, exercise machines, massage, laundry, sleeping arrangements: you can find them for yourself.'

She nodded, impressed.

'This is America mobilising,' he said.

'Right,' she said, and sat down at Southern Group Three.

It soon became clear to Herrick that every second of the day, RAPTOR was producing a vast amount of information which in turn spawned endless new investigative possibilities. Field officers were being sent to check out the most casual contacts made by the suspects while a lot of work was being done on the helpers who had eased the men into their hiding places. A separate data bank was dedicated to this information as it constantly threw up possible links and cross-references in the backgrounds of people and organisations across Europe. Already, interesting connections had been made – men who had attended the same university or were from the same Middle Eastern tribal grouping; clerics who had visited mosques in Stuttgart and Toulouse; businesses belonging to the fixers which had arrangements with cities where suspects were present; the use of the same banks or hawala agents to transfer money.

The range of activity was bewildering. The hackers based in Crypto

City at Fort Meade were penetrating the defences of every relevant public agency, including in a few instances the computer records of European intelligence services. Vast amounts of data were sucked up and flung unedited in the direction of London, where the systems people had breakdowns trying to absorb the flow of information and make sensible arrangements for its analysis. Added to this was the work of the Special Collection Service, a joint unit run by the CIA and NSA, based in Beltsville, Maryland. Known simply as 'Collection' it had sent a substantial proportion of its staff to Europe to eavesdrop on the suspects and their helpers. A similar outfit run by MI6 and GCHQ was also on the ground, erecting eavesdropping antennae disguised as TV aerials and dishes, and attaching devices to the suspects' phone lines. But circumspection was called for because a few of the helpers and two of the suspects were seen carrying out anti-surveillance routines while on the street. This meant they would also be alert to the possibility of electronic eavesdropping and might have access to the equipment to detect it. Electronic surveillance added another swollen tributary to the flow of intelligence that the Bunker attempted to process each day.

The British and American service chiefs let it be known they were already exceptionally pleased with the detail being gathered and sifted – they were already far in advance of their previous understanding of terrorist methods and planning, and most importantly there had been no breach in security.

'In due course,' said Spelling in a rallying speech at the end of Isis' second daily briefing in the Bunker, 'these networks of sleeper cells and enablers will be lit up like an air traffic control board. We will know the routes, the timing, the intention of these people before they know themselves. This is a very great step in the war against terrorism.' Beside him were Barbara Markham, Director of MI5, and Walter Vigo.

The Americans had all fallen in love with Vigo. They said he knew what it was like to be at the sharp end. Herrick observed that he often wandered over to the investigation desks and chatted to Lyne. On Friday evening he had made a crucial suggestion. The Rome suspect had disappeared for two days after losing the surveillance at the city's northern rail terminal.

'Have a look at the Muslim student groups in Perugia,' said Vigo. 'There's a foreign university there and our chum may be in contact with the radical groups around the Italian university.'

This advice turned out to be spot on, and two Arabic-speaking Americans were sent to the Umbrian town to sign up for Italian language courses. After this, Vigo made a point of coming over to them at least once a day. He would pull up a chair and sit with his hands folded across his Anderson and Sheppard suit to attend to detailed questions about the beliefs of the Wahabis or the transfer of gold through the Gulf States. His manner was that of a concerned PhD supervisor. The vibration of sophisticated menace Isis felt in the late night meeting with Spelling a week before had been replaced by an almost amiable focus.

Her misgivings about Vigo and the operation receded at equal pace mostly because of the pressure of work. Lyne was demanding and insisted that every avenue was investigated thoroughly. He nagged them constantly to remember the two central questions: what were the eleven planning and when were they going to move?

Lyne knew which buttons to push. When he wanted a favour out of the embassy in Riyadh he dashed off a cable and routed it through the State Department, marking it for the attention of several diplomats, even though he knew they couldn't read it because of the special encryption used by RAPTOR. What mattered was that America's spies knew their performance was being watched by the highest levels of government in Washington. On scrambled phone lines to CIA stations all over the Middle East, Lyne harried officers to make that last call. Late one night Herrick heard him organising funds to bribe an official in the Qatar immigration service. It was four in the morning in Qatar but he ordered the station chief round to the man's house and told him to email copies of the passport applications to the Bunker by morning Middle Eastern time.

Herrick pushed the British embassy officials in a similar fashion, though most of the MI6 officers working undercover in British embassies already sensed the urgency of the situation, even if they did not know precisely what was going on.

It was Herrick's conversation with Guy Laytham, the MI6 man in Oman, that produced a crucial breakthrough. Laytham remembered a reception early in the spring when a director of one of the country's bigger banks had pointedly asked him about the funding of rebuilding programmes in Sarajevo. The question struck Laytham as odd because he hadn't served in the Balkans and was unfamiliar with the levels of corruption. The banker said he was worried about a client's money that was being sent to a Muslim charity he had not heard of, through the Central Bank of Bosnia CK. Could Laytham make inquiries about the bank and the charity? Thinking about the conversation later, Laytham realised that his contact was not asking him to check out the bank and charity; he was telling him that one or both were involved in something that would interest him.

Herrick hung up and arranged to speak to Dolph in Sarajevo. Dolph, no slouch when it came to Middle Eastern banking practices, said he welcomed the distraction since the RAPTOR team was tripping over itself in Bosnia. The local suspect was only a little more active than a pregnant sloth, he said.

Fifteen minutes later he came back to her.

'How about sending a second donation from the same bank in Oman using the name of the original remitter, but with instructions that the money be picked up in cash at the bank in Sarajevo? I'll see to it that we have someone inside the bank to tell us when the transfer comes through. Then we'll simply watch who collects it.'

There was some prevarication at the British Embassy in Masqat, but eventually $5,000 of British taxpayers' money was released and sent on its way by the bank in Oman. Twenty-four hours later, Dolph was on the line saying they had surveillance pictures of someone picking up the money. Dolph suggested that the look of surprise on the man's face meant one thing: he had been the one to send the first donation from Masqat and was therefore the primary financier.

Photographs of the helper were sent back to Laytham. A bank official remembered the man from a year before when he had changed a very large sum of Saudi riyals into the local currency and US dollars. Records showed that the man's name was Sa'id al-Azm. He had produced a Saudi passport and an Omani driving licence when setting up two business accounts. The driving licence meant he had been resident in Oman for some time. A search was ordered of the country's driver and vehicle licensing authority records. On the application form he gave his occupation as construction engineer and property developer. Further search of Oman's corporation registry yielded the fact that al-Azm was from a well-known professional family in Jeddah with business connections all over the Gulf.

Late that night, as Lyne and Herrick ate a meal in the Bunker canteen with the rest of Lyne's crew, Herrick suggested that al-Azm must have known suspect Four before they both ended up in Sarajevo.

'You got a point. The Parana suspects knew each other in Rome.'

'Right, maybe they attended the same Islamic college or worked together.'

'Everything says Four's got to be a Saudi, like al-Azm. We got pictures of both so why don't we start with those and get the Wallflowers to trawl through the picture agencies?'

It took just a day for the hunch to pay off. Sa'id al-Azm's professional life didn't merit a published photograph, but in a brief newspaper description of his work as project manager for a sewage works in Oman, it was mentioned that he had played for the Saudi national under-eighteen soccer side. Pictures of the side were sent to the Bunker, but Four was nowhere to be seen. Lyne wasn't about to give up.

'Maybe he made the local side with al-Azm.' A search of the newspaper libraries around the Gulf eventually produced pictures of the Jeddah touring team from 1984 and 1985. Al-Azm was seated in the front row holding the football. Standing in the back row was the man currently under observation in Sarajevo. His name was Abd al Aziz al Hafy. 'The servant of the Almighty,' said Lyne, translating the first part of the name. Then to anyone in earshot he announced, 'We've ID'd another wood pussy. He's in the cross hairs, brothers and sisters.'

A small celebration was held – champagne in throwaway cups and cheesecake bought from a pâtisserie near the US Embassy. Spelling and various American officials emailed their congratulations to Lyne. Vigo came over to them, made a courtly bow and said they were about to get a line into al-Azm's phone.

'With their usual lack of regard for our convenience,' said Vigo, 'it's quite possible that the suspects are passing messages by word of mouth – Chinese whispers from person to person. But somewhere along the line, someone has got to make a telephone call.'

We know that, thought Herrick rather testily. The satisfaction she got from the identification of Four had not done much to reduce her unease about RAPTOR, which seemed to her to be displaying the classic growth of bureaucracy. When later someone wandered over to ask Nathan Lyne whether they should mount an operation to get DNA samples from the suspects, she shot a look of cold fury at the man. 'Why the fuck would anyone want to know their DNA profiles? The only thing that matters is what these men are planning, not whether they drink *café macchiato* in the morning or have a predisposition to male pattern baldness.'

'I agree with Isis,' said Lyne, looking a little startled at her outburst. 'I think that's a really dumb idea.'

When the man had left, Lyne steered her away to a coffee machine. 'Something eating you, Isis? Maybe you need to go get some daylight. I know I feel like a goddam earthworm down here.'

'Yes, but that's not what's bothering me. This thing is too remote. We're no nearer to knowing what they're planning. We have no concept of their leadership, although that was what my people said they wanted when they told me about all this.'

'Hey, the whole point is to watch these guys at work. We're learning all the time. It's a long process and it may go on a year or more. That's what a good intelligence operation takes – sweat, frustration and hard labour. Who said it was going to be fun?'

'All that's true. But doesn't it strike you that in this microscopic observation we're missing some of the big things?'

'Like what?'

'Like what happened to Youssef Rahe, the MI6 agent who was found murdered in Lebanon. Like what happened to the twelfth man who got on the same flight as Rahe and is presumed to be responsible for his death. We don't *know* that, yet no one has bothered to find out where he went or who he was. We just assume he was the hit man and that he's disappeared into the sands of the Middle East. Why are we ignoring him?'

'You got a point about Rahe,' said Lyne. 'But the rest of what you say challenges the policy, the whole purpose of RAPTOR. You signed up for it.'

'Well, someone needs to challenge it. Remember, these men are masters at flying under the radar. What we have here is a fantastically complicated radar system designed to detect everything but the obvious.'

Lyne shook his head sympathetically but didn't agree. 'What do you want, Isis? Arrest the suspects and lose the chance to learn who's pulling their strings and how they receive money and instructions? What we're doing here is gathering life-saving intelligence that's going to be important for maybe the next five years. It's a real opportunity you created. As Walter says, it's your baby, Isis, for chrissake.'

She nodded. 'Yes, but we're missing something. I know it, but I can't tell you what it is.' She didn't like saying this. She knew that graft, logic and occasional inspiration solved problems in their world, not some kind of daft women's intuition.

'I like having you work with me,' said Lyne. 'You're solid talent right through. The real thing. But if you're going to buck against this, you may feel you're more comfortable quitting and going back to Vauxhall Cross.' Then he slapped his forehead. 'Hey, you know what, I have an idea for getting you out of here for a while but not losing you entirely.'

'What is it?'

'I'll tell you when I've talked to Jim Collins and *Lord* Vigo. Meantime, get your ass back to work.'

She returned to the desk, picked up the phone and dialled a number in Beirut. After a little while a familiar English voice answered. Sally Cawdor was placing her ineffably sunny nature at Herrick's disposal.

In the headquarters of Albanian State Security in Tirana, Khan heard the other prisoners being beaten and brutalised during the day, and at night the groans and terrified whispers between the cells. Yet the interrogators did not lay a hand on him and after a week he was beginning to recover some of his health. They fed him well, or at least regularly, with pasta and potatoes and chicken broth. On the third day they even called a doctor to stitch the lip split by Nemim's cane. The doctor smelled his breath and gave him antibiotics for the abscess. Throughout the visit the man did not say a word, but before leaving he touched Khan's shoulder lightly and gave him a strange look, as though measuring him in some way, gauging his character.

PART TWO

CHAPTER TEN

Robert Harland inched upwards from his chair in the café on 31st Street and waited for the spasm to shoot from his lower back into his leg. He gritted his teeth as the pain reached a point behind his knee in a pure molten form. For a month now he had not been able to lie down, and had to sit perched on one buttock, holding his leg out at a particular angle. When he walked, he had first to stand, slowly stretching his frame, then move off with his right side leaning down and his head turned up to the left. The pain was unrelenting and lately, as he dragged himself between specialists, he'd begun to wonder if it would ever leave him.

He shuffled out of the way of the people on the sidewalk and reached a gingko tree where he fought for a space with a dog that scurried round him before squirting the other side of the trunk. He breathed in. Eva had once told him he could breathe into pain, but it didn't help. What did help was the neat whisky he had poured into the black coffee. It blunted his senses, and he resorted to it increasingly even though he had been warned not to mix it with the anti-inflammatory drugs, pain-killers and sleeping pills.

He started looking out for a cab to take him just six blocks to the Empire State building. A couple cruised by with their lights on but did not see him flap his arm wanly from the kerb. Finally a waiter came out of the café and asked if he could hail one for him, but Harland had changed his mind. New York cabs were as much of a problem for him as a convenience. The only way he could travel in one was by almost lying across the back seat, exposing his spine to the full force of the jolts as the cab surfed over the bumps and metal plates that lay in

Manhattan's streets. That was his life today, a querulous, narrow existence filled with obstacles. The pain had come to occupy his whole being and it was now a matter of making small gestures of resistance. He decided to walk, whatever it damn well cost him, and moved off slowly, forcing himself to take notice of the early summer sun pouring into Park Avenue. He summoned Benjamin Jaidi to his thoughts.

The Secretary-General had called him at home that morning from a plane somewhere over North Africa and ordered him to phone Dr Sammi Loz. With a thousand things on his mind and a Middle East crisis, he was apparently worrying about Harland's mysterious condition. True, the injury had prevented Harland from carrying out a mission on the West Bank in advance of Jaidi's arrival in the Middle East and he had been irritated. Still, it was thoughtful of him to have phoned and elbowed a space in Loz's schedule late that afternoon.

'The appointments with this man are like gold, you understand,' said Jaidi. 'He *will* cure you, I have no doubt of that. But in return I will expect you to look after my friend. I believe he may be about to enter a difficult period. This is the deal, Harland.'

It was typical of Jaidi to leave the conversation without specifying the doctor's difficulties or how Harland could be expected to help. But Harland had heard of Loz and dared to hope that, after the procession of chiropractors, nerve specialists and bone doctors, this man would do something for him.

He reached 5th Avenue and turned right towards the Empire State building. Now the sun was on his back and with the effort of walking like a clown he began to sweat profusely, something that Harland, once so fit and trim, loathed intensely. He paused and looked up at the building thrusting into the brilliant, almost white sky above Manhattan and remembered lines that Jaidi had pointed out to him. 'This riddle in steel and stone is at once the perfect target and the perfect demonstration of non-violence, of racial brotherhood, this lofty target scraping the skies and meeting the destroying planes halfway.'

Jaidi had said, looking out over the city from his suite in the UN tower, 'That was written in forty-eight by E.B. White, about the very building we're standing in now. "A single flight of planes no bigger than a wedge of geese can quickly end this island fantasy." A great artist must be prescient, don't you think, Harland? He must know things even though he doesn't understand where they come from. Troubled times, Harland. Troubled times.'

Harland reached the entrance where a line of doughty American tourists stretched round the corner into 34th Street, passed through security and took the elevator to the sixty-fourth floor. He was grateful to be in the cool and when he got out of the elevator, he rested a while, mopping his face and neck, regretting the whisky which he knew had caused the sweating fit and made him smell. He looked around. The corridor was quite silent, except for the gasp and whine of the elevators as they rose and plunged through the 1,200 odd feet of the Empire State. A door opened and a man in shirt-sleeves looked out and examined Harland pointedly before turning back inside. At the far end of the corridor another man in a suit and tie showed a close interest in him. Harland called out to ask where Dr Loz's office was. The man gestured with a turn of the head. 'Four down on the right,' he said and returned to his newspaper. As Harland crept along the wall, he passed a third man, sitting just inside an open door. This one was armed and wasn't bothering to hide it.

He pushed on the door that announced Dr Sammi Loz DO FAAO and found a slender man in a smoke-blue tunic buttoned to the neck, standing behind the reception desk. He moved out to greet him.

'You must be Robert Harland. Forgive me, I've sent my assistant off to organise the clinic at the hospital this evening.' He stood still for a moment, his eyes running over Harland. 'Yes, you *are* in a lot of pain.' Loz was in his mid-thirties, with a high forehead, wavy, well-groomed hair, a thin, slightly aquiline nose and a generous mouth that spread easily into a smile. Harland guessed he was Iranian or Armenian, though he spoke with an unimpeachable English accent and his voice was modulated with concern as his eyes made easy contact with Harland's. 'Yes, we're going to have to do something about this immediately. Come,' he said, gesturing to a room. 'Come in here and take the weight off your feet.'

Harland perched on a raised bed, now nauseous with the pain. Loz began to take down his medical history, but seeing that Harland could no longer really concentrate, helped him off with his trousers and shirt and told him to stand facing the wall. After examining him from behind for a minute or two, Loz moved round to his front and looked at his patient with a gaze directed about five inches to the right of him, in order, Harland assumed, to see his whole. He placed one hand on Harland's sternum and the other in the middle of his back and exerted a tiny amount of pressure for about five minutes. His hands began to dart around his torso, pausing lightly on his upper and middle chest, neck, spine and the top of his pelvis. He was like a Braille reader finding meaning in every bump and depression, and once or twice he paused and repeated the movement to make sure he had not misunderstood. Then his hands came to rest on the marks and scars on Harland's contorted body and he peered up into his face to seek confirmation of what he suspected. 'You've had a rough, tough old life, Mr Harland. The Secretary-General told me you were the only survivor of that plane crash eighteen months ago at La Guardia. I remember seeing your picture on the television news. That was something.'

Harland nodded.

'And these burn marks on your wrist and ankles, the scars on your back. These are older, aren't they? What caused them?'

Harland was embarrassed. He didn't like to use the word torture – it shocked people and tended to evoke a sympathy that he had no use for.

'It's a long story. I was held prisoner for a while back in the nineties.'

'I see,' said Loz gently. He told him to sit on the couch then lifted Harland's legs up so he was able to lie on his back.

'I don't think I can take much manipulation,' Harland said, at the same time noting that the pain had subsided a little.

'Nor do I,' said Loz. His hands moved to Harland's feet. He bent first one leg then the other, holding the kneecap in the palm of his hand.

'What are the men doing in the hallway?' Harland asked.

'That's a long story.' Loz's attention was elsewhere.

Harland's eyes came to rest on an Arabic inscription hung in a simple frame. 'What's it say?' he asked.

'Oh, that. It's a warning against pride and arrogance. It was written by a man named al-Jazir two hundred years after the Prophet died. It says, "A man who is noble does not pretend to be noble, any more than a man who is eloquent feigns eloquence. When a man exaggerates his qualities it is because of something lacking in himself; the bully gives himself airs because he is conscious of his weakness." '

'Very true,' commented Harland.

Loz had moved behind him and, after holding his head and working his neck very gently, slipped his hands down to the middle of his back, his fingers moving with the whole of Harland's weight pressing down on them. Although the pain still lurked beneath the surface, the heat had been taken out of it and for the first time in four weeks Harland felt free to think.

'The air crash,' said Loz suddenly. 'This has caused your pain. The trauma you experienced has come to the surface.'

'After all that time?'

'Yes. You've kept that shock at the centre. You are a very strong and controlled individual Mr Harland – impressively so. But it was going to happen some day. The body has to get rid of it.' He paused. 'And the other things in you. These too will have to come out.'

Harland ignored this. 'You can treat it then?'

'Oh yes, I *am* treating it. You will recover and you'll be able to sleep tonight without the use of alcohol.' He peered at him with an expression of deep understanding that unsettled Harland. 'We'll need to work on this over the next few months. It's a very serious matter. You will feel not quite yourself for twenty-four hours, as though you have a mild case of 'flu. Rest up and get as much sleep as you can.'

He continued working for another twenty minutes on the hips and pubic bone. Harland's eyes drifted to the slightly tinted glass of the window and the glistening silver helmet of the Chrysler building. 'The Empire State is an unusual place to have your practice,' he said.

'Yes, but I am disinclined to go to the Upper East Side where many of my patients are. It's an arid part of the city, don't you think? No heart. Too much money. Besides, I love this building. You know they began it just before the Crash, continued building it through the Depression and finished it forty-five days ahead of schedule. It's a lucky building with a strong personality, and not a little mystery.'

'A riddle of steel and concrete.'

'Ah, you've been talking to Benjamin Jaidi. He told me he had found that passage when I visited him the other day.'

He left Harland's side and went to a small glass and steel table to write something down. He returned and placed a note in Harland's hand. 'This is the time of our next appointment.'

Harland read it to himself. 'Sevastapol – 8.30 p.m. tomorrow. Table in the name of Keane.' He looked up at Loz, who had put his finger to his lips and was pointing to the ceiling with his other hand.

'Right, we will see each other in a week's time. But now I must go to the hospital. Rest here for ten minutes then turn off the lights and pull the door to. It will lock automatically.' He smiled and left Harland in the cool solitude of the room, watching the light slip across the buildings outside. He looked round the room again, noticing five battered postcards of the Empire State lined up along a shelf, copies of the Koran and the Bible and a fragment of stone, which looked like an ancient spearhead.

He left after about half an hour and went to the apartment in Brooklyn Heights, where he ordered in a Chinese meal and settled down with a book about Isaac Newton.

The Sevastapol was much more than a restaurant of the moment. The same writers, film and money people and city politicians had been haunting the same tables for decades. It was above fashion. Harland had been twice with Eva, who was fascinated by the place and its noisy owner, a Ukrainian named Limoshencko, a pet brigand of the downtown crowd.

Harland passed through the tables outside, consciously putting Eva from his mind, and asked for Mr Keane. He was pointed in the direction of a table that was obscured by the bar and by a tall young woman who was gesticulating in a manner designed for public consumption. Loz was seated with his hands folded on the table, looking up at her with an unwavering if rather formal politeness. He rose to greet Harland but did not introduce the woman, who then left rather resentfully.

'It's good to see you,' he said. 'You're looking a different man.'

'Thanks to you. I'm a bit fragile, but a lot better. Look, call me Robert or Bobby, please.'

'You know, I prefer Harland. It's a good name.' They sat down. 'It's a good dependable name.' He moved closer. 'I'm afraid we had to come here because the FBI couldn't get a table in a thousand years.'

'The men in the hallway were FBI?'

'Yes, they've been with me since the first postcard arrived. Did you look at them when I left?'

'The postcards of the Empire State? Of course not.'

'That's interesting, an investigator with principles.'

'I'm not an investigator, Dr Loz. I do research work for the UN. Most of my time is spent on clean water issues. It's pretty unexciting.'

'Jaidi told me you were due to go to the Middle East to talk to Hamas. That isn't just research, surely?'

Harland ignored the remark. 'He was rather oblique about you, Doctor. He said you were about to have some problems. I will certainly help if I can.'

Loz flashed a discreet, slightly awkward smile at him. 'You see them out there? The black van down the street by the mailbox? I know that vehicle as if it was my own. It's the FBI. They follow me everywhere. They're making my life very difficult indeed and I think it's quite possible that I will be arrested. I've seen a lawyer – a patient of mine – and he told me to be utterly open in all my dealings, but I couldn't be more open. I live a very simple and uncomplicated life. Apparently there's nothing I can do to fight this kind of harassment. America is no longer the land of the free, Mr Harland. People like me with Muslim backgrounds can disappear into jail and never be heard of again.'

'I think they'd have to have strong grounds for arresting someone like you. You're very well connected.'

'Oh believe me, that's not true. How many innocent people have they detained without charge or trial? Here in the United States of America people are disappearing as though it's a police state in *Latin* America. I love this country beyond any in the world. I believe in it. That's why I became a US citizen. I sometimes think I was born to be an American and to work in the Empire State building.' For a moment his eyes flared with hurt and indignation. The waiter who had been hovering to take their orders beat a retreat.

'When did this start?' asked Harland.

'When the first postcard arrived, at the end of last year. I guess some mailman with a keen eye thought it was odd for a postcard of the Empire State to be sent to the Empire State with a foreign postmark. They read my name and saw the signature Karim Khan and came up with a plot. Who knows what they think these days.'

'Who is Karim Khan?'

'A friend.'

'What was written on it?'

'In essence each one told me of my friend Karim's progress from Pakistan to the West. The first one was from Pakistan, then there was one from Mashhad, a town in Iran, another from Tehran, one from Diyarbakir in Turkey, and the last came from Albania.'

'But why pictures of the building? It does look odd. Is there any significance?'

'No, I just kept a stack of cards of the building. I have done since I first visited New York in the eighties. And when Karim went off to Afghanistan I gave them to him with my address written on because I knew that while I might move apartment I would never move my practice.'

'Do the FBI know your friend was in Afghanistan?'

'Maybe. They have lists of these things. I am certain.'

'You're telling me he fought with the Taleban?'

'Yes, but he used a *nomme de guerre*. He had one before he left.'

'You must expect this kind of trouble. To all intents and purposes he may be regarded as a very likely enemy of the state.'

'No,' Loz said with finality. He smiled at Harland once, a brief piece of punctuation that closed the issue. He turned and ordered for them both – caviar, blinis and Kobi beef with spinach. 'Will you have some wine? I don't drink.'

Harland shook his head.

'Good, I'm glad to hear you're giving your system a rest.' He paused. 'What if I told you I was going to be arrested tonight?'

'I would be very surprised if you had advance notice of that.'

'It's a feeling. The pressure has been increasing over the last few days. I cannot be arrested and I cannot submit to confinement. I want your help to avoid it.'

'Tell me about your friend,' said Harland, noticing now that nearly every woman in the restaurant had either waved to or was stealing looks in Loz's direction.

'We were both sent to Westminster School in London to gain qualifications to go to college in England. Karim was from an affluent family in Lahore – very old, very pukka. I was brought up in Lebanon, though my father was Iranian; my mother had a Druze background. We were outsiders in an English public school so it was natural that we became friends, despite being unlike each other in practically every way. He was wilder, more gregarious, more daring and I suppose more fun. I think we relied on each other's strengths.'

'Tell me about these postcards.'

Loz took five postcards from his pocket and laid them out in their order of arrival. Harland examined the images then turned them over. On each there was a short message in an educated hand. The first said:

Greetings, my old friend. I am in Pakistan and hope very soon to be in London. I may need a little help from you. I have good news. I am returning to complete my medical studies, as you always said I should.

The next two were less upbeat and gave only details of where Khan was in Iran. The card from Turkey told how much of his money had been stolen. He still had $400 that his mother had given him and he hoped to use this to get to London. But there were unspecified visa and passport problems.

Harland read them again. 'They seem harmless enough,' he said eventually. 'But these days intelligence services are likely to look at them with an eye for codes and hidden messages.'

Loz wasn't listening. 'Karim needs my help,' he said, looking straight past Harland into the mêlée of diners and table-hoppers. 'The last postcard, from Albania, was followed by this letter. I assume they read this as well, but there were no signs of the envelope having been opened.' He withdrew a single sheet of lined paper from his jacket. The letter was signed by a Mr Skender. It told of Karim Khan's arrest and imprisonment and his transfer to the state security centre in Tirana. The letter mentioned that Khan had made the local TV news in the context of a massacre in Macedonia.

'I know something about this incident,' said Harland. 'The UN has been asked to investigate by the Albanian minority in Macedonia.'

Loz turned to him. 'I had a friend go through the Balkan news websites – it's clear those men were murdered. They had come from Turkey. Karim must have been travelling with them.'

'Then why wasn't he killed?'

'Because he knows what to do in such situations.' He produced a printout of a web page from a Greek newspaper and pointed to a photograph of a bedraggled man, dwarfed between two policemen. 'That is Karim, though he is barely recognisable. You can see that he is very thin and has been hurt.' A troubled look swept his face and he reached for the bottle of water. Neither of them had eaten much of the first course, and when he had drained his glass he pushed his plate aside and waved to the waiter.

'I had the caption beneath the picture translated.' He handed Harland a piece of white card.

Terrorist snared after gun battle in Macedonia.

Jasur al-Jahez, the man who escaped from Macedonian security forces in a raging gun battle has been found to be a Palestinian terrorist wanted in connection with outrages by the Israeli authorities and also by Syria, Egypt and Lebanon. Jasur al-Jahez, also known as The Electrician, was believed to have died of natural causes eighteen months ago and has not been heard of since. Israel, Syria and Egypt are now seeking his extradition.

Loz took back the card. 'This *is* Karim, but for reasons I cannot comprehend they believe he is Jasur. Jasur has killed many, many people. Apparently he split with Hamas in the early nineties and formed a group that assassinated moderate clerics and politicians all over the Middle East.'

'I have heard of him,' said Harland. 'Your friend is in a lot of trouble if they think he's Jasur.'

'Now you see why I cannot be arrested,' he said, placing his hand lightly on Harland's. 'I must help him.'

Whether or not something was transmitted in the touch Harland could not say, but he was aware that a part of him submitted very easily with the pressure of Loz's hands, and something made him try to resist. 'What can you do?'

'I don't know, but I must try. Now I think we should go. There's a letter on your desk from the Secretary-General. He wrote it before he left and asked me to let him know when it should be released to you. In that letter you will find his instructions.'

'Does he know about Khan?'

'Some of it, but he left before I discovered the business about the mistaken identity.'

'And this letter, what does it say?'

'I don't know.'

'Right, I'll pick it up tomorrow,' said Harland.

'Why not this evening? You are feeling better, are you not? We should go now. I have a small bag at the back of the restaurant and we will leave through the kitchens. It has been arranged. I will go first and wait for you at the rear entrance. The bill has already been settled.'

With this he got up. On his way to Sevastapol's kitchens he paused at two tables, shaking hands and saying hello. Harland noticed how he made contact with each person, drawing a palm across a shoulder, touching a bare forearm or clasping a hand for just a second or two longer than was usual. This casual laying on of hands over, he moved without haste to the kitchens and vanished through the swing doors.

Harland got up a little stiffly and walked through the kitchens to find Loz waiting with small black bag at the rear door. He worked the double lock, moved out into the warm evening and indicated to a car across the street. Just then a man hurried to them clutching one of his pockets.

'Mr Loz. Federal Bureau of Investigation. Agent Morris. I need you to come with me, sir.'

Harland stepped forward. 'I'm afraid that's not possible. This man is in my custody. I'm taking him to the headquarters of the United Nations under the explicit instructions of the Secretary-General.' He showed him the UN police badge that Jaidi had issued him during an internal investigation six months before.

'I'll check this out sir,' he said, pulling the microphone on his lapel towards his mouth.

'You do that Agent Morris,' Harland replied, knowing it would be a matter of seconds before his colleagues at the front of the restaurant came on the scene to seize Loz legitimately. 'But I have to take this man with me now. It's a matter of the greatest urgency.' The agent, who was saying something and pressing his hand against his ear at the same time, put himself between Harland and Loz. 'Back off, sir,' he said to Harland. 'This is a Federal matter.'

'Go to the car,' Harland told Loz.

'No, you stay right where you are, sir,' the FBI man replied, moving for his gun. Harland clamped his hand round the holster and moved his forearm up against the man's Adam's apple, forcing him back to Sevastopol's door. He held him there and wrenched the gun from its holster. 'This is one occasion the United Nations takes precedence over the United States – okay!' He ran over to the car and scrambled in, but as he reached round to pull the door closed he felt his back go, and fell in agony across the seat. 'Take us to the UN building,' he shouted to the driver.

The Ukrainian chauffeur supplied by Limoschencko warmed to the task of out-driving the FBI and shot up 6th, running lights on Houston and West Four, then crossed to the East Side along the top of Washington Square Park. In less than five minutes they were on 1st Avenue, speeding towards the sanctuary of the United Nations. No car followed.

CHAPTER ELEVEN

'Harland, pick up! I know you've got that goddam back doctor with you.' Harland recognised the voice of Special Agent Frank Ollins of the FBI. Ollins had led the air crash investigation two years before. For a time they had been uneasy allies during the investigation, but then Ollins had been warned off by the Bureau.

Clutching his back, Harland moved to the phone. 'Hello, Frank. How can I help you?'

'I guessed right,' said Frank.

'How'd you get my direct line – the switchboard isn't working this time of night.'

'I got a phone directory for the UN, for chrissake. What's it to you?'

'Then do me a favour and look up the number of the Secretary-General. Ask the duty officer what Mr Jaidi's instructions are concerning Dr Loz. After that, find the number for Senator Howard Staple. You know who he is, Frank? He's one of New York's two senators. Mr Staple is a long-time patient and friend of Dr Loz's. You ask him whether he thinks arresting an innocent American citizen on the grounds that he is a Muslim is either fair or just, or indeed tactful at this point. You ask him, Frank, then come back to me.'

'Look, we just want to talk to him.'

'Then book an appointment like everyone else. You know where to find him. You know his schedule. Your men have got his office covered twenty-four hours a day.'

'Why don't you just put him on the street now, Harland? We know he's with you.'

'Good for you. But to answer your question, no, I'm not going to give him to you.'

'For Christ's sake, Harland, you do realise you could be aiding a major terrorist? We can file any number of charges for your treatment of Agent Morris in the street this evening.'

'I don't think so, Ollins,' said Harland, laughing. 'You want me to have a word with the fellows in the press department? By noon tomorrow I'll have a story about the FBI harassing UN officials on every news service in Europe and the Middle East. I take it you're aware of the situation in the Middle East, Frank? I know it's not your beat, but even you understand that the US is in a bind. What do you think the State Department is going to say to Justice and the director of the FBI when you try to arrest Dr Loz? You're out of your depth, Frank. Leave this man alone.'

'I hear you threatening me,' said Ollins calmly. 'And I'm sure you're acting with the best motives, but you don't want to be caught up in this, believe me. I'll be waiting outside.' There was a click as he hung up.

Harland turned to Loz, who seemed unfazed by what he'd heard. 'How's the back?' he asked. 'I'm afraid it's not going to get any better with me treating you on a desk. But what I did should work for a day or two. You want a glass of water? You should drink more water, you know.'

Harland replied that there was whisky in his assistant Marika's room – his whisky, but kept in her cabinet at her insistence. When Loz had gone into Marika's office, he stretched a little and moved to an armchair where he opened Benjamin Jaidi's letter.

My dear Harland,

If you are reading this, Sammi Loz has signalled that he is in need of our help. This should be offered unconditionally by you on my behalf, and you should regard all United Nations facilities and the influence of my office as being at your disposal. Your role will be simply to watch Dr Loz and watch over him. I stress the distinction between those roles, though he has performed numerous services for this office and I believe we owe it to him to help him through his present difficulties. I enclose a letter which states that you are working for me and directs anyone who challenges or questions you during the course of this assignment to my office. This, I hope, will be of some use to you, my dear Harland.

Yours with gratitude,

Benjamin Jaidi (signed in his absence)

He folded the two sheets of paper and placed them in his pocket. Loz returned with the whisky.

'You read the letter. I was right, wasn't I? Jaidi wants you to help me.' He handed the glass to Harland. 'What do we do now?'

'I'm thinking,' Harland replied. 'Perhaps you'd better tell me what you want, apart from avoiding arrest?'

'To go to Albania,' said Loz simply.

'Just like that? It's not Atlantic City you know.' He exhaled heavily and took a mouthful of whisky. 'If you turn up in Tirana waving a picture of your old school pal they're likely to put you straight in jail. And when it comes to prisons, I'd choose American over Albanian any day.'

'I have to go. You must understand that there's no other way.'

'Even if you get there, you have to realise your man will have been seen by the CIA. Despite all protestations to the contrary, the CIA and FBI *do* talk. When you show your face in Albania the CIA will tell the FBI and that is likely to confirm all the suspicions they have about you. You'll wind up in prison for a very long time. Much better to go to the FBI. Tell them the story of Khan and then go to Albania if you must.'

Loz was unmoved. 'That is not possible.'

'It's your only course.'

'And where will you be, Harland, if they lock me up? What will you do for your back? You have a very serious condition and I am confident that I'm one of the very few people who can treat it. The Secretary-General told me you had tried everything before coming to see me. Is that right?'

Harland shifted in the chair and drank some more whisky, wondering about the imperturbable man in front of him.

'I want to know more about you and Karim Khan – all the things you left out in the restaurant. If I think you're keeping anything from me, I'll put you back on American soil straight away.'

'What do you want to know?'

'Why you owe him.'

'He saved my life.'

Harland revolved his hand. 'More, Doctor, I need more.'

'In Bosnia he offered his life for mine.'

'When were you there?'

'Ninety-two to ninety-three. I had finished my course at Guy's, Karim had one year to go. We joined a convoy taking supplies from London to Sarajevo. We went for the adventure and we didn't imagine what we'd find when we got to Bosnia. The trucks never reached Sarajevo of course and most of the stuff was looted in Krajina, not far from the coast. But Karim and I managed to communicate with the peacekeepers and became involved.'

'You fought the Serbs?'

He lowered his gaze. 'We were Muslims. Although neither of us had attended a mosque for many years, we felt obligated to help our people. I was there for a short while; Karim remained until nineteen ninety-six.'

Loz took off his jacket and started unbuttoning his shirt. He slipped off the right side and turned to reveal a patch of mottled light skin on his back, matched by a similar, smaller patch on his front to the right of his diaphragm. 'These are the grafts I received after being wounded by a mortar shell.' He did up his shirt and put on his jacket, fastidiously nipping at his collar and sleeves. 'We were serving with the brigade in the north of the city. We were in a trench, very much like you have seen in pictures of the First World War, facing the Serb lines. Ahead of us was an outcrop of rock where the Serbs had a heavy machine gun and mortar. Snipers used the rock also. They could look down almost into our trench and we were losing a lot of men. The outcrop was about fifty yards from the Serb lines and we believed if we captured it we'd save many lives as well as improving our concentration of fire.' As Loz talked he moved his hands through the air and glanced up to give an idea of the angles of fire.

'We launched an attack but were beaten back. As we retreated across no man's land they got the mortar range right and I was hit in the back and the leg. I was lying out there all night. The Serbs didn't finish me off because they thought my cries would demoralise our lines.' He stopped and moved to perch on the side of Harland's desk. 'Karim got back safely. He could not stand to hear my pain. He shouted to the Serbs that they could have him in exchange for allowing me to be taken back to our lines. The Serbs agreed, although we knew they would try to trick us and kill Karim and his helpers, as well as me. The arrangement was that two of our men would accompany Karim to the spot where I was lying and bring me back. At the same time two of their men would walk out and take Karim. All six of us would be exposed and both sides knew their men could be killed instantly. It was all about timing.

'Karim reached me and walked on with his hands in the air to meet the two Serbs, leaving our two guys by me. As he left, the two men who had come to pick me up began to count the seconds away. One... two... three – very slow, like that. It looked to the Serbs like they had the advantage because they could get their men back to safety and pick the rest of us off. When Karim reached the Serbs they called out, and this big Algerian man, very strong in the legs, lifted me on his back and we set off to our trench with the other man counting out loud. They knew they had thirty seconds to get me back because Karim was counting also. As they reached thirty they lowered me into the trench. Then Karim put his plan into action.'

Loz stood up, put his hands behind his neck, then continued. 'He had strapped hand grenades under the hood of his jacket, attached by the pins, so when he pulled the grenades away, the pins came out. Remember, his arms were raised like this, so he was able to let them drop back behind his neck. Just as they reached the trench with me, he took hold of two hand grenades, slipped behind his escort and threw them in the direction of the Serb lines. He could throw a cricket ball a hundred and fifty yards and aim it like he was dropping a penny into a glass. Two more followed. By this time our side were firing to cover him, but the Serbs couldn't get a clean shot at him because their men were in the way. He had many more grenades in his pockets and a couple of handguns concealed in his waistband. He dealt with the Serb escort and then went on to take that rock outcrop by himself. God knows how many people he killed in those few minutes but it was certainly the bravest act any of us had seen. And it didn't end there. He took me to find treatment and waited until he knew I was going to be okay.'

During the telling of this story some of the polish had slipped from Loz's manner and Harland sensed that he regretted his vehemence. Loz's eyes returned to his shoes and he smiled to himself.

Harland said nothing.

'You know, Karim was soft. He liked the easy life in London, *la dolce vita* – the women, the clubs, the alcohol, the restaurants. When he got to Bosnia he couldn't take the cold, the lack of sleep and the food. But instead of crawling back to London with his tail between his legs, he became a real soldier, one of the best men defending Sarajevo. He buckled down to it.'

'When did you last see him?'

'In London – 1997.'

'So by then you had moved to New York and set up your practice in the Empire State?'

'Yes.'

'But you weren't trained as an osteopath by then?'

'No, I took the premises while I was training.'

'Expensive.'

'Mr Harland, that's what I wanted. I was a rich young man. So was Karim. It wasn't a problem for me, you understand.' He paused. 'So, have you heard enough about us?'

He shook his head. 'I am not going on the run with you, Doctor. You're going to see the FBI and tell them what you told me. Straight. Explain who Karim is.'

'They'll put me in prison.'

'They won't be able to: Ollins will come in here and talk, then he will leave.'

The interview went on until dawn in Harland's office. Ollins insisted that Harland leave so he went off and found himself somewhere to stretch out. He was woken by the toe of Ollins' well-worn black brogue at six, but had to be helped up.

'You're too old for this shit, Harland,' said Ollins, without letting the slightest sympathy crack his face. 'Why don't you stick with the water sports in Dubai?'

'Water supply, Frank – drinking water for people who don't have it.'

'You know what, Harland? Your back quack doesn't ring true to me.

Just because we can't lay a glove on him now doesn't mean we're going to quit trying.'

'But you got some of what you wanted?'

'Nowhere near.'

'Still, you have to agree you've had unobstructed access to someone in UN custody.'

Ollins levelled his gaze at him. 'I just want to know one thing. What are you and the Secretary-General going to do if this guy is a terrorist, as we believe he is? How are your boys in the *press department* going to spin that one? "Jaidi Aide Gave Terrorist UN Haven." Don't imagine Jaidi will stand by you for that. He'll stiff you, Harland, and then where will you go – a guy with a back problem who knows about water? Huh?'

'I'll get someone to show you from the premises, Special Agent,' said Harland.

When he returned to his office he found Loz gazing meditatively along the East River. 'What do you want me to do, Harland?' he asked.

'What did you tell Ollins?'

'Everything I told you.'

'Good, that should keep him quiet for a while. The canteen will open soon. You should go and have breakfast while I think and make some calls.'

As Loz wandered off, Harland received two calls in rapid succession, the first from an assistant Secretary-General who was with Jaidi in Cairo, wanting to know the situation. The second came from a man named Charlie Coulson, one of several MI6 officers attached to the British Mission to the UN. Coulson had somehow heard about the situation and tried to impress upon Harland the need to get Loz out of the UN as soon as possible.

'We don't want this to turn into a stand-off between the Americans and the UN with a Brit in the middle,' he said. There was something about the way he was speaking that made Harland think that there were others listening. 'Look, is there any chance of you leaving your chap and having a cup of coffee with me? There's a place called The Sutton Coffee House on First Avenue. I'll see you there in twenty. Your man's not going anywhere without you.'

Coulson was in a booth reading the *Financial Times*. He was exactly as Harland had guessed from his voice – a combination of military briskness and social ease. He was in his forties and wearing a dark blue suit, suede loafers and a spotted tie.

'We'd like to know what you're up to with this character,' he said, after the waitress had brought coffee.

'That's UN business, I'm afraid.'

'We think it goes beyond that,' said Coulson. 'We understand Secretary-General Jaidi is involved. That makes it very high profile. Tell me, what do you know about Loz?'

Harland didn't reply.

'For instance, did you know that before he started squiring half the available crumpet in New York, he fought in the Balkans and is very, very rich?'

'He doesn't make any secret of it.'

'Right,' said Coulson, looking slightly disappointed. 'But we think he's important and I know the Chief is most concerned.' This was a common enough ploy. The Chief wants this; the Chief thinks so and so; the Chief has placed the highest priority... It was all bullshit. When Harland was in the Service he used it often, implying to some greedy little defector that his case was under the constant scrutiny of the head of the British Secret Intelligence Service.

'I'm sure he is. Even in his final days at Vauxhall Cross, Sir Robin Teckman is watching developments in a thousand intelligence arenas with the keenest interest.'

'In this instance it happens to be true.' Coulson got up.

Two men had materialised by the booth. One of them was the unmistakably patrician figure of Sir Robin Teckman; the other was his bodyguard. Teckman placed a hand on Harland's shoulder. 'Don't get up, Bobby,' he said.

Harland couldn't help returning the smile. He had always liked and admired Teckman. 'What the hell are you doing here, Chief?'

'Oh, you know, routine stuff. But I must say it's very pleasant to be in New York at this time of year. The city gives one a spring in the step. I used to love it when I was doing my time at the UN.'

His guard dropped back to the bar and the three of them were left alone.

'We were talking about the situation at the UN,' said Coulson.

'I dare say,' said Teckman, fixing Harland with an interested gaze. 'Bit of a mess, is it Bobby?'

'I don't think so.'

'I'm glad you say that, because from the outside it looks rather as though it is. I mean, he can't live in your office for ever, can he?' He paused. 'I think we ought to be open with you. This man Loz interests us. We've been watching him, though not as intensely as your friends in the FBI.'

'Why?'

Teckman gave him the stonewall smile. 'Suffice it to say, we were never totally convinced by his story.'

'But why would you even be aware of his story?'

'We're always interested in the Secretary-General's friends. Loz came to our notice a year or so ago and we felt he was not quite twelve apples to the dozen. We want you to stick with him. Find out everything he knows.'

'I don't work for you,' said Harland testily.

'But how does this compromise your position, Bobby? You would simply be doing what Jaidi asked you and letting us know as you go along. And of course you will want to keep in touch with Dr Loz because of your back.' He let out a chuckle. 'I hear he's very good but I wonder whether he has done all he can for you. That would be one way of keeping your interest, wouldn't it?'

That thought had occurred to Harland as he had lain face down on his desk the previous evening. 'My impression is that Loz is far too sophisticated and too successful to be involved in any kind of terrorism,' he said defensively. 'He's got everything to lose.' He wondered how much they knew about Loz's friend Khan. Probably nothing if they hadn't already mentioned him.

'Sophistication doesn't rule out evil. But in substance I agree with you. Still…' He leaned across the table and lowered his voice. 'I believe he can lead us to something very important, and I want you to let him take you with him. You won't even have to tell us anything. Just be aware that we'll be behind you.'

'If you're so sure he's got something to hide, why aren't you working with the FBI? You share intelligence on all this. Why not now?'

'He's got something to tell; not something to hide. I'm certain they don't see the difference.' The Chief shook his head anxiously. 'It's become awfully complicated, this business we're in, hasn't it? Now, tell me how you are.'

Coulson got up and went to join Teckman's guard.

'Nothing much to say,' said Harland.

'Any news of her? I had heard things hadn't been easy.'

Harland didn't like to talk about Eva, because it was almost impossible to utter a coherent sentence about her disappearance, especially to Teckman, who had been privy to her work for British intelligence and knew their story. Harland had been away in Azerbaijan for a few days. On his return he found that Eva had cleared out some, but not all, of her things and resigned from her Wall Street job where she'd worked on an Eastern European investments desk. No note, no calls, not a single transaction on their joint account or on any of her credit cards. So he had gone to the Karlsbad in the Czech Republic and searched for her. There was no trace. The large apartment where she had once lived with her mother had been re-let and there was no forwarding address. Eva Rath had disappeared again. No, things hadn't been easy.

'Bobby, we'd be more than happy to help on this. If there's anything you think we can do, you know you just have to say the word.'

'Thank you.'

'You think she's alive?'

'Yes.' Why not tell someone, he thought. Why not say what you actually think instead of this fucking secrecy? 'I believe... I believe she just decided it wasn't going to work, and rather than going through the distress of explaining, she just cut out. That's her.' Articulating it didn't make him feel better.

The Chief nodded. 'Well, I really am very sorry indeed. You deserve happiness more than most.' He paused. 'On this other business, I think you understand that I wouldn't ask you unless I thought it was of the utmost importance. It really is. All you have to do is keep tabs on this man and we'll follow along at a discreet distance.'

He nodded. He knew it would be more than that, but what the hell. It might pay to have some help on hand.

'And this meeting hasn't taken place. Even with our own people, you haven't seen me. I can't stress the importance of this too much.' He got up, gripped Harland's shoulder and squeezed it. 'Look after yourself old son, and get that back better.' Then he was gone, slipping across the stream of office workers into a black Lincoln.

Coulson's exfiltration skills were not required. When Harland took him to his office in the UN building, he found a note from Sammi Loz on his desk.

I have discovered a way of leaving the building undetected. I shall be in the Byron hotel in Tirana in two days' time and will expect you there. Before flying, take a day's rest on your back and drink plenty of water.
   With warmest regards,
   Sammi Loz

'He won't get out of the country,' said Harland.

'I'm not so sure,' said Coulson. 'After all he's not on the watch lists and if he's managed to dodge the FBI outside the building, they'll assume he's still in here. They won't be looking for him at the airports yet.'

'That's true,' said Harland. 'Ollins must believe he's with me for as long as possible.'

'And when they eventually demand you give up the man in your office, you can shove a surprised British diplomat out into the sunshine. That is to say, yours truly.'

CHAPTER TWELVE

Herrick and Nathan Lyne took to having a drink together after a late shift, during which a kind of truce operated and they talked about anything but RAPTOR. One evening Lyne told her to hang around because a decision had been taken to arrest the suspect in Stuttgart the following morning at 1.30 a.m. local time. The man known as Furquan, the third member of the Parana group, had in fact turned out to be called Mohammed bin Khidir. His voice had been recorded while he was speaking on a payphone a few hundred yards from his apartment. By chance someone at GCHQ had compared this with samples in their archive and matched it with what was known as the Bramble video.

Lyne explained that Mrs Christa Bramble, a young widow from Woking in Surrey, had been visiting the ancient sites of Carthage in Tunisia. At one of the sites, she and her party came under attack from a group of seven men armed with machine guns. Twelve tourists were killed and twenty-one others, including Mrs Bramble, were injured. As she fell to the ground, she kept her finger on the record button of her video camera and captured some blurred scenes and – crucially – the sound of the terrorists shouting and talking. From these came three distinct voiceprints, one of which was that of bin Khidir. Enhancing techniques, applied by the FBI to the film, clinched the identification. One of the moving figures matched Furquan's height, weight and gait exactly, and that man they knew to be Mohammed bin Khidir.

Under the terms of RAPTOR, any of the suspects confirmed to have been involved in international terrorism had to be killed or taken off the street – as Lyne put it, 'stiffed or lifted'. The former seemed a great deal easier, but they knew that a professional killing would act like a bird scarer for the other ten suspects. So a plan was developed, in which bin Khidir would be kidnapped from his apartment in the Turkish district of Stuttgart, and taken to an airfield nearby.

Herrick and Lyne went to their desks and hooked up to the live feed from Stuttgart. There was a commentary of sorts from a van parked near bin Khidir's apartment and they caught the clipped sentences of the armed members of the snatch squad.

Lyne sat tensely. 'If this fucking thing goes wrong…' he said.

'I don't see why they're taking him,' Herrick said. 'We know they're all terrorists. Why's he any different?'

'They're the rules we're playing by.'

'I'm not sure there should be any rules,' she said.

'That's not a very smart thing to say.'

Her gaze drifted to the glass box, where the operation was being run. Everyone was there – Spelling, Vigo, Collins and the nameless head of the Special Collection Agency who had flown in from Washington DC in order to escort bin Khidir from Northolt back to an unknown destination outside the United States for interrogation.

They listened as the team gained entry into bin Khidir's apartment without difficulty. Bin Khidir and his flatmate were drugged before they even woke and he was bundled into an airline services truck and driven to a plane waiting at the airfield twenty miles away. The plane took off for Northolt, but over Luxembourg the pilot reported that bin Khidir had come round and was proving difficult to restrain, even though his hands were tied behind his back. He was lashing out with his feet and throwing himself around the fuselage.

Herrick picked up the summaries of Southern Group activity from that day and went to the control box. As she entered, Vigo nodded to her from the table where he sat watching Jim Collins.

'Tell them to give him another shot,' said Collins.

There was silence until the pilot said that 'the horse' – the plane was normally used for transporting racehorses – had gone to sleep of its own accord. Vigo looked straight at Herrick.

'I expect you understand what's happened, Isis.' Then, without waiting for her to answer, he turned back to Collins. 'You'd better tell them to turn the plane around.'

'Why, for chrissake?' Collins demanded.

'I think you'll find the horse has swallowed a cyanide capsule concealed in its teeth.'

Confirmation came in a matter of minutes. The crew had found a dribble of foam on bin Khidir's chin.

'I don't imagine there'll be many takers for mouth-to-mouth resuscitation,' said Vigo, without mirth. 'Tell me, Isis, what would you do now?' Spelling and the rest of them turned to her.

'I'd get him back to his own bed, if possible.'

'Which is exactly what we should do, gentlemen, though quite how they're going to get the body off the plane is another matter. The transport arrangements only worked *into* the airport. We have not allowed for the return journey.'

Herrick went to call up satellite maps of the airport on her screen, printed them off and returned to Vigo and Collins with her idea. Twenty-five minutes later the plane landed at the airport, the pilot having complained to the German air traffic control of two un-commanded aileron movements. As the de Havilland Dash taxied through the first light of dawn towards the end of the runway, a hatch in the belly of the aircraft opened and four members of the Special Collection Service, who had cut their way through the perimeter fence, sprang from the darkness to receive the body. Forty-five minutes later, they reported back to say bin Khidir was in bed and the other man was still out cold. Everything was as it should be in the apartment, and bin Khidir's helpers would assume that he had bitten through the capsule in his sleep. RAPTOR was safe.

'It will be interesting,' mused Vigo, 'to see if they report this to the authorities and risk the pathologist discovering the cause of death. My bet is they'll dispose of the body and get in touch with the man running things. That provides us with an unusual opportunity.'

Isis watched the glitter of Vigo's eyes fade as he became absorbed in his thoughts. Then his head turned slowly to the men from GCHQ and the National Security Agency. 'We should pay great attention to phone calls from Stuttgart over the next few hours, for we know they must deliver a message that their man is dead.'

Next morning, Herrick went back to her house. The isolation of the

Bunker and its eerily regulated conditions – the fact that it was neither hot nor cold, humid nor dry, light nor dark – were getting to her. She and Lyne were getting on each other's nerves, which had as much to do with her bad temper as his unwavering faith in RAPTOR. She was still sure that RAPTOR was missing something in the flood of information, yet when challenged by Lyne found it difficult to be precise. At that point, he gave her a twenty-four-hour break. 'Take off, go to a hair stylist, see a movie, get laid,' he had said, without looking up from his screen.

Just one of those would be enough, she thought. She booked an appointment at the hair salon opposite Rahe's bookshop and submitted to the pleasure of a hair wash and head massage. As she had done a couple of weeks before, she moved to the seat that enabled her to watch the bookshop as her hair was being cut. This was how it started, she thought: an average-looking bloke, a bit on the chubby side, bustling from his bookstore to meet a cab and then a plane. She stared at the shop front, imagining him there in his ludicrous green jacket; Vigo's man rushing to a terrible death in his Sunday best.

She left the hairdresser and walked up and down the street, noticing a couple of *bureaux de change*, a printing shop and a Lebanese restaurant. Then she went into the Pan Arab Library – despite Rahe's absence, the bookstore was still open and doing a reasonable trade. She stopped at the cash desk, smiled pleasantly at the young woman, and asked if the store had a book called *The Balance of Power in the Jordanian Islamist Movements* by Al-Gharaibeh, a title she remembered seeing on one of the Wallflowers' desks. The woman explained she was new and wasn't sure which section the book would be found in: she'd check the computer stock list. As her varnished nails skittered across the keyboard, Herrick's gaze came to rest on the smears of grime on the return key and space bar – grime accumulated in tens of thousands of keystrokes by Youssef Rahe. She realised suddenly that she had found what she was looking for.

'That's a Dell computer, isn't it?' said Herrick. 'I've had the exact same one for three years and it's never caused me any trouble.'

The woman looked at her oddly. 'Yes, it seems to be very reliable.'

'Can I look?' asked Herrick, leaning over and memorising the model number. The woman was still trying to find the book on the stock list. 'I can always come back later,' said Herrick. 'I've quite a number of purchases to make. Perhaps it would help if I brought a list this afternoon.'

The woman seemed relieved. Herrick left the shop and caught a cab to Notting Hill Gate where she began to search the second-hand shops. Very soon, she found a Dell for sale, slightly newer than the one in the bookstore, but with an identical keyboard. She examined the socket at the back of the computer and practised pressing the plug home. Then she negotiated with the youth behind the counter to buy the keyboard separately. Clutching her prize in an old supermarket bag, she walked a few doors along the street and entered a large book-shop. The back of a recently published book in the politics section called *Jihad* had an excellent bibliography, from which she took the titles of half a dozen obscure-sounding books on the Middle East.

This done, she returned to Rahe's bookshop with the list and the keyboard, but the obliging young assistant at the desk had been replaced by a rather stout and ill-tempered woman wearing a hijab to cover her hair and neck, who must have been Rahe's wife. She told Herrick to leave the list overnight and return to collect the books next day, then picked up the phone and began speaking. Herrick placed the list on her desk and moved to the door, taking from her pocket another piece of paper now nicely compressed into an oval pellet. As she reached the door, she again checked for an alarm, then wedged the pellet into the metal opening of the lock and slipped into the street.

She made her way to Westbourne Grove and took lunch in a brasserie – sea bass with half a bottle of Mersault – and read the *Guardian,* which had a detailed analysis of the Norquist shooting and raised the possibility of a stray police bullet. She was interrupted by a man who said she reminded him of an American film actress, whose name he couldn't quite recall. She tolerated him for a little while, admitting to herself that being complimented wasn't such a bad expe-rience after nearly a fortnight in the Bunker. But at length, she made her excuses and went to a department store, buying a small plastic pill container, a make-up powder brush and a thin, very flexible metal spatula.

With these she went home to wait. In the hours that followed, she made some calls, took a nap and packed a fresh set of clothes for her return to the Bunker. At midnight, she drove her car to a road leading off Forsythe Street and parked opposite Rahe's bookshop. At 1.00 a.m. she left the car and crossed the road. There were still one or two people about, so as she approached the bookshop door she pulled out her own flat keys and lifted them as if to unlock it. At the same time, she shook the head of the spatula from her sleeve, raised it to the door-frame and worked it in at the point where the wad of paper had prevented the lock from sliding home. One firm push and the door opened.

She removed the keyboard from her bag and went round the desk to face the computer. As she stretched behind the box to remove the keyboard plug, she knocked the mouse. The computer whirred and the screen flashed on. Instinctively, she moved to block the light from the window, but as she did so, she noticed the aquarium screensaver appear and begin to animate. It was exactly as Dolph had described, but what interested her now was the noise coming from the hard drive. Behind the picture of the fish making their progress across the screen, something was going on. She changed the keyboards, knowing this would not affect the computer, and put Rahe's into her bag, never letting her eyes leave the screen. A few seconds later, she heard the modem dial out. Suddenly she was looking at a web page in Arabic. She read the words 'Ansar Allah' – helpers of God.

A noise came from the door. 'Is there a problem here, Miss?' A policeman was standing in the doorway with a flashlight.

'Oh, you gave me a shock, officer.'

'What are you doing here?' he said, moving from the door.

'Just changing the keyboard – I've had a nightmare trying to find the right one. Mrs Rahe wanted it here by morning.' She pointed to the ceiling. 'We'd better keep our voices down. I don't want to wake her.'

The policeman looked doubtfully at her. 'You work here? I've never seen you in the shop.'

'I read Arabic, so I look after the stock at the back and do the re-ordering from publishers in the Middle East. I'm part-time.'

'Let's have some light, shall we? Where's the switch?'

'By the door,' she said. 'But I'm going now.'

'It must be difficult to learn Arabic. What's that say there?' he asked, pointing to a card.

'This? It says the Pan Arab Library welcomes you. Our staff will be happy to offer every assistance in finding your purchases – Youssef Rahe.'

'Very impressive,' said the policeman. 'I don't know how you manage it.' His radio crackled with a voice and he turned down the volume. From upstairs, there was the sound of a light footfall.

'I'll just shut down the computer,' she said. 'They left it on.' She got up and moved around the desk. 'I must say it's very reassuring to see you, officer. You hear so much about there being no police on the beat.'

The policeman nodded. 'Would you mind if I took a few details from you, Miss? Just as a precaution.'

'Not in the least,' she said, leaning against the door and letting her forefinger remove the pellet of paper from the lock. 'My name is Celia Adams. I live at 340 Ladbroke Grove.' She smiled again, this time more coquettishly. 'You could give me a lift there.'

'Just a moment,' he said, writing in his notebook. 'Celia… Adams. Do you have some form of identification with you?'

'Yes, of course.' She made as if to look in her bag, but just then a voice called out from the back of the shop. She looked up to see the woman whom she'd spoken to on her second visit. 'My apologies, Mrs Rahe,' she said in Arabic. 'We have woken you up. This officer was worrying about your lock but I told him there was a knack to it.'

The woman stared at them uncomprehendingly. Herrick knew she had to make a run for it or be arrested. She stretched her hand to the door, flipped the latch upwards and jumped into the street, pulling the door shut behind her. She ran straight across Forsythe Street, dodging a bus, but did not immediately make for her car. Instead, she turned into another side street, glancing behind to see the policeman tearing towards his patrol car with his radio to his mouth. She was badly out of condition, so she took the first possible escape route, a short driveway leading to a high wooden gate. She scaled the gate and found herself in an untidy London garden. Thanking God there were no intruder lights, she negotiated a wall covered by a rambling rose, and lowered herself into the next garden. She was aware of the blue light flickering in the gap between the houses behind her, but kept going through several gardens until, eventually, she ended up in the street where her car was parked. Out of breath and feeling slightly silly but elated, she moved without haste to her car and drove off in the direction of Paddington.

Ten minutes later, she parked under a street light, placed the keyboard on her lap and unscrewed it with infinite care. She prised it apart and began to stroke the inside surfaces with the make-up brush, gathering the dust and strands of hair that had worked their way down through the keys, and sweeping it all into the pill container. She wasn't surprised at how much matter had accumulated in the keyboard, for she had once unscrewed her own to repair a jammed key and found a mass of hair and a couple of dead insects. After a few minutes of brushing, the bottom of the box was covered with a few millimetres of debris. She closed the box and placed it in an envelope that bore the address of an establishment in South Parks Road, Oxford. This she fed into a nearby postbox, then drove home.

Next day, Isis got to the Bunker early and passed through the numerous security checks to find that her place at the archipelago of investigation desks was taken. Nathan Lyne saw her and rose. 'We have some business, you and I, in the conference room,' he said, jabbing his finger over her head.

Vigo and Spelling were ranged on one side of the table. Lyne took up a seat at the end, leaving her standing.

Spelling didn't look up. 'We understand you broke into Youssef Rahe's shop last night. Can you explain why?'

How did they know? Surely the bookshop couldn't still be under observation. 'I wanted to take a look at his computer,' she said. 'His role in all this still seems unclear.'

'Unclear?' said Spelling. 'In what way unclear?'

'It doesn't seem sensible to put all this effort into the eleven others without trying to work out what happened in Lebanon: why Rahe fell for it; who the other man on his flight was. We're missing something.'

The room was thick with pious male complacency. Spelling finally looked up, his reading glasses magnifying the anger in his expression. 'I specifically instructed you not to press your personal inquiries further, for the very good reason that if these people understand we know Rahe is dead, they're very likely to conclude their entire operation is compromised. I assumed you had grasped this elementary point and yet you go off on your own, break into the premises and provide the police and Mrs Rahe with a very good idea of what you look like. What if you had been apprehended and charged? How would you have explained your presence in the shop?'

'But I wasn't caught.'

'Don't be bloody stupid. I'm talking about the risk you took.'

Vigo shifted in his chair. 'We were extremely lucky,' he said. 'The local police were aware of our interest in the shop and alerted Special Branch about the break-in, so we were able to acquire the film from the security cameras outside the adjacent premises.' He slid a photograph across the table. She looked down and saw herself moving from the door with the plastic carrier bag in her arms.

'What was in the bag?' he asked, fixing her with utterly expressionless eyes.

'I took a keyboard. You know, to look as if I had some business being there...'

'A little amateurish for you, I would have thought,' said Vigo. 'What would anyone be doing mending a computer at that hour?'

'It nearly worked,' she said. 'If Mrs Rahe hadn't come down, I would have been okay.'

'That's beside the point,' said Spelling. 'Your actions threatened RAPTOR. It was exceptionally irresponsible of you.'

She held her temper and spoke deliberately. 'I concede that I may have been a bit rash. But I don't agree that my actions jeopardised anything.'

'I'm not going to argue with you,' Spelling shot back. 'Mr Collins and I believe you've forfeited our trust and therefore your place in RAPTOR.'

Lyne clenched his hands together and turned them out to click his knuckles. 'Look, gentlemen, we all agree this was very dumb of Isis, but in her defence I'd like to point out that she's easily one of the best investigators we have – you saw how quick she was the night before last. Hell, she really gets it. I'd hate to lose her.'

Herrick tipped her head in thanks.

'What were you hoping to find on the computer?' asked Vigo. 'You know we had all that covered. Did you imagine we had overlooked something?'

'To be honest, yes. I feel we're all missing something. I've told Nathan this, countless times.'

'I can vouch for that,' said Lyne. 'She's been a real pain in the ass.'

'And you think that because you spotted the switch at Heathrow, you have some superior insight into this operation?' said Vigo.

'Well, at least my *personal inquiries* achieved something on that occasion.'

'So you felt you had the right to go off piste again?' said Spelling.

'I suppose so, yes.'

'And did you see anything on the computer that interested you?' asked Vigo.

'As a matter of fact, yes, it was in sleep mode and when I touched the mouse it automatically logged on to an Islamist website. I didn't have time to read much, but it struck me as interesting that the messages were still coming through to a man they knew was dead. I wondered whether his wife had knowledge of the way the screensaver operated as a gateway. I wondered about the site I saw. The internet address showed it was based in Malaysia.'

'The screensaver – did you know about it before?'

'I made it my business to find out as much as I could about Youssef Rahe. I still feel he's important.'

'But where from?' demanded Vigo.

She returned his stare and gently shook her head. 'My sources,' she said defiantly. Damn Vigo: he'd still be selling second-hand books if it hadn't been for her. He owed his resurrection to her. She turned to Spelling, determined to get off the subject of the computer for good. 'I've done nothing wrong, and if you don't mind, I repeat that we are ignoring an essential part of this case. What happened to Youssef Rahe?'

Spelling rested his chin on his hands, then removed his glasses. 'That will be all,' he said.

Twenty minutes later the three men emerged, and Lyne came over to Herrick. 'You're off the team,' he said. 'They're sending you to Tirana. A suspect is being held there, and we think he's interesting.'

'Why me? We've got our own people at the British Embassy. Why can't they give him the once-over?'

'The resident officer is ill – cancer. His stand-in is too inexperienced and besides, he's not in on the big secret. Maybe the suspect has something to tell, and if he does, I want you to be there to hear it. There's a really good case for going. I was arguing for them to send you before you started burglarising bookstores. Hell, Isis, this is a reprieve. They want you back in a couple of weeks. Jim Collins thinks you're shit hot.'

'I wish you could persuade Spelling of that.'

'I think he's already there. But Christ, you're a fucking handful. You know that?'

She smiled sheepishly. 'By the way, thanks for sticking up for me in there. It's not everyone who would do that.'

'That's okay. You're flying out tomorrow morning to Zurich, then Mother Teresa airport, Tirana. Spelling says you'll have the usual diplomatic status, but they don't want you mixing too much at your own Embassy, so you're to stay at the Byron – it's Tirana's only good hotel. You'll see a lot of the guys at the US Embassy, but again, I don't have to tell you to stay off the subject of RAPTOR. Some of them may have got wind of it, because of the involvement of so many personnel, but you're Garbo – right?'

'Who am I reporting to?'

'Me – this is an officially sponsored RAPTOR tour. Just see the guy interviewed, turn in a report and bring your butt safely back here in a couple of weeks. It's a piece of cake. You'll probably end up with a beautiful tan.' He paused and placed his hand on her shoulder. 'But you be careful. There are some bad, bad people out there.'

'Then I'm going to need a story. That requires a little preparation. I don't know if I've got enough time.'

'You got all day. But make it better than the keyboard story. That was bush-league stuff, Isis – just terrible.'

She stayed for a further two hours to read the file on the Tirana detainee and draw some money – $7,000 in hundred-dollar bills – from a character who came from the US Embassy and stressed that every last cent was to be accounted for.

CHAPTER THIRTEEN

Around five-thirty in the afternoon, the public areas of the Hotel Byron in Tirana began to fill, mostly with Albanian gangsters who left their bodyguards out in the car park. They moved through the bar to a crescent-shaped area bordering the gardens, trailing an air of listless menace, and sank into the Lloyd loom chairs to drink, smoke without pause and fiddle with their cell phones. There were some foreigners too; insanely risk-averse businessmen, low-level diplomats and a few edgy American evangelists sipping soft drinks and wearing hiking gear, as if the mere fact of being in this godless, chaotic country required rugged clothing.

The tableau was not difficult to decode, and as Herrick waited on her second evening for Lance Gibbons, her contact from the local CIA station, she realised that more or less the same groups appeared and seemed to settle at regular tables. Bashkin, the driver who had attached himself to her at Mother Teresa International airport, told her the Albanian men were mostly engaged in drug trafficking, prostitution rackets and smuggling people, cigarettes and fuel.

Gibbons arrived late, a large, shambling man who quickly announced that he was a veteran of the war against al-Qaeda in Afghanistan, or the 'Big A' as he called it. After a couple of drinks, Isis brought up the purpose of her trip and asked when she could see the suspect.

'Look, that's going to be kinda difficult right now,' he said, toying with the scarf loosely hung round his neck. 'We have to tread carefully with the Albanians. He's their prisoner. We're just observing.'

Herrick gave him a sceptical look, pulled out her phone and dialled

Nathan Lyne. 'I'm having some unexpected difficulty inspecting the goods,' she said to Lyne. 'I wonder if you could intervene with the local representative and tell him there'll be hell to pay if he doesn't cooperate. I'll put you onto him now.'

She handed the phone to Gibbons, who listened silently then said, 'You got to understand, Nathan, that these goods are not in our possession yet. They're still being held by the customs service.'

He hung up and handed the phone back. 'You know, that was real unfriendly of you.'

'I have to see this man quickly and report back to London. That's all there is to it.'

'You and your man Lyne don't cut any ice here. Here is dif–fer–ent. Period.' He sipped his drink then lit a cheroot. 'So, Isis Herrick, tell me about RAPTOR. What the fuck is going down? We hear something big's happening. All our guys pulled in from the field. Operations suspended without warning. What's the deal?'

She shrugged. 'That name doesn't mean anything to me, but if there is something going down, as you put it, you better be sure that I see this suspect. It comes from the top.'

He laughed. 'The top of what – my organisation? No way. The British Secret Intelligence Service? Hey, that would be something, wouldn't it? I'll stand to attention and drink to Her Majesty.'

'Where's he being held?' she asked.

'That's classified information.'

'The intelligence headquarters, the prison – where?'

He shook his head and stroked the three-day-old stubble on his chin.

'What's the problem with giving me access? If this man is talking, you must have transcripts.'

'Oh yeah, he's talking.'

'Then you'll get the transcripts to me?'

'I can't be certain of that.'

'I'm not fooling around,' she said icily. 'If I don't get your agreement this evening, I'll have Nathan Lyne call his friends in the State Department and Langley. By morning your communications centre will be jammed with cables. Give me what I want and I'll get out of your hair.'

'Don't misunderstand me, Isis. I'd like you *in* my hair. This town gets pretty tedious and you're definitely the best thing to happen to me all week, but this is real difficult. I don't see the Albanians letting you visit the suspect. Hell, you're a woman. You know what that means to these people, right?'

'Mr Gibbons…'

'Lance.'

'If you've heard that something unusual is going on,' she stopped while the waiter placed another drink in front of Gibbons, 'you should know that the authority behind it doesn't get any higher.'

Gibbons exhaled a low, sarcastic whistle. 'Hey, you already said that. Look, I'll see what I can do, okay? But you have to understand that this is not a Western jail and right here they don't have Western standards of prisoner care – you follow me?'

She nodded. 'I want the transcripts this evening.'

Gibbons shifted the small, black pack from his lap – the standard cover for an automatic weapon – shouldered it and rose from the chair. 'Maybe tomorrow,' he said, looking down at her.

'This evening,' she said.

'We're on Albanian time, Missie. Tomorrow.' He gave her a two-fingered salute and loped out of the hotel, beckoning to his driver on the way.

She had dinner and then went to her room to smoke a rare cigarette on the balcony overlooking the gardens. At ten-thirty her cell phone rang and she dived for her bag.

'Hello, darling. It's your father.'

'Dad, what are you doing?'

'Merely phoning my daughter to find out how she is and what she's up to. Can you speak?'

'Yes. Did you go on your trip to the West Highlands?'

'Yes, yes. Saw a lot and did a good bit of sea trout fishing.'

She was smiling to herself, swamped by a rush of affection for the old man. 'That's exactly what I'd like to be doing now,' she said, glancing around the bleak hotel room.

'Then we should take a trip together when you have some time off. I know how much you love being driven in the Armstrong.' He laughed. 'Look, I gather from friends that you're in Albania. The first thing to say about that is, be careful. They're a treacherous bunch. I was there at the end of the war when I was no longer needed in France and witnessed a very ugly side of them. Anyway, the reason I'm calling is that I have a message for you. It's from my old student.' She understood he meant Sir Robin Teckman. 'He wants to talk to you on a secure line. So you're booked to go and see our ambassador tomorrow.'

'Dad, why's he using you to talk to me?'

'No doubt you'll find out. He wants you there at eight-thirty sharp. You should go to Skenderbeg Street. Our Embassy is next door to the Egyptians'. Be discreet, Isis. If you have a driver, don't use him. Take a taxi. The student says the driver may be unreliable.'

Herrick found herself reluctant to let her father go and asked him a succession of questions about Hopelaw and its inhabitants, the tap-room gossip that she missed, about barns burning down, sheepdogs going wild, poachers being caught and people running off with each other. Her father, though elliptical about himself, was an acute observer of village life and she liked hearing him speak about it. At length, she said goodbye, re-lit her cigarette and began to read a book about Albania she'd picked up in the hotel shop.

Just as she thought of turning in, the room doorbell rang. She looked through the spy hole and saw Gibbons standing with his thumb hooked in his shirt pocket and another cheroot hanging from his lower lip.

'Hey there, Isis. Brought what you wanted,' he said when she opened the door. His eyes scanned the room. 'Any chance of a little of that Johnny Walker Black Label?'

She had bought the bottles as useful bribes. 'Help yourself, Mr Gibbons.'

'Lance,' he said. 'That stuff you have is from the first ten days. Most of what he's said is in there. You'll see that this character is quite fly. He's educated in Britain and speaks good English. He's not the usual Mujahadin type. He's sharp and kind of civilised. Tough too. He got over the border and managed to survive long enough to be taken by the police. We think there is something more to him. For one thing, he was carrying the documentation belonging to a man thought to be dead, name of Jasur Faisal, otherwise known as The Electrician or The

Watchmaker – a wanted Hamas terrorist. Maybe you've heard of him? So you see he's a deal more interesting than the average holy warrior. We don't know what he's doing in Europe and why he's flat broke, but he's the kind of guy who could form the nucleus of a very big terrorist attack. We think one tough sonofabitch lies beneath the polite exterior.'

'And what happens now? They've had him for ten days. Can't be much more to get out of him.'

'You're wrong. There's a truckload of stuff he can tell us about. He's been ID'd by people in Camp X-Ray and elsewhere. Beyond that, we're not sure. He may have served in Chechnya.'

'But it's been established that he's a Pakistani national?'

'Who knows, Isis. The way he looks, he could be either Pakistani or Palestinian.'

'So what happens to him?'

'Anyone's guess.'

Herrick looked at the first few pages while Gibbons sipped and swilled the whisky round his mouth, making pain-pleasure grimaces.

'Well, thank you for bringing this round so quickly. I take it I can keep this?'

'For sure, but don't leave it lying around.'

'Is there much more?'

'Some,' he said, rolling the tumbler in his hands. 'But it's pretty much the same as what you got there. They're doing a slow job on the stuff they know he'll talk about. This is not a Defense Intelligence Agency operation – it's the Company. We're doing it thoroughly. The Pentagon knows shit.'

She moved to the door and opened it. Gibbons got up with a sigh. 'If you need anything or any company while you're here, this is my mobile number.'

'Thanks again,' she said.

'Hey, we're all on the same side in this thing.' He gave her another salute and went out.

'Exactly.' She closed the door behind him and returned to the chair on the balcony. For the first time that day, the air was fresh and cool. She looked across the gardens to the lights illuminating the Palace of Congress and noticed a swirl of bats feeding on the moths that had gathered beneath each lamp. Then she turned to the interview transcripts.

She rose early the next day and left the hotel by a side entrance, knowing that Bashkin would already be waiting for her at the front. She crossed the city's main boulevard and cut through the old politburo compound, passing Enver Hoxha's villa, built in a curiously open style and surrounded by gardens now partly taken over by a McDonald's restaurant. A little later she came across the diplomatic quarter, a haven of police patrols, well-barbered hedges and almost no traffic.

At the Embassy she pushed past a dozen locals, showed her passport and was led to a communications room in the basement, stuffed with equipment and a couple of large computers. The ambassador was drinking a cup of coffee and chatting to one of his staff.

'Ah, Miss Herrick, welcome, welcome. Take a pew. The line is all set up for you.' He left her alone with a copy of the *Spectator*.

When the call came through, Teckman was at his most distilled. He explained that he wanted her to make contact at the Byron with a former SIS officer named Harland, who at his request was escorting an osteopath named Sammi Loz, 'a rather unusual figure from New York high society', who he felt was interesting. She had heard of Harland, and knew he'd had something to do with the demise of Walter Vigo, but stopped herself from mentioning it. Instead she asked if he thought Karim Khan was important, or merely an excuse to get her out of the Bunker.

'Both, though they won't suspect that he is important. I think the fact the osteopath is interested seems to indicate something. Harland says that Loz owes Karim Khan for saving his life in Bosnia and feels obligated to try to free him. This is probably true, but there may be something else, and you and Harland are going to have to get it out of him, even if you have to mislead him about the possibility of achieving Khan's release. I should warn you that the Americans are already alert to Loz's possible significance but, like us, they don't know why he's important. Also, it's unlikely there has been much serious communication between the FBI, who have been watching him in New York, and the CIA in Albania. He's not on any watch list, and you know relations between everyone in Washington are at an all-time low.'

'What do I say to the Americans? They're being a bit tricky about access.'

'I'll see to it that you get in this afternoon. Present yourself at the US Embassy at three unless you hear from me.'

'And RAPTOR?'

'Just see Khan, do your stuff and send back a report to the Bunker. Believe me, they're very preoccupied with the other nine active suspects and it will only confuse things if you start kicking up in your usual way.' He paused and laughed quietly. 'So, no break-ins for the moment, Isis. Keep your powder dry and use those observant eyes of yours. I'm afraid I can't brief you more clearly than this, because things are very fluid: I'm relying on you and Harland to respond in a way that I know you're both capable of.' He gave her a number, then hung up, leaving her sitting in the cool of the communications room, wondering what the hell was going on. Her father had observed that the Chief might be waiting to make his move, but with only three or four weeks left of his tenure, it seemed a little late. Besides, everything he was interested in seemed way off the point.

She left the Embassy and walked out into the dust and noise of Rruga e Durresit, along which she had noticed some shops. She entered one of the boutiques, a sad little place with almost no stock, bought two brightly coloured T-shirts and a canvas shoulder bag she had seen some of the Tirana women carrying. In another, where there was more sense of actual commerce, she chose a belt and some jeans with studded seams. She moved on to a market and threaded her way into a rickety wood and tin structure pierced with shafts of light. Beyond the pyramids of vegetables and boxes of live chickens, she found a woman with a tray of cheap costume jewellery, and bought some imitation gold bangles and a necklace of white and black plastic beads. She turned to the adjacent stall, which was run by a young man with a wispy moustache, and bargained for a black fish-net shawl and a pair of high-heeled ankle-length boots with a cowboy fringe at the top. She placed all her purchases in a white supermarket bag, together with some fruit, and walked purposefully through the stall holders, who had now cottoned on to the presence of a foreigner and were plucking at her jacket.

By ten-thirty, she reached the hotel and, deciding that she would wait for Harland to contact her, went to the swimming pool with a couple of books and a newspaper.

When the doctor first came to Khan in the headquarters of SHISK, the Albanian intelligence service, and treated him for the abscess and broken lip, Khan assumed he was Albanian, but through the days of his interrogation he had learned that the man was Syrian. The SHISK interrogators referred to him as The Syrian or The Doctor, the latter always accompanied by a brief ironic smile that puzzled him. The Doctor also had a habit of making notes when Khan was answering a question. What did a doctor need to know about his past in Afghanistan? More unnerving was the way he interrupted proceedings by leaving his chair near the window and walking over to grasp one of Karim's arms or dig his thumbs into the tendons at the back of his leg. While the doctor went about his curious inspection, the two Albanian interrogators would sit back and light up; the Americans, of whom there were never fewer than three, stretched, rubbed their necks and murmured under their breath.

At first he was reassured by The Doctor's presence, thinking it would protect him from the treatment meted out to the other prisoners, but he gradually came to resent, then loathe the strange prodding and pinching that went on. Besides this, the expression in the man's face had hardened in blood-chilling appraisal. He wished fervently never to be left alone with this man.

The interrogations had followed the same pattern since the first days, when he had given them the outline of his story from Bosnia to Afghanistan. Their interest focused on the last four years. They took it for granted that he met and knew the leadership of the Taleban and al-Qaeda, although he told them over and over again that he was just a mountain commander and had little experience of the regime, and none of the terrorist training camps. But, prompted by the Americans, the Albanian intelligence officers went on asking: 'Where did you train? Who trained you? What methods were you taught – car bombs, sniper attacks, butane bombs, timing devices? What about dirty bombs?' Did he know of any radioactive material coming over the border from Turkmenistan, Uzbekistan or Tajikistan? He had admitted being in that area during the summer of 1999, they said, so he must have known of the shipments of strontium and caesium chloride. He insisted that he didn't know anything about these shipments, but would not have hesitated to tell them if he had known. He was numb with repetition, going over the details so often that the words lost meaning for him.

They showed him books of photographs, brought by the Americans in two metal cases. This was a welcome break in the routine. He used these to show that he wanted to cooperate, and for all of two days they went through the four or five hundred faces of men who were suspected of having trained in Afghanistan. He gave them names of about a dozen he had fought with, and pointed out that three of the men – a Saudi, a Yemeni and another Pakistani with a British passport – were dead. He had seen the young Yemeni killed in front of him by a Northern Alliance rocket, and he'd buried him with five others under a mound of rocks, the ground being too hard to dig.

The interrogators returned again and again to the al-Qaeda camps. Khan explained that he had gone already trained, battle-hardened from Bosnia. As far as tactics and weaponry went, he knew much more than any of the men he fought with, but he had absolutely no contact with the terrorist training camps. During the last two winters, he had been trapped at the front with no supplies, freezing his arse off, men dying of cold and illness all around him. They had radio contact with Kabul but nobody seemed to care about them. 'I was a soldier,' he concluded wearily. 'I was nothing to them, and the Arabs mostly kept to themselves.'

'But you were the big hero from Bosnia. You commanded Arabs in battle with the Northern Alliance and on the Tajik border,' said one of the interrogators.

'The Arabs without money stayed with us, yes. And they became good fighters. But the rich ones always bought their way back south. I saw them come and knew they would not last more than a few weeks. You may have heard of the different Arab words for them. *Tharwa* were the rich ones, *Thawra* were the revolutionaries. It is an old joke in Arabic – a pun, I believe.'

'Why didn't you leave earlier?' asked one of the Americans. 'You say you hated the Taleban and you had no respect for the Arabs, yet you stayed in Afghanistan longer than anyone we have interrogated. Why?'

'I was committed to the men I fought with. There were ten of us who'd been together since ninety-eight. We survived all the hardship together, the dangers and the crazy decisions that came from men in Kabul who didn't have to fight. We ate with each other, shared our possessions; we saved each other and buried our brothers. When you're out in the mountains like this for years, depending on one another, without supplies, you don't think about what is going on in the outside world. It's easy to become cut off...'

'Myopic,' offered another one of the Americans.

'Yes, myopic. I was guilty of that. Yes.'

'Horse-shit,' said a man named Milo Franc. He was leading the American team and was easily the most hostile. 'That's hypocritical horse-shit, Khan. You're a mercenary and you fought for a regime that executed women for reading school books!'

'I didn't support those things.'

'You enjoyed killing. That's the truth, isn't it? You're a professional killer. And when your people in Afghanistan were thrown out, you were ordered to the West to kill again.' He paused and lowered his voice. 'You left Afghanistan in December – is that right?'

Khan nodded, and stared at the patterns of chips in the wall paint. He knew every square inch of the room and was familiar with the routine noises coming from the street: the surges of traffic, the calls of vendors who appeared at exactly the same time every day, and the sound of students issuing from an academy up the road.

'So,' said Franc, hitching up his trousers. 'At the same moment the leadership disbanded all al-Qaeda fighters and told them to continue the struggle from their own countries, you get it into your head to return to London to complete your medical studies. You go over the border at Spin Boldak and dodge around until you make contact with your family in Lahore. You went through Quetta, travelled north to the tribal areas then doubled back westwards to Iran. We have the Inter-Services Intelligence Agency report, so we know all this. It just so happens that at *exactly* that moment, hundreds of al-Qaeda fighters took the same route from Mashhad or Zabol in Iran, two cities you admit visiting. And you're saying that all this is coincidence?'

'Yes, I wanted my old life back. I realised I'd made mistakes with my life. I wanted to go back … to leave the killing and become a doctor.'

'That's crap. You were a lousy student and your professors in London – the ones that remember you – say you didn't give a shit about medicine. Screwing around and drinking, yes. Medicine, no. We checked with them. Your attendance record was terrible and you never turned in your term papers.'

Khan shook his head. 'I was a silly, misguided young man. I know that. But I have committed no crime.'

Franc looked at the two SHISK agents to see if they minded him continuing. One made an exaggerated flourish with his hand, as though to say 'be my guest'. Franc approached him and knelt down by the table so he was looking up into Khan's face.

'You see, Karim – or whatever the fuck your name is – you've had it good so far. Regular meals, a bed, treatment for your injuries. That's like three star service here. But it can all change. We can just leave you to these people. I guess you know what that means.' He turned and glanced at The Doctor over his shoulder and smiled with his harsh, grey eyes boring into Khan's face. 'This man is a real doctor. Like any real doctor he cures people and saves them,' he paused. 'That is, after he has hurt them so much that they want to die. But he doesn't let that happen. Oh, no. You see, he preserves the life of his subjects and then starts over with the pain. With your medical training, maybe you have an idea of what he can do. It's not just scalpels, draining the blood from your body; it's not electricity, or beating, or drowning. No, The Doctor is very scientific. He does things from the inside as well as the outside. He feeds you drugs, acid and every goddam shit you can imagine. The pain is total, you understand that, Khan. Total. He takes you to another place, a place that no man alive can imagine, because it's so terrifying, so relentless. He can keep you in that state for *years*. Imagine that, Khan. He's had a lot of practice because he worked for Saddam Hussein. He had so many people to experiment with there that he became the best in the business. No one has ever failed to tell him what he wants to hear.' He got up and raised his voice. 'And you know what, you little prick sonofabitch? We've got you an appoint-ment with The Doctor. His time is booked for you, baby, and he's willing to start work whenever we give the word. So you better cooperate and answer our questions.'

Khan stared at the table and composed himself. 'I've told you everything I know,' he said. 'I have committed no crime. I fought a war as a foreign soldier in a foreign land, much like your people did in Vietnam. We both found we'd made a bad mistake and I wish to repay my debt to humanity.'

'You're a terrorist. That's the difference, buddy.' Franc went over to his chair, picked up a folder and returned to the table. 'Now you know about The Doctor, let's see what you say about this.' He withdrew the two remaining postcards of the Empire State. 'Can you explain these cards, which were found in your possession?'

'Yes, they were given to me by a friend a long time ago to remind me to keep in touch. That's why he addressed them to himself.'

'Yes, Dr Sammi Loz. You studied together in London and then went to Bosnia, right?'

'Yes.'

'Why the Empire State? What's the significance?'

'My friend had a love of the building, an obsession with it, you might say. He said he would always work from the Empire State because of its spirit. He said it was a lucky building. He can tell you this. I'm certain he's still there.'

Franc gave him a sardonic smile. 'We were going to ask Dr Loz, but he went missing when federal agents approached him four days ago. He is currently being sought in the United States. When we find him we will of course ask him, but at the present time we're going to have to rely on you.' While Franc paused to consult some photostats, Khan absorbed the news that Sammi was a suspect too.

'These postcards are written in code, aren't they? Our analysis has shown they may include an attack date and target information.' He placed five photostats on the table. 'I want you to read them for us and explain the code.'

'I can read them, but there's no code.' He shook his head and looked down at the surface of the table, then picked up the photostats and read the first one. 'Greetings, my old friend. I am in Pakistan and hope very soon to be in London. I may need a little help from you. I have good news. I am returning to complete my medical studies, as you always said I should. With warmest wishes, Khan.' He stopped. 'That is all there is – there's no message.'

'You sent that from Quetta, Pakistan, where you got the passport doctored. Is that when you received your instructions? From the same people who gave you the name of the man who did the work on your documents?'

'No, I did everything I could to avoid those people in Quetta. My family told me the ISI were looking for me. I had to be very discreet.'

'So you managed to find the man who does work for al-Qaeda by yourself?'

'I didn't know he worked for them.'

'Continue,' said Franc.

He read the postcards and, when he had finished, slammed his hand on the table with frustration. 'These mean nothing, I tell you. Nothing.'

Unmoved, Franc produced a second set of copies and put one in front of him. In the first postcard sent from Quetta, Khan saw that the capital letters were ringed in red:

*GrEetings, **My** old friend. I am in **PakIstan** and hope veRy soon to be in London. I may neEd a little help from you. I have good news. I am returning to complete my stuDIES, as you always said I should.*

Karim looked up at him, mystified.

'Let me remind you about this,' said Franc. 'All the letters you made into capitals spell EMPIRE DIES.' He ran his finger along the message, stopping at each capital letter.

Khan shook his head incredulously. 'This is stupid. It is like a school kid's code. You think I wrote this to my friend? Honestly?'

'But you did. Take a look at the first one you sent from Iran. It's a little more complicated.'

He placed a grid of letters alongside a phrase from the postcard, which read, 'I want to hide in Lundun for all time. KariM.'

'This is the way you concluded your postcard from Iran. It's certainly an odd phrase, especially when you compare it to the rest of the postcard, which reads pretty naturally and is correctly spelt. So our analysts had a look at it and they came up with this.' He indicated the grid.

```
A  L  K  U  F
R  M  I  L  A
T  U  N  W  A
H  I  D  U  N
```

'What you wrote was a near anagram of a well-known Hadith, a saying of the prophet – 'Al kufr milatun wahidun' – meaning unbelief is one nation. It's a call to arms against the unbelievers.'

Khan stared at the letters. 'I don't understand.'

The American took a pencil and ticked off the letters that appeared in the Arabic phrase.

'But it doesn't work. There are too many letters in my postcard.'

'It's near enough. Why would anyone spell London like that? And again you use capital letters where they don't belong – the M in Karim is a capital. We're working on the next two cards but we think this is enough to put you and your friend Dr Loz in jail.' He paused. 'Unbelief is one nation. You people! What kind of shit fills your minds?'

'This is crazy.'

'All you have to do is tell me where the target information is hidden. I want the date and time of the attack and the names of your associates. What does the Empire State building have to do with all this? Is that your target? We need answers, Khan.' He was shouting now.

'There isn't a plot. I am innocent. I wasn't used to writing English – writing anything. The capital letters are a mistake and the codes you've found are coincidence. They don't exist.' He was sweating profusely, his throat parched with fear, and he had to hold his hands under the table to stop them shaking.

'Yeah, like the other coincidences in your story. Right now, we're all a little tired of listening to your crap so we're gonna leave you for a couple of hours with The Doctor. When we come back, we want answers.'

CHAPTER FOURTEEN

At two, Herrick walked from the pool with a bitter taste in her mouth, the result of inhaling Tirana's polluted air for most of the morning. She walked through the lobby to the elevator bank and pulled out a card which acted as both a lift and room key.

'May I?' said a voice at her shoulder. She was aware of a friendly, dark face and a wide smile.

'Thank you,' she said, and stepped back. He pressed three, and asked which floor she wanted. 'That's okay, my floor's after yours anyway,' she lied.

The doors closed.

'Would it interest you to know that I'm going to Robert Harland's room?'

'If I knew who he was, it might,' she said, looking away.

'Oh, I'm sorry. I understood you were a colleague of Mr Harland's. He told me to find you in the hotel.'

'And who are you?'

'Dr Sammi Loz. I'm afraid circumstances have forced me to go under another name while travelling. I am calling myself Charles Mansour, which I like even less than my own name.' Another smile.

She studied him in the mirror. He was wearing a linen jacket, dark blue, unstructured trousers and a white, probably silk, shirt, fastened at the neck. He was evidently rich and took care over his clothes. There was also self-assurance, vanity and deliberateness in his movements.

'Dr Loz, why didn't Mr Harland find me himself?' she asked.

The lift came to a stop and the doors opened.

'Because he is laid up with a bad back after three separate flights and since I am his doctor, I have ordered total rest. He's getting better gradually and should be on his feet tomorrow. The room's three twelve. I'll wait here if you would prefer it.'

'Thank you. I would.'

She knocked at the door and glanced back to the elevator where Loz stood with his arms folded.

The door opened and a tall, but stooped middle-aged man held out his hand and said hello. 'I'm sorry I had to get Loz to find you, but I'm pretty immobilised at the moment. Come in.' Robert Harland returned crookedly to his bed and lay down very slowly. 'I gather you were at the Embassy, so you know what I'm doing here.' He laughed grimly. 'Actually, I don't know what the hell I'm doing here, so I can't expect you to.'

'The Chief has got me in to see Karim Khan this afternoon. I'm due at the US Embassy at three. Perhaps we should talk after that?'

'I'd like you to talk to Loz first.' He frowned, more out of perplexity than pain, she thought. 'I'd like to know what you think of him. He got here under his own steam, with a fake passport. Teckman believes he knows something, but God knows what, which is why I'm sticking to him. Your brief, I gather, is to help me.' He stopped and felt the front of his pelvis. 'Look, I've been thinking it may be worth letting Khan understand that you're with Loz, but in a way the Albanians don't appreciate.'

'Why?'

'Because I want to know what his reaction is, though that's not what I've told Loz. Let's have a talk with him, shall we?'

She opened the door to find Loz waiting outside. He came in and Harland explained what he needed.

'I see,' he said. 'You're looking for some code word or phrase which Karim will recognise.' He leaned against the desk, placed one hand at his elbow and stroked his nose. 'You could ask him about The Poet.'

'Who the hell's the Poet?' said Harland rather bad temperedly from the bed.

'That's the point,' replied Loz. 'Nobody knows. The Poet was a commander in Bosnia, but none of us knew who he was or where he operated from. Karim did. It was The Poet who persuaded him to leave for Afghanistan in 1997. If you mention him, Karim will know you have spoken with me because only I could have told you that.'

'Fine,' she said, thinking that this was all pretty daft. 'I'd better go now.'

A couple of hours later, she drove with Gibbons and a guard from the US Embassy to an anonymous four-storey building with blinded windows. They passed through some blue metal gates into a large car park where there was an unusual sense of order, regimentation even. Several off-road vehicles were lined up and were being hosed down, and the yellowish run-off was being swept into a drain by a young man in army fatigues. Around the high wall surrounding the SHISK head-quarters were coils of razor wire, cameras and movement sensors, all of which she assumed were bought by the American money that had poured into Tirana during the mid nineties. About half a dozen armed guards were in the yard. Two at the entrance to the building came to attention, while a third inspected their IDs before leading them to the second floor and along a dark corridor. They were told to wait.

'The big man in there is Milo Franc,' said Gibbons out of the corner of his mouth. 'He'll do most of the talking, together with the SHISK officers. I guess I don't have to tell you that it's best if you keep your yap shut. They don't like having a woman here.'

Herrick said nothing.

Her first impression when they got into the interrogation room, was of a gang of schoolboys caught tormenting an animal. All but one looked at her with a slight awkwardness. That man, heavy-set with a thick, black goatee, did not look up from a bag of nuts. Khan sat shrunken at the table, bedraggled with sweat and clearly at the end of his tether. As the two SHISK officers turned to look her up and down, his eyes darted to hers with an expression of utter bewilderment. She saw immediately that his right cheek was affected by a tic, and once or twice he put his hand up to swat the movement.

Gibbons pointed to a chair along the wall, next to the three Ameri-cans. She glanced at the one who she guessed must be Franc, another man in his thirties with a clean-cut and well-policed parting, and a clerical type who had a sheaf of documents on his lap.

No explanation about her arrival was offered to Khan, but his attention now fixed on her and she realised he was looking for a sign that she could offer him a way out of that room. She removed her gaze to a point between the two Albanians at the table, but felt uncomfortable doing so. 'Please continue,' she said.

One of the Albanians leaned forward. He was a slender man, with a russet complexion and a high forehead. He spoke with a somewhat stilted American accent.

'We have some confusion here. You were carrying two documentations. One related to Karim Khan and the other to Jasur Faisal al-Saggib, known also as Jasur al-Jahez and Amir al-Shawa. You say you saw this man killed in Macedonia two weeks ago. But our American colleagues have asked the Macedonian authorities to look for the body of this man. They searched the area where the incident took place and found no dead body there.'

Khan looked perplexed, as if they had suddenly started talking about architecture or botany. 'The man died with me. He was not killed – I told you that. He died of a heart attack. Maybe he was suffering from asthma. I don't know.'

Herrick was surprised by his upper-middle-class English.

'But they could not find this man,' returned the interrogator. 'What is the proof he was with you in these times?'

Khan did not answer, but shook his head hopelessly.

'What is the proof that these documents are not yours?'

'The pictures are not of me. Anyone can see that. They belong to a man who doesn't look like me. He was an Arab.'

The interrogator examined a photocopy. 'This looks like you to me.' He showed it to his colleague, who nodded vigorously. Herrick glanced at the copy on the CIA officer's lap. There was no resemblance whatsoever to Khan. However, she took out her notebook and wrote down Faisal's name and the other aliases.

'But it is natural that you do not want to look like a member of Hamas. The man Faisal is wanted in Damascus, Cairo and Jerusalem. *Everyone* wants to speak with Mr Jasur Faisal because he is responsible for many explosions and killings. In Syria they want to see Mr Faisal for two murders. In Egypt, Mr Faisal assassinated a politician and a newspaper editor and was sentenced to death by the courts in Cairo. Maybe Jasur Faisal – The Electrician – is sitting here in this room with us. Maybe we have big shot terrorist here, right here in front of us, a real soldier of Islam?'

'Why are you asking me questions I can't answer? Proof that I am not Faisal lies in front of you, but when you say you do not believe this, how am I meant to answer you? It's the same with the postcards. There isn't a code in the postcards. You have found what you wanted to find and I am to be punished for this.' After this speech Khan hung his head. The sweat trickled down his cheek and collected in the stubble at his chin.

There was silence. Franc turned to her and gave her a big, fat wink.

'May I ask the suspect a question?' Herrick said to the room. Then looking directly at Khan she asked, 'Who are you?'

'I am Karim Khan.'

'And you haven't used any of these other names – Faisal and the rest?'

'No. I found the identity on the man I fled with in Macedonia.'

'Have you ever been known as The Electrician, or The Watchmaker, or The Poet, or any other name?' She said it lightly, as though the names had come to her randomly, but Khan raised his head and his eyes filled with recognition.

'No,' he said, 'but I once knew a man who was nicknamed The Poet – a long time ago, in Bosnia. My friend Dr Loz knew of him.' There was no doubt he understood what she was saying. They had made contact.

Franc turned to her. 'A moment outside, Ms Herrick.' He steered her to the door, beckoning Gibbons to go with them. In the corridor, he pushed her to the wall and leaned into her face with his arm resting beside her head. 'I don't know what the hell you're doing in there, but let me tell you that you're here on my sufferance and those remarks were unacceptable. This is front line procedure, Miss Herrick, an extremely delicate interrogation, the result of coordination between us and officers of the Albanian intelligence service. I can't allow you to butt in with any damned thought that comes into your head. You *copy*, Ms Herrick?'

She moved her face from the blast of his breath and remembered Nathan Lyne's approach. 'Mr Franc, I am here under a joint Anglo-American authority, the likes of which you cannot even dream, and I will behave in the way that I believe is appropriate to the operation. If you want to test this, why don't you call your station in London and speak to the Deputy Director of the CIA, Jim Collins?'

Franc took his arm from the wall. 'What was that crap in there about?'

'I wanted to know if he recognised the code name for a Bosnian commander. You saw how he reacted to it. That means he can't be Faisal, and that the story of the man dying in Macedonia is probably true.'

'That proves nothing,' said Gibbons.

'You really believe he's a member of Hamas?'

'We have to explore all the possibilities, Ms Herrick,' said Franc, 'and if I am going to let you back inside that room, I need a guarantee you won't interrupt again. Lives could depend on us finding out what this man was sent to do. We know from the codes he sent to his associate, Loz, that he is part of a plot to mount a major attack in the US.'

'So why are you asking him about Faisal?' asked Herrick innocently. 'You know he isn't Faisal – that's clear to me from the early transcripts. Why waste the time?'

'The fact that he was carrying papers belonging to a member of Hamas, the most feared terrorist group in the Middle East, means there may be a connection between al-Qaeda and Hamas. I don't have to explain how important that is.' Franc had become avuncular, telling the little girl from England about the realities of 'front line procedure'. A look in his eye spurred her to wonder exactly what was going on.

'Okay,' she said, apparently placated. 'Shall we go back inside? I haven't seen enough to write anything sensible yet. By the way, who's the man with the bag of nuts?'

'He's a doctor,' Gibbons drawled. 'He's looking after the welfare of the suspect.'

When she went in, The Doctor was perched on the interview table offering Khan a pistachio nut. Relief spread over Khan's face as he saw Isis and his eyes leapt in hope, but then The Doctor leaned across and said something to him. When she saw him again his expression was blank and compliant.

She took her place as the questions about Hamas resumed, most of which Khan refused to answer, at one stage saying that he might as well be questioned about Colombia. An hour passed and although the sun was sinking outside, the room remained stifling. Suddenly Isis jumped up and left the room, this time to the sniggers of the two Albanians and The Doctor. Franc followed her out looking angry.

'You're yanking my chain,' she said. 'You're not interested in Hamas. In fact, I think this whole session has been arranged for my benefit. You're taking the interrogation up a blind alley so I don't get anything.' She stopped and looked at his glistening, fleshy face. 'I'll let you into a secret, Mr Franc. I am not here on some kind of training programme. There are literally hundreds of CIA and SIS officers engaged in a secret operation in London and all over Europe – one vast intelligence operation. I am here as part of that. Do you understand? So let's forget this Hamas business. It's a load of shite, and you know it. When I go back in, you steer the questions to the matter in hand.'

For a moment Franc was taken aback by her vehemence, but then he stretched and wiped his forehead. 'You're quite a spitfire, Miss Herrick, I'll grant you that. But you got to understand that this is not my interrogation. The man is in Albanian custody! We are here as their guests, for chrissake.'

'I don't give a fuck,' she hissed. 'If you want me to keep you out of my report, you will go back to the line of questioning you were pursuing in the transcripts.' With this, she turned and walked into the room again.

Evidently much of their exchange had been overheard. The Albanians were barely able to contain themselves and the other two Americans were smirking. Amidst all this brutal jollity, Khan looked even more pathetic. Suddenly he rose from his chair, but the restraints on his feet held him and he lurched onto the table. 'They're torturing me,' he shouted. 'This man, they call him The Doctor, he is the torturer. Tell him to show you the plastic bag he suffocated me with.' One of the Albanians was now at Khan's side, forcing him down and trying to clamp his jaw shut, but Khan ducked from his grip and continued shouting. 'Everyone here is tortured and brutalised. Is that what you want? Is that the policy of the British and American governments? Get me out of here and I will tell you anything you want.' He was silenced by The Doctor, who had got behind him and slipped a large forearm around his neck, locking it into the crook of his other arm. Khan coughed and slumped to the chair, staring at Herrick.

'Stop that,' Herrick screamed. 'Stop that now.' But the Americans were already leading her from the room. 'My government does not condone this,' she said out in the corridor.

'Nobody gives a damn what the British government thinks,' said Franc, physically handing her to Gibbons. 'Get her out of here, Lance, and make sure she doesn't come tomorrow.' He turned and went back into the room.

As the door opened she caught a glimpse of Khan, the whites of his eyes shining in the shadow cast by The Doctor's form.

It was dusk outside. The clouds above were mottled with the last rays of the sun and in the east the mountains were brushed with a dirty pink. The noise of the hot, swarming capital came to Herrick's ears like a roar.

Gibbons pushed her into the Toyota and climbed into the driving seat. 'You have some fucking balls,' he said, starting the engine. 'This is the way it is, you know! The way it has to be with these people.'

'What? Torture?'

'Hell, that's not torture. He's been slapped around a little. That's all.' His lips pouted downwards with a kind of patronising disgust.

'Oh, for Christ's sake! The man is going to be tortured because you can't get the answers you want. Has it occurred to you that he doesn't have anything else to tell you?'

They went a few hundred yards, swerving to avoid the worst of the potholes and the kids running into the street with iced drinks and cigarettes. Then, in a quieter spot, Gibbons pulled up and swivelled round in his seat, one arm hooked around the steering wheel. 'I know this is tough, but it is the only way. We have a man who could be part of a plot to kill thousands of people. We have learned our lesson about these guys. We have to fight fire with fire and be every bit as ruthless and cruel as they are, because we're here in this shitty little country, charged by the American people to protect them – at the very least, to give them warnings of terrorist attacks. How the hell do you think we're going to do that? Huh? I mean, like we treat Khan nicely when al-Qaeda's going to blow up this fuel tanker or drop a truckload of nuclear waste in DC, so he tells us? Get real, Isis. We're in a different kind of war now. We got to respond with all available means and, hell, if that entails one of the murderous little bastards being hung from a beam for intensive questions, I for one don't give a shit. What matters is that we get the result and protect our people. It's the same with the British. You think the average Brit cares a damn what happens to some Paki terrorist thousands of miles away? Of course he doesn't. He wants you to go out and get the answers and prevent these people from destroying his liberty and way of life. That's your job. It's as simple as that, and if you don't have the stomach for it, you should find yourself another line of work. This is the way it is from here on in, Isis. A long, cruel war between civilisations.'

'Civilisation,' she said, without looking at him, 'is exactly what this is about. That's what we're fighting for, the standard that says torture is wrong. There is nothing more absolute than the absolute wrong of what you're doing to that man. Don't you see that?'

'Don't be so fucking pious. You think this is an exclusively American vice? Give me a break, Isis. You Brits have been torturing people all over the goddam empire for a couple of hundred years. Hey, you even used those methods on your own citizens in Northern Ireland – bags over the head, sleep privation, beatings. And as long as the people were safe, they didn't want to know about it.'

She exhaled heavily. 'Torture and internment didn't stop the IRA. In fact, there's a good argument that the Peace Process only happened once those things had been abandoned. I didn't say we were perfect, but I know that if we start pulling people's fingernails out now we lose a sense of what we're fighting for.'

'The moral high ground, et cetera, et cetera.' He lit a cheroot and blew a stream of smoke through the crack in the window. 'You know about the guy who planned to crash a dozen airliners into the Pacific? He was arrested in the Philippines and after *intensive interrogation* he told them what was going down, and the whole goddam cell was detained. Maybe they broke a few bones on the way, but what's that compared to the people they saved, the vast numbers of Americans who aren't grieving because some nut says their lives offend the Prophet's teaching? You know what? We should go further. Every time they attack us, we should go after them, take the fight to every goddam mosque, every meeting held by every crummy imam and ayatollah, and if they don't get the point with a few smarts, we'll show what a little instant sunshine can do. It's about power, and using that power to dissuade.' He swept his hand at the street and the teeming life ahead of them on the Boulevard of National Heroes. The evening *volta* had begun, a procession of people walking up and down in the dusk, admiring each other's babies in a formal ritual found all over southern Europe. It seemed to speak of an ordered civil society. 'The only reason I can park up and talk to you is because those people know this is a US Embassy car and inside there's a guy with Lieutenant-Colonel Uziel Gal's finest invention on his lap.' He touched the sub-machine gun through the knapsack. 'Otherwise they'd strip the car and take you away.'

'What happens if you torture that man and get the wrong answers? What if you're asking the wrong questions?'

He smiled. '*We* are not going to be hurting anyone. *We* don't have any control over what happens in the state prisons here. It's like Colombia's baby brother. Everyone's corrupt, the gangsters are running the politicians, the police, the judges – everything. They sell their neighbours' children into sex slavery and when the kids get pregnant the gangs take the baby and put it to work for a living in the arms of some beggar. America doesn't run Albania, Isis. We got a toehold in the heart of darkness, that's all, and we use it to try to protect our own people.' He paused. 'We should have a drink back at your hotel and talk some more about this. There're things you should understand.'

Her first instinct was to say no, but then she thought there was every possibility of Gibbons getting drunk and talking about Khan. Besides, she wanted to see Khan again and she would need Gibbons to get her in.

'Why not?' she said. 'Yeah, why not?'

They passed through the lobby, Herrick drawing sullen, hungry looks from the knot of bodyguards, and went to the bar where Gibbons ordered whisky and a Diet Coke which he drank separately, downing each in one before Herrick had touched her glass of Albanian white. Another full glass of whisky followed and they went to the terrace and sat down, where Herrick recognised a piece of Schubert playing in the background. One or two of the evangelists were still earnestly hunched over lemonades. How odd, she thought, that in one part of town Americans were standing by as a man was tortured, while in another they were preparing a mission to convert the faithless masses. She made the point less harshly to Gibbons.

'Before you get too self-righteous, remember the British in India – missionaries and massacres. The sub-continent was virtually enslaved to the British Raj.' He paused and made a conciliatory gesture. 'You're a good person, Isis. I know your type from college. You've got genuine, honest to God goodness at your centre and, like all those people I knew, you believe in the healing power of liberal argument.'

She smiled a little vulnerably. 'Well, you have to believe in something, Lance.'

'Maybe we do, but belief doesn't work here. You got to see this as a vacuum. Since the communists fell, every goddam religion and ideology has been trying to fill it. That's why there're Christian evangelists in the mountains with a Bible in one hand and machine gun in the other, and why every kind of shady Muslim charity came here and started building mosques. But these people don't give a shit about either of them.' He drank the whisky, eyes patrolling the tables on the terrace. Then he clutched his belt. There was a faint buzz. 'Hey, that's my phone going. I better make the call.'

'That's fine. I have a couple of calls to make, too.'

'Don't you get lost,' he said, and vanished into the gardens in a conspicuously clandestine manner.

Herrick dialled Harland's mobile.

'Who's that with you?' he asked.

'Where are you?'

'It doesn't matter. Who is he?'

'The guy from the US Embassy.'

'There are some developments,' he said. 'One, you can't use the phone in the hotel, but I imagine you already knew that. Two, my charge has gone missing. Probably nothing to worry about, but I need to find him. He said the consignment you inspected this afternoon is much more important than anyone imagined. In a conference call to head office from the Embassy he blurted this out and now the MD is really interested. They're getting back to me. Meantime, you're to find out everything you can. Any movement of the consignment from the warehouse and they want to know about it.'

'Just like that?'

''Fraid so.'

'I'll do my best, which in the circumstances won't be much. How's the back?'

'Comes and goes. Your man's returning to the table. I'd better hang up.'

Out of the corner of her eye, in the darkened part of the terrace, she saw Harland get up from a table and walk to the dining room door, which she knew could be used to bypass the terrace. He was no longer bent double, but he was moving stiffly.

Gibbons flopped down beside her again. 'Hell, I thought I had more whisky than that. Isis, you been sneaking my booze?' He ordered another. 'So where were we?'

'What's going to happen to Khan?' she asked.

'That's all you ever ask.'

'Well, we would like to talk to him in slightly less threatening circumstances. Maybe he would tell us more. '

'He'll tell us.'

'Then what will happen to him? Where will he be tried?'

'Who the hell cares?' He drank some more and looked at her with sudden sharp focus. 'Forget about Khan. We just had word from London. I guess they told Milo Franc that you were a royal pain in the arse. They sent you here to get you out of the way. He talked to Collins, then a guy named Vigo, and he said you had no authority whatsoever. The way you threw your weight around has made Franc awful pissed. He said to tell you that you should write your report and get the hell out of Tirana. He doesn't want to see you again.' He laughed. 'Hey, have another drink for chrissake, you're making me feel awkward.'

'Vigo spoke to Franc?'

'Yeh, Vigo, he knows a lot of our guys at Langley.'

'I'll take that drink,' she said, brightening. 'It's a relief not to have to go to that place. I don't know how you stand it.'

'Goes with the territory,' said Gibbons in a manly, stoic way.

They drank while Herrick listened to Gibbons' theories about the lack of car mechanics in Albania and the fact – according to him – that no one was able to read a map because the communists had banned them for forty years. She was amenable, smiled a lot, and was certainly guilty of implying that things might develop further that evening. But just past nine o'clock he leapt up and said. 'Got to leave you, Isis. Date at the Valleys of Fire.' He said it as if it was a film title.

'What's that?'

He looked down at her without a trace of humour. 'A place where questions are asked and answers are given. I'll check in tomorrow. Hey, why don't we do dinner at Juvenilja?'

He navigated a pretty straight course through the tables of Tirana's underworld and hopeful reformers, which she thought was due more to momentum than any residual balance.

CHAPTER FIFTEEN

Herrick left the terrace and went upstairs, trying Harland several times on the way, but his phone was either switched off or out of range. Once in her room she spread the contents of the plastic bag on the bed, and after trying various combinations, opted for jeans, red T-shirt and knitted shawl around her shoulders. She tied her hair back, put on some lipstick and blueish eyeshadow, then slipped along the corridor to the fire exit. Outside in the boulevard she merged with the *volta,* which was still in full flood, but quickly dumped the shawl behind a bush because she suddenly felt it made her look like a street walker. She was glad she'd chosen to wear her trainers instead of the fringed boots.

As she made her way across the broken pavement in badly lit side-streets, she realised that a woman equipped herself with one of two attitudes on the street in Tirana – a kind of brassy hauteur, or beaten-down, famished servitude. The former implied that you had protection, which was everything in a town full of northern immigrants who had brought with them the ancient clan code *Kanun of Lek Dukagjin* which she had been reading about that morning. The dishonouring of a woman associated with a powerful man – the very smallest slight – could result in death and endless vendetta. So she strutted her stuff until she reached the SHISK compound, where she became more discreet and circled the place, noting the infra-red camera and the number of cars parked in the street leading to the headquarters. In the back of her mind was her father's advice about getting to know somewhere before attempting any kind of surveillance, and she had to admit she was woefully unprepared. If Khan was suddenly moved, she would have no way of following. The area was several degrees more sinister at night. There was no street lighting and the little light that came from the headquarters and the bar directly across the road only served to hint at what lay in the shadows. She was aware of people watching her from the darker recesses where they'd put up for the night. When one of the city's regular blackouts came, casting the neighbourhood into total darkness, she fumbled in the canvas bag for her mobile and called Bashkin, knowing that he would still be loitering hopefully outside the main entrance of the Byron. He agreed to meet her outside a newly renovated Catholic church a couple of streets away and flash his lights twice. She hung up and was about to switch off her phone when it vibrated in her hand.

'Yes,' she said hurriedly.

'It's Dolph – Andy Dolph!'

'Can't talk now, Dolph. I'm really busy.'

'Okay. Quickly then, you've got a message from Beirut. Your friend has news for you. She said you'd need to know straight away.'

For a moment Herrick couldn't think what he was talking about. 'Oh yes. Where are you?'

'At your old desk to fill in for you. I'm sitting next to sweetie Lyne. You didn't tell me about him, Isis.'

'But he *is* sharp.'

'Oh yeah, he's good, but re–lent–less.'

'Look, I've got to go. We'll speak soon. And, Dolph – thanks for ringing.'

'Be safe.'

About ten minutes later, just as the lights came back on, a pair of identical white Landcruisers with US diplomatic plates appeared in the street, crashed over the potholes and pulled up to wait for the compound gates to open. Herrick turned on her phone and dialled Harland. This time he answered.

'There seems to be some movement and Gibbons mentioned he was going to the Valley of Fires, wherever that is. The people from the US Embassy are here. Two cars. Maybe something is happening.'

Harland thought for a moment. 'Have you got transport?'

'Yes, but I don't know how reliable he's going to be.' She gave him Bashkin's mobile number because her battery was low, then hung up and made her way to the Mercedes where Bashkin was sunk down in the driving seat, smoking. She tapped on the window and he let her in. 'What we do now?' he asked.

'We wait,' she said. 'We wait, Mr Bashkin.' To pass the time she told him about her father coming to Albania in the war and fighting with the partisans.

Inside the SHISK headquarters, Karim Khan heard the sound of several men walking along the corridor between the cells. One of the prisoners had suffered some kind of convulsion earlier and despite cries of help from the other men no one had come until it was too late. At least, that is what Khan concluded from the wailing in a language he could not understand. He wondered wretchedly what they would do with the body and whether the man's relations would be told.

For a few moments the lights were thrown on and there was the sound of men moving something. But instead of the footsteps dying, they approached his cell and keys were turned in the lock. Two men came in and dragged him from the iron bed. Another pulled his arms roughly behind his back and bound them with a plastic restraint. He was marched along the cell block, fearful eyes watching him from the cages nearest the door, and taken outside into the night where he was hooded and rolled into the back of a vehicle. Now he'd better make his peace with God, he said to himself. There had been many nights before now when he'd known he would never see daylight, but the dawn had always come and Karim Khan had somehow survived. But tonight he was certain that his life would end, and the knowledge brought him an odd solace. For him the struggle was over.

They watched as the gates were shut and then opened again. Herrick had been urging Bashkin to take the handbrake off and allow the Mercedes to creep forward but he insisted on keeping his distance. The SHISK were people you didn't mess with, he said. The mere fact of watching the headquarters was enough to land him in jail. When they glimpsed the figure being brought outside she leaned forward to the dashboard, wishing she had a pair of binoculars. The build of the man was about right and he was wearing a blue T-shirt, as Khan had been, but she didn't get a clear view of his face before he disappeared behind the vehicles. Seconds later the cars emerged from the compound and moved off down the street.

'We have to follow them,' said Herrick, stabbing at her phone to call Harland.

Bashkin shook his head. 'It's no possible.'

'Of course it's bloody well possible. How much do you want?'

'For this?' He looked extremely doubtful, as if no amount of money would compensate for the risk he was about to take. 'Two hundred dollars.'

'Done,' she said.

Unable to hide his astonishment, Bashkin started the car.

Herrick put the phone to her ear. Harland had already answered. 'There are two cars,' she said. 'I'm ninety per cent certain that they're moving Khan. I'll follow them. They're going towards Skenderbeg Square.'

'I'll join you. Keep in touch.'

They followed the cars for about five miles to the western fringes of the city. The evening was still warm and a lot of people were milling on the side of the road, buying watermelons and cold drinks from fridges hooked up to the public power supply. Bashkin slowed down several times, once for a dog-fight that spilled into both lanes of traffic and then for a broken-down truck. As a result, they lost the two Landcruisers, and when they eventually cleared Tirana's chaotic outskirts and hit the dual carriageway to Durrës she shouted for him to put his foot down. For once Bashkin did as he was told.

They shot past the new Coca-Cola plant and a detergent factory, both incongruously neat and well-lit, like giant pieces of Toytown, then realised they must have missed the Landcruisers on the turning to Krujë a few miles back. They turned round and took a much smaller road. It passed through several villages and began to climb into a forest of low pines. Bashkin explained that this had once been Enver Hoxha's private hunting ground and was now the place where they made charcoal. There were fires up here that burned night and day, he said. She asked to borrow his mobile, and after haggling over the price for a call, she phoned Harland for the final time and told him she had found the Valleys of Fire. This was where they must have brought Karim Khan, for what purpose she could not say. Harland seemed oddly unimpressed, but said he was on his way.

After rounding several more bends they came to a headland over-looking a bowl in the landscape. Along the far side were about ten furnaces gouged out of the bedrock. Each one had an opening about the size of a door and a little above this was a hole which let out viscous smoke and muddied light. Herrick climbed out of the car saying she'd pay Bashkin another hundred dollars to wait. She also told him to direct a tall Englishman who was about to arrive down into the valley.

She started down the slope, picking her way through the scrub, all the while glancing ahead of her and up to the road above. As she drew near to the point where the bushes had been cleared, she saw dozens of young men and small, emaciated boys scurrying between the fur-naces and heaps of rubber tyres that were responsible for the poisonous air. Their skin and clothes were blackened and the sweat on their bodies gleamed in the light. She crouched down and watched for a few minutes, almost hypnotised by the sight of them rolling tyres up the incline, then heaving them into the furnaces. Occasionally, down-drafts from the mountains caused the fires to blow back without warning and those nearest the furnace doors had to jump for cover. She saw one of these tar-black creatures, no more than four foot six tall, use a long metal poker to vault out of the way with great agility. When he landed he performed a jig like a monkey-demon cavorting in the flames of hell.

Maybe it was the roar of the underground fires, or the idea that she was witnessing a spectacle brought to life from Hieronymous Bosch, that dulled her attention. Either way, she was utterly caught off guard when they seized her from behind, lifted her bodily onto the clear ground in front and began to frisk her. She managed a little yelp but otherwise put up no resistance.

There were three of them, all armed. She recognised one from the SHISK headquarters. He gestured to the other two to bring her a little way down the hill and they walked to a pile of wood. The two men holding her relaxed their grip, and one – covertly it seemed to her – slipped his hand down to feel her bottom. What did this mean? Did it presage gang rape, or was this man's interest something she could use? Could she snatch a gun and run for it?

'You do know I'm a British diplomat?' she said in a voice that sounded all too thin and powerless.

The SHISK guard laughed without turning towards her. He was searching the track below them, shielding his face from the heat of the fires. 'No Ingleesh diplomat,' he said, wagging his finger without looking at her. 'You Ingleesh spy. Missease Jeemes Bond.' All three laughed. At this point, the little man she had seen leaping from the flames came over with a seesaw walk, holding the metal pole over his shoulder like a javelin. He had a round, hairless face with elfin ears and eyes that were too close together. They knew his name – Ylli – and beckoned to him, although his strange looks clearly made them feel uncomfortable. Ylli put out a hand and was given a cigarette and some notes which he stuffed into his back pocket. Then he strutted around Herrick, making observations about her in the high, unbroken voice of a boy. Twice he tried to touch her but was shooed away by the guards. Then he withdrew and let himself down onto a pile of four tyres where he smoked with quick, childish puffs and made gestures that suggested he was sitting in the finest armchair ever made.

The little man heard the cars first, and scrambled up to balance on the tyres with prehensile bare feet and waved excitedly with the pole. The two Landcruisers, now joined by a Jeep and BMW sped up the remainder of the hill and tore past them about fifty yards away. Herrick strained forward but couldn't make out any of the passengers because they were thrown into silhouette by the light of the fires and a lot of dust had been kicked up by the lead vehicle. They reached the top of the bowl and stopped just beyond a layer of black fog, at which Ylli jumped down and scampered over to them. Several men got out and started making for the higher ground above the furnaces. They were dragging someone with them, the man in the blue T-shirt, who evidently had his hands tied behind his back and was offering no resistance whatsoever. Behind them came The Doctor, who struggled up the slope with Ylli bringing up the rear. Something passed between this group: it almost seemed as if they were trying to reason with the prisoner. But at length all but two stepped away. The man was marched forward and without further hesitation pushed into the flue opening. Ylli rushed up to the hole and could be seen thrusting and jabbing at the body with his pole. Then a couple of car tyres were thrown in. These instantly caught light and belched a column of smoke and sparks into the night. Without a second look, the party descended to the cars, drove back down towards them and pulled up. A man she hadn't seen before got out. He was in his late forties, dapperly dressed for the evening in a light sports jacket, a thin polo shirt and well-cut trousers. He took off the jacket, hung it round his shoulders and dusted off his hands with a quick slapping motion.

'It was your choice to be here tonight,' said the man. His English was perfect; the manner reminiscent of the polo ground. 'You were spying, and unpleasant things sometimes happen to spies, as you are no doubt aware.'

Herrick was almost too shocked to speak. 'Why did you kill him?' she said. 'And like that?'

'We have no use for a filthy terrorist. He would not answer our questions. We gave him his chance as you saw this afternoon. How many people have been burnt and mutilated by the actions of men like Khan? You ask yourself that before you judge us. We believe in decisive solutions here in Albania.'

'Burning people alive,' she said quietly, 'is not an option in any war.'

'You have a phrase in English, do you not, Miss Herrick? If you can't stand the heat of the fire ... well, I'm sure you know it.' He gave a little chuckle, took a small notebook from his pocket and held it up to the headlights of the leading car. 'Your address in London and your telephone number are written here, and that belonging to your father, an old war hero, I believe. He lives in Scotland in a place called Hopelaw – a pretty name – and he has a servant there named Mrs Mackenzie. You see, you are no mystery to me, Isis Herrick.'

She shook her head. 'Who are you?'

'I am Marenglen.' He paused and took a folded handkerchief from his trouser pocket and held it under his nose. 'You see, we Albanians have been locked up in this land for many years, so when the communists fell we acquired a taste for travel. Many Albanians have left and set up enterprises all over the world. In some cases, regrettably, these did not meet with the approval of the authorities. However, in London my countrymen encountered little opposition to their activities and they were able to establish themselves in many different fields of endeavour. You will be familiar, perhaps, with the way they have taken over certain businesses in Soho, but they also have many other tricks up their sleeves. One is contract killing.'

He returned the handkerchief to his pocket and snapped his fingers. The guard who had first apprehended her handed him a cigarette and lit it. 'So,' he let out smoke from the side of his mouth, 'allow Marenglen to tell you now that if you place so much as a word of what you have seen in your report to London, I will have you and your father and his loyal servant killed. Naturally, these contracts will be issued in the order that causes maximum pain. If, however, you feel you cannot guarantee your silence to me now, then I don't see why we shouldn't advance things a little. You have met Ylli. I believe Ylli is a virgin, at least with humans, although the same cannot be said for sheep and goats. We can leave you with Ylli, he can take his pleasure with you and then, well, you will disappear. I think you can imagine that this would not be a happy end.'

She nodded.

'So why don't you go back to the Byron and prepare to leave Albanian soil within, say, thirty-six hours. That should give you time to send a convincing report saying you were given access to the prisoner Khan and that he was in every respect unforthcoming and uncooperative. Oh yes, there is one other thing. Take Robert Harland with you. I don't see that there is any point in his staying on after you've left.' He smiled, not very pleasantly, and walked the few paces to the car.

The men holding her let go and jogged over to the cars. When one of the doors was opened she was sure she caught a glimpse of Gibbons. A few seconds later the convoy bumped off down the hill. She turned and made her way to Bashkin's Mercedes, sickened and choking on the smell of the Valleys of Fire.

CHAPTER SIXTEEN

One question stayed in Herrick's mind on the ride back to the hotel, and when she was sitting on the balcony of her room with a packet of crisps from the minibar she said it out loud. Why would the CIA and SHISK go to such lengths to question Khan about a planned terrorist attack, then kill him without getting an answer? Even if Khan had talked in the few hours between her leaving the headquarters and seeing him taken off, that would be no reason to kill him. Surely it would be the moment for the Americans to produce him to the world's media as evidence of another thwarted terrorist plot, a triumph of vigilance and interception to be shared with their Albanian friends. There was only one solution. Khan had not been killed.

She phoned Harland's room and then his mobile. There was no answer on either. She waited for half an hour, drinking a little of the whisky opened by Gibbons the night before, not really enjoying it, and gazing across the garden. Then she went to the bathroom and washed the smell of burnt rubber from her hair under the shower. This took only a few minutes and when she came out she saw that a note had been slipped under the door. 'Rooms and phones bugged. See you at Embassy soonest.'

She dried her hair, changed and was downstairs in less than five minutes. Bashkin was still out in the car park. 'What is this, a twenty-four-hour watch?' she asked him.

He looked at her a little ruefully. 'Mease Errique leave soon? Tomorrow Bashkin drive you to airport.'

'You know my plans before I do,' she said, climbing into the

Mercedes. 'Perhaps you could tell me what you thought of what we saw up in the hills?'

'Bashkin see nothing. Bashkin asleeping.'

'Right,' she said, 'Bashkin asleeping. But not tired enough to go home after he's dropped me at the hotel. Who do you work for?'

'For you Mease Errique.'

'And for Mr Marenglen also, I shouldn't wonder,' she said. 'Drive me to the British Embassy, please.'

Harland was waiting for her just inside the Embassy gates with one of the Hereford-trained guards, who introduced himself as Steve Tyrrel.

'Where the fuck did you get to?' she said to Harland. 'I thought you were following me. Where were you?'

'We'll talk inside.' He gestured to a door where another armed man stood. 'We've got Loz here, but I haven't told him anything and I think we should keep it that way until we know what's going on. There's more to him than you could imagine.'

They found Sammi Loz seated nonchalantly in an outer office with a cup of tea and a copy of the day's *International Herald Tribune*, looking for all the world as though he was about to go out in Manhattan on a warm summer's evening. 'Reunions later,' said Harland roughly as Loz got up and made an elaborate fuss over Herrick.

As soon as the metal door of the communications room thudded behind them, Herrick gave Harland a brief account of what she had seen on the mountains. When she reached the end she said, 'This wasn't for real. I know that. Gibbons dropped the stuff about the Valleys of Fire like a pile of plates after he had spoken on the phone – obviously to Milo Franc. They wanted me to go up there and watch someone being thrown into the fire.' She stopped and looked around. 'I don't suppose you've got any food, have you?' Harland phoned Tyrrel and asked him to scratch something together.

'Where'd you get to?' she asked when he put the phone down.

Harland gave her an odd, crooked smile. Now that his back was on the mend the strain had left his face. 'I went with Steve Tyrrel. I didn't tell you because I think the Americans are listening to our mobiles. So I had to pretend that I was following you up there. Steve had a hunch they were taking Khan out of the country and he was exactly right.

Khan was driven to the airport and put on a private jet. The plane is being tracked by GCHQ and our people on Cyprus. I have no word yet as to where it's headed but the Chief will be on as soon as he knows.'

'So that's more or less that,' said Herrick. 'We've lost our man and I can go home.'

'Better hear what the Chief says,' he said with another smile.

Khan had known nothing after being rolled into the back of the car because a needle was plunged into his buttock. When he began to recover consciousness on the plane, all he was aware of was a raging thirst. He had been given no water during the previous day and whatever drug they'd used to knock him out had heightened the need for liquid. This blocked out his fear at finding himself on a plane, still hooded and bound, but now also with his mouth taped over and his ankles tied together. After a little while he started to explore his surroundings by moving his legs. He touched what he assumed was the seat in front of him and then angled them into the aisle and started to kick out, making as much noise as he could behind the tape. Someone stirred in front of him and he heard Lance Gibbons' voice, then the big CIA man, Franc. He kicked some more and became aware of them consulting each other. 'Look,' said Gibbons. 'Langley says he might have a capsule in his teeth.'

'He would've used it by now,' growled Franc.

Khan had no idea what they were talking about and heaved his torso forward so he was almost out of the seat and in the aisle.

'Hey, hey, hold still there, buddy,' shouted Gibbons.

The hood was removed and Gibbons' face peered into his. Khan stared back, eyes popping and cheeks blown out.

Gibbons examined him in the dim light of the cabin, then pulled back the tape so it hung from the corner of his mouth. When he heard what Khan wanted he grunted and fetched a clear plastic beaker of water which he lifted to his lips. He replenished it twice from a bottle before Khan's thirst was slaked and he was able to croak thank you.

'Now I'm gonna put this tape back. There's no use you getting excited. We got a lot of flying time ahead of us and unless you want us to give you another one of those shots you'll take a nap.'

Khan saw that he was considering whether to replace the hood so shook his head vigorously. Gibbons hesitated, then folded the cloth and placed it on the headrest in front of him. Before returning to sprawl in his own seat he jabbed his finger in front of Khan's face and said, 'Now, sleep, buster.'

Khan wasn't reassured by the water. These tiny acts of kindness meant nothing and indeed they often seemed to foreshadow some new, unpleasant turn in his story. In all the thousands of miles he had travelled he realised he had met almost no one he could trust, except perhaps in the case of Mr Skender – the consumptive interpreter who had accepted his money and the postcard with a look of solemn obligation. He was sure that Skender had posted the message and that it had arrived in New York. Moreover he understood that the pretty young English diplomat was letting him know she had met Sammi when she mentioned The Poet. It wasn't just chance she used that name because he caught the look in her eye as she said it. And yet she couldn't have any idea what it meant. Loz must have told her to drop it into the conversation, knowing he would recognise it while she would remain utterly ignorant of its meaning. That was smart of Loz.

But just as there seemed to be hope it was snatched from him. He was almost certainly on his way to Camp X-Ray, which he knew would be impregnable to all Loz's money and cunning. He had heard enough about the place while travelling through Iran to know that no one left unless the Americans wanted it. What hope did a veteran of the jihad in Bosnia and Afghanistan have of persuading the interrogators that he was simply a soldier? He wriggled a little to ease the pain in his ribs where The Doctor had hit him. The discomfort reminded him that at least the Americans did not practise torture. They may have been prepared to leave the room while The Doctor suffocated him and pressed his thumbs into his eye sockets. But that wasn't the same as doing it themselves. He could at least survive at Camp X-Ray and soon they would understand that he was cooperating with them and represented no threat whatsoever. Yes, he would make them understand that.

Although the drug made his mind sluggish and he was desperate for sleep, he kept on returning to the young woman. He had forgotten what a Western woman could be like and she brought back memories

165

of his time in London. This woman was poised, intelligent and brave. It had taken courage to shout out in his defence when they tried to stop him talking.

He managed to doze for half an hour or so but then woke to a new kind of light in the cabin. He looked to his left and saw dawn rising through the window, an orange light below the wing tip, graded through azure to a deep mauve in the stratosphere. He watched it for a while before realising with a sudden, sharp dread that the sun rising on the port side of the aeroplane could only mean one thing – they weren't headed west for the Caribbean and Camp X-Ray, but due south.

Harland and Herrick sent a long encrypted email to Vauxhall Cross about Khan being taken out of the country while the CIA and SHISK had set up a diversion in the mountains, then sat back to consume a meal of bananas, Marmite sandwiches, digestive biscuits and coffee, rustled up by Steve Tyrrel from the Embassy kitchen. Herrick found she couldn't eat enough.

At 3.00 a.m. the Chief came on the phone. The British listening station in Cyprus had picked up the unscheduled flight an hour before and noted that, having executed a wide circle over the Mediterranean, the jet turned east into Greek air space and then followed the commercial air corridor down the coast of the Mediterranean, skirting Turkey's southern flank, Lebanon and Palestine.

'They're going to Egypt,' said Herrick, leaning into the conference phone.

'It looks like that,' said the Chief.

'It fits with today's line of questioning,' she said. 'The only thing they wanted to demonstrate in front of me was that Khan was Jasur Faisal – the man whose papers he was carrying. Faisal is wanted all over the Middle East, and in Egypt for the murder of a newspaper editor.'

'Yes,' said the Chief quietly. 'It means of course that the Albanians wouldn't want to be answerable for the degree of torture they're planning. This has happened before, in 1998.' There was a long pause during which Harland and Herrick wondered if the line had dropped. 'It complicates things a great deal.' Another pause. 'Yes, what we shall want you to do for the moment is to have that serious talk with Loz, using the information I sent you earlier. See how he responds. I'll get back to you. Oh, by the way, we're going to change encryption on the next call.' He told Harland to enter a six-digit code into the computer through which the phone was routed, then hung up.

As Harland worked at the keyboard, Herrick asked, 'What did Loz say to you that made you and the Chief so interested?'

'He told me that Khan knows the identities of two terrorist leaders who were already talking about al-Qaeda activity in the mid-nineties. He and Khan talked to at least one of them when they last saw each other in ninety-seven.'

'But surely Loz is just trying to get us to spring his friend?' she said. 'He's bound to exaggerate the importance of Khan's information.'

'It's a tip that the Chief's not prepared to ignore. He has very good reasons to think Loz is telling the truth, but I don't know what they are.'

'But what's the point?' she asked. 'If Khan is in Cairo, we can forget it. The only thing the Egyptians are concerned with is what target he's planning to attack, who his contacts are, and where he was trained. They'll be asking the questions the Americans want answers to, but with a cattle prod. When he denies being involved in a specific plot they'll torture him to a point where he has to dream up some cock and bull story. Meanwhile they'll miss the really valuable information.'

'One of the minor problems with torture,' said Harland grimly. He picked up the phone and told Tyrrel to bring Loz in.

Loz's buoyant expression collapsed when they told him that Khan had been taken to Cairo. 'This is very, very bad news,' he said, shaking his head and working his hands.

'Well, we're still evaluating what this means,' said Harland, steering him to a chair away from the computers. 'But it doesn't look good, I grant you that.' He paused and rubbed his chin, as though wondering how to proceed, then he focused on Loz. 'Isis had an encounter with one of the nastier scumbags of our time tonight, a man called Maren-glen who is head of the local secret service here. It's a curious name which I understand is made from the first three letters of Marx, Engels and Lenin – a name forged in desperate communist times when people needed to ingratiate themselves with the regime.' He stopped again. 'Interestingly, it's the same kind of formation as TriBeCa in

New York, the Triangle Below Canal. But I probably can't tell you anything about TriBeCa, Doctor.' He let that hang in the stuffy atmosphere of the Communications room and looked down at Loz intently. Herrick wondered where the hell this was leading.

'This Marenglen,' continued Harland, 'was picked up when he came to the LSE in London on a scholarship in 1987, and he was trained by former colleagues who of course had no idea that communism was about to collapse in Albania. He was a good spot because he was exceptionally clever, and useful to us after Enver Hoxha's death, but Marenglen turned out to be a rotten apple, as bad a man as you could ever meet. There is literally no crime in Albania that Marenglen does not in some way supervise from the safety of his position. Coming in contact with this man is like handling a test tube of bubonic plague. I do not exaggerate.' Loz looked mystified. 'We are here because of you, Dr Loz, and because of your friend. Isis took a big risk this evening to see if she could help Khan and that's when she came across Marenglen. It could have ended very badly for her but she took that risk because of you and your friend. But you know something? We don't really have any idea about either you or Khan. So, I want you to help us. Tell us everything about you.'

'Absolutely,' said Loz, eagerly leaning forward, hands clasped around his knee. 'But what more do you want?'

'You should understand your position,' said Harland. 'You're in Albania illegally. You travelled here on a forged passport and have none of the correct visa requirements. Remember, this was Khan's only crime in Albania, and yet he was held and beaten up. If they find that his main contact is also here, they are very likely to do exactly the same to you. Who knows, you may even end up in the same Egyptian jail.'

'But your responsibility is to help me.' A fleeting, rather professional smile crossed his face. 'That's what the Secretary-General instructed you to do.'

Harland shook his head. 'Believe me, Doctor, what happens to you is entirely my choice now.'

'So what do you want me to tell you?'

'Ninety-seven. What were you doing in 1997?'

'I was in New York, studying osteopathy. You know that!' he smiled at Herrick as though Harland was now being quite impossible.

'And the real estate business? How did that fit into your life?'

Loz's gaze hardened. 'What do you mean?'

'We know all about that. We know that while you were studying, you were also investing large sums in Manhattan developments. I have a figure of sixty million dollars, but London believes the amount transferred to you through twenty accounts may be two or three times that figure. All of it was placed at your disposal to buy real estate in Manhattan – mostly in Chelsea and TriBeCa. TriBeCa was the big killing of your operation, wasn't it? You made a profit of 15.7 million dollars on one deal in the Triangle Below Canal. There were many others.' He stopped and examined his notes. 'You know how we began to trace them? We started by looking up the name of a company that let your premises in the Empire State building – and still does – the Twelver Real Estate Corporation. That name rang a few bells in London. Anyone who knows anything about Islam knows that the Shi'a sect is called in Arabic *Ithna Ashariya* – the Twelvers. The movement of money from the Shi'ite banks in Lebanon to New York had been noted between 1996 and 1999 and so had the name of the Twelver Real Estate Corp. What they didn't know was who was controlling the investments. A week ago, they began to dig again and found your signature on documents held by the City Authority in New York. Who were you investing the money for, Dr Loz?'

'Some former associates of my father.'

'And these people were connected with the Hizbollah organisation?'

'No. But I cannot say definitely, of course.'

'But you agree that the utmost was done to disguise the origin of this money before you invested it and, given your father's Shi'ite background, it is likely that it came from Hizbollah?'

'It's a possibility.'

'But more interesting is that you deceived almost everyone about the extent of your wealth and your real occupation.'

'But I *am* an osteopath.'

'Yes, you are, and a very good one. But you are also a property tycoon. You've made many millions of dollars for your partners *and* for yourself. A rough estimate puts your wealth at fifty million dollars

– enough, as someone observed in London, to finance one hell of a terrorist operation. Enough money to buy as many sets of fake identity as you could need. That's why you found it so easy to leave the States and bribe your way through the Balkans.'

Loz sank into the chair. 'I had to leave the US, as you are very well aware. I spent what was necessary.'

'Yes, but what other back doctor has your sort of contacts – members of Bosnian crime fraternities outside Chicago, gun runners, people smugglers in Southern Bosnia and Montenegro? We've only just begun to research you, but it's already clear that you are seriously "connected". Your pose as a society figure in Manhattan is a carefully constructed cover.'

Loz shook his head. 'I *really* am an osteopath. That's what I do! It fulfils me in a way I cannot describe. Why else would I run free clinics every week in three New York hospitals? Yes, it is true I have made a lot of money, but I can arrange for you to talk to my lawyers and they will tell you that I have donated much of my fortune to charity. In other circumstances I would not mention this, but you should know that I have made grants and donations of nearly twenty million dollars in the last three years. This can all be confirmed in New York, by my lawyers, my accountant. Even the charities will tell you.'

'But you still have a tidy sum in the bank.'

Loz uncrossed his legs and threw his hands out hopelessly. 'Of course, but the money was gained honourably on the rising market of the late nineties. Would it be any different if I had invested in new technology and sold at the right moment? What's the problem with real estate?'

'The difference to us is that you were investing on behalf of a Middle Eastern terrorist organisation. Where the profits from those deals went is certainly interesting, and you will face questions on this when you return to the United States. That is a legitimate concern of the FBI and I will make sure Special Agent Ollins is fully briefed with the information we have. No one can protect you from that. But for the moment I want to know what occurred when you met Khan in London in 1997.' He raised a hand. 'Before you answer, be clear that I have the authority to turn you over to Marenglen if I'm not satisfied with what you say.'

He nodded. 'Look, there isn't a problem about this. Karim phoned me in New York and said he wanted my advice. He was like that. He relied on me, trusted my judgement.'

'And you agreed to go to London?'

'Yes, I flew the next day and we spent a couple of days together, seeing old haunts, talking about Bosnia. Eventually he got round to the subject of Afghanistan. He told me he had decided to join The Poet in Pakistan. As I explained this was our name for a man he had met in Bosnia whose real name we did not know. Anyway, Karim was offered a role in Afghanistan training fighters. That can mean a lot of things. Karim understood it to mean that he would be continuing the war against the oppressors of Islam on Afghanistan's northern borders, the republics of the former Soviet Union. But he was torn between Western and Muslim values and wanted the moral view of what he was going to do. He felt I would understand because I had suffered the same agonies of guilt in Bosnia. I told him that he should stay in London and return to medicine. But he was caught up with the idea of himself as this great adventurer, even though he knew the horrors of war and had seen the very worst things in Bosnia. We had an argument – a terrible argument – because I could not believe he was going to make this mistake. I was appalled, disappointed. I accused him of being addicted to killing and failing to face his responsibilities as a human being, a doctor and a good Muslim. For his part he said I was a coward and running away from my duties as a Muslim. We made it up the following day, which was when I gave him those postcards and some money.'

'How many postcards?'

'Oh, a handful. I can't remember.'

'And how much money?' asked Harland.

'I don't recall exactly – fifteen thousand dollars, something like that.'

'Did you hear from him again, apart from the postcards?'

'No.'

Herrick looked at Harland then asked, 'If you haven't changed your address in the last six or seven years, presumably your phone number hasn't changed either?'

'No, it's the same.'

'So why didn't he call you instead of sending these postcards? There was very little guarantee of them getting through to you. Why didn't he just pick up the phone and ask you to wire him some money?'

'I have wondered about that,' said Loz. 'Maybe he was worried about the calls being monitored.'

'Yes,' she said. 'But it still doesn't really make sense, unless of course he had to send those cards because of the coded messages in them.'

Harland stood up and let his right arm slide down his thigh.

'You shouldn't do that yet,' said Loz gently. 'In a week's time you can begin the exercises I showed you, but not yet.'

'Isis makes a good point,' said Harland, removing his hand and straightening.

'I agree,' said Loz, 'but I can't answer her question.'

'You must have some idea of The Poet's identity,' she said. 'There can't have been many Bosnian commanders that Khan was friendly with.'

'I believe he was originally a scholar… but I only inferred that from what Khan said.'

'Where was he from?' asked Herrick.

'The East, maybe Pakistan or Iran, but I do not know.'

'And you think this is the man that Khan can tell us about? What reason do you have for believing he's still alive?'

'Because he was very smart. Khan was in awe of him. He said he was the most civilised and dangerous man he had ever met. Those were the words he used – civilised and dangerous.'

Herrick took out a piece of paper and wrote 'Phone Dolph', then on a second line, 'Beirut'. She had suddenly had an idea.

'But all this is guesswork,' said Harland contemptuously. 'I need a lot more.'

'We really need to know everything that you know,' said Isis, leaning forward and looking into Loz's eyes. 'Trust us for Christ's sake. We've certainly earned that.'

Loz breathed in deeply, seemingly to savour the air. 'Eighteen months ago I was phoned by a man in New York. He was a foreigner, but well-spoken and educated. He said something like, "I expect you have heard of me. I am The Poet." I knew he must have been given my number by Khan, so I listened and he told me straight away that he wanted thirty thousand dollars. He said there was no question of my not giving it to him – he made it sound as if I owed him. In the background of what he was saying there was a threat and I understood that he would harm me if didn't give him what he wanted. So I got the money together the next day, put it in a bag and began to walk to the agreed meeting place in Union Square. He specified that I should walk, even though it was winter and there was a lot of snow on the ground. On the way, a homeless beggar came up to me asking for money. He wouldn't leave me alone and followed me down the street, then he grabbed hold of my arm and handed me a card which said, "The Poet thanks you for your donation." He reached out and took the bag from my hand.'

'You gave thirty thousand dollars to a New York beggar?' said Harland incredulously.

'Yes. When I got back to the building there was the same message on my answerphone. "The Poet thanks you for your donation." '

'You were had,' said Harland.

'I don't think so. Two days later I received an Arabic inscription in a frame. You remarked on it when I was treating you. If you remember, it says, "A man who is noble does not pretend to be noble, any more than a man who is eloquent feigns eloquence. When a man exaggerates his qualities, it is because of something lacking in himself. The bully gives himself airs because he is conscious of his weakness." Also in the package was this …' he opened his jacket, then handed Herrick a small black and white photograph wrapped in cellophane. It was of Karim Khan dressed in tribal costume and sporting a boldly patterned turban. 'This was proof that he was in touch with Khan and had seen him recently. I suppose it was also proof of his own identity.'

'Why didn't you show me this before?'

'Because you're of a sceptical disposition, Mr Harland. If you don't mind me saying, you're too nervous to believe.'

'I would have believed a bloody picture,' said Harland, holding it away from him.

'You need glasses,' said Loz.

Harland took no notice and put the photograph in his wallet. 'I'll keep this for the moment.'

'What did this man look like?' asked Herrick.

'A homeless person,' he smiled. 'I'm being serious. He was covered in coats and wore a long beard. I couldn't see his face beneath it all and anyway he was a few inches shorter than I am. Maybe only five foot five or six.'

'So you're telling us you may have seen The Poet?'

'I have no doubt about that.'

'When was this?'

'The winter of 2000, just after the millennium celebrations.'

Harland walked to the door and opened it. 'Right, that will be all for the moment. We will talk later.'

When Loz had left he looked at Herrick and said, 'Well?'

'We either believe all of it or none of it. Either way, there's nothing we can do about Khan.'

Harland frowned. 'Does this overlap with anything you've been doing for RAPTOR?'

'No, but I would like to make a call on this phone if you wouldn't mind. I have a friend who may still be up.'

She got through to Dolph, whose brisk hello rang out on the conference speaker.

'Why're you up so late?' she asked.

'Waiting for you.'

'But what are you doing?'

'Turns out that the Americans are keen poker players. We've got two full tables on the go, playing for a monkey – that's five hundred nicker in your language, Isis.'

'Don't you sleep?'

'No one knows whether it's day or night down here. We're like beagles in a smoking lab, or labs in a smoking beagle. Whichever way you like it.'

'Are you drunk, Dolph?'

'No, merely rat-arsed.'

She was aware of Harland's disapproving gaze. 'Dolph, I need your help, so pull yourself together.'

'I love it when you're strict.'

'I want to know about Bosnia – the siege of Sarajevo.'

'Okay.'

'We're interested in a commander of Muslim soldiers. We have no name apart from The Poet, but this was not commonly used.'

'Well that narrows it down,' said Dolph, laughing.

'Come on Dolph. I haven't got time…'

'Well, there was Abu Abdel Aziz or Barbaros – the guy with the two-foot beard.'

'No, someone less obvious. Perhaps a scholar of some sort, but a good fighter.'

'So we're looking for a member of the Mujahideen Brigade that was disbanded after Dayton?'

'Maybe. We're right at the beginning with this one, so we're interested in anything.'

'I'll talk to some of the hacks who were there during the siege. They may have come across him. Any idea where this character came from?'

'Pakistan or Iran are possibilities.'

'Have you got a description? His age at the time?'

'No – we know he is about five foot five or six.'

'Don't burden me with detail, Isis,' he laughed. 'I'll call you if I get something. Where're you going to be?'

'On my cell phone.'

'Hey, Isis. You got to hear about Joe Lapping before you go.'

'Okay.' Herrick sat back smiling.

'So Lapping is left in Sarajevo instead of me. The French tumble him in precisely three and a half seconds and start making his life hell. Lapping can't move without one of the Frogs whispering "Rozbeef spy" in his ears. He gets completely freaked, changes his address and then can't find his way home and has to put up with some aid worker while the apartment is found. Meanwhile the Frogs have moved every bird with a dodgy past into Lapping's place and opened it as a brothel.' Dolph broke off. She could hear him helpless with laughter and thumping something in the background. 'So when Lapping eventually gets home he's greeted by some lovely wearing the top of his Marks and Spencer pyjamas smoking a spliff, at which point the Frogs arrange for the place to be raided by the Bosnian vice squad.' He stopped again. Herrick glanced at Harland, who was smiling. 'You got to hand it to him,' continued Dolph, 'I mean there's never been anyone like Lapping in our business. He's classic.'

'Where's he now?'

'Still in Sarajevo. They're making new arrangements but there's no rush coz the suspect's gone to ground.' He paused. 'You know, Lapping could be really good on this. Seriously. He's a prize researcher, loves nothing better than sifting through dusty files in Serbo-Croat. That's like a threesome to Lapping. I can easily put him on to it through RAPTOR. Nobody will know.'

'Good.'

'And don't forget your friend in Beirut,' he said.

'I won't.'

The Chief did not phone until 6.30 a.m. local time. The plane carrying Khan had touched down at Cairo and been greeted by members of the local CIA station and the Egyptian intelligence service. As far as the local MI6 people could make out, he had been taken straight to police headquarters. There was some suggestion that he would make an appearance in court that day in connection with the slaying of the newspaper editor, but the Chief thought this unlikely because any lawyer appointed to Khan's defence would be able to demonstrate that he was not Jasur Faisal, and would move to have him released.

'Who else was on the plane?' asked Herrick.

'Two of the men from the Tirana station and the Syrian gentleman. He turns out to be Dr Ibrahim al Shuqairi, an extremely nasty piece of work. He has a Syrian passport but is from one of the Sunni tribes in Iraq. In any sane world he would be tried as a war criminal.'

'So, there's nothing we can do.'

The Chief mumbled, 'We'll see about that. Now, tell me, what did you make of Loz's answers?'

Harland and Herrick looked at each other. 'I'd say it's worth looking into the business of the Bosnian commander known as The Poet,' offered Harland. 'It appears he was in New York in late 1999. But you know it may be all nonsense. There's nothing hard.'

The Chief digested this.

'We're working on the Bosnian angles,' said Herrick. 'Andy Dolph is going to ring some contacts.'

'Can he be discreet about this? He can't talk about it at RAPTOR.'

'There's no one more reliable,' said Herrick.

'Good. Right. Well, Isis, I think you'd better get back here. Harland, I wonder if you could help us to get Loz out. Nothing complicated. A boat ride to Italy. That's all. I'm putting the arrangements in place now. You'll get further instructions during the morning.'

Herrick noticed the expression in Harland's eyes had darkened a little.

'You do realise I'm not working for you, Chief,' he said.

'Of course, of course. Forgive me, Bobby. You know how grateful we are to you, I'm sure. I'm glad you've reminded me you're helping as an *irregular*. We're indebted to you. Oh, by the way, I have some movement on that trace we discussed in New York. I think it looks very promising.'

Harland said nothing.

'Eva – I think she's alive. Perhaps you would rather discuss it another time. We're likely to get some more.'

'Yes,' said Harland quietly. 'Yes, thank you. You understand I must consult with the Secretary-General about my movements. I have to answer to his brief.'

'Yes, you're quite right,' said the Chief emolliently. 'I just pray that you will be able to see your way to helping us on this one. Do you think there's any chance of Mr Jaidi letting you do your bit?'

'What is my bit?'

'We'll talk when you're in Italy. In the meantime, expect to be joined by several friends at the Embassy. They'll get Loz out. And Bobby, thank you again for all you're doing. I think you know how important this is.'

Isis watched his effortless manner sedate Harland. It occurred to her that he was susceptible only because there was some part of him that privately felt he still belonged in the Secret Intelligence Service, or at least was animated by the challenge and felt he could still rise to it better than most. In that way he was not unlike Munroe Herrick. She wondered about the woman mentioned by the Chief, and Harland's curiously subdued reaction. What the hell was that about?

He must do away with himself. That was his only thought as the plane touched down and sped along the runway to a desolate spot on the airbase where some vehicles waited. Gibbons cut the plastic restraints on his ankles and hooded him again. He avoided Khan's eyes and said nothing. Khan already knew he was to be tortured. During the last twenty minutes of the flight, as the light flooded the cabin, he had strained round to see who was behind him and caught sight of a powerful, fat leg jigging in the aisle. Then he heard the rustling of The Doctor's bag of nuts.

They hauled him from the seat and steered him towards the door, down the short flight of steps. Several men were shouting in Arabic and tugged at his arms, but Gibbons held on and guided him towards one of the vehicles where he was formally handed over. Beneath the hood Khan saw the shadows of the men and the outlines of the vehicles. The smell of the great city nearby came to his nostrils, a mixture of exhaust, wood smoke and shit. Gibbons said 'Welcome to Cairo, Mr Faisal.'

Someone spoke to him harshly in Arabic. When he didn't respond, he was hit in the small of the back with a rifle butt, and sank to his knees. He was picked up and the same phrase was repeated over and over. Gibbons shouted, 'Look, you fucking goons. His mouth is taped!' Someone took off the hood and ripped the tape back. He saw faces staring at him, men eager to hurt him. They spoke again, using the name Jasur Faisal, and although he understood better this time, Khan realised that it would be stupid to respond. Arabic was not his language; Faisal was not his name.

CHAPTER SEVENTEEN

Speaking in a damp, official monotone, Vigo attempted to wind up the meeting with Herrick in the Bunker. He shifted in his chair and pushed her report on Karim Khan away from him as though confronted with a poor examination paper. 'And you're satisfied that Khan was the person executed on the hill?' His eyelids seemed heavy; his hands lay limp on the table.

She nodded. 'Yes. I observed him being loaded into the car by his Albanian guards at the SHISK headquarters. I noted his clothes and saw the same man taken from the same vehicle to the fire's edge. There's nothing more to say. They disposed of him.'

'Were any of our people there?' asked Nathan.

'No, just Albanians,' she replied. 'A man named Marenglen was in charge of the operation.' She stopped and looked at Vigo. How would Marenglen's tutor respond to that?

'We know of him,' said Vigo neutrally. 'And what was your impression of Khan? Did you believe he had any potential, or was he no more than what he claimed to be – a refugee, a disillusioned fighter?'

'As a veteran of the jihad in Bosnia and a field commander with years of experience in Afghanistan, he could have told us much that was useful, yes. But the constant threat of violence and the actual abuse during his interrogation were counter-productive. Aside from this, there was disagreement between the Albanian interrogators and the agency personnel, who seemed concerned only with proving that Khan was in fact the Hamas operative Jasur Faisal. It's clear to me that Khan's story about taking the identities from Faisal's body following the attack in Macedonia is true, but the presence of these papers was

179

used to harass and intimidate him. Khan was guilty of no crime, whereas Faisal was wanted by several countries. And they wanted to pin Faisal's crimes on Khan.'

'Quite so,' said Vigo. 'Well, there's evidently nothing more we can do on this.'

She nodded.

'Now, as to your role here…'

'I have a few questions about this,' said Lyne. 'It doesn't make sense. I looked at the transcripts and it's obvious that the questioning was unfocused, but what explains the change in direction when Isis went to the jail? You were having difficulty getting access, right? Then the moment you get in the room they start talking about Faisal. Why would they do that? And then why would they suddenly kill him? Whether they believed he was Faisal or Khan doesn't make any difference. He was still useful by any standards.' Herrick studied him. This was no play act. Lyne was genuinely puzzled, which meant he didn't know about Khan being flown to Egypt.

'In some respects it *is* regrettable,' conceded Vigo. 'But as you know, the American government has taken a firm line on terrorist suspects. They are to be eliminated…'

'Sure, if they're escaping through the desert like the al-Qaeda suspect in Yemen, but not if they are already in custody. I'm telling you, this doesn't make any sense, especially as our guys were involved in debriefing the suspect. They wouldn't let it happen like that.'

'I can only say what I saw,' said Herrick. 'I was certain it was him in that valley and my conversation with Marenglen confirmed it.' Vigo's eyes glittered with concentration. The Chief had taken pains to rehearse her and warned that if she appeared too credulous or too sceptical he would suspect she knew Khan was alive.

'But you, Isis,' said Lyne accusingly, 'the reigning queen of doubt, you know this doesn't add up.'

'Look, we weren't in charge of the operation. Your people were. There's a hell of a lot going on in Tirana that I couldn't find out because Lance Gibbons wouldn't tell me. You're in a much better position to discover why this happened. Call your friends at Langley.'

'I will do,' said Lyne.

Vigo's eyes moved from Lyne back to her with a slow, reptilian blink. 'In the meantime we must discuss whether you're willing to rejoin Nathan's team without indulging your wilder impulses. We just can't have that sort of behaviour, Isis. We must work together as a unit on this.'

'It's up to you,' she said. 'I apologised for the last incident and now I genuinely want to help with the ten remaining suspects.'

'Nine,' said Lyne. 'The Turkish guy in London is in a coma. Complications from surgery. He's not expected to recover.'

'Right,' said Vigo, evidently having made up his mind. 'You can start at the next shift in an hour's time. You better bring her up to date, Nathan.' He moved from the room with a slight limp on his left side.

Isis raised her eyebrows to Lyne.

'Gout,' said Lyne.

She smiled. 'Good.'

Lyne seemed to be weighing something in his mind. 'It's great to have you back, Isis. But I got to say I don't believe a word about Tirana, even though it's you telling me. What about the torture? Were our guys involved?'

'Not directly.'

'That's something, I suppose. I remember Lance Gibbons when I was in the DO. He was old school, crazy but brave as hell – and effective. He was captured in Kurdistan after the Iraqis penetrated one of the Kurdish groups up there in the mid-nineties. When he was being driven back to Baghdad he took out his guards with a concealed Beretta hidden on his ankle and then hiked back to Kurdistan and over the Turkish border through a fucking mine field. We need more people like him. I can't see him sitting in some fly-blown jail turning thumbscrews.'

'Can I ask you a question, Nathan?'

'Shoot.'

'What do *you* feel about the torture of terrorist suspects?'

'Depends on the circumstances. Clearly, if you know a man is in possession of vital information that may save thousands of lives, like the location of a dirty bomb or a suitcase full of smallpox, well, then I can see the argument that the harm done to one man, repellent though it is, may be excusable in the face of protecting thousands of innocent people. Eventually you have to do the math.'

'Even so, there's a moral problem, isn't there?' She was aware of herself sounding priggish.

'Yes, if you're dealing in absolute terms, I guess there is. But the war on terrorism is not about moral absolutes. This isn't a clash of moral systems of equivalent worth. The attacks on ordinary people aren't justifiable in either Islam or the Judaeo-Christian systems. What we are dealing with is a profound, undermining evil that threatens everyone, and I suppose it's understandable, if not forgivable, if the West tortures one or two men to save large numbers of people, some of whom may be Muslims.'

'But a line is being crossed. Once we condone it, we lose the thing we're fighting for.'

'I'm not persuaded of that. You could easily argue that killing someone is worse than torturing them. When those guys were targeted by a missile in the Yemeni desert, that was clearly extra-judicial killing and wrong by any moral standard. Yet almost no one objected because people saw it as the justifiable elimination of a threat. Why is torture any worse than that?'

Herrick thought for a moment. 'Because the slow and deliberate infliction of pain on any human being is in most instances worse than death. And then there's the question of whether it produces the information that you want, assuming you know the individual is in possession of that information in the first place.'

Lyne leaned back. 'Mostly I agree with you, Isis. A few years ago I wouldn't have condoned it in any circumstances. But say one of these guys we're watching is about to let loose a virus on the continent, a virus that might kill millions. No one could stand in the way of extracting the information by all available means. That's the nature of the inglorious, shitty war we're fighting. It's rough, but these guys chose it and now you and I are in the front line of the response. That's our job right now.' He put a pen to his lips and examined her, rocking silently in his seat. 'How badly was Khan tortured?'

'Not while I was there.'

'What would you say if I told you I believed he was still alive?' Lyne asked.

'The official version, the version that your people have decided will be the record, is in my report. By your people I mean the high command of RAPTOR – Vigo, Jim Collins, Spelling, the head of bloody MI5, God bless her. Who am I to doubt their wisdom?'

Lyne threw himself forward. 'You're shitting me. What do you know?'

'Nothing. I simply asked you about torture because all this took place with the CIA involved. I wanted to know what you thought about the issue.'

'No, you were sounding me out for another reason.'

'I thought you were sounding me out!'

'Either way, tell me what's up.'

'Honestly, Nathan, I think it would serve both our interests if you were to accept everything in my report and then forget about it.' She looked down.

'I hear you.' He raised his fingers in a boy scout salute. 'Don't tell. Don't ask.'

She smiled again. 'So what's been happening here?'

'It will be easier if we go out onto the floor,' he said, brightening. 'Andy Dolph is looking forward to seeing you. I think he carries quite a flame for you.'

They went together to Lyne's desk. On the way Herrick noticed new spaces had been opened in the short time she had been away, and there was a lot of new equipment manned by people she didn't recognise.

'Forget those guys,' said Lyne, gesturing in their direction. 'They can only talk number theory and they're losing their backsides in Dolph's poker school. One of them has been running a program based on the cards he draws, trying to figure out if he's cheating.'

'He is,' said Herrick.

Lyne also told her that 'Collection' had bugged all the apartments where the suspects were hiding. The live feeds from these could be seen on every computer hooked up to the RAPTOR circuit. The behaviour of the nine men – their toilet routines, exercise regimes, diet, reading patterns, religious observance and evidence of sexual frustration – was subject to minute scrutiny by behavioural psychologists.

'Did they find anything interesting?'

'Uh-uh.'

They arrived at Southern Group Three to find Dolph leaning back in his chair wearing a pair of lightly tinted sunglasses and a black trilby with a small rim.

'Hey, Isis, what's cooking?' he said, getting up and giving her a brief hug.

'Andy's won the Blues Brother award for investigative excellence,' explained Lyne, 'which means he gets to wear John Belushi's hat until someone betters his achievement. The shades and ghetto-talk are optional.'

'How'd you win it, Dolph?' she asked.

'The Haj,' said Dolph, sitting down again. 'My man here will explain.'

Lyne grimaced. 'Andy did some research which tied all the suspects together. They basically all went on the Haj pilgrimage. Every single one of them arrived in Mecca on the fourth of February. They each went as one person and came away with a new identity.'

'A variation of the Heathrow switch,' she said.

'I told you she'd take credit for it,' said Dolph, raising his sunglasses to the rim of the hat.

'Okay then, tell me how it worked,' she asked, bowing in mock respect.

'How much do you know about the Haj?'

'A bit.'

Dolph put his feet on the desk. 'The Haj takes place every year for five or six days. Nearly one and a half million people from all over the world are issued with special visas by the Saudi Ministry for Religion. The pilgrim goes stripped of his worldly possessions, with nothing but a two-piece white cotton wrapping and a money-bag tied round his waist. The whole point is that you go as one person and return as another. "Re-chisel then your ancient frame and build up a new being," says a Pakistani poet. That sentence rang a bell with me and I realised the Haj was the perfect occasion for these guys to swap identities.' He stopped.

'That's the traditional break for applause,' said Lyne drily.

'I just knew that's what they had done. And after just forty-eight hours we found three had travelled to Mecca on the same day in the first week of February. The whole thing is so damned easy because the

Saudi authorities insist that each pilgrim hands in his passport when he enters the country. They only give it back when he leaves. How much organisation would it take to do that switch? Answer, nil. By the way, all of them travelled in that period and acquired the identities they're currently using. They re-chiselled, Isis. And there are more. We think a total of seventeen men moved through Saudi Arabia during that week and came away as other people.'

She thought for a moment. 'But would they do this – sully the holiest pilgrimage of the year with a terrorist plot?'

'Of course they would. Anyway, I think it happened as they were leaving, after the visit to the holy sights was done and dusted.'

'You deserve the hat,' she said. 'But what would be the point of the second ID switch at Heathrow? If they'd already established a very efficient way of doing it on Arab soil why the hell would they risk everything by repeating the operation at Heathrow?'

'Aye, there's the rub,' said Dolph.

'So what's happening about this?'

Dolph looked pained. 'They put it on the back burner. They were interested, but the focus is on these nine men. We're going to hunt down the others at some later point.'

'Still, it was very smart of you.'

'That's what I keep saying,' Dolph exclaimed.

'I can vouch for that,' said Lyne.

Five minutes later, Herrick asked, 'You remember when the Stuttgart suspect killed himself and Walter Vigo ordered an intensive surveillance of calls from the Stuttgart helpers? He thought they would make contact with the leadership. Was a call traced?'

Before she had finished Dolph's eyes were revolving.

'Yep,' said Lyne absently, 'there was a trace to a satellite phone in the Middle East, but that's all I know. It's Umbra.'

'Umbra is NSA-speak for very restricted knowledge,' said Dolph.

'Right, so shut the fuck up,' said Lyne without smiling.

'Why's that so sensitive?' she asked. 'Anyway, where in the Middle East?'

'Search me,' said Dolph.

Lyne got up and made for the water machine shaking his head.

*

Herrick spent the next few hours doing what the Chief had instructed, roaming the system and reading anything that caught her eye. 'Go into the garden and pick what flowers you like,' he had said. 'Then come back to me.' She concentrated on the connections between the Lebanese-based terrorist group Hizbollah and the suspects who had visited the tri-border region in South America. It was a random thread, but she followed it because of Sammi Loz's background and her particular interest in Beirut.

When Lyne asked what she was doing, she told him she was familiarising herself with the new material and then added, 'You know, the suspects still seem like they're all half-asleep. Why haven't they been arrested?'

'Maybe they will be,' said Lyne wearily.

'When?' she demanded. 'When are they going to take these people into custody?'

Lyne revolved his chair and used his feet to wheel it round to her. 'You've been back precisely ten hours, Isis, and you already want access to the policy decisions. You understand the deal here. We gather the intelligence, okay? And the guys living up in the beautiful English summer get to make the policy, right? I don't see why you need to raise this again. If you want to decide policy, go see your Prime Minister. He and the President will decide when to take the suspects off the street. Not you, Isis. Not me.'

'But what kind of advice are they getting?'

'Twice daily assessments. The President and the Prime Minister value the information we're getting here. That's what we're told, and I believe it.'

'Nathan, I accept it's good material – really impressive in a way – but doesn't it strike you as odd that there's no movement, no sign of what they're planning, no hint of a target or of a battle formation? They're inert. '

'But this is exactly what they do. The key men always lie doggo before an attack, right up until the moment they're needed. In the files you've just read there are cross-references to the capture of a Spanish cell and their plans to drive a truck full of explosives and cyanide into the US Embassy in Paris. None of the principals cased the joint, none went anywhere near the target. That's the way they operate.'

'So if we already know their MO, why the hell are we studying it further?'

'You know, you're a very smart, very beautiful woman Isis. But you can't run the whole goddam programme.'

'You're beginning to sound like an old-fashioned male suprema-cist, Nathan.'

'That's not true. But you *are* becoming a royal pain in the ass.'

'Aha, the same phrase used to me by a member of the CIA in Tirana after a briefing from your Jim Collins. Were you in on that conversa-tion, Nathan?'

'No, but I did overhear a little of what they said. Collins and Vigo were talking on the phone to Milos Franc. I heard that – yes.'

'Right. During that conversation, information about me – my address and my father's address – was released so that the Albanian Intelligence Service could threaten me.'

'I wasn't party to that,' said Lyne, looking her straight in the eye.

So Vigo was responsible, she thought. That was hardly surprising, but she was puzzled by his motive. 'Why do you think he would do that? It's not as though Karim Khan was remotely important to RAPTOR. Why would he go to the trouble of threatening me?'

'Has it occurred to you that he might just have wanted to scare you a little? Clearly you were causing trouble in Tirana. Maybe it's Vigo's way of warning you to toe the line.'

'By releasing my father's address, which is still classified informa-tion? That's a serious breach of security. Vigo is breaking the Official Secrets Act.'

'Look, Isis, my patience is kind of running out here. I saved your ass when you were in trouble with Vigo and Spelling over the break-in. Will you just give me a break and shut the fuck up? Okay, so you were threatened a little. So what? You're back here and now you're expected to work for a living.'

'You know I'm right, Nathan.'

'Right about what?'

'About RAPTOR. It's not working.'

'I'm not going to discuss it any longer. We both have work to do.' He pushed himself back to his screen.

Dolph had been watching the exchange. He got up and came over.

'Permission to give Herrick a jolly good spanking, sah.'

Lyne didn't smile.

'Failing that, perhaps we could go for a smoke up top?'

'Fine, I'll see you back here in half an hour.'

Herrick checked her watch. It was 4.20 a.m. Beirut was two hours ahead and she could just about get away with calling Sally Cawdor. She picked up her bag and followed Dolph to the elevator bank.

A minute or two later they walked out of the modest brick building which capped the Bunker and strolled a little way to the airfield, surrounded by the scent of mown grass mingled with dew. Dolph took out a pack of Marlboro and offered her one. She looked up with the first drag. 'No stars,' she said.

'Did you make the call to Beirut?' he said, flicking the match away.

'No, I will in a few minutes.'

'What are you up to, Isis?'

'Following my nose.'

'And what a nose. Tell me.'

'Not for the moment.'

'It's got something to do with you breaking into the bookshop?'

She shook her head.

'Why don't you just tell Dolph about it?'

'Because I can't,' she said.

'You think I'll tell Vigo?'

'You did work for him once.'

'That doesn't mean I'd grass you up, Isis.' He looked at her. 'You know, there's a really fascinating intelligence problem here. These guys are a mystery. They are not following any of the usual patterns. They're not making the connections with al-Qaeda, the Armed Islamic Group or any of the other groups – Salafist group for Call and Combat, for example. They're like a parallel group. There is no communication between the individual members. They're—'

'What about the money transfers from the Gulf, the network of helpers, the training in Afghanistan and the tri-border region? It looks pretty standard to me.'

'Yeah, but it's not. There's something else, isn't there?'

'That's what I've been saying. You're trying to draw me out by repeating my arguments to me. It's the oldest trick in the book, Dolph.'

A look of theatrical hurt passed across his face. 'Captious, that's the word for you. Even when someone agrees with you, you find a reason to doubt them.'

'I'm sorry,' she said distractedly. 'What about the foreign intelligence services? They must have got wind of RAPTOR by now.'

'Yeah, they have. In Hungary the local plods are showing interest in suspect Eight, the Yemeni, and the French are definitely on to the Saudi in Bosnia, though we don't believe they've sussed the operations in Toulouse and Paris. It's a matter of time though. In Germany the BND are showing interest in the late Mohammed bin Khidir, in particular his fake passport.'

'Time,' said Isis, screwing the butt of the cigarette into the ground with her toe. 'The whole thing is based on the assumption that we have time. Somewhere there's a clock ticking. We seem to have forgotten that.'

'Nathan hasn't. He wants to know when, where and how. He's just working within the system. He's a genuinely good guy.'

She nodded. 'Yeah, I know. Hang around, will you? I want to ask you about Lapping but I do need to make this call first.'

She walked off into the dark and dialled the Beirut number. A bleary male voice answered after half a dozen rings and she asked to speak to Sally Cawdor. Sally came on, also a little sleepy.

'It's me – Isis. I'm sorry to call so early but—'

'You picked your moment,' said Sally. 'We were up half the night trying to get me pregnant.' She paused and giggled. 'That's on a need to know basis.' In the background there was the sound of male complaint.

Isis smiled. Sally had been in the Service for four years before marrying a Lebanese businessman. Herrick had known her at Oxford but they were recruited independently. Sally was already in SIS when Isis joined.

'You know that problem I had…?' started Isis.

'Yes.'

'Did you manage to do anything about it?'

'I emailed you and sent a message through Dolph to call me.'

'Sorry, I was out of the country.'

'I gained access – for which you owe me lunch – and managed to get a sample which I've sent to your home address.'

'You didn't! That's terrific. Thank you. Thank you. Thank you.'

'I know it's there because it was delivered by one of Rafi's couriers.'

'How the hell did you pull that off?'

'Rafi disapproves so I'll explain when I see you. I pray I got enough of what you want.'

Herrick thanked her profusely and said she'd let her know how things turned out.

'What was that about?' asked Dolph.

'Did Lapping find out anything in Sarajevo yesterday?' she asked.

'Not much, but I know he will.' Dolph had taken off the hat and was brushing his hair back.

He caught her look of appraisal. 'What're you thinking?'

'I was blank – sorry.'

'Well,' he said, replacing the hat so it was tipped forward over his brow. 'I did find something for you. There was a woman I knew, Hélène Guignal, a terrific looker. She spent most of the period from 1993 to 1995 in Sarajevo filing for Agence France Presse. For part of that period she had an affair with a man who was one of the defenders of Sarajevo. He was important, a kind of liaison between the Bosniaks and the foreign Muslims.'

'Has she got a photograph of him?'

'I didn't ask because she had no time to talk. I have tried to reach her but she's proving remarkably elusive.'

'Where does she live?'

'Brussels.'

She thanked him and gave him a peck on the cheek. Dawn was breaking and a thin layer of mist had settled over parts of the airfield.

'We need to get Joe Lapping onto this.'

'Yeah well, it's difficult because we've all got our hands full. I mean Lyne and the other guys never let up. We don't seem to be able to flit about the place like you, Isis.'

CHAPTER EIGHTEEN

Three hours later a cab dropped her at the end of the one-way system on Gabriel Road, which was now decked out in the full municipal splendour of almond and cherry blossom. With her bag over her shoulder, she walked the remaining hundred yards to her house, telling herself that once she'd showered and had breakfast at the café round the corner she wouldn't feel so tired.

She reached her front door and lowered the bag to the ground to search for her house keys. As her hands moved from pocket to pocket, her eyes ran over the house and came to rest on an upstairs window where the curtains were drawn. She was sure they hadn't been left that way because when she was leaving for Tirana she had stood at the window watching for the cab. She put the key in one of the two locks and found it had already been turned; only the Yale lock was keeping the door shut. She placed her ear to the letter-box. The cool air from inside the house brushed her cheek like a breath. There was something wrong – a smell of someone, a sense of occupation.

She turned the Yale lock and slipped inside. There was a sound coming from upstairs: someone was moving about at leisure, unaware that she was in the house. She stepped back into the garden and dialled the emergency services on her mobile. The woman instructed her not to confront the intruder but to wait at a distance from the house, which was what she planned to do once she had retrieved a baseball bat she kept in her umbrella stand. She darted inside again, but as she seized the bat a dark shape appeared at the top of the stairs. She dived from the house, conscious only of the need for room to swing the bat. In almost no time at all, the man had rushed the stairs and taken hold of her, and was trying to drag her inside. She screamed and slipped from his grasp, then let the bat slide through her hands until she felt the knob at the top of the handle. She drew it back over her shoulder and brought it down against the side of the man's head, causing him to yell out. A second, much cleaner shot concentrated all her energy into the fat end of the bat and felled him, unconscious, into the path of another man who had come down the stairs. The obstruction gave her a fraction of a second to run through the gateway and dive behind the hedge, but in that moment she registered that the man had pulled a gun from his waistband. A bullet whistled through the hedge and tore into a car parked in the road, setting off its alarm. She spun round and ran a few yards down the street to shelter behind a van, hearing the screech of a police patrol car in the road. Two officers tumbled out just before bullets exploded in the bodywork and windscreen of their vehicle. A stocky man in trainers and an oversized leather blouson stepped into the road. The policemen had dropped behind the patrol car, but instead of running off, the gunman kept moving forward, taking aim and firing with cool deliberation. Herrick popped up and saw his close-cropped head through the front windscreen of the van and decided that unless she did something, he would kill the officers.

Crouching low, she hurtled along the gutter and rounded the front of the van. The man was obscured from her, but from the sound of two further deafening shots she judged he was only a matter of feet away. She moved a few paces, saw his back then lunged at him, leading with her left foot and bringing all her weight down with the blow. She connected squarely with the back of his neck and knocked him forwards. But the gun was still in his hand. She jumped to the right, knowing that she had just one chance, and struck him with all her might across the shoulder, aware of the tennis-serve grunt that escaped her lungs. The man was still on his feet, but the gun had flown from his hands and landed under the van. For a split second they looked at each other, then he scrambled away, his feet slipping momentarily on the snowfall of almond blossom, to flee down the centre of the road with his arms working double time like a character from a silent movie. Herrick crouched to retrieve the gun and without straightening, swung round and fired at the retreating figure. She missed, aimed again but didn't pull the trigger because one of the policemen yelled at her. 'Hey, Stop that. Put the gun down!' She stood up and handed it to him, and both officers set off after the man, but by now he was fifty yards away and opening a car door. In one movement he slid behind the wheel and started the car engine. Seconds later his car had vanished.

With a burst radiator and a flat, the police car was hardly in a state to pursue him. The officers radioed details of the fugitive and returned to examine the injured man, who had come round but was still lying on the ground in a daze. His head was bleeding copiously and Herrick went to fetch a cloth from her kitchen to stem the flow. She told the policemen that the incident should be regarded as a security matter and that she would need to make a call. They stood looking a little bemused as she phoned one of the Chief's assistants at Vauxhall Cross and asked him to get in touch with the local station.

The injured man struggled to a sitting position and began to curse and wail in a foreign language.

One of the officers knelt down beside him. 'What the hell's he speaking?'

'I think you'll find it's Albanian,' replied Herrick. She looked down at the stocky little man with russet-coloured skin and slightly protruding ears. He could be the Albanian interrogator's brother.

'With the way you must have hit him, miss, he's lucky to be alive.' He pressed the cloth to the gash on the side of the man's head. 'But by heck, I'm glad you dropped the other fellow. He meant business.'

The other officer looked at the gun and read the inscription on the side of the barrel. 'Desert Eagle fifty AE pistol – Israel Military Industries Limited.' He paused. 'You only have to see what it's done to the car to know you don't want to be in the way of that thing.'

People began to gather in the street and soon afterwards an ambulance and three other squad cars arrived. The man was taken away for treatment under guard while Herrick went inside with one of the two constables to find the house turned upside down. The policeman observed that burglars normally made a pile of the things they intended to steal, but in this case the obvious items of value – the TV set, jewellery, CD player, and odd bits of antique silver – had been left untouched.

'What would two Albanian villains be wanting to search your house for?'

'Your guess is as good as mine,' she said.

She made a statement, which he took down at laborious speed in his notebook, contriving to extend two or three minutes' action into a forty-minute feature. Herrick tidied and filled the drawers and cupboards while he spoke.

'What do you do for a living, Miss Herrick?' asked the constable finally.

'I'm civil service,' she replied. 'And I have a very important meeting in an hour.'

'We could give you a lift into town and I can fill the gaps in your statement while my colleague drives.'

'Fine, but I have to shower and eat and clear up a bit.' She thought for second. 'It would make my life a lot easier if you would get me two bacon and egg sandwiches and a cup of coffee from the café on Rosetti Road, just round the corner.'

'Two!'

'Yes, two, unless you both want something, in which case I'll treat you.' She proffered a twenty-pound note. 'Really, it would be a big help.'

He examined her. 'Are you sure you're all right? Not suffering from shock or anything?'

'As a matter of fact, I'm feeling pretty damned good. It's not every day you get the chance to knock out a man with baseball bat.'

He took the money and went to the door, just as the bell rang. Herrick looked round from the kitchen to see him open it to a man in a chauffeur's uniform.

'Yes?' she called out.

'Miss Herrick? A package from the Nabil Commercial Bank. You are expecting me. I have it for you, here.'

It was only when she took the fat brown envelope from him and recognised the handwriting on the address label that she realised this was the package Sally Cawdor had promised her.

It occurred to her that the contents of the package were the only thing that anyone could want from her. But why were two Albanian thugs looking for it? Some twenty minutes later as she sat at her kitchen table, working her way through the crusty bread bacon sand-wiches, she began to put a theory together.

'Cunning is the dark sanctuary of incapacity,' said the Chief quietly. 'Are you familiar with that aphorism, Isis? It comes from the Earl of Chesterfield, who knew that cunning is a substitute for talent and originality. In this particular situation someone is being very cunning indeed, so perhaps it is simply a matter of looking around us and set-tling on the least talented.' She knew he was referring to Richard Spelling and Walter Vigo.

'Despite everything, I wonder if the business at my house is really a side issue, Sir Robin,' said Herrick, wanting to get off the subject of what the men were looking for and why they might have been sent by Vigo.

'If you really think that is the case,' he said, 'I am happy to leave it, at least for the moment.' He turned to the window with his glasses lodged in the corner of his mouth. 'Do you know how many people are under surveillance by the Security Services, Special Branch and us, Isis?' he asked suddenly.

'No.'

'About five hundred and fifty require close attention. And that's in this country alone. Outside, the number reaches into the thousands.' He paused and turned from the view. 'Yet the preponderance of our effort is deployed watching nine people.'

'I feel rather responsible for that. I'm—'

'You did your job. It is the reaction to the discoveries you made at Heathrow that is flawed, and I am more than responsible for that.'

'But the Prime Minister only has to say the word and we bring all the foreign intelligence services into the operation and immediately diminish the commitment as well as the exposure.'

He nodded slowly. He couldn't say it, but she understood that Spelling and Vigo had monopolised the advice going to the Prime Minister. 'Who knew that you would not be sleeping at the Bunker after your shift? You had your bag with you, so it was a fair assumption that you would be staying there.'

'Only Andy Dolph, I think.'

'So anyone else might imagine your house was free to be searched at leisure today?'

'I suppose so.'

'And you say they were definitely Albanians?'

'The second man wasn't apprehended, but the one in hospital is certainly Albanian.'

'Interesting,' said the Chief. 'But as you say, this is beside the point. I think we should move on to Karim Khan.'

He pressed a button on his desk and got up. 'I have made a lot of calls on your energy and I'm going to ask that you give a little more over the coming week. I hope that will be in order.'

He showed her to the door at the side of his office and they made their way to a room sealed off from the outside world, reputedly armoured and protected from every known surveillance device. They sat down at the table and the Chief looked expectantly at the door. After a few seconds it opened and Colin Guthrie, the head of the joint MI5–MI6 anti-terrorist controllerate and his main aide, Gregor Laughland, came in. They were followed by Charles Harrison, head of Security and Public Affairs, his deputy Christine Selvey, Philip Sarre and three men she had not seen before. The group had a marked conspiratorial air about it and Herrick was intrigued that both Guthrie and Selvey were in attendance, since they had originally been supporters of RAPTOR. Perhaps they'd thrown their lot in with the Chief knowing they'd be thrown out under the new regime. More likely the Chief had encouraged them to attach themselves to RAPTOR to find out what was going on and report back to him.

The Chief began speaking in a quiet, uncertain tone that gave the impression he did not know quite what he was going to say. 'Time is short and I believe we have only a matter of days to act.' He gestured to the three strangers. 'These gentlemen are from a security firm that specialises in hostage negotiation. In a moment I will ask the firm's head of operations, whom I will call Colonel B, to speak about the plan he has been putting together for us in the twenty-four hours since we heard that Karim Khan had been flown for interrogation to Cairo. Colonel B's team will remain anonymous to all but myself and Colin Guthrie. It is Colonel B's condition that their involvement in this matter will not be referred to outside this room and so I stress to you all that the need for secrecy has never been more imperative.'

He stopped and looked round his staff, seeking a sign of consent in each person. Herrick understood that it was not simply for the consultant's peace of mind. The Chief was going beyond his powers as specified by the Foreign Office and Parliament. Despite the studied calm and modulation of his voice, this was a desperate last move and might very well also be Herrick's last work for the Service.

'Over the next few days,' he continued, 'we plan to remove Karim Khan from the custody of the local intelligence service and question him in the proper manner. It is my belief that this man possesses crucial information about future terrorist attacks in the West. In particular he can identify two, maybe even three, terrorist leaders who have so far escaped our attention. The first problem is that Mr Khan is being questioned simply as an operative who may, or may not, be involved in a particular attack. Mr Khan's knowledge is, I am certain, of a much more general and historic nature. He knows much, but is not in a position to appreciate what he knows, or how valuable it could be.

'The second problem is that our American friends are convinced Mr Khan knows things that are of immediate worth. They are therefore content to allow the Egyptians to torture him until he talks. Previously the Egyptians have been constrained by the requirement to produce foreign suspects in court, which entails exposure of their methods. But there will be no court case for Mr Khan because he is being held as Jasur Faisal and a sentence has already been passed on him, in his absence. So the Egyptians will have a free hand. Hence our need to move quickly.

'Now, we already have good information about where he is being held. Up until 6.00 a.m. today he was in a holding cell in police headquarters in central Cairo. At some stage he will be removed to a facility attached to a very secure prison on the southern outskirts of the city, at which point we may give up all hope of freeing him. According to our people, there are no signs of that yet. We have pulled out all the stops on this one and the sources of information are proving fast and responsive to our requests, so I am confident that at least in this regard we're not working in the dark.

'Before Colonel B outlines his thoughts, I want to say what happens after we have got Khan. The immediate aim will be to restore him to a condition where he is able to talk about what he knows. This will not be a simple matter. He is likely to be quite badly injured, to say nothing of the psychological trauma of torture. What I have in mind is this: we do not attempt to exfiltrate Khan immediately, but keep him in Egypt at the safe location being prepared at the moment by some unusual associates of ours. It is important that Khan sees some friendly faces – people he knows he can trust.

'His oldest friend, Sammi Loz, will be on hand. Loz is an excellent doctor and I am hoping we can rely on him to treat Khan. Also at this location will be Robert Harland who has been shadowing Loz, and Isis Herrick who saw Khan in custody in Tirana a couple of days ago. It will be Isis's job to question him, and since she has already attempted to intervene to prevent him being hurt, I believe he will be inclined to trust her. There will be backup but we will keep them out of sight. Once Khan has given us what we need, we will bring him to this country and provide safe asylum. Any questions?'

The only question in Herrick's mind was why the Chief believed Khan knew enough to risk mounting the operation, but no one asked a question and she decided to keep quiet. It was clear the members of SIS in the room had decided to pay him the supreme compliment of taking him on trust.

'I should point out that if any of you are caught in Egypt,' continued Teckman after a brief pause, 'Her Majesty's Government will deny all knowledge of you. However, I am satisfied that we stand a very good chance of success, and that even if we do not get Khan out, all of you will be able to disperse and leave the country without difficulty. The one problem is that our friends at the CIA will be in evidence. We should of course make every effort to avoid injuring these people. They may be misguided, but they are still our allies, and in the end I believe they will come to see the error of their ways in this matter.'

He handed over to Colonel B, a compact man in his mid-forties with sandy hair, a freckled tan and pale crow's feet at the corners of his eyes. The colonel stood and opened a laptop which sent a series of maps, diagrams and satellite photographs to a large screen at the end of the table. Over the next hour and a half, he roughed out several plans, each of which required intensive surveillance of the route between the police headquarters and the prison. Meeting places, covers and arrangements for communication between members of SIS and the snatch team were then settled.

After two hours, including a break for coffee and sandwiches, the colonel closed his laptop and looked around the room. 'Generally, I find in these operations that we have to be very light on our feet and willing to adapt to new circumstances. Everything we have sketched out may fall apart. Success *will* come, but only if we are prepared to change our plans at a moment's notice.' He shook the Chief's hand with military firmness and made for the door with his two silent lieutenants.

Before leaving, Teckman drew Herrick aside. 'A lot of this operation relies on your ability to gain the trust of Khan and Sammi Loz, but you will have to watch Loz like a hawk. Harland will be with you, armed. He is on his way to Egypt with Loz now.'

He reached over to a dark blue plastic box the size of a computer case. 'This is the medical equipment which Loz will need to treat Khan after his ordeal. It contains all the usual drugs – antibiotics, vitamins, anti-inflammatory drugs, painkillers, sleeping pills – and some unusual ones, together with bandages and syringes. Our people have tried to allow for the sorts of injuries Khan will have sustained at the hands of The Doctor. Loz will know what to do with them. If not, there are instructions for each. In the unlikely event of your being questioned by Egyptian customs, you will say this is the emergency pack for the elderly patient you and Christine Selvey are accompanying.'

'Which elderly patient?' she asked.

A flicker of a smile escaped the mouth that had been set in grim purpose for the past two hours. 'I'm afraid I haven't been entirely open with you, Isis, but there has been very little time. Your father has agreed to take part in the operation.'

'What! You can't be serious. He's in his eighties.'

'It's only a very minor capacity and I still have the highest regard for his abilities.' He put up a hand to silence her objection. 'Besides, what would be better cover than you and his devoted nurse travelling to see the Pyramids at Giza and Saqqara?'

'But it is such a liability. I can't think of a worse way of going about an operation.'

'Nonsense. The moment Khan is in our hands, your father will travel home with Christine Selvey, with whom, by the way, he gets on splendidly.'

'With Christine Selvey!'

'Security and Public Affairs are not all she knows. She gave up field-work a dozen years ago because there was no one to look after her ailing mother in the evening. She was an excellent operative. Quite superb.'

Herrick shook her head in disbelief. 'It's so bloody unorthodox, sending two related people on the same job.'

'The whole thing is bloody unorthodox, Isis.' He didn't smile. 'Now, all you have to concentrate on is getting Khan to a point where he can tell you what he knows. I believe you are right about Bosnia and I'm sure that line of inquiry will prove fruitful. In the meantime I will tell Spelling that you're doing some work for me.'

She wondered fleetingly whether to tell him about the package from Beirut that she had forwarded to the address in Oxford before getting to the office, then decided that there wouldn't be any point until she had got the results.

CHAPTER NINETEEN

A large wheel was fitted into a wooden beam in the ceiling. Through it ran a dirty brown rope that had been stretched and pulled until it had the appearance of a rusty cable. One end of this hawser led through a pulley fixed on the stone floor, then to a two-handed winding mechanism, allowing the load to be lifted to the ceiling and held there by a ratchet. The other end was attached to a number of chains and manacles designed to be fastened round human limbs.

Though elementary, the capstan provided several options. A man could be hauled up by both arms, or just one; he could be suspended with one arm behind his back and bound to his leg; or he might be winched up by his neck only, so that for what seemed like many minutes he experienced the sensation of being garrotted. Usually, being hung by his arms for several hours was all any normal man needed to persuade him to talk.

The man in charge of the interrogation understood perfectly well that most people would talk when confronted with the prospect of this treatment, but in his trade there was a saying, which translates as 'squeezing the lemon dry'. It summarised the belief that when a man was broken he could always find something more to blurt out – the name of a street or a person, some old gossip about the activities of a neighbour. There is always another drop to coax from the crushed fruit. Even if the persistence of the interrogators produced stories and lies – for it was often the case that the man really had nothing more to tell the security forces – the process was still vindicated. The suspect was *talking*, wasn't he? And talk in all its forms – babbling, whispering, crying, pleading or cursing – is less threatening to the state than silence. Put simply, the information that came from a man experiencing such brutality was the operation's product and, like any diligent workforce, the men who stepped into this hellish place every day had standards of productivity, a yardstick by which they measured their output. The stories and lies were merely the husk of the operation, the off-cuts that would eventually be discarded after the creaking security apparatus had checked out the statement through its thousands of investigators and informers and established which parts were unlikely to be true. But even this might result in some innocent being lifted from the street and given similar treatment.

Karim Khan entered this brutal world at precisely 7.30 a.m. local time and was straight away hoisted by his arms so that his whole body was suspended four feet from the ground. The Doctor was in the cell with him but an Egyptian was in charge and gave the order for Khan's feet to be beaten by two men with long rubber truncheons. Khan cried out that he would tell them anything they wanted. They stopped and the Egyptian shouted questions at him in Arabic. Khan pleaded that he could only speak English. The men returned to beating him and soon the pain in his feet, together with that in his arms and shoulders, took hold of his mind, though he did experience a fleeting astonishment that strangers would take such care to hurt him. After several minutes they let him down to the ground with a bump so that the force of his weight shot through the injuries on his feet.

The Egyptian officer approached him and spoke in English. 'You will talk to us now.' He said it like a reprimand, as though Khan had been impossibly obstructive.

Khan nodded.

'And make full statement of your plans to make terrorist attacks.'

'I will do this.' Khan understood the pretence that he was Jasur Faisal had been dropped.

He was put on a tiny stool which required him to use his feet to balance, and the only way of doing this was to turn them in so that the outside of his soles rested on the floor. The Egyptian lit a cigarette and offered one to The Doctor, who shook his head, and then with fastidious care replaced the packet and lighter in the pocket of his jacket. With the cigarette in his mouth and one eye closed against the smoke, he put out a hand to one of the men who had been beating Khan and snapped his fingers for the truncheon. He slapped it gently into the palm of his left hand, then leaned forward and brought it down on Khan's collar-bone. Khan fell from the stool screaming and had to be lifted up and held straight by the two thugs.

'I was... in Afghanistan,' he stammered. 'I was trained to use explosives. I was trained for political assassination and to eliminate large numbers of civilians. I know the plans. I know what they are going to do.' He threw these lines scattershot, hoping that one of them would interest them.

'We know all this. Where were you trained?'

'Khandahar... for six months in 2000. I learned about political assassination. I know the plans to attack buildings in the West.'

'Which buildings?'

'Christian buildings, embassies and water supplies also.' This was remembered from one or two newspapers that Khan had read in Pakistan and Turkey.

'Which buildings?'

'A big church in England – London.'

'When are these attacks due to take place?'

'Soon – next month.'

'Next month? Then how were you expected to be in place? A man like you with no money walking through the mountains?'

'That was the plan, to enter Europe illegally. Then if I was caught, I would say that I was a man looking for work. That is all. They send you back to where you came from, but they don't put you in jail. They know terrorists have money and travel on planes, so they are watching the airports. But with all these men on the road they don't know who people are. It's much safer. I came with many other men. Many, many men. And I know who they are, where they went, what their plans are.'

The Eygptian turned to The Doctor, who shook his head. 'These are stories,' said the Egyptian.

Khan looked up at him. 'Ask yourself why you're questioning me. Ask yourself if I would lie about these things when I know what you can do to me.'

The officer threw the cigarette away into the gloom of the cell and returned the look. Khan noticed the whites of his eyes were muddied and that his skin, a degree or two darker than his own colour, was very thick and plump, as if blown up slightly from the inside. The Egyptian shook his head and without warning stepped behind and hit him several times. '*You* will answer my questions.'

'I am,' he cried out. 'I am trying.'

Khan now understood the game he had to play. The Egyptian must be seen to win. If he failed to make this happen The Doctor would take over, and this he had to avoid at all costs. So the Egyptian became a kind of ally. Khan had to work with him and make it look as though it was his skill that was persuading him to talk, and that there was no need of The Doctor's expertise. But this meant he would have to endure much more pain while letting the information out slowly.

He was terrified by this conclusion. He was taken up to the ceiling again and began to experience a quite new level of pain. He lost count of the times he passed out during these hours but the investment of pain seemed to be working. The gaps between the beatings grew longer and a man was summoned to write down what he said in English, which was a slow process because he had to stop and ask Khan how to spell certain words. This gave Khan time to collect his thoughts, however, and add convincing detail to the story of his training in an al-Qaeda camp. He found that the things he just made up out of desperation were the most readily accepted by the Egyptian.

Night came and the questions continued under a naked bulb. At some point in these hours, Khan's faith in humanity, more particularly his assumptions about his fellow men, slipped away. He had been changed, although his mind was in no state to hold such an idea or to know what it meant.

Herrick noticed that the prospect of the adventure in Egypt instantly took ten years off her father. His eyes shone with animation and he seemed to be moving less stiffly. Besides the essentials of the plan, he had mastered the hand-radios, the encryption phones and the topography of the district of Cairo where Khan was believed to be held. On the way to Heathrow he explained to Herrick and Christine Selvey that he'd spent two weeks in Cairo before leaving for Palestine in 1946, exploring the medieval quarter and the area around Khan al Khalili souk. He understood that little had changed.

They were booked, not into one of the modern hotels along the

Nile, but the more central Devon Hotel that once acted as a kind of officers' mess for the British Army. Munroe had stayed there when the more exclusive Shepheard's had been full. He was astonished to find the same 1930s switchboard behind the front desk and the ancient lift that carried guests up to the rooms in a steel cage and stopped short of each floor by about a foot. He was even more taken by the scorched canvas which had once been a hunting scene and still hung in the dining room as a reminder of the anti-British riots that coincided with Nasser's coup in 1952. 'Of course they were right to kick us out,' he murmured. 'We had no business being here.'

'And what about now?' asked Herrick.

'That's another matter, as you well know, Isis.' He shook his head with affectionate despair. 'Anyway, we haven't time for this. We've got a rendezvous to make.'

They left Selvey at the hotel and caught a cab to the Sunset café, which was still nearly full even though it was well past midnight. They didn't know which member of the team to expect, just that someone would arrive with details of the next day.

When they had ordered tea and a hookah, Herrick said, 'You have to admit this is bloody weird, Dad.'

'I suppose it is,' he said. 'I was even less keen than you, but I believe the Chief needs our help, and you have to admit I'm an excellent cover.'

'But you're part of the operation, not just cover. That's what worries me. And what about the Chief? Even if we manage to pick up the package, this is bound to get out sooner or later.'

'I'm certain you're right. But he's not furthering his own interests. He's only trying to protect the Service from Vigo and Spelling.' He looked at her with a sudden, intense concern. 'The Chief told me what happened to you. He said it was almost certainly Vigo who'd put those two bloody Albanians on to you. You did well to fight them off. I'm impressed and immensely relieved.'

'That's what I mean. You shouldn't know about this stuff. How can I possibly be expected to work if I know you're being told about every minor danger? Anyway, they weren't after me. They were searching the place and I happened to turn up.'

'What were they looking for?'

'I don't know,' she said. It had now become almost a matter of faith that she told no one about the package from Beirut.

He smiled sceptically. 'But Vigo knew it was there.'

'Yes, that means he was listening to a phone conversation I had a few hours before with a friend. Though God knows why he would bother.'

'Come off it, Isis. You surely understand?'

'No.'

'He's jealous of your talent. You're a natural. The Chief never stops telling me how good you are. The idea that anyone could possess the sort of flair he once showed would certainly grate with him. Besides that, you're critical of his operation. He's bound to be put out.'

She shrugged and moved a little closer. 'What chance do you think we've got here?'

'Fifty-fifty. It relies on quick, accurate information and if we don't get that, we're jiggered.'

'Jiggered! Where did that word come from?' She looked at his eyes moving over the café's customers, discreetly noting who was showing an interest in them. 'Well, I suppose this is better than looking at snail shells through a magnifying glass.'

'Not a patch on it, but the change is certainly refreshing.'

They waited a further half hour gossiping about Hopelaw, and then a young man who had been browsing along a magazine stand twenty yards away came to sit at their table and ordered a pipe and coffee. He was pale and sickly looking with eyes set wide. Herrick noticed he moved awkwardly as though he had damaged his back or pelvis, and she asked him what was the matter.

'Big lorry jump on little car. Everyone dead except Mr Foyzi.'

'I'm glad you survived, Mr Foyzi,' she said.

'Yes, but treatment at hospital very, very expensive. Mr Foyzi needs money to make back straight. You want buy papyrus?' He handed Munroe Herrick a card. 'This address of best papyrus shop in all Cairo.' His arms danced in the air as he described the splendour and size of his brother's factory. 'Okay, you come. We have coffee and make party.'

'This sounds exactly what we want,' said Munroe. He handed the card to Isis. It read, 'Go with Foyzi – Harland.'

'What time should we come?'

'But of course now. There is not long distance to factory.'

They left money on the table and were ushered from the alley by Foyzi, who made a great show of leading his new and valued clients to the factory. They crossed at the intersection of two large streets then plunged into another alley. Either side of them rose elegant turn-of-the-century apartment blocks with balcony windows that jutted over their heads. They passed men labouring over tiny fires in dimly lit workshops and others loitering, picking at grilled corn cobs, smoking makeshift hookahs and offering advice from the street with the exaggerated movements of a mime troupe. No women were about and Herrick, dressed in jeans and a shirt, felt conspicuous, although Foyzi's presence seemed to reassure the men and they gave her barely a second glance. For fifteen minutes they dodged back and forth, moving through the dark maze of alleys until eventually they came to a courtyard where a man with welding equipment squatted by a car door. The sparks flew into the dark, illuminating three trees and washing lines that swayed in the warm breeze.

Foyzi stopped and beckoned them to the side of the courtyard. 'No speaks now,' he whispered, putting both hands to his lips, then turned to watch the entrance of the courtyard. A minute or two later the welder lifted his visor and snapped off the flame. The courtyard became utterly dark and silent. Foyzi guided them to an entrance, knocked on the door and spoke through a grille. Locks were turned heavily and bolts drawn back. Inside there were some candles in red glass pots and a figure wrapped in white cloth and a headdress who immediately slipped away into a recess. Without explanation, Foyzi hurried them along a corridor heavily scented with flowers and the smell of candle wax, then they burst into a brightly lit room with chandeliers and show cases full of bottles.

'Where the hell are we?' asked Herrick.

'A perfume factory, I think,' replied her father.

'Gentleman is correct, but we not stay here,' said Foyzi officiously. 'You buy lotus oil some other time, missus. We see your friends now in next store.'

A communicating door was opened and they were propelled into another cavernous space hung with carpets and huge brass lanterns.

Foyzi took their arms and navigated them through the piles of rugs on the floor. When they reached a better-lit part of the shop, Herrick checked her father's face. He showed no signs of strain whatsoever.

'Isis, I will say this once,' he murmured as they approached a room where they heard voices. 'Do not fuss over me. I am perfectly all right.'

Inside, she saw Harland, Colonel B and, to her surprise, Colin Guthrie, who explained that it had been decided in London at the last moment that he would oversee the operation. Harland greeted them both with an enigmatic grin and said that Loz was already under guard at the place where they would take Khan. Foyzi sat down at one of the chairs and tipped a little liquid from a flask into a cup of coffee.

Guthrie unrolled a map on the table. 'Over the past twenty-four hours we have been observing the route taken from the police headquarters to the jail on the southern margins of the city. Without exception the trucks and cars making this journey have travelled along the streets marked in red. We have no reason to believe they will vary the routine for Khan. At the moment our sources say that the security people are exhausting their methods and are likely to hand over to The Doctor sometime tomorrow. That leaves us with very little time, yet also too much of it. While we have to be ready to go tomorrow we must also remember that it will be a considerable challenge to mount any kind of watch in an area which is at all times crawling with police and security personnel.'

Guthrie laid four A4 photographs on the table and joined them together to create a continuous picture of the street named Bur Said. He pointed to a three-storey stone Italianate building and a much larger and more modern office block, painted white and turquoise. 'The older building holds the courts. This is joined on the right to the police headquarters. At the back is the jail complex where Khan is being held. The truck carrying him will leave an entrance at the rear and take the crowded side-street to Bur Said. Beginning at this junction there is a run of shops, restaurants and cafés where The Doctor – Ibrahim al Shuqairi – has been observed talking to a CIA man whom Bobby Harland has identified in surveillance photographs as Lance Gibbons. He has been seen there four times in the last thirty-six hours and it is believed that he has been unofficially briefing the American on the progress of the interrogation. On the last occasion, earlier this evening, the couple appeared to have a falling out. We think Gibbons has failed to recommend that the responsibility for the interrogation should be given to The Doctor. Information from the police HQ, produced by Mr Foyzi this afternoon, would seem to confirm this. We know also that communications traffic from the US Embassy has featured the interrogation and its results. Unsurprisingly, Khan has admitted to being involved in a plot to blow up a number of churches and other prominent targets, but he has given them no definite date for an attack. Perhaps he senses that this is the one thing he still has to play with.'

Guthrie looked up from the pictures and moved a lamp to shine on them. 'This run of cafés is where you will be stationed, Isis. Your job will be to observe Gibbons and try to overhear what he says. We will have other people in the café, but you will be the person to signal the operation is on. Foyzi will be with you. The important point of course is that Gibbons and The Doctor both know you, which means you have to go well-disguised.'

Herrick nodded agreement that this would not present the slightest problem.

Guthrie turned to Munroe. 'The first part of your day will be spent in the newly restored Islamic Museum directly opposite the courts. This should not be arduous. The museum is air-conditioned and I believe possesses an unequalled collection of manuscripts and ornamental art. You will remain there with Selvey until such time as you receive a message. Then you will make your way out and look for a blue and white Peugeot with the words Zamalek Limousine printed on its side. You will be driven to this point here in the Northern Cemetery, about ten to fifteen minutes away, depending on the traffic. You will see that there are a number of right-angle bends there which require the truck to slow down to about ten miles an hour. It is here that the interception will take place. You will remain in the car until you hear from Philip Sarre and Gregor Laughland who will be positioned close by in the cemetery. One of them will radio you when they have visual contact. At this point, you will both get out and prepare to create the diversion we've already discussed. Once the wagon has stopped you will move as quickly as you can to the Peugeot and make your escape. It is likely to be hot so you will need to reserve all your energy for that walk, Munroe.'

Guthrie sat down. There was silence in the room for several seconds. This was the signal for Colonel B to speak.

'What you all need to know about the end of the operation is minimal,' he said. 'We will be in the area of the cemetery, but you won't see us before the truck arrives. We've spent most of the day recceing the area and in many respects have found it the perfect spot. There is very little traffic and the road there is poorly made. Our main object of course is to release Khan without loss of life, but there will be one or two bangs that will attract attention, so we'll be aiming to move out of the area with Khan very quickly.' He placed a packet of earplugs on the table and shoved them towards Munroe. 'These are for you and your colleague, sir. Once you've got the signal, be sure to ram them right in.'

'And me?' said Herrick. 'How do I hook up with you? Where's Harland going to be?'

'Harland is going to be with us, so we will need the medical kit you brought out from England.'

'Right, I can get that to you. But after the truck has passed what do I do? Follow it?'

'Exactly. We want you to watch for an escort. Generally these trucks travel alone, but given the interest in Khan there may well be a couple of cars following with some armed police. They shouldn't present too much of a problem, but we'll need a description of the vehicles and the number of men inside.'

'There's one thing I don't understand,' said Harland. 'Why does Isis have to hang around the café and then pursue the truck? Wouldn't it be a lot simpler to put Sarre or Laughland there to do the initial watch and have Isis tucked away in the cemetery ready to leave with me and Khan?'

Guthrie shook his head. 'No. For one thing Isis will be far less conspicuous. Two, she can dress in the traditional manner for an Egyptian woman and be to all intents and purposes unapproachable. Three, she has a rather special talent which I was reminded of only the other day by one of our colleagues in the Company.'

Munroe nodded and smiled. Harland looked mystified.

'She can lip-read English, and as long as she gets a good line of sight on Gibbons, we shouldn't have any problem finding out what's going on.'

'That's excellent,' said Foyzi in the perfect intonation of a middle-class Englishman.

Herrick and her father turned round to see him lying on a pile of rugs with his tea precariously balanced on his chest.

'Mr Foyzi is not what he appears to be,' said Guthrie. 'In fact Mr Foyzi is not even Egyptian.'

Foyzi gave him a demure nod.

'So between Isis and Foyzi we should be in business. Now communications. The first call will be made by Isis on her mobile phone. That will go to me in the control van, positioned halfway between the police HQ and the cemetery. Thereafter we should use the radios, earpieces and clip-on mikes which you all have. But chatter should be kept to a minimum. Specific details of the truck and any escort should be phoned to me and I'll pass them on in suitably obscure terms. Right, Foyzi will take you two back to the Devon and Harland can collect the medical bag. We should aim to be in place by 10.00 a.m. and let's hope we get a hint of movement sooner rather than later.' He gathered up the photos and map and stood up.

Later at the hotel Herrick told her father, 'This is just about the daftest plan I've heard. Practically everything can go wrong.'

'Well, there's an awful lot of room for manoeuvre. And that's no bad thing.'

'That doesn't make me feel any better.'

CHAPTER TWENTY

Khan knew neither night nor day. He was fed once with a plate of slop and given water, which the guards snatched away after he had drunk only a little. And he did not sleep. When the Egyptian and The Doctor were out of the cell he was let down to a sitting position on the floor with his arms still held above him by the rope. Except for an intermittent prickling sensation caused by the lack of circulation, he had lost the feeling in his hands. When he nodded off, or simply fainted during moments when the pain became extreme, the guards kicked him or banged the door with a truncheon.

Time had ceased to exist. Thoughts came in snatches of telegraphese. He knew he could not manipulate the situation to save himself from The Doctor because he had already begun to tell him what drugs he would use. He said they would paralyse him for hours, turn him mad, set rats loose in his mind, make his skin burn, cause his eyes to flinch at the light of a candle and give his body such discomfort he would neither be able to rest nor sleep.

Khan thought, I did this… I brought myself here… a journey of my devising… God have pity on me… The Prophet (peace be upon him) please stop these men… Stop these men, please… this is not your way… I beg you, stop these men… I am … I am hurting … I don't know myself… Let me die.

Prayers and self-recrimination circulated in his head for hours, or just seconds, he could not be certain. He had the strange idea that his mind was somehow becoming detached from his body, yet he knew this was not true because he had never been more aware of his physical self. They had locked his mind in a cage with a beast and the beast was his pain. Why? He had no answer to that question. The question no longer existed because there could not be an answer.

Perhaps he should have told the truth instead of all these fabrications about terrorist training and targets. But he *had* told them the truth. That's what he had done when he had first seen The Doctor, and it hadn't worked because the man had begun to hurt him.

It was cooler now and he guessed it was night. One of the two guards had propped himself against the door and hung his head in sleep. Khan's mind rambled and he thought of the now unbearable sweetness of his early life. Was it really his, or had he imagined it?

Then the cell door opened, sending the sleeping guard into the centre of the cell. When he recovered himself he struck Khan twice with his truncheon as though punishing him for a violation that had just taken place. In the light from the corridor, Khan glimpsed the guard's guilty, moronic face turn obsequiously to the Egyptian and The Doctor as they walked in. Then he caught sight of the trolley being wheeled behind them.

It was about the size of a cocktail trolley, although like everything in the prison it had been knocked together from scrap – an artless contraption with wires coiled on the top, a box and a wooden board on which there was a switch and a lever. One of the guards unravelled the flex and ran it to a power point outside the cell. The other uncoiled the wires lying on top. At the end of these were a couple of metal crocodile clamps such as might be used to charge a car battery.

The Doctor picked his teeth while the Egyptian bent down and dipped a rag in a pail of water, then handed it to the guard so it could be wrung out.

Herrick slipped out of the hotel early and went with Foyzi to buy a hijab, the head scarf that covers the hair, ears, shoulders and part of the face. Foyzi, himself wearing a long white jellaba and a red and white cloth on his head, assured her that once she was wearing a hijab, no one would look at her, particularly if they were together. She bought a black one with a severe cut.

Already the air was thick with pollution and the roads were teeming with every form of motor vehicle, hand-cart and wagon. They reached Bur Said by 9.00 a.m. and took a turn round the traffic system, cruising past the court and police buildings, then the museum where Munroe Herrick and Christine Selvey were to be kept on ice amongst the collections of incense burners and weaponry. They parked a little distance from the café near the police headquarters and waited for Gibbons to show. On the previous day one of Foyzi's men had observed him arrive at 10.30 a.m., but an hour and a half passed without sign of him. Guthrie called Herrick twice on the mobile to tell her to get out of the heat and into the café so she'd be sure to have a place by the time either of them arrived. She insisted that she must wait until she knew which table they were at.

The day dragged on, and although the density and noise of the traffic did not subside, there were fewer people walking on the streets. The women who had improvised a vegetable market on the other side of the road suddenly packed up and vanished in swirls of brightly patterned cloth. The men who had been listlessly hoeing and watering a narrow flower border separating the two streams of traffic had sunk to their haunches in the shade of a tree to watch three hooded crows fight over the seepage from their hose.

Just past midday a hot wind blew up, whipping eddies of dust along the road and tearing at the flags outside the court. The crows took to the wing and flapped in the air above the traffic. Herrick and Foyzi slipped down in their seats and took sips from a bottle of mineral water. They moved the car several times to keep in the shade and at two o'clock saw a convoy of three police trucks making its way up the side street. The back of each vehicle was open, and as they swung into Bur Said, Herrick saw past the guards to the tiny steel cubicles which held the prisoners.

'They must roast in those things,' she said.

Foyzi nodded sadly then straightened in his seat. 'Here's the American. Look! Look! In the mirror!'

Herrick glanced in the right wing mirror and saw Gibbons stepping out of a taxi. She pulled down the sunshade to check the hijab and the Jackie O dark glasses and then plugged in her telephone earpiece and the microphone that ran up her right sleeve. He passed quite close to them and made straight for the café. After some indecision, he settled at an outside table in the breeze. They watched him while he ordered, then got out and walked together, rowing in Arabic about Foyzi's driving, and sat down just inside the door where there was both shade and a breeze. Foyzi had his back to Gibbons which meant that she could observe quite easily over his shoulder while talking. They ordered tea. Twenty minutes passed during which Gibbons made two short calls on his cell phone, allowing Herrick to test her skill on him. He was speaking to The Doctor, asking where the fuck he was. A few moments later she saw The Doctor lumbering up the side street in a pale green robe. He was with another Arab, a much smaller man who wore a jacket over his shoulders that flapped in the wind and revealed a pale blue lining. This man had a rather fussy manner and brushed the chair before sitting down with his back to Foyzi and Herrick, then plucked at the crease in his trousers. The Doctor let himself down heavily in profile to them and produced a bag of sunflower seeds which he proceeded to eat.

Once they'd given their orders, Gibbons leaned forward and began to speak. Herrick dialled Guthrie, raised her right hand to her face and murmured into her sleeve, looking away slightly but never letting her eyes move from Gibbons' lips. She gave Guthrie a verbatim account, only sometimes pausing to say which of the men he was addressing. 'What have you got for me?' Gibbons asked the Egyptian. He replied at great length. Gibbons examined him closely. 'Do you have definite dates? What about names? Did you get the names of his contacts?'

The man shook his head and The Doctor interrupted, slicing the air with his hand.

Gibbons ignored him. 'You say this was going to happen in Paris and London simultaneously. What about the States? Did you get anything about the postcards?' He nodded as the Egyptian replied. Again The Doctor interrupted, but Gibbons' eyes remained fixed on the other man. 'So he admits they were coded messages? Right, what about the Empire State? Is he saying the attacks will be coordinated in the States as well as Europe?' As they both attempted to answer, Gibbons began shaking his head. 'You guys gotta realise that's what we're all here for. We need to know. Right now, all I'm hearing is maybe this, maybe that, maybe now, maybe later. We have a ticking bomb here. My people need accurate information.' He stubbed his index finger on the surface of the table then slumped back in his chair and looked away in frustration. The Doctor also turned his gaze elsewhere, leaving the ball in the other man's court.

He made a long speech that seemed not to impress Gibbons, who ordered another drink and then dialled a number on his phone.

'No information… no real details of the plan… right… okay… sure… I'll tell him… that's right… yeah, yeah. Leave it to me.' He lowered the phone and spoke to the Egyptian. 'Okay, so my people think we should pursue the second option. I'm sorry Mr Abdullah, but that's what they say. It's out of my hands. You got to see I'm in a bind here. We're very grateful for what you have already done and the US Embassy will make a formal recognition of your service to us with a letter of thanks. Here is something to be going on with. A kind of personal thanks.' He reached for the top pocket of the man's jacket and stuffed a roll of money into it.

Herrick now gave the first piece of commentary. 'He's paying off the Egyptian security officer. The interrogation is going to be handed over to The Doctor.'

'Tell Foyzi to activate his sources and find out when Khan's going to be transferred,' rasped Guthrie. 'We want to know which bloody vehicle he's in.'

Foyzi didn't need telling and gave Herrick a nod to say he understood.

Gibbons looked at his watch and said something she couldn't read, because he had raised a glass to his lips and held it there for some time without drinking. The Doctor felt in his robes for something and pulled out a set of black worry beads which he handled like a rosary, then repeatedly flipped over his index finger.

Gibbons lowered the glass and said, 'We need something tonight or tomorrow. The work has got to be finished by Monday.'

All this she communicated to Guthrie. Occasionally she heard him speaking on other lines to her father and Colonel B.

She hung up and started to speak to Foyzi in Arabic. Had he checked the car? Didn't he think he ought to be leaving? Foyzi allowed himself to smile at Herrick's portrayal of a nagging wife and made as though to grumble. He paid and left the café saying that he would see her in twenty minutes.

Herrick planned to return to the car the moment The Doctor left. From behind the sunglasses she looked ahead of her without acknowledging their presence or bothering to see what they were saying. Gibbons lit a cigarette and threw occasional interested glances in her direction, but she was certain he wouldn't recognise her and sat with what she hoped was the unapproachable poise of a young middle-class Arab woman.

After a desultory exchange The Doctor got up. Gibbons did not rise or offer a hand. Herrick thought she saw a fleeting look of distaste sweep across his expression. 'We'll speak soon.'

Herrick decided to leave, but just as she stood up, her phone began to vibrate. The momentary distraction meant that she did not pay attention to the wind, as the Arab women on the street do, and a gust took hold of the hijab, revealing her hair, neck and some of her face. She pulled it down swiftly and made for the car. As she opened the door she saw Gibbons rise, sling some money onto the table and start purposefully towards her. In a matter of seconds he had reached the car and shouted through the window. 'I'll be damned if that isn't Isis Herrick.' He bent down to her level. 'Shit! That *is* you, isn't it?'

She looked ahead of her without moving, realising that she couldn't just sit there – one call from Gibbons and the whole operation would be blown. She got out, pushed him away and shouted in Arabic to the passers-by that the American was bothering her.

'Well, what do you know,' he said, leering down at her. 'The cold-assed British spook has followed me all the way to Cairo for a little loving.' He felt in one of the pockets of his photographer's vest and pulled out a phone. She knocked it from his hands and spun round, cursing him in Arabic. The filthy American was making indecent suggestions – wouldn't someone help a virtuous woman?

Gibbons seem to find this funny. 'Oh, you're good,' he said, unhurriedly bending down to retrieve his phone. 'You're very good, Isis. But I just gotta tell my people you've gatecrashed the donkey roast.' He stood up and placed a hand on her shoulder, dialling a number with the thumb of his other hand. Suddenly Foyzi appeared from nowhere and pulled Herrick away from him.

'Who's this? Omar Sharif?'

Foyzi smiled up at him. 'I have gun aimed at your heart, sir. Get into the car.'

'Yeah, and I'm King Farouk,' said Gibbons. 'Step aside, buster. This lady and I have business.'

Foyzi manoeuvred so he could show Gibbons the gun without displaying it to the rest of the street. 'I *will* kill you unless you get in the car, sir.'

'Okay,' said Gibbons, trying to maintain his dignity. 'So you're going to kidnap an American citizen. You can't get away with this, Isis – you and your little towel-head friend.'

'Such company we have to keep,' said Foyzi despairingly. He opened the back door and prodded Gibbons. 'Get in.'

Gibbons obeyed, but with a thunderous look that said he would soon have the upper hand. 'I'll see you on the fucking rack for this.'

She climbed behind the wheel. 'What now?'

'No problem,' said Foyzi, pointing ahead of them. 'No problem at all. Drive!'

She edged the Fiat into the traffic.

'Oh, I get it. You're going to try to spring Khan!' said Gibbons, laughing. 'Jesus, I'm gonna be ringside on fucking amateur night.'

'Last thing I heard, you said he was Faisal, not Khan,' said Isis over her shoulder.

'Right,' said Gibbons sourly.

They passed the police HQ and courts, then turned left to travel in the opposite direction. Foyzi wrested Gibbons' phone from him and crushed it underfoot on the floor of the car. Then he called someone on his own phone and spoke rapidly.

Gibbons talked over him, affecting not to mind the silencer lodged in his armpit. 'You understand what you're doing, Isis? You're interfering with the legitimate investigation of a terrorist suspect by the United States. If an attack should result from your actions you and your friend will be named as accessories. They'll come after you, wherever the fuck you are.'

'I understand just one thing about your activities,' she said calmly. 'You've instigated the torture of a man who hasn't been found guilty of a crime and—'

'That's the trouble with you fucking Europeans,' interrupted Gibbons. 'You want all the benefits of American power but you don't want to get your hands dirty.' He paused. 'Let me tell you, this is the big new game, and it's played with a whole new set of rules. Frankly, you don't cut it. You don't even come near.'

'There's nothing new about your *big new game*,' she said. 'You told me that yourself. You were right. Torture was used by the regimes in South America, all of them endorsed by the US government. Torture is actually a very old, very desperate game and it doesn't work. You don't get results by tearing a person's body apart.'

This gave Gibbons some pause. 'We're against the clock. There's no other way now.'

'There is,' said Isis. 'There always is.'

They were alongside the museum and Foyzi told her to drive two hundred yards further and take the first turning right. She negotiated a hand-cart loaded with crates of vegetables and swerved right into a shaded street where huge pieces of awning and cloth hung vertically from wires overhead. Foyzi was on the phone. They turned right again into a yard where there was a white Nissan van. Four men in jellabas rushed towards them. One opened the door on Gibbons' side and rammed a needle into his arm. Almost immediately the American's eyes closed and his body went slack. He was dragged from the car, carried off to the van and lifted into the back. Two of the men jumped in with him and the van moved off in a cloud of dust. Foyzi got out, ran round to take the wheel from Herrick and reversed out of the yard at a furious speed, span 180 degrees and rushed to rejoin Bur Said.

'Who were they?' shouted Herrick, thinking it was certainly fitting that Gibbons had now himself been drugged and driven off uncon-scious.

'My backup, my people,' he said.

'Who're your people?'

'Another time,' he replied, straining left and right to look for an opening in the traffic. 'The transport is about to leave the police building. We must get into position.'

'What will they do with Gibbons?'

'Take him somewhere and dump him. He'll be fine, but he won't remember who he is or where he is for a day or two.'

They found a way through the jam that brought them near to the café, and stopped alongside a line of minibuses disgorging passengers and admitting others with equal numbers of cumbersome packages. For a few minutes they waited in the sweltering heat. Foyzi's eyes darted between the screen of his mobile and the throng of people around the car. Then the phone beeped twice with a text message.

'It's coming,' he said. 'He's on the next truck.'

He nosed forward through the crowd and within a very short time they saw the truck moving out of the side street. It was accompanied by a car that had edged round the truck and was forging through the traffic with occasional blasts on its siren. Herrick relayed all this information to Guthrie. There were four policemen in the car, and two guards carrying automatics could be seen through the open back of the truck. She caught sight of The Doctor in the passenger seat of the truck. Khan had to be inside. Guthrie told her to use the radio from now on so that everyone could hear.

Foyzi worked the little Fiat into position, about three vehicles behind the truck, which was moving at about 15 mph. There was much competition among the other cars around them to fall into the truck's slipstream, but Foyzi held their place effortlessly.

They reached the Kahn al Khalili souk where the traffic became less responsive to the police siren, and they stopped for minutes at a time. Herrick used the fan fixed to the Fiat's dashboard to cool her face and glanced idly down the warren of passages into the souk. A further ten minutes passed. Then the traffic seemed suddenly to ease and the truck moved away at a speed of 40 mph. Foyzi dodged to keep in touch, but was forced to stop at some traffic lights where they knew the first lookout man was positioned. They heard his terse commentary over the radio and then shot off in pursuit of the truck, which to their relief followed the predicted route, turning left on a road called Salah Salem and then right into the cemetery. Herrick called out, 'Three minutes to landing. Repeat. ETA – three minutes.'

Harland had moved very little in the heat, but when he heard Herrick's voice he got out of the Isuzu and lifted his binoculars to the cemetery road. From his vantage point 150 yards away, he had seen the blue and white Peugeot stop some ten minutes before and Munroe Herrick leave the car with Selvey. Despite Munroe's reputation, Harland was extremely doubtful about allowing a man in his eighties to take part in the operation. However, he observed him now, moving without the slightest sign of age or heat fatigue. He was dressed in a light summer jacket and a broad-brimmed straw hat. Selvey was in a long floral skirt and a hat tied with a scarf under her chin. Together they looked as though they were about to attend the Chelsea Flower Show or a vicarage garden party.

Harland saw Munroe set up an easel in the shade of one of the monuments that bordered the road. Very soon he was sitting on a collapsible fishing stool, sketching the view that Harland had been staring at these past few hours – the parched sandstone necropolis and, beyond it, Cairo and the flood plain of the Nile in a dusty blue haze. It was a pity he'd never finish the picture.

In almost every respect the place was perfect for an ambush. The traffic was very light indeed. Just four cars had passed in the previous five minutes. The walls either side of the road were never less than ten feet high, so no one would be able to see what was going on when the police convoy was intercepted. And there would be very little danger from stray bullets. There were many open doorways into the cemetery either side of the road and the numerous smaller byways which crisscrossed the area. At two different points these held the vehicles that the snatch squad would use in their escape.

For a moment Harland's attention was caught by three or four black kites wheeling in the sky high above the cemetery. His concentration snapped back to earth and he moved the binoculars down the incline to settle on a group of barefoot children playing in the stretch about 200 yards from Munroe. He hoped they wouldn't get wind of the old man. If they were drawn to him for baksheesh it would badly complicate things. He swept the cemetery on the far side of the road, pausing to examine the figures moving between the memorials. One or two people were sleeping in the shade of the more elaborate tombs. He wasn't sure which of these belonged to Colonel B's squad of SAS veterans, but he knew they were there because of the radio checks every ten minutes.

He saw the police vehicles leave the main road and begin the steady climb towards Munroe. The car in front moved a little too quickly for the truck and twice had to slow down to wait.

Harland got back behind the wheel, started the engine and, leaving it in neutral, let the handbrake off so that the Isuzu began to creep down the narrow stony track to the cemetery road. If all went well, he would arrive behind the police truck, ready to receive Khan, Herrick and Foyzi. But the timing had to be just right.

The radio sprang to life. 'Final positions, please. Runway clear.' Then Sarre's voice could be heard counting away the distance – 'Five hundred yards and closing. Four hundred. Three-fifty.' When he reached two hundred, Munroe got up, felt in his pocket and handed something to Selvey. They were replacing their radio earpieces with earplugs.

Not far from them, a bundle of rags moved slightly – a beggar dozing in the dappled shade of a eucalyptus tree shifting something hidden in the sackcloth. Across the road a cart loaded with sugar cane seemed to move of its own accord. Harland could just make out two pairs of boots beneath it.

The police car showed round the first part of the Z bend and climbed the rutted stretch towards Munroe. Then came the truck, heeling as it took the potholes. Some way off, the little Fiat driven by Foyzi tore through the dust kicked up by the two bigger vehicles.

As Harland inched forward, his view of the road remained unimpaired. The whole plan began to unfold in front of him. Munroe was the first to move. He got up from his seat and managed to dislodge his hat, which rolled off across the road. This seemed to cause the old man some distress and he went in pursuit of it, holding his back and moving with great difficulty. He added further to the impression of frailty by waving a stick in the air and knocking over his easel. At this moment the police vehicle came round the bend and, without slowing down, drove between him and the hat. Munroe seemed to become disorientated in the cloud of dust, fell forwards and rolled onto his side. Harland prayed the driver of the truck would see him. He did brake, but only just in time, at which point several things happened. Smoke grenades went off in the road behind and in front of the two vehicles. The load of sugar cane erupted and three men wearing gas masks jumped into the road, shooting out the police car's tyres and radiator. The vehicle juddered to a halt with its blue light still flashing in vain. At this, another man sprang from an opening in the wall and propelled a small canister of knockout gas through the window. None of the four men had any time to react.

A second or two before, Munroe rolled over in the road and aimed a machine pistol with one hand at the truck's front tyres and engine. He was joined by Selvey, who raised her sidearm in a textbook two-handed aim. The rear tyres were cut to ribbons by two other men who had leapt from behind a wall, and for good measure they threw a stun-grenade in the general direction of the truck. The driver had been on the point of jumping down when it exploded and he fell to earth like a dead bird.

Harland plunged through the narrow opening, scraping the underside of his vehicle on a boulder, and landed in the road just behind the truck. He saw the Fiat parked with both its front doors open and Isis Herrick running up the road into the smoke. This was the very last thing she should have been doing because three police-men, who had been protected from the worst effects of the stun-grenade, had spilled from the open door at the back of the truck with their rifles. Harland had no choice but to steer the Isuzu into one and then slammed a second by opening his door while the vehicle was still moving. The third man had scuttled round the truck and was taking aim. Harland got out and sprinted to tackle him. The gun went off at the moment he collided with his upper thighs and sent him into the dirt. Harland was aware that his back wouldn't take the jolt but pushed the thought to the back of his mind. While Colonel B's men disarmed the three policemen, Harland picked himself up painfully and went to the front to find Isis bent over her father. He appeared to have sprained his right wrist but that was all. The Peugeot getaway car had already been summoned, and before long Munroe and Selvey were being rushed towards it through the smoke. Isis stood looking utterly stricken, but then her father bent down to pick up his hat and waved a cheery goodbye over his shoulder.

It was a bizarre sight, and no one was more astonished than The Doctor, who remained in the passenger seat of the truck as if he had suffered a seizure. Foyzi opened the door and pulled him down into the road at gunpoint uttering many imprecations under his breath, then took him by the scruff of the neck and marched him to the rear of the truck. Harland and Herrick followed.

They went through all the cells. Two men were released but neither bore the slightest resemblance to Khan and were told to make a run for it while they could.

'Maybe they've got him on another truck,' suggested Colonel B, wiping his face. 'Inform this cunt that you will shoot him if he doesn't tell us where Karim Khan is.'

Foyzi placed the silencer of his pistol against The Doctor's temple. After a moment of deliberation, The Doctor lifted his head and pointed inside the truck.

'There's a compartment in the floor,' shouted Isis. 'Look, there are two hinges.'

They wrenched the door up with crowbars. Beneath the steel plate Khan was lying bound, gagged and blindfolded in a space not much larger than a coffin. His feet were a blackened mess and his groin was stained with blood and urine. The rest of his clothes were sodden. They lifted him from this hold with infinite care and moved him to the light. Herrick took off the blindfold and gag and told him he was in safe hands, but he seemed not to understand and moved his head rhythmically from side to side like a blind singer.

'For the love of God…' said one of Colonel B's men.

'No,' said Harland, remembering with an almost physical pain his own time at the hands of a torturer. He shook his head and turned to The Doctor ready to kill him.

The Colonel put up his arm. 'We'd better be about our business,' he said. 'Get Khan into Harland's vehicle and give him a shot of morphine.'

'What about this man?' Harland asked, pointing to The Doctor. 'He knows Isis. We can't leave him here.'

The Colonel nodded. 'I rather thought we'd take him with us.'

'And?' said Harland.

'Well, obviously we can't take him all the way home to Syria or Iraq, or wherever the devil he comes from, but we can certainly give him a ride to, say, the middle of the Sinai desert.'

Harland, Isis and Foyzi got in with Khan and made their way through the remainder of the smoke. Colonel B's men melted into the cemetery, two of them running The Doctor towards a container lorry waiting with its engine ticking over a little way off.

The radio came to life again. It was Guthrie. 'I'm sure you'll want to join me in thanking the Captain for a perfect landing. Local time is 4.25 p.m. The temperature is ninety-two degrees. Welcome to Cairo. Please remain seated until the aircraft has stopped moving.'

CHAPTER TWENTY-ONE

The island where they took Khan lay some two hundred miles south of Cairo, below a great bend in the Nile. Thirteen hours after leaving the cemetery they made a rendezvous with a boat named Lotus, hidden at the edge of a sugar plantation. Khan's stretcher was loaded across the bow and secured with ropes. The boatman pushed off into the current and, using only a long oar at the stern, steered them downstream towards the island. There was no man-made light to be seen for miles around and the moonless night had an infinite clarity. When the boat found a breeze in the centre of the river, Herrick peered down at Khan to see if he was cold. She watched his eyes open and then his entire face spread and relax. A curtain was being drawn back.

The Lotus glided silently towards a cleft on the island and the boatmen punted the last few yards to the bank with the oar. The shapes of several men appeared and moved down to the river's edge to catch the boat and lead it into a berth of ancient wooden piles. One man waded through the water holding up a white robe. It was Sammi Loz. He bent down, touched Khan's shoulder and said something. There was no response.

'How bad is he?' he asked Harland.

'Not good.'

The stretcher was borne up the bank by four men to a group of single-storey buildings arranged loosely around a courtyard and hidden from the river by a screen of vegetation. At the corner of the courtyard, light came from an open door, revealing a room with a faded mural of flowers and exotic birds, a low wooden bed, some chairs and a couple of oil lamps. They lifted Khan from the stretcher and laid him on the bed. He stirred and seemed to recognise Loz, then Herrick, but he plainly doubted what he was seeing and tried to reach out to touch Loz's face.

Loz told him to stay still, lifting Khan's head to give him some water and a sleeping pill. When Khan's eyes closed a few minutes later, Loz set about removing the rags from his friend's emaciated body with a pair of surgical scissors he'd found in the medical bag. He took each strip of cloth and dropped it neatly into a pile. Then he asked Foyzi to run a light over Khan very slowly so he could see the extent of his injuries. He stopped to look at the burns on his genitals where the electrodes had been applied. He sponged away the grime and blood and dabbed the livid red and black weals with anti-bacterial ointment. With Herrick's help he rolled Khan onto his side so that he could treat similar injuries on his back, buttocks and the inside of his thighs. Then he cleaned and dressed the chafe marks on his hands and ankles.

Khan's feet presented a greater problem. They were so swollen and bruised that it was hard to distinguish the toes from the rest of the foot. Loz suspected there might be one or two broken bones but said he wouldn't be able to tell until Khan had had an x-ray. There was little he could do, apart from giving him painkillers and arnica to help the bruising. He said that many weeks of physiotherapy lay ahead.

Throughout the hour he spent tending his friend, Loz paid as much attention to the general trauma as to the particular injuries, judging the position of his spine and shoulder blades now that he was in repose. He touched the back of his head, neck and pelvis lightly, gazing up to the flickering light on the ceiling to concentrate better on the distortions and misalignments that his fingers found. Occasionally he shook his head but said nothing. At length he asked Foyzi for a pen and paper, and made some notes on his lap.

Harland signalled to Herrick that he was going outside. She followed. They had agreed during the journey that one of them should always be with Khan and Loz to hear anything that passed between them, but Khan was obviously going to be out for some time and Foyzi was keeping a close eye on both of them.

They sat down on an open terrace a little distance away. For several minutes Harland stared down at the insects that had gathered round a light, then shook himself from his reverie and looked at her vacantly.

'Yes,' he said slowly. 'What we need is a drink and a smoke. I've got some whisky in my bag. Have you got any cigarettes?'

She shook her head.

'Damn.'

Foyzi came through the door and tossed him a packet of Camel Light. 'Compliments of the establishment,' he said, turning back to Loz.

'Who the hell is Foyzi?' asked Herrick quietly.

'He's in your business, actually – a freelance, as fly as you get. But he's reliable and loyal.'

'And all this?'

'He must have done a deal with the local Islamist nutters for the island. This area is crawling with them. They hide out in mountain caves either side of the Nile.'

'Where's he from?'

'He's Jordanian, based in Turkey. He had something to do with the Iraqi opposition but now works all over the Middle East. I came across him about a year ago when the UN needed a line to Hamas. Foyzi fixed a meeting in Lebanon.'

'And you trust him?'

'Yes, so does the Chief.'

They drank for a further fifteen minutes, then Harland looked at his watch and said they should call Teckman. He set up the satellite phone in a clear patch of ground nearby and plugged it into a laptop equipped with powerful encryption software. He dialled three times before getting through to one of the duty officers at Vauxhall Cross. There was a further delay while the office patched through the unscrambled call to the Chief. Harland passed the handset to Herrick. 'You're the secret servant round here,' he said. 'I'm just the help.'

The Chief came on. 'Your father is going to be fine – a suspected fracture in his wrist, that's all. They'll be back with us by midday today. What about our friends?'

'He's sedated, and the osteopath is doing a good job, as far as one can tell.'

'Well, we'll send reinforcements to you later. Two of your colleagues are nearby.' He paused. 'You've all done very well, but now comes the hard part. I need you to get as much as you can, as soon as possible. I know the fellow is in a bad way but you should make a start tomorrow. You can use the computer to send your reports. I'd prefer you do that than spend any time speaking on the phone. If you log on now, Harland will find a message.'

Harland was signalling that he wanted to talk to Teckman, but before she could tell the Chief, he had gone.

'What's the bloody hell's he playing at?'

Herrick told him about the message. For the next ten minutes Harland struggled with the decryption program. Eventually she took over and retrieved the email.

'Good news, I hope?' she said.

He shook his head.

'Well?'

'It's nothing important.'

'Anything that comes through that computer is important. I need to know what it says.'

Harland lit another cigarette. 'This is personal. A deal which I don't propose to discuss with you.'

'If it has a bearing on this situation, I insist you do,' she snapped.

'It doesn't, except that I may have to leave the island over the next day and a half. This is your business now. I don't work for HMG. I've got another job to go to. And I *do* have to go – the Secretary-General is leaving for Syria and Jordan tomorrow. I must find a way of joining him.' He paused and looked at her. 'You've got Foyzi. You won't have any problems.'

'Oh yeah, stuck on some bloody island in the middle of the Nile with a known Afghan veteran and a man who has direct links with Hizbollah. That's to say nothing of the minor interest the Egyptian government and the Americans have in finding Khan and apprehending those who freed him. And when you throw in the Islamic jihad skulking in the mountains, the whole thing is a mere picnic. You bloody well can't leave me here. I need you. Tell me why you're really going. It's not your job.'

Harland shook his head. 'Look, you knew I had a deal with the Chief. In return for helping to get Sammi Loz out of Albania and bringing him here, the Chief said he would find a friend of mine. And he has now given me the information. This is something I have to do.'

'Well, which is it? This friend or the job?'

'Both.'

She sighed heavily and swallowed the remainder of her whisky. 'I need sleep. I can't think about this any longer.'

They got up and went to Khan's room. Loz was sitting on a three-legged stool watching him sleep. He looked up.

'Thank you for rescuing my friend,' he said. 'You have undoubtedly saved his life.'

'We weren't doing it as a favour for you,' said Herrick.

'I know,' he replied, 'but you risked much. I am grateful to you both and so will Karim be when he's able to speak.'

'Which will be tomorrow. We need to talk to him as soon as he wakes in the morning.'

'That will be too soon,' said Loz evenly.

'Too bad,' she said.

'Perhaps you need some rest, Isis. You look tired.'

'Don't tell me what I need. Just make sure he's ready to speak to us by morning.'

Loz was taken aback. Even Harland was surprised by the sudden flare of temper.

She woke six hours later, and for a few minutes stared through an open door, astonished by the intense, green lushness that surrounded her. Apart from a few bird-calls there was a strikingly profound stillness, and she felt that only now had Cairo stopped ringing in her ears. She swung her legs from the bed and glimpsed a reed bank through the trees.

A few minutes later Harland called out from the courtyard and announced he was bringing her coffee. She drew over her the blue cloth that had served as a blanket during the night and said he could come in.

'Feeling better?' he said, as his head came round the door. He handed her a bowl of thick, black coffee, and held up a dark blue robe with a hood. 'It's been suggested by Foyzi that you might be prepared to wear this while you're here. He says you won't be so conspicuous to people passing in boats. If it makes you feel any better, they've found me one as well.'

'That's fine. Leave it over here,' she said.

He dropped it on the bed.

'What about Khan?'

'He's still asleep.'

'Something came to me in the night,' she said. 'I can't quite put my finger on it – a sense that we're looking at the wrong thing.'

'Maybe.' Harland's shrewd eyes narrowed. 'Let me know when you think of it. I'll go back to them now. One of us should be there when he wakes. Why don't you get something to eat from Foyzi and then relieve me in an hour or so?'

She put on the robe and trainers and walked around the building until she found Foyzi standing by a clay oven. With him was an old man in a brown skull cap and dirty shift who, on seeing her, whisked a roundel of unleavened bread from the fire. Foyzi cooled it by flipping it between his hands, then spun it through the air to her. He walked a little distance to a patch of bare earth and looked up at the smoke from the oven curling to the top of the trees.

'You should look around,' he said. 'It's quite a place. A piece of paradise.'

'You're moving better,' she said. 'You've lost your limp.'

'Oh yes, the doctor took a look at me last night and pressed a few buttons,' said Foyzi. 'He's got quite a touch.'

She nodded. '"Big lorry jump all over little car," I liked that. Were you actually hurt in an accident?'

'Yes, a long time ago in Manchester, England. I worked there for eighteen months. Four of those were spent in hospital with a broken hip bone.'

'What were you doing there?'

'This and that,' he replied.

She smiled at the evasion.

'Okay, I have a question for you,' he said suddenly in the manner of an eager college student. 'How did you learn to lip-read?'

She told him about catching meningitis when she was young, the deafness that followed and the operation to cure it a few years later.

'Only in English, not other languages?'

'Maybe I can lip-read as many languages as you can do accents, Foyzi,' she replied.

'Never,' he said.

A little later she took Foyzi's advice and began to look around. From the buildings clustered on the rock plateau in the south to the northern end, the island measured about three-quarters of a mile. At its widest point it was about five hundred yards. The banks were covered in dense shrubbery, but at the centre there were citrus groves, palms and several large dark green trees which bore fruit Herrick didn't recognise. There were also a few square fields cultivated with strips of lucerne, bananas, maize and flower crops, mostly roses and marigolds. Between these grazed tethered water buffalo, goats and a lone donkey.

There was very little noise as she walked – the rustle of a lizard over dead leaves, a bird call or the cough of buffalo – and because she barely glimpsed the river, the only sense she had of it was the smell of heated mud banks and an occasional distant whoosh caused by the current tugging at an obstacle on the bank. In a glade at the northern end she came across the old bread maker, who had made his way there along a more direct path, and was contemplating a wall constructed of drainage pipes and mortar. From the openings spilled swarms of bees that hung in the sun like skin pelts drying. He lifted the swarms with a stick, talking to them in a falsetto.

She made her way back and found a spot where she could see all the buildings and realised they had been designed to look like the blunt prow of a ship forging up the river. They were almost completely hidden from both banks of the Nile by vegetation, and even from where she stood they appeared deserted, a ruin from a colonial past.

She continued walking, deep in thought. She had never been so impressed by the beauty and stillness of a place, yet was aware of its dangerous isolation. The Chief had planned it this way, she was sure. He expected something to happen, some revelation to occur. And when it did, he wanted Loz and Khan away from the world and unable to communicate.

She went to Khan's room and saw that he was still asleep.

'I think you had better wake him,' she told Loz.

He shook his head. 'We've tried.'

She looked at Harland who nodded to agree with Loz. 'I want him conscious by midday,' she said, 'even if it means throwing water over him. Is that understood?'

'We will do our best,' said Loz.

'Just get him to the point where he can answer my questions,' she said, and turned on her heel. Harland followed, leaving Foyzi to watch them.

They walked to the most shaded part of the island in the east where a tree grew out into the river. Herrick perched on a low branch.

'So now you're going to tell me about this woman?'

He looked at her for a while, then shrugged. 'She left six weeks after nine-eleven,' he said. 'November first to be precise. Just vanished. No letter, message or phone call; no activity on her checking account; no record of her having left the United States or having bought a plane ticket in her own name. Nothing.'

'Had you been together long?'

'About a year. I fell for her nearly thirty years ago. That didn't work out, then we got together a couple of years back. It was after the business in the Balkans. You probably heard about it.'

'I know it did for Walter Vigo – at least temporarily. You had a son together?'

'Yep. When he died it was a very deep shock to her. She moved to be with me in New York but never settled down. She didn't know anyone there and turned in on herself. My job took me away. It was difficult.'

'And you tried to trace her?'

Harland nodded. 'She knew how to disappear. She did it once before when we were young.'

'Where is she?'

'In Tel Aviv.'

'She's Jewish?'

'Yep, though it was never particularly important to her, apart from the fact that her mother's family in Czechoslovakia was wiped out in the Holocaust. Her mother was the only one left.'

Herrick thought for a moment. 'Maybe she was reclaiming her Jewish ancestry. Trying to put herself in some kind of context.'

Harland nodded. 'Something like that.'

'How did they find her?'

'Spotted her at Heathrow, followed her and then traced her to Israel.'

She thought, he's holding something back. Either that, or there's something else he doesn't understand.

'So you'll try to see her?'

'Yes, I'll go directly from here. I've got work in Damascus anyway.'

'And you have to go now?'

'Yes.'

'Why?'

'Because I've got a bloody job to do.'

By the early afternoon the mercury in an old enamel thermometer in her room reached the 105-degree mark. Nothing moved. The leaves on the trees hung limp and the birds and insects had long ceased to make any sound. In search of some movement in the air, Herrick climbed to a covered turret and looked across the swathes of green either side of the river to the unforgiving mountains in the west and east. Harland spotted her and shouted up that Khan was awake. She rushed down the narrow stairway and went to the room with him.

'How are you?' she asked, approaching the bed.

'He's doing very well,' said Loz.

'That's good,' she said, smiling at Loz.

'I was just telling him that he must have lost forty pounds since I saw him last,' said Loz. 'I can't believe he's still alive.' There was certainly love in his eyes but also an expectant look.

'Have you explained that we have to ask him some questions?' she asked.

'It is too soon,' he replied. 'I don't think he has the strength.'

She crouched down so that she was at eye level with Khan. 'We know you've suffered terribly,' she said softly, 'but I was wondering if you wouldn't mind talking to us for a little while?'

He glanced at Loz. 'That will be all right,' he said. Again the perfect English she'd heard in Albania surprised her. 'I can try to help.'

She put the notepad and digital recorder down and touched his hand. 'I'm really sorry about this, Karim. The moment you feel too tired you must tell us.'

'It's okay,' he said. 'But there are some things that are … not very clear at the moment.'

'He's on very strong painkillers,' Loz interjected.

'Can I ask you about The Poet?'

'I've already told you about him,' said Loz.

'I know, but we really do need to find out more about him.' She turned to Khan. 'The Poet, who is he?'

'The Poet was a man in Bosnia. But this was only our name for him.'

'What was his real name?'

Khan shook his head helplessly.

'You know that a man calling himself The Poet went to see Dr Loz in New York to ask him for money? He mentioned your name and after Dr Loz had given him the money he gave him a photograph of you. Mr Harland has it here.' Harland delved into his shirt pocket and handed it to her. 'Is that you?'

'Yes, this is me... but I thought...' he looked towards Loz doubtfully.

'What?'

'I don't know... I'm confused.'

She waited. 'Who took the picture?'

'A man in Afghanistan. I don't know his name.'

'Did you give the picture away? How did it get into the hands of the man calling himself The Poet?'

He shook his head. 'I do not remember... I'm sorry.'

'That's all right. We'll come back to it when you've had a chance to think.' She paused and looked down at the recorder on the floor. 'You know why we're asking these questions, don't you? We believe that one of the men you knew in Bosnia is now a terrorist leader.'

He blinked slowly with a gentle nod.

'Are there any other individuals you remember from Bosnia – or from Afghanistan, for that matter – who expressed the kind of views we associate with al-Qaeda or other extremist groups?'

'There were many in Afghanistan but I kept away from them. I was not interested in attacking the West.'

Loz nodded in agreement.

'But it must have been difficult not to be affected by the atmosphere. You are a Muslim and most of the people who came back from Afghanistan were very opposed to Western beliefs and lifestyle.'

'I believe in the teachings of the Prophet. I prayed to him when I was in prison... I prayed to Allah... in these last days I have prayed... and I was saved... but I have suffered moments of doubt. There was much cruelty in Afghanistan. Much violence. But I never hated the West.' This all came out very slowly. Quite suddenly his eyes closed and his forehead creased. Tears began to run down his cheeks.

Loz put a hand on his shoulder, but there was something in the gesture that made Herrick think Loz was content with the situation.

'Will you describe The Poet for me?' she asked when he had recovered.

'He was about five foot five or six... small build... He had dark hair, thinning at the front. His cheeks were sunken, which made him look older than he was, but this was because we had little food in Sarajevo. He went days without eating. I did not recognise him later...'

'Later? That was in Afghanistan,' said Herrick quickly. 'The Poet asked you to join him in Afghanistan in ninety-seven. And you saw him there. Is that right?'

Khan nodded. 'But he left.'

'Yes, we know he was in New York receiving money from your friend. And the only way he could do that was if you had given him Dr Loz's address and the picture of you to use as his *bona fides*.'

He nodded.

'Did you know he would use your picture in this way?'

'I do not remember.'

'But you must do. It was like the postcards you sent him recently. It was proof that you were still in the land of the living.'

Khan's brow furrowed. His eyes moved rapidly from her to Loz.

'It's okay, Karim,' said Loz.

She waited until his gaze returned to her. 'I would like to run a few names past you. They're men you may have come across while in Afghanistan.'

She went through a list of suspects. Some she had remembered from RAPTOR, others from the FBI watch list. She hoped the process had a ring of authenticity and thought she noticed a certain interest in Loz's eyes. Khan appeared to hesitate over one or two but was unable to say definitely whether he had met or seen any of the men. In any normal interrogation the failure of memory would have been unacceptable, but she let it pass and asked him instead to list the key men he'd met and describe them. He gave her a score of names, many half-remembered. Then she returned to ask him where he had last seen The Poet.

'It was in the south in the first three years. I stayed with him several times. He was with the men from the Taleban. The men who were giving us the crazy orders. He asked me to take the struggle to the West but I said no. After the second time he lost patience.'

'So he did try to recruit you as a terrorist?'

He nodded.

'With your background in London he must have thought you were an ideal candidate.' She wondered whether she was sailing too close to her actual target and before he had time to answer added, 'So when you refused, you helped him another way – by giving him the photograph and Dr Loz's address?'

'Yes...I felt...'

'You felt you had to compensate for not going along with his wishes?'

'Yes.'

She spent some time asking about his journey from Afghanistan to the West. 'There's something I don't understand,' she said. 'Why didn't you come back before the attacks in 2001? You say you were disenchanted with the Taleban and that you had seen too much bloodshed. The ambition to return to medicine must have developed in you before then. Why didn't you act on it? And why these postcards? Finding a phone to call Dr Loz was surely not beyond you – not in all that time.' She thought she was exerting just about the right degree of pressure, but then Khan looked around the room as though he suddenly didn't recognise anyone.

'That's enough,' said Loz. 'I think you are confusing him. You must remember what he's been through.'

'Yes, you're probably right. We'll take a break there and return to all this later.' She switched off the recorder and left the room. Harland followed her out while Foyzi made his presence felt by putting the chairs against the wall and lowering a canvas blind on a window that had suddenly been filled with sunlight.

'You know what you're doing?' he said when they reached the shade of a tree fifty yards away.

'I think so ... I hope so.'

'You don't seem to be getting much.'

'I don't expect to,' she said.

He wiped a trickle of sweat on his cheek with the back of his hand. 'Then what the hell are we doing here?'

'Well, as you're about to bugger off, I hardly think I need to answer to you. This is my operation and I'm going to run it the best way I can think of.' She paused. 'When are you leaving?'

'I'm waiting to hear from Foyzi, probably this evening. I would like to help. Really.'

'You can, by setting up the sat' phone. I need to send the recording I've just made plus an email.'

She went to the table where they had sat the night before and composed a message on the laptop.

At five the sun began its rapid descent into the western desert and the temperature eased a little. All around the riverbanks the steady call of frogs suddenly started up. Herrick moved from her room to the courtyard and came across Harland in a jellaba, getting his things together.

'Thanks for saying goodbye.'

'I was about to,' he said, and explained that he would try to catch the Luxor Cairo Express at a halt sixty miles away. If he waited until the following day for a train he'd fail to meet up with the Secretary-General in Tel Aviv on Thursday.

'I don't get it. If you're so bloody important to them why did they let you spend all this time with Loz?'

'I was no use with my back. I couldn't travel, let alone sit at a desk. Benjamin Jaidi put me in touch with Loz and things followed on from there.'

'It can't have been accident that gave you Loz's name.'

'Jaidi is also a patient so knew how good he was.'

'That I hadn't realised.'

'Whatever one's doubts about Sammi Loz, I have to admit he's a bloody good doctor. I'm pretty much all right now, even after the twinge in Cairo.'

She thought for a moment. 'And then as if divinely coordinated, just as you come under the care of Sammi Loz, the Chief pops up in New York and asks you to watch him. And what the fuck was Teckman doing in New York anyway? He doesn't travel abroad almost as a matter of policy.'

'He was there because of Norquist's death – a meeting.'

'Yes, the Norquist murder… where this whole thing started.' She thought again. 'So both the Chief and the Secretary-General were steering you to Loz but without giving you their reasons. What was going on?' She started to pace up and down, then moved to the shade of a tree. 'I should have thought about this more seriously. What do they know? Why haven't they told us?'

'Look, I don't think Teckman or the FBI or the Secretary-General knew much. The information about Loz's property deals only came together when we were in Albania. And that's the most they've got.'

'Right. But they still must have suspected a connection between Loz and the assassination of Norquist.'

'And Khan?' he said.

'Khan? No, I don't think so.'

'You're very certain of that.'

'Yes, Khan is an innocent, in as much as any fighter with his kind of record can be innocent. The point of Karim Khan is that Sammi Loz loves him. You've seen the way he looks at Khan in there. Actually I find it quite moving to think he would cast everything to the wind because of this man. But that's the point, that's why we're here. It's Sammi Loz they're interested in.'

Harland's eyes had come to rest on a beetle doggedly making its way across the path. 'I see,' he said eventually. 'You think the Chief has put both of them on ice here, taken Sammi Loz out of circulation?'

She nodded impatiently. 'Sorry, have I been going a bit fast for you?'

He didn't smile.

'Tell me about Loz's life in New York,' she said. 'What kind of man are we dealing with here? I need to know more.'

'He's well-connected. He has beautiful consulting rooms in the Empire State building. He dines at the best places. Knows the best-looking women. A perfect life for a certain type of bachelor.'

'Any permanent girlfriend?'

'I would guess not. Why?'

'I'm wondering if that's his weakness. We know he's prepared to risk everything for Khan, so clearly he is a man who follows his emotions. To that extent, he's impulsive.'

'The one woman I saw him with in a restaurant was dismissed from his presence without much ceremony.' He stopped. 'You're not thinking you…'

'Jesus, no. He's attractive. Anyone can see that. But I'm hardly his type. Besides, I've always thought that seduction was overrated as an interrogation technique.'

Harland started to say something but decided against it.

'What?'

'Nothing… Look, I want you to be careful over the next few days.' He took her arm to move away from the buildings. The sun was plunging towards the mountains leaving the landscape bathed in a creamy apricot light. Through a gap in the trees she saw a pair of purple-green herons stalking the waters below. Beyond them a kingfisher hovered.

'Foyzi was right,' she said. 'It's extraordinary here. Almost too much to take in.'

'I mean it, Isis,' said Harland severely, pulling her round to face him. 'If for one moment Loz realises you're stalking him through your questioning of Khan, you'll be in trouble.'

'Foyzi's here,' she said. 'His men are all over the island, though one never sees them. And I've got one thing going for me: the fact that we went to so much trouble to spring Khan. No one could doubt the value we place on him, not when nearly a dozen people flew from Britain to free him. Not even Loz. That was brilliant of Teckman. I just wish he had told us, that's all.'

They walked back to the villa where Foyzi told them that the truck was already waiting on the east bank. Harland picked up his stuff and they walked down to the river's edge where he gave her an awkward kiss that missed her cheek and landed on the fabric of her hood. 'Foyzi, you look after her,' he called up the bank.

'What were you going to say back there?' she asked.

'That Teckman has left you on this island without the standard backup of a lot of puffing, red-faced SIS officers, for a reason.'

'Thanks,' she said. 'I'd got there.'

He produced a Walther P38 from his jellaba, together with half a dozen clips of ammunition, and offered them to her.

'I hardly know how to fire one of those things,' she said.

'You might as well take it. I'll have to dump it or give it away before I leave the country.'

'Right.' She took it and let it drop into the pocket of her robe.

'You've got my mobile number – it's good for anywhere. Call me.'

'What, for dinner?' she said sourly.

He shook his head with mild exasperation, wedged his bag in the bow of the little wooden skiff and clambered in, knocking his shin against the rowlock and swearing. Herrick smiled and began to climb the bank. She did not give the boat a second glance as it slipped downstream into the dusk.

CHAPTER TWENTY-TWO

She slept deeply that night and woke at six the next morning. After bread and coffee she went to Khan's room, taking her recorder and the notepad on which she had ordered a series of questions. Khan was propped up, smiling tentatively, as if a dream was about to come to an end. Beside him Loz worked in the morning light at a cane table, setting out the medicine and throwing solicitous glances in his friend's direction. Foyzi stood by the door and nodded to her as she came in.

'I must congratulate you on these supplies,' said Loz. 'I haven't wanted for anything yet, though we may need a little more of one or two drugs and I'm running low on the ointment. Any chance of a fresh delivery?'

'Maybe we can get something from Luxor,' she said pleasantly, sitting down on the opposite side of the bed from Loz. 'You're looking a lot better, Karim. You seem to have put on a little weight.'

'I hope so,' he said.

'We were just reminiscing about our life in London,' said Loz. 'We were trying to think of a restaurant we used to go to where there was a very pretty waitress that Karim took a fancy to. She was Polish. The food and service were atrocious but Karim insisted we had to eat there because of her. What was her *name*?'

Khan shook his head, unable to help.

'Katya!' said Loz triumphantly. 'That was it. She was a real beauty. She's probably two hundred pounds today, five children and a vodka habit.' He paused. 'The restaurant was in Camden High Street. We played snooker nearby, then went round to order just before the

241

kitchen closed. You see, Karim wanted to walk her home at the end of the evening but after spending all that money we discovered she was having an affair with the owner.'

Karim was smiling, borne along with Loz's enthusiasm.

'Actually, I also wanted to talk about the past,' Isis said.

'If Karim feels strong enough,' said Loz.

'I'm sure the rest last night will have done him good. When you were on your way to Bosnia you travelled together, is that right? In a lorry?'

They both nodded.

'What date was this?'

'February 1993, I think,' said Loz.

'And you were prevented from going all the way to Sarajevo by Serb troops?'

'Actually the Croats,' said Loz.

'I'd prefer it if Khan answers,' she said, switching the recorder on and resting it against the chair leg.

'Yes, the Croats,' said Khan.

'So you made your way with UN vehicles into Sarajevo. What was the point of that?' She glanced at the recorder to check its light was pulsing in time with her speech.

'No, we got a lift in a plane. We took all the medicine we could carry.'

'Did you travel with any fellow medical students?'

'No.'

'So this expedition was your own idea?'

'Yes, we felt for our fellow Muslims. It was something we thought of together. I raised the money and we took two other people, one of whom could speak the language. But they both turned back with the truck.'

'So you got to Sarajevo and delivered your supplies. Then what?'

'We both worked in the hospitals. A lot of people were being injured by the snipers and in the daily bombardment. Thousands of people died in the siege.'

She nodded. She had the exact figure in her head – 10,500.

'How did you end up on the frontline?'

'It just happened. Sammi met someone who said they needed

ammunition at the front. A big attack was expected. They asked us to help carry the boxes.'

'And…'

'There was an attack going on as we arrived. Many of our men were being killed and they were over-running our lines. We picked up the guns of the dead and started firing. It was as simple as that.'

'As simple as that – from doctors to fighters in a few seconds?'

'Yes,' said Khan. ' But we still helped out as medics. We did both.'

Loz nodded approvingly.

'When did the incident take place when Sammi was injured?' Herrick said, raising her hand to stop Loz answering.

'Sometime in the winter of that year,' Khan replied.

'Of 1993?'

'Yes.'

'Where were you treated?' she asked Loz.

Loz replied that he was taken first to a hospital in Sarajevo and then to Germany. He recovered in London.

'Which hospital in London?'

A private one.

'Which?'

'King Edward's – this was for the skin grafts. They didn't do a very good job in Sarajevo.'

'But you, Karim, stayed on, for nearly two years. Why?'

'I was committed. I couldn't understand why Islam did not declare a proper jihad against the Serbs. To leave those people when they had so little help, no heavy guns, no fresh troops, would have been desertion.'

'So you were moved by very much the same emotions as The Poet. You were both men of peace who were turned into soldiers by the extreme conditions in Sarajevo. Tell me exactly where you met him.'

'On the front. He was just an ordinary soldier like me then.'

'Was that in the lines to the north of the city?'

He looked surprised. 'Yes – north-east actually.'

'Near where Sammi was wounded?' she said quickly.

'Exactly there. It was during that period.'

'At the same time?'

'No…'

Loz got up and said, 'Karim, I think I need to change the position of your legs. The way you have them will do no good to your hip. I've told you about this before.' His tone was gently admonishing.

Herrick sat back as though she hadn't noticed the diversion. 'So you came across The Poet before Sammi was wounded?' she said.

'I don't remember now,' he said. He winced as Loz moved him.

'Maybe another painkiller,' said Loz, reaching for the table.

Khan shook his head. 'I'm okay.'

She waited.

'Yes it was sometime about then… before or after, I'm not sure.'

'But it is perfectly possible that Sammi met The Poet during that time.' She paused and looked at Loz. 'Did you?'

'Yes,' said Loz, looking unsettled. 'I told you that we met him but I can't remember exactly when.' He got up again and started fussing over Khan's feet.

'I'm sorry, this is not going to work,' said Herrick. 'I think I'd prefer to talk to Karim alone.' Foyzi moved from the top of the bed and steered Loz from the room.

She smiled at Khan reassuringly. 'Sammi has told me about the brave way you saved him. I must say it's an extraordinary story. Was The Poet there to witness that?'

He shrugged helplessly.

'Let's say he was,' she said. 'What date was that – roughly?'

'It was winter – November 1993. I think.'

'Not after Christmas?'

'No, definitely not.'

'I just wanted to make sure, because we're looking for pictures taken by an English photographer at that time.'

Khan absorbed this.

'In fact, it would be helpful if you could identify as many people as you can when I eventually get the picture.'

Khan grimaced.

'I'm sorry. You're in pain.'

'Yes, my feet hurt a little.' He stopped. 'Maybe Sammi could help with the pictures?'

'That's a good idea.'

Gradually she returned to the subject of the winter of 1993–94. She made notes, taking particular care over places, dates, weather conditions and names. Khan's memory was hazy, and it didn't work in a linear fashion, so building a chronology was difficult. He relived the terror of that winter in epic flashes – the din of bombardment from all directions; the incursions of the Serbs into the streets of Sarajevo, the danger from snipers and the hunger and cold. It was in the account of this time that he made several mistakes. She made a note of them, but her smile did not fade as he stumbled between what actually happened and what Loz had prepared him to say.

The air was oppressively heavy and with each blink his eyes stayed closed for seconds at a time. She rose and left the room, at which Loz returned with a slightly exaggerated look of concern.

She returned at four, sat down and placed the recorder in its usual position. Loz had straightened Khan on the bed and was holding his legs just above the ankle bone with his thumbs and forefingers. The rest of his fingers were splayed out so that they didn't touch the bruised flesh below the ankles. Then he lifted the legs, almost as if comparing their weight, and tugged each one gently. He moved to the knees and thighs with a gentle stroking motion, pulled up the shift and covered Khan's groin with a cloth.

She made to leave.

'Stay, I've already examined him there.'

His hands moved to the hips and he again seemed to weigh Khan's body. Then he went round to the side and slipped both hands under his back, working his fingers into place while looking away to the corner of the room. Herrick was struck by the concentration in his face.

'You see,' he said after a little while, 'by hanging him from the ceiling they stretched his body so everything went out of line. Apart from the damage this did to the muscles and ligaments, there are various skeletal problems. These will take longer to heal.'

'Have you treated this kind of injury before?'

'Yes, a young man – a New York cab driver from Cameroon. He had been tortured very badly three years before I saw him. The damage was hidden for most of the time, but came out at moments of stress. The man was mystified because the spasms seemed to be unconnected with the method of torture.' He paused. 'The body does not forget, you see.'

There were periods of inactivity over the next half-hour during which Loz's slender hands simply rested on Khan's chest, under his neck or at the back of his cranium. At other moments they became animated, brushing and pressing the skin and then once or twice flicking it with a screwing motion of the finger knuckles. The way he moved around Khan's bed was so precise and fluent that it had an almost hypnotic effect on her. When he had finished, it was clear Khan was having difficulty in keeping his eyes open.

Loz shook his head apologetically.

'That's okay,' she said. 'I want to talk to you anyway. We'll go under the trees.'

They walked out into a second perfect sunset.

'It's been interesting to hear about Bosnia,' she said conversationally. 'I'd forgotten about the brutality of it all.'

'People do,' he said.

'Of course, both sides did terrible things. People forget that too.' She was on more certain ground now.

'No, just one side.'

'There were Muslim war criminals too.'

'We were the defenders of Sarajevo,' he said, shaking his head. 'People were being killed every day by the snipers and artillery.'

'Even so, atrocities were also committed by the Bosniaks. Raiding parties on the Serb lines. Men were butchered and tortured.'

He continued to shake his head. 'You're mistaken.'

'It's true,' she said. 'The War Crimes Tribunal has the names.'

'Yes, but there were no indictments of Muslims. The only Muslims who appear at the tribunal are victims – women from the rape camps; men who saw their friends and family murdered.'

'But it did happen,' she said. 'We should always remember that Muslims are as capable of crime as Christians.'

'Not then,' he rounded on her, a startled look growing in his face. 'The market square bomb – what about that? What about those people?'

'I'm sorry,' she said. 'I don't recall…'

'These things are in the news for a few days and then forgotten, but for anyone who was there... One shell aimed into the central market place at midday. Seventy people killed. The carnage...'

'Yes of course, I remember. You mean, you saw that?'

'This is what I am saying.' The veins in his neck and in his forehead were bulging.

'That must have been terrible.' She knew the exact details of the massacre. The round had killed sixty-nine people and injured two hundred when it impacted on a plastic canopy just above the heads of hundreds of shoppers in the central market. More important to her was the date – Saturday February 5, 1994 – at least two months after Sammi Loz said he had been injured in another mortar attack and air-lifted out of Bosnia to Germany and then London. How could he have made such an elementary mistake?

She nodded as though it was all coming back to her. 'There was some suggestion that mortar came from the Muslim side to gain sympathy from the world.'

'No, no. I was there! I was standing just a few streets away. The Serbs fired it from the hills above.'

'But you can't tell where a mortar comes from,' she said. 'It's lobbed up in the air with very little noise.'

'Listen! What Muslim would do this to his own people? Tell me that.' He was shaking. 'I was there. I saw it. Men and women blown to pieces – decapitated. Arms, legs everywhere.'

'I'm sorry... but that was the rumour at the time. I think our people in Sarajevo even investigated it.' She wasn't going to pursue the point because she'd got exactly the information she wanted: Loz was still in Sarajevo in 1994. And that meant his entire account of the last decade had to be called into question.

She wrote an email to Teckman at Vauxhall Cross with a series of terse requests, pretty certain it would end up with Andy Dolph. There was no need to outline her theory to him – he would get it straight away from the drift of her questions – she just prayed that he'd have the resources to follow up the idea. She stayed on line but nothing came, so she hung up and put the phone away, realising as she unplugged the leads that she had failed to send the latest recording of her interview with Khan. She'd left the damned recorder in with Khan and Loz.

She went again to the room and sat down beside Khan. Loz's composure had returned, but he was evidently worried about Khan, whom he was attempting to feed with small pieces of bread and goat's cheese. There were plates of tahini and sliced fruit on the bed, untouched. Khan's head moved from side to side, avoiding the food as a child would do. He wasn't hungry, he said, and there were pains in his chest and stomach. Loz explained this was indigestion and that he must eat if he was to build up his strength. The tussle went on until at length Loz set down the plate and turned to a bottle of vitamins. As he did so, Herrick's hand slipped down to the leg of the chair where the recorder was. She glanced down and noticed the flashing light that indicated that the memory was full.

'Look,' she said with a certain amount of irritation. 'I think we're probably done for the day. We need to have a good session tomorrow though. I'm going to eat now.'

'Thank you for being so understanding,' said Loz softly, without looking up.

Khan nodded goodnight.

She found Foyzi by the oven with the old man. A pile of flat breads was fast accumulating in a palm-leaf basket balanced on top of the oven.

'I'll be eating with my men,' said Foyzi, gesturing into the dark. 'There's food for you on the table. I won't be far away.' He adjusted the strap of a machine pistol over his shoulder, picked up a box of provisions, put the bread on top, then padded off into the dark, followed by the old man who was wheeling a container of water on a little carriage.

Isis set a lamp on the table and remembered the whisky, still lodged behind a stone on the ground. There were also some cigarettes there. She bent down, took one from the pack, lit up and tipped the chair so that she could rest her head against the wall and look at the necklace of stars strung across the tops of the trees.

A few moments later Loz appeared. 'Can I join you? Karim's asleep.' His tone was ingratiating.

'Yes, do. He didn't seem too good to me.'

'It's to be expected. He has got a slight intestinal reaction to the antibiotics. We have to remember what he's been through. It's not just the torture, but months of not eating or sleeping properly. But he will recover.'

'Thanks to you.'

'No,' he said, sitting down opposite her and placing his hands on the table. 'This is all due to you, Isis. You saved him and we are indebted to you.'

'Where will you go after this?'

'I've been thinking about it,' he said, surveying the food on the table. 'I have contacts and some money in Switzerland. I shall probably take Karim there, and after that … well, we will have to see.'

Did he really believe they would let him slip away like that? 'I thought you would be tempted to disappear into South America for a year or two,' she said.

'I've never been, but I'm certain it wouldn't suit Khan.' He paused. 'And you?'

She pushed herself from the wall and stubbed out the cigarette on the ground. 'I'll go back to work in London.'

He massaged his neck and looked up at the sky. 'You know, in an odd way the time spent here has done me good. I may change my life after this.'

'You may be forced to,' she said sharply. 'The FBI want you in New York and they expect you to explain about the money you sent to Lebanon.'

'I don't think so,' he said simply.

'Will you continue with your practice?'

'Who knows what happens. Did you have any idea a week ago that you would be on an island in the middle of the Nile with us?' He paused for an answer but got none. 'I read an article in the newspaper a few weeks back about a man who was driving along a road near his home in Connecticut. He had been to the local stores; the weather was fine; there was no traffic on the roads. As he reached the driveway of his home, a tree that had stood for hundreds of years suddenly fell down on his car and set it alight. His family and neighbours were unable to rescue him, and watched as he burned to death. In the newspaper, there were expressions of puzzlement from his family. Why should this good man – a loved and loving man – be taken in the prime of his life? Why? Who was behind it?'

'Do you believe in God, Dr Loz?'

'Yes, naturally.'

'How do you explain the wisdom of dropping a tree on an innocent man?'

'I don't need to. That's not for me to understand.'

'But you must try to fit it into your system of belief?'

He shook his head. 'I don't. And you, Isis, do you believe?'

'Maybe, but I don't think God intervenes in human affairs.'

'Why?'

'Compare the intricacy and scale of the universe,' she looked up at the sky, 'with the mess and pain of human life. There's no one running this thing except us, and we should take responsibility for it. When we do, things will improve.'

'That's an atheist speaking.'

'No, a rationalist.'

'Surely you believe in fate – destiny?'

She picked up some bread. 'They're words used to explain chance, luck, accident and coincidence. I don't believe in a pre-ordained life. No.'

He began eating also, smiling as though in possession of superior knowledge. 'With your name, Isis, you could have guessed that you would eventually end up here. That's fate.'

'Actually, I wasn't named after the Egyptian goddess,' she said. 'My name comes from the end and beginning of my mother's first two names – Alazais Isobel.'

'From two beautiful names comes one beautiful name – like a child.'

'Right,' said Herrick.

'But seriously, here you are on an island in the Nile. Did you know that Isis's greatest temple is on the Nile, somewhere south of Luxor, and that she is associated with the river and the growing of corn?'

'Yes, I did,' she said without interest. 'How come you know so much about this?'

'I find Isis the most appealing of all the ancient deities because to begin with she used her magic to heal the sick. She brought her husband Osiris back to life, and nursed her son Horus. Also, she is made of contradictory passions: on the one hand she was ruthless and cunning; on the other, a loyal and devoted wife who went to the ends of the earth to find her husband's dead body. She is like all interesting people – a paradox. In her case, both deadly and caring.' With this he broke a piece of bread and scooped up some tahini.

'If anything, Dr Loz, the paradox is nearer to your character. I mean here you are healing your friend but in other lives you are, or have been, a soldier and fundraiser for a terrorist organisation. So perhaps the lesson is that we should never judge someone by one observation, but wait until the whole picture emerges from many observations, then decide which is the dominant trait.' She stopped. 'Would you like a drink?' she asked.

'I don't drink,' he said.

'Well, I'm going to have one.'

Loz wrinkled his nose.

'When I was at school,' she continued, 'I did read something about Isis, in particular about her relations with Ra, the sun god. Do you know about Ra, Sammi?'

He shook his head.

'Ra's might depended on his secret name, a name that only he knew. You see, the ancient Egyptians believed that if someone learned your secret name they gained power over you. Isis made a cobra from Ra's spittle, which had fallen to the ground on his journey across the sky. The cobra bit Ra and injected poison. Only when Ra told Isis his secret name did she agree to relieve his pain.'

'In other words, she tortured him. I told you she was ruthless.'

She smiled. 'I was wondering whether you had a secret name. Something that would give another person power over you if they knew it.'

'Why do you do this job? This spying.'

'It's very simple. I believe in the freedoms that we have in the West, and I am happy to work against those who want to destroy them.' She paused to sip the whisky she had mixed with a little mineral water. 'Also, I'm good at it,' she said, putting the glass down. 'Very good at it.'

His forehead puckered with disbelief. 'You want nothing else in your life?'

'You're making the assumption that I don't have anything else in my life.'

'You lack something,' he said, 'possibly love.'

'Oh, give me a break. Let me tell you I'm happy and utterly fulfilled in what I do.'

'No, I think not.'

'On what evidence?'

'Your body. The tension in your shoulders, the way you stand and move, the set of your mouth, the expression in your eyes. There are a hundred signs. You're a very attractive woman, but neither happy nor satisfied.'

'I guess that's the line you use on all the girls in New York,' she said.

'I'm serious,' he said. 'You should take more care of yourself, maybe visit an osteopath when you return to London.'

'There's nothing wrong with me.'

'Except your hip, which hurts when you get up in the morning, and your shoulders, which rise up during the day and cause you headaches, and perhaps a difficulty at night when you try to find a comfortable position for your neck on the pillow.' He sat back, satisfied. 'You could certainly use some help.'

She reached for a carrot and sliced it lengthways into strips.

'I would guess you've been very seriously ill at one time in your life. There seems to be some residue in your body of that sickness. When was that?'

'What is this – the osteopathic seduction?'

He shook his head. 'No, I am trained to observe people very closely. That's all. An artist's eyes do not stop noticing the shape of things or their colour when he leaves the studio. It's the same with me. When I saw you in Albania I noticed these things immediately.'

They sat in silence for a while, then she picked some fruit from the basket and got up from the bench. 'I have work to do now. I'll see you in the morning.'

CHAPTER TWENTY-THREE

Khan looked up into Loz's face when he returned from grinding the pills into a solution. He was glad Sammi had found something to ease the pain that was growing in his chest, to say nothing of the constant throb in his feet.

'No man has ever had a friend like you,' said Khan. 'I don't deserve you. I cannot believe my good fortune.'

'Don't tire yourself, old friend.'

'What's the matter with me, Sammi? Tell me. What is it? Why can't I keep my eyes open?'

'Because you have had years of ill treatment and hardship. You need rest. I will give you this shot, then you will feel much better tomorrow.'

'But you wanted to leave tonight.'

'That's okay. We can wait. The important thing is for you to get better. Then we'll talk about what we're going to do.'

While Loz wiped his arm and slapped it to bring up the vein, Khan's mind returned to the hillside in Macedonia and the wonder he'd experienced one morning as he watched the sun come over the hill and saw the light filtering through the trees. Now he could smell the dying embers of the fire, mingled with the rich, damp scents of the morning; taste the mint tea that the young Kurd had made him. The memory of those moments had been clouded by the terror that had followed less than half an hour later, but now he understood that the completeness he felt when walking down the track was something important. He should remember it.

'There was some kind of a bird there,' he said suddenly.

'A bird?' said Loz as he slipped the needle into Khan's vein. 'What kind of bird?'

'The smallest bird I have ever seen. It was almost round with a tail that stuck up. It had made its nest just where we camped. The fire was right below the vine where it lived … it stayed there all night and the next morning it was still there to feed its young.'

Loz smiled down to him. 'And you liked this bird, Karim?'

He nodded. 'Yes, it seemed very brave and determined.'

'Like you.'

'No, like you, Sammi. You never give in.'

Loz sat down on the stool. 'Now, sleep, old friend. We need you to be strong in the morning.'

Khan nodded. There was much he wanted to say. He opened his mouth but then he felt his eyes close and could not bring to mind the words he needed.

Sammi seemed to read his mind and said it for him. 'There was never true love like this before. Never between a man and a woman; never between two men.' He picked up Khan's hand and clasped it in his, then bent and kissed him on the forehead.

Khan smiled and opened his eyes. The smooth plane of Sammi's forehead was broken with a single crease of anxiety, and there were tears running down his face. 'Thank you,' said Khan, and closed his eyes to a multitude of fleeting images: his mother opening her arms to him on a shady terrace; the mountains of the East and the dancing, spirited eyes of the fighters. *His* men, the men who'd fought with him and shared the hardship. *His* men.

Herrick climbed to the turret with her computer, satellite phone and digital recorder, and sat on the warm tiles to concentrate on the recording she'd inadvertently made. The machine had gone for a full two and a half hours before switching itself off. That time included the forty minutes she had spent watching Loz treat Khan, then a period during which Khan had been left alone while she and Loz talked outside, and finally about forty-five minutes of them alone together. She went through the recording, stopping at random, but found little of interest, so she copied it into the computer, encrypted it, then dispatched it to Vauxhall Cross. She would listen to it later when she was in the bath.

She logged off from the secure server and dialled Dolph's numbers one after the other, each time getting a message service. She decided to try him again in a couple of hours and left the computer and satellite dish on the ledge surrounding the turret, knowing they would be just as safe there as in her room. Then she descended to the courtyard, where she smoked a cigarette and thought about her strategy for the following day.

From somewhere on the other side of the building came the faint sound of music – strings overlaid with the chant of a male singer. Occasionally she heard snatches of the same voice as the previous night. Foyzi had told her it was the CD player of one of his men, a Sufi addicted to his sect's music. She listened until it stopped and silence fell on the island. Above her, the stars had been partly obscured by clouds moving from the north, which explained why the evening was still so stifling. She rose and took a few paces towards her room, then stopped in her tracks as she caught the sound of a motor some way off to the south. Her ears strained to the night, but she couldn't tell if it was coming from the sky or the river. After a few seconds it died away completely. She listened for a further five minutes but heard nothing more and reached the conclusion that it must have been a boat.

Sleep was impossible because of the heat. Besides, she could not stop thinking about Loz and Khan. She gathered up her sponge-bag, a set of earphones and the digital recorder, and went with a lamp to the bath-house. It lay at the corner of the main building and was constructed from large granite blocks which even during the heat of the day retained a deathly chill. At the centre of the room was a square bath made out of porphyry, which in other circumstances might be mistaken for an ancient sarcophagus. She set down the lamp, but before plugging the waste pipe with a rag, she had to remove the insects and lizards that had accumulated in the bath, and kill a scorpion that scuttled into the light on the floor.

The water had a slight metallic odour, but she let herself down into it gratefully and found that she could lie almost fully stretched out. As the water rose, she noticed the light catch pieces of feldspar in the granite. She washed, then made a pillow for her head out of part of her robe and shifted the lamp so she could see the machine's display.

Having forwarded the recording to the seventy-five-minute mark, she began to listen again.

There was nothing for the first fifteen minutes, apart from the even noise of Khan's breathing. Then she heard Loz come into the room. This must have been after he had lost his temper with her under the trees. Khan seemed to pick up on his mood and weakly asked what the matter was. No reply came, but then Loz moved close to him and began to whisper.

'We have to leave, Karim.'

Khan replied, 'Why?'

'Because we have to. This girl is not so stupid.'

Silence followed. Then Karim said, 'You go without me. I'll be all right here... Does she know?'

'Know what?' His voice was far sharper than usual.

'That you were...'

'No... But now you are rested we must leave.'

'I cannot.'

'You must. We need to get away from here. It is too dangerous for us to remain. I have some help. You will be well cared for. A night's rest and you'll be fine, old friend.'

Both voices faded at that moment and for several minutes she listened to the muttering she had heard when she first sped through the tape before sending it to Vauxhall Cross. Then something suddenly occurred to her and she switched the machine off and sat up in the bath. 'Jesus wept, I'm an idiot,' she said aloud. She lay back again, this time not into the bunched material of her robe but into two hands which caught her head and then slipped to her neck. She looked up to see Loz.

'I don't think you're an idiot,' he said, relaxing his grip but not letting go.

'What the hell are you doing in here?' she demanded. 'Get the hell out.'

He drew back and studied her without saying anything.

'Get out!' she shouted.

'I have seldom seen such beauty in a woman – particularly in one who does not know it.' He moved from behind her, one hand still holding her neck so that it pressed against the side of the bath.

She struggled a little, but the pressure of his hand increased. 'Get out now.'

'But we need to talk. I wanted to thank you for what you have done for us.'

She covered herself with her hands as best she could.

'Don't do that,' he said playfully. 'If you could see yourself, you'd understand why I am lost for words.'

'But you're not lost for words.'

There was something different about his expression. The easy charm was there, but also an odd, embarrassed savagery. His face was streaked with sweat.

'I'm warning you. Please leave now.'

Loz pulled the robe from the end of the bath and felt the material. 'Ah yes, I thought you had something in here.' He pulled out and examined the pistol, then let go of her neck and drew back. 'I mean it, Isis, I'm awed by the sight of you. The way the light surrounds your body, yet does not reveal you completely.' He paused to contemplate her further. 'They say that each woman experiences a perfect twenty minutes during her lifetime when everything – her skin, hair, body, the expression in her eyes – is perfect. Have you heard of this?'

She said nothing.

'I believe I am witnessing that moment in your existence. You're truly radiant. I am overwhelmed.'

Herrick took stock. There was absolutely nothing she could do. The question was, what did he plan?

He smiled and moved to sit on the side of the bath. 'In my culture the use of water – the preparation and purification of the woman's body – is part of the act of love. Properly, there should be no division between the two.'

'In my culture you are committing a crime and behaving like an arsehole.'

'I mean you no harm. I took this away from you so that you didn't shoot me as we talked. That's all.' He pulled up his sleeve and slid his hand into the water, then ran it up and down the inside of her calf, stroking her other leg with the backs of his fingers. 'What were you listening to when I came in? Can I hear it too?'

'Please stop doing that.'

'What were you listening to?'

'One of the recordings I made of our conversations. You were there.'

'There's nothing to hear. We have done nothing. We are what we seem.'

'In which case you don't have anything to worry about. Would you please stop touching me?' She lifted his hand out of the water and placed it on the side of the bath. He dried it on his sleeve, then touched her face.

'Another place and another time, Isis, and we…'

'Give me my towel and my clothes, then leave!'

'We haven't had our talk,' he protested. His hand went to her face and played on her forehead and cheek, then slipped round to her neck. 'You know, this would be as great a pleasure for you as it would be for me.' His finger traced a line round the depression at the base of her throat. 'I could do so much for you.' He paused. 'After all, we may never see each other again and I for one would regret that we did not take the opportunity that has been given to us here.'

Herrick shifted her position in the bath and tried to read his expression in the light of the lamp. 'Look,' she said, her tone softening. 'You *are* an attractive man. Anyone can see that. And yes, in other circumstances I might be tempted. Even now I find myself drawn to you. But threatening me is no way to seduce me, and you *are* threatening me.'

'I am not,' he said with a note of injury.

'But you must see that to walk in here, take my gun and then use your advantage to touch me is very threatening behaviour.' She paused. 'Now, I am going to get out of this bath and I want you to hand me my clothes.' With this she stood up and faced him, without bothering to hide herself. He picked up the lamp and stood.

'Really, you're quite beautiful.'

'My towel,' she said, putting out her hand.

He did not move.

She lifted her foot to the flat rim of the bath.

'Stay,' he said. 'Stay there. I want to look.'

'For God's sake, give me my towel!'

Instead he reached out and touched her right breast, then moved to her left side. They looked at each other for a few seconds. She shook her head and removed his hand. 'No.'

'Let's start this scene again,' he said with a sudden boyish enthusiasm. 'Believe me, it will be worth it. This is how we will do it. I will come in again and you will be dressed, and then we will take our ease together. You can drink a little of the whisky – but not too much – and we will talk.'

'Yes,' she said. 'But you will have to stop pointing that gun at me.' She stepped onto the damp floor and made for the towel herself, feeling ridiculous and very angry. As she bent down he seized her and held her in both arms so that the gun reached round to the back of her head. Then he placed his lips on her mouth and kissed her with incongruous tenderness. She did not return his kiss but pulled her head away and looked into his eyes.

'You're not going to do this. It's against everything you stand for. You render yourself a criminal in the eyes of God and a pathetic creep by the standards of the American society you profess to love.'

'No,' he said, in a tone that seemed to mock her unreasonable behaviour. 'This is what we both want. You do not understand yourself, Isis. I know this.' He bent down and kissed the top of her breast then moved to her neck with his lips. But he did not relax his grip on the gun.

'Stop,' she said, as his free hand began to explore her behind and the top of her leg. 'Why don't we talk for a while? That's what you said you wanted to do.' She shivered suddenly, knowing she would now have to scream or attempt to beat him off.

'Sure. Why not? We will talk. There's no hurry.'

'Then let me get my clothes,' she said. Without waiting for an answer she picked up the robe and put it on. Then she reached for the recorder, unplugged the earphones, and placed it in her pocket.

'What do you want to talk about?' he said indulgently.

'It was you who came to speak with me,' she said, 'but since you ask, I would like to talk more about your past.'

'You never give up,' he said.

She began to make for the door. 'Let's go and have that drink.'

'No,' he said sharply, then modified his tone. 'It's good in here. More romantic, don't you think?'

She turned. 'You said you wanted to thank me. That is exactly what you should be doing, instead of threatening me. You owe me. Without me, Karim would never have been freed. And now… well, this is a very strange way to show your gratitude.'

Loz thought about this. 'I am grateful to you. But you were doing it for your own ends as well. You wanted to know about Karim, just like the others did.'

'With good reason,' she said. 'We're fighting a war and Khan made some connections we're interested in.'

'Is this the way to fight your so-called war against terror? With torture, holding people without trial or legal representation, bombing innocent civilians? You know those people being held by the Americans? Nobody even knows their names.'

She shook her head. 'You know what I think about torture and that goes for the whole of the British government and scores of other countries in the West. Whatever the deficiencies of the war against al-Qaeda, it must be obvious that we did not start this thing.'

'But you did. Don't you see that?' Again the sudden flash of temper. 'Look at the conditions of the Middle East, the people in Palestine. Look at the poverty here in Egypt. Look at Africa. These people are suffering because of the West's greed and selfishness. No one can argue against this truth.'

'Look,' she replied quite calmly, 'we all understand that the West must help less wealthy nations and that we all have to do something about the social problems, but let me just remind you that in Arab countries torture is routine. Remember why the CIA brought Khan here – because he was being strung up to the roof of a prison cell by an Arab government. So don't give me a lot of bullshit about the mistreatment of suspects in the West. Torture and imprisonment without trial is the norm in your world.'

'You do not understand! You have not seen how our people suffered in Bosnia, in Palestine. Everywhere. That's what we are fighting for.'

'Fighting for, Dr Loz? Who are you fighting for? You're a US citizen and you enjoy all the delights and riches of the West, yet you say you're fighting. For whom? Against what?'

'No … I mean, the Arab peoples. This is what *they* are fighting for. They struggle for… justice.'

She exhaled heavily, realising that he was on the point of making an admission, and once he had there would be no turning back. He would have to kill her. At the moment there was still a residue of the urbane Manhattan doctor, the pretence of reason and consensus, but it had slipped twice already that day and she was certain he would not leave that room without getting what he wanted. 'Let's go and sit down outside,' she said quietly.

He shook his head.

'Look, it's you who needs to relax. You've barely had any sleep in the last three days.'

'I am fine,' he said. 'We will stay here.'

'Then let me get a cigarette.'

'No.' He raised the gun. 'Sit there.'

She wiped the edge of the bath with her towel and sat down.

'Let's not pretend any more,' she said. 'We're on different sides. You know what I do and I now have a pretty good idea of what you are. For example, I guessed you were injured in Afghanistan, not Bosnia, and that Karim Khan saved you there and took you to Pakistan to be treated. All along you have been worried not about Karim – poor, misguided Karim – but about what he might reveal. You knew you couldn't rely on him because, let's face it, he's really quite naïve, and the only reason he didn't tell them about you was because his interrogators didn't know precisely what questions to ask. Until you got the first postcard, you believed that the only man who could harm you was safely tucked away in Afghanistan, maybe even dead. Then the card came and you realised he was on the loose and – more dangerous to you and your organisation – untraceable in the shifting population of migrant workers coming from the East.'

Loz's eyes were utterly expressionless. 'Go on,' he said.

'Well, it's pretty simple really. The picture you had of Khan wasn't given to you by a homeless man in New York. You brought it back with you from Afghanistan. For some reason I recall that in 1998 all photography was banned by the Taleban except for official purposes. The portrait of Khan looks very much like the ones from the Taleban's records recently handed over by the Northern Alliance. So my guess is that you were in Afghanistan in 1998 or 1999 for a period of training and planning. And you managed to get a copy of one of those pictures. You were there. I'm right, aren't I?'

'You're forgetting that I'm a Shi'ite.' He said evenly. 'The people in Afghanistan were all Sunni Muslims, like Karim.'

'That's a detail. The point about your war is that it's not really about religious practice, despite all that bullshit about jihad; it's about the inequalities between the West and Islam. That's what you're fighting against, although the foot soldiers like Khan really have no notion of this. You don't believe it's a religious war any more than I do. It's about economics.'

'You're wrong,' he said.

'But look at your life in New York – the material wealth, the women, the fornication. What does the Koran say? "Approach not fornication; surely it is an indecency and evil as a way." But that is your way. Or is this just the sacrifice you've made to create a convincing cover? I think not. I think you genuinely bought all that stuff and you're such a fucking freak that you manage somehow to reconcile it with your other lives.'

He shrugged good-naturedly. 'You think I am a split personality, Isis.'

'Nothing so simple. You have compartments with communicating doors. Each side is conscious of the other and fully aware of what it is doing, but you can close the doors.'

'Maybe you see into me a little.'

'And The Poet?' she said rhetorically. 'The Poet doesn't exist, not in any relevant way today. But I do believe there's another man you have been protecting, an individual whom Khan knows but doesn't, *or didn't*, see the importance of. He gets it now because you have been schooling the answers he gives me.'

He shook his head. 'You won't be asking Karim any questions now.' He looked down. 'But since you have chosen to press the issue, which is certainly an unwise course for you, I can tell you that The Poet exists – it was the name we used in Bosnia when this individual, as you call him, refused to tell us his real name. This lasted a matter of days and when we learnt his real name we stopped calling him The Poet.'

'And this man is running your organisation – another Shi'ite perhaps?'

'I cannot answer you.'

'From Lebanon?'

He grinned. 'I can't tell you these things, Isis.'

'But you can. What good is it to me now? I know what you intend here. What is his name?'

He thought for a moment and smiled to himself. 'His name is John.'

'John?'

'Yes, John.' He laughed. 'Now, we do have some unfinished…' He looked down. A small green frog had hopped into a pool of light on the floor and remained there, blinking. This was the moment she had been readying herself for. She launched herself from the edge of the bath towards his stomach, but he had anticipated the move. He stepped out of the way, caught one of her arms and pulled her round like a rock'n'roll dancer into his chest. Then he lifted her with a strength that took her by surprise and placed her on the side of the bath, forcing her legs apart.

'No! Not like this,' she shouted out.

He stopped and held her by the shoulders. The gun was pointed at her right temple. 'Then you will behave.'

She shook her head, thinking only of how she could wrest the gun from him.

Then he did something odd. He stroked her face, brushing his hand across her lips and eyebrows. He considered her once more. 'You are a real beauty, Isis. You have a secret beauty. That's it – a secret beauty.' He pressed his mouth to hers hungrily and moved between her legs. 'You understand,' he said under his breath. 'I didn't want it this way. I wanted us to make love like equals.'

The gun had slipped down and now she was sure it must be pointing at the wall behind her. She put her arms around his neck. As she did so a triumphant smile flickered at the corners of his mouth and he kissed her neck.

'Tell me you want me,' he said.

'I want you,' she replied.

He was touching her breasts. She now felt such loathing for him that she was prepared to risk anything to stop him. The only way that presented itself to her was to use the purchase she now had on his shoulders to headbutt him. But she was slightly above him, and any blow would only connect with the top of his head. She had to get him to look up to her. 'I want you,' she said, smiling with as much acquiescence as she could muster and drawing back as though to see him clearly.

'I knew you desired me all along,' he said.

Then she hit him, not with her head, but with a chop of her hand at the carotid artery. He fell back but still managed to hold onto her with his left arm. And then she felt the incredible, athletic energy of him as he spun her round so that she was facing the bath, and forced her head down to within a few inches of the water. He was cursing, pulling her robe up and working her legs apart.

It was then that the first explosion occurred.

Herrick was thrown upwards and flipped over like a leaf so that she landed half in the bath, her body bent backwards. The blast seemed to have caused the room first to depressurise and then fill with a second deafening thunderclap. She knew nothing for several seconds, but then recovered enough to tell herself that she was still alive. She rolled into the bath and covered her head with her hands, concerning herself only with the masonry and timber falling from the roof. She had heard a cry from Loz at the moment of the explosion, but that was all.

A few seconds later there was another, equally demonic explosion, but this time another part of the area was hit and she was able to better comprehend what was happening. There were three distinct stages after the initial impact: a huge reverberation that must have been heard twenty miles away, a whoosh of air, and a short time afterwards, sounds of collapse and pulverisation.

She waited for a third blast, now convinced that the island was under bombardment from the bank of the river. But nothing came, and the only noise she could hear was a fire taking hold somewhere across the courtyard. She began to push upwards against a mass of debris that was trapping her in the bath. It was no good. For minutes on end she grappled with a beam and what seemed to be a large chunk of plaster attached to some stone, which lay across the top of the bath and gave her room to manoeuvre. All the time she could smell the fire taking hold. She lay back in the water, deciding that her best chance was to work at an opening she had found with her foot near the tap.

This required her to bunch her legs to her chest and force herself forward in a somersault. It took many contortions and compressions of her frame before she managed it and then she was so out of breath that it was several minutes before she began working to enlarge the hole. At length she thrust her head and right shoulder through it and was able to start shifting larger pieces of stone and wood. A few minutes more and she was free, scrambling through the roof of the bath-house to see the damage in the light of two fires.

The first explosion had occurred in the rotunda and completely obliterated the structure, together with the stairway and the rooms either side. The second had hit the buildings on the far side of the courtyard. Where Harland and she had sat talking the first night, there was now a crater measuring thirty feet across. The wooden terrace and building had been atomised. She clambered down, cutting her foot on a piece of metal, and reached the ground. Two figures were running towards her from the north end of the island shouting her name. She sank to the ground, and before she knew what had happened, she was looking up into the anxious faces of Philip Sarre and Joe Lapping.

'Are you all right?' said Sarre.

'Yes… I think so. Where the fuck … did you?' she stopped, spat the dust from her mouth and wiped the blood and sweat from her face. Her eyes and hair were caked in a kind of clay. 'Where did you two come from?'

'We were over there,' said Lapping pointing to the east bank.

'Since yesterday. We were told to keep our heads down while you were getting so much from Sammi Loz.'

'But what the hell happened?'

Sarre shook his head. 'Joe'll explain – where are Loz and Khan?'

She pointed to the bath-house. 'Loz was in there with me. He must be dead. Khan might be alive. He's over there in the part that wasn't hit. I don't understand,' she stammered. 'What happened?'

'We think it was friendly fire,' said Lapping. 'It looks very much as though you were hit by a couple of Hellfire missiles delivered by a Predator. We heard it earlier and were halfway across the river when we saw the first strike.'

They heard Sarre shouting.

265

'Right, you stay here, old girl,' said Lapping. 'I'm just going to see what he wants. Be back in a tick.'

She looked up. Between the gaps in the smoke the cloud was beginning to clear, and one or two stars were showing again.

PART THREE

CHAPTER TWENTY-FOUR

As Harland moved towards Immigration at Beirut, acutely conscious that he would benefit from a shave, haircut and a new set of clothes, he noticed a group of three men standing a little way off from the visa counter. One nudged the other two to look in his direction.

Instead of making for the counter, he arrived in front of them and dropped his bag. 'Hello there,' he said pleasantly. 'Tell me, are you Syrian or Lebanese intelligence?'

The men shifted and pretended not to understand.

'I was hoping one of you could give me a ride into town.' He searched their faces expectantly. 'No takers? Oh well. Just in case you're wondering, I'm with the United Nations. Robert Harland, Special Adviser to Secretary-General Benjamin Jaidi.' He opened his passport and offered it to them. They looked the other way and began to walk off, one flicking worry beads, the other two finding the need to consult their cell phones.

He moved to the kiosk to pay his twenty-five dollars for the visa, then to the counter where his passport received a little stamp showing a sailing barque. Finally he passed through Immigration and Customs and made for the taxi rank, where a shabby Mercedes waited in the warm summer night.

Both Benjamin Jaidi and Sir Robin Teckman had told him to go to Beirut and, most importantly, it was the only place Eva Rath would agree to meet him when he phoned the number Teckman had given him. The reaction of his vanished partner had been surprising: she offered neither an expression of astonishment about his finding her, nor remorse for her disappearance, but simply forbade him to visit the apartment block in Shabazi Street, Tel Aviv, where she now lived with her mother. She had told him that Hanna Rath was now in her last weeks and she would not stand for Harland disturbing her peaceful end.

As the Mercedes bumped through the vast new developments in the central district that had risen on the ruins of Beirut's civil war, Harland found he was curiously at ease with the situation. The pain of her rejection of him had in the last week or so miraculously ebbed away. He was now concerned only with getting answers about her behaviour. Of course he now understood she must have left to look after her mother, who as one of the few Jewish survivors of the Holocaust in the Czech Republic, had presumably gone to Israel to die. But there were other aspects of Eva's departure which Teckman had told him about. SIS was certain that she was working for Mossad in a capacity requiring her to move between London, New York and Tel Aviv, possibly as a courier. Having been trained by StB, the security services in communist Czechoslovakia, then by the KGB spy school, Eva would have interested Mossad high command. Harland imagined she must have done a deal that allowed her mother to live the remainder of her days in Tel Aviv with medical assistance, in exchange for Eva's talents as a spy. It was unsurprising to him. If he'd been asked to describe the unseen parts of his lover, the first would be her need to deceive, the second was her habit of placing herself beyond control by vanishing, and the third was the unbreakable bond with her mother, Hanna. These were to a very large degree the drives of Eva Rath, although the things that had attracted him when he was barely twenty were her nimble intelligence and startling, intimate beauty.

Why hadn't she told him? Why not explain? She could never reasonably have doubted his devotion to her. It had spanned nearly three decades and, even in the long period when their son Tomas was growing up and he had no idea of his existence or where she was, he had still nursed his love for her.

But now, as he thought of her, he felt strangely unburdened. He was amused by things, which quite apart from anything else accounted for his twitting the graveyard shift of intelligence officers at the airport, usually an unwise move.

He arrived at the Playlands Hotel – specified by Eva and suggested by Teckman – and checked in. There were no messages for him and he tramped off to his bedroom in the southern wing of the hotel where he poured two miniatures from the fridge into a glass and took it into the shower. Fifteen minutes later he was standing on the balcony letting his hair dry in the sea breeze, when there was a knock at the door. He opened it to Eva, who stood in the corridor with a tight, drained smile. He instinctively bent down, took her by the shoulders and let his lips skate across each of her cheeks.

'You'd better come in,' he said.

She circled a finger in the air, which he took to mean that the room was probably bugged, and they walked through to the balcony.

'Where the hell did you go?' he said, unable to hide the anger of fifteen months. This was not how he'd planned it.

'Bobby, don't start…'

'Don't start! I thought you were dead. I searched everywhere. You just walked out with no explanation, no idea of the hurt you caused me or the effort I would put into finding you.'

'I knew you would eventually.'

'I didn't – Teckman did. You remember him?'

'Of course. I worked for them, like you, Bobby.'

He shook his head, wondering at his own earlier nonchalance about seeing her.

'Then why not tell me in the first place? You only had to explain about your mother. I'd have understood.' He examined her in the light from the illuminated swimming pool beneath them. Her hair was much shorter and as yet unflecked with grey. She was using less make-up than before and had put on a pound or two that showed in her cheeks. If anything, it made her look younger. 'You look good,' he said quietly. 'Really, a lot better than you did in New York.' He stopped, studied her, then exploded. 'Jesus … are you incapable of understanding what I felt for you?'

'And you?' she asked, calmly turning towards the sea. 'Did it occur to you to ask what *I* was going through in New York?'

'But I did. I tried to talk about Tomas with you. You said so little that I thought you… Look, I tried. You know that.'

'I knew no one. Only you. You were the one person who knew what I had been through. I had no other witness to my life in New York. Do you understand what I mean? No one who knew that I'd lost Tomas and what that meant to me.' She stopped. 'It was never going to work, Bobby. Never. We… our love…'

'Was overwhelmed by circumstances,' he said.

She grimaced. 'Yes, if you want to put it that way. But it was also destroyed by you, Bobby. You didn't know *how* to talk to me. Maybe that's because there was an inequality between us. I *lost* my son; you hardly knew yours. He was an acquaintance for a few weeks. That's all.' Her jaw clamped shut and her eyes welled with tears.

He touched her on the shoulder. 'It's okay,' he said.

'No it isn't!' she hissed, recoiling from him. 'That's the point. It's not okay. I'm not English. I have to be able to talk about this and be with someone who understands what his death means to me now – today. It doesn't go, you know. It doesn't just end like that.'

'I'm sorry,' he said, moved by the pain flaring in her eyes. 'I admit this is a failing of mine, but I wasn't responsible for his death. I did everything to try to save him.' He paused. 'And you know if you and your mother had not been so close to Viktor Lipnik, Tomas would never have seen the things he did in Bosnia. He wouldn't have been a danger to Lipnik. It was Viktor Lipnik – your lover – not I, who killed Tomas…'

'Don't!' she said. A passionate hatred passed across her face. Without looking down, she felt for the arm of the metal chair and sat at the table.

'I'd like some vodka if you have some.' This was unlike her. He had only ever seen her drink wine. He went to the minibar, resolving to be calm.

When he returned with the drinks, he laid his hand on the table near hers. 'Eva, I'd have done anything to keep you with me. Anything. You knew how much I loved you. You should have helped me, shown me how to talk and listen to you.'

'You can't tell a man this. Either he knows or he doesn't know. You don't, Bobby. That's why I stopped loving you.' She paused to consider this. 'No, that's not true. I didn't stop loving you. There are many parts of you that are wonderful; it was just that my love for you was not deep enough to tolerate the way you were ignoring me.'

The self-evident truth of this stung Harland. That was exactly why she had left. She hadn't told him because she had been hurt and resented him.

'Christ, I'm sorry,' he said. 'Really, I don't know how to make it—'

'It's no use. You are what you are. I know why you're like this. You went through a lot when you were tortured, and with your cancer. That's why you're so bad at talking. You should have seen someone at the time. It's gone so deep.'

'I did. But that wasn't the reason I was so bad with you. I didn't know what to say. You erected a pretty impenetrable wall. You know that.'

'Yes,' she said, her head nodding in agreement. 'I know.'

They drank in silence, then he asked about her mother.

'She has cancer. It moves very slowly, but each day she is reduced in some way. The doctors are very good and we have two nurses who stay at the apartment, so I can leave when it's necessary. They have been good to…' She stopped when her voice cracked.

'It's very distressing – your only living relative.'

'I find that the strangest part,' she said, moving her head from side to side so that the sea breeze reached her neck.

Harland nodded. 'Well, you have my sympathy. I do understand what she means to you.'

She nodded thanks, lit a cigarette and looked at him more softly. 'Why are you in the Middle East?'

'Trying to hook up with Jaidi. They were due here yesterday but they aren't leaving Damascus until tomorrow.'

'Teckman called me before you. Did you know that?'

'So you wouldn't be caught on the hop,' he said. 'That was the right thing to do.'

'But this is not the first time you've been in the Middle East this year, is it? We heard that the UN talked to Hamas three months ago. Was that you?'

He shrugged. 'If I was talking to Hamas, I couldn't tell you about it, Eva.'

'I didn't say *talking* – present tense. I said *talked*.'

'My answer is the same.'

'I'll take it as a yes then.'

After that exchange he couldn't help but press her. 'They picked you up at Heathrow and followed you to the safe house in Kensington on the day Norquist was killed. They went over the security film for the day and found you.'

She didn't react to this but said, 'Look, if we're going to have this conversation, we should go down to the pool or the beach.'

They went down one floor, slipped through the fire exit and walked towards the beach where they removed their shoes and made for a line of parasols.

'You were waiting in line with Vice-Admiral Norquist at Immigration,' he started. 'He became suspicious after you dropped your stuff a couple of times. He knew you were trying to strike up a conversation with him and told our people to follow you.'

'Is that so?' she said indifferently.

'They realised your flight arrived several hours before his and that you only went to the Immigration desk when his flight from Reykjavik was disembarking. You were timing it. Were you going to trail him to the hotel? Pick him up ... that kind of thing?' No answer came. 'I guess Norquist was a big prize for you. To know what he was saying to the British government?'

'Teckman told you all this,' she said huskily and then cleared her throat. 'Are you still working for British Intelligence, Bobby?'

'Nope,' he said.

'They don't just give out information like that. What did you do for them?'

They were fencing again. He wondered how much this game had been part of their attraction. 'They owed me,' he said. 'They wanted me to keep an eye on someone and I did. In exchange I got your number.' He thought for a moment and decided to take a chance. 'A lot else went on at Heathrow that day.'

Her expression became animated.

'A dozen or more terrorist suspects passed through Terminal Three and exchanged identities at precisely the moment you arrived.'

She said nothing.

'What were you doing there?' he asked.

'It's complicated.'

'Surely you can answer that. It doesn't affect you or your security. Also it's important. There has to be a connection between the arrival of Norquist at Heathrow and the identity switch of the terrorists. The current theory is that the Norquist killing was a diversion.'

'See! You're talking like you're still working for SIS.'

'That's because I can't avoid the conclusion that your movements that day could provide a clue. If you knew of Norquist's arrangements, it follows someone else could.'

She looked out into the dark towards the waterline, where the waves caught the light as they reared before breaking on the sand. 'Tell me more about the switch,' she said.

'No, you tell me something, Eva.'

'My name is Irina. It always has been.'

'You were Eva when I fell in love with you in Rome. You were Eva in New York.'

'But I *am* Irina,' she said with quiet defiance. 'That is my name, Bobby.'

'Look at us! We're still at it. Fencing with each other over some bloody secret. Why? Why're we still doing it?'

'Because that's our work. That's what we're good at.'

'Look, if there's anything you can tell me, please do. I'm instructed to tell you that you'll receive no hassle when you pass through London again on your regular trips. Everything will remain as it is.'

'There won't be any more.' The breeze lifted her hair at the front and for a moment he saw Tomas, standing in the cold outside his apartment in Brooklyn on that first night when he learned that he had a son.

He shook himself. 'How did you know when to follow Norquist?'

She said nothing.

'We know you were booked into the St James's Hotel, as Norquist was. We don't understand why you went to the safe house first, but we assume you were going to make your way to the hotel later, maybe make a pass at him?'

She shook her head despairingly.

'Well… what *was* the plan then? You do realise that SIS can blow your cover and render you useless to Mossad?'

'I need the money. I need their help in Tel Aviv. Don't threaten me. After all you have done… don't threaten me.'

'How did you know when to fly?' He demanded. 'Norquist's schedule was secret.'

She put her hand to her cheek. 'It was easy. Norquist started life as a naval helicopter pilot in Vietnam. His aircraft was hit and he crushed several vertebrae when it crash-landed. Every time Norquist was planning a long flight somewhere, he got treatment for his back problem in New York.'

Harland stiffened but said nothing about Sammi Loz. 'And?'

'We are interested in the man who treated him. It seems their relationship went beyond the normal doctor–patient thing. They did business together. That's all I can say without jeopardising my position. Please think of me and my mother.'

'What kind of business?'

'Some deals.'

'What deals? Stocks, restaurants, futures, real estate? What?'

She looked at him quizzically, then said, 'Real estate?'

'Why would you be interested in this?'

'Come on, you can't ask me that. Please.'

'Yes, I see.' He paused, several calculations going on in his mind at once. 'Information on high-ranking American officials is very useful to the Israeli government, but only if there is some impropriety that can be used against them, or even better, used to influence American policy in Israel's favour. So you were seeking evidence of this nature. But why in London?'

She shook her head. 'I can't tell you.'

Harland slapped his knee. 'Ah, I get it. You already had the evidence you needed and this meeting was part of a regular arrangement. He was working for you already. Was he telling you about American intelligence policy?'

She uncrossed her legs, leaned forward in the wicker chair and looked him in the eyes.

That was all he needed. 'Thank you.' He thought for a moment. 'We both know we're talking about the osteopath.'

Her gaze held his eyes.

'So let me suggest this. Not only was Norquist telling you about US intelligence planning, he was also keeping you informed about Sammi Loz, specifically the transactions in New York that enabled you to work out the money flow to Hizbollah. But of course it wasn't easy for Mossad to see Norquist, so your people had to fit into his arrangements. You never contacted him by phone or email; instead you popped up at some moment during his travels, to receive information and give instructions. Each time a different person would make contact, so Norquist's security wouldn't be suspicious. That explains why he didn't know who you were at Heathrow.'

She nodded, but by the way she looked at him he knew there was something more.

'What is it? What else?'

Again she shook her head. She was prepared to give a mute confirmation, but only if he reached the right solution without her aid.

'So let's think about this,' he said, wishing he had brought a couple of miniatures down to the beach. 'There was something unusual about the message you were going to give him that day. That would explain why you followed him from New York and waited before passing through Immigration with him. If it had been routine you would simply have bided your time until you saw him at the St James's Hotel. What was it? Did you have knowledge of the hit? Were you trying to warn him?'

Her eyes pulsed and he knew he was right. He was also momentarily aware that his attraction for her still moved deep in him. 'Does that mean you knew about the switch that was going on in Terminal Three?'

'No, we didn't. You have to tell me about that.'

He then proceeded to give her everything he had learned from Isis Herrick, aware that this was specifically against the instructions of Sir Robin Teckman. But he had no illusions that he was still being used by Teckman, and reasoned that he could consult his own judgement about what to tell her. She listened intently, memorising the salient details, logging and filing them away to be recalled in a matter of hours for the benefit of her controllers in Tel Aviv. After he finished, she asked him a series of penetrating questions about the tracking of the suspects, not all of which he could answer, but she nevertheless soon grasped the significance of the exclusive Anglo-American arrangements.

'Why is this? Why don't they use the other services in Europe?'

'Because they don't trust them.'

'But that is wrong. Only a few months ago the French told the British of some Algerian suspects. We help all the European agencies on Islamist terror cells, sharing information about the movements and backgrounds of suspects. This is the only way.'

'I'm sure there are many who agree with you, but I didn't design the policy.' He stopped and looked at her again. 'Has it occurred to you that this is the level we work best at – when we're discussing some fucking intelligence problem?'

'Yes,' she said, as though this had long been evident to her.

'Well,' he said with a bleak smile, 'let's think about the connection between Sammi Loz and the switch at Heathrow. How much notice did you have of Norquist travelling?'

'Eighteen hours.'

'And how did you know where he was going?'

'Other intelligence,' she said.

'Oh come on, Eva. What other intelligence?'

'I cannot say. Operational security.'

'Okay, okay,' he said, raising his hands in surrender. 'So when did you hear there was a threat to his life?'

'Just before I got on the plane at JFK. Our people had been monitoring a website. There was nothing definite, but we thought that Norquist was the likely target, and I was told to get to him as soon as possible at Heathrow and warn him.'

'Your service was ahead of everyone else on this. As far as I can gather, the British had very little notice of the threat.'

She shrugged.

'Right, so you did get to him at Heathrow. Did you warn him?'

'I was about to, but then I saw armed police waiting and I knew they must be there to protect him, so I thought it would be better to wait and talk to him about the other things later. I thought he was safe.'

'Is it the assumption of your service that Sammi Loz tipped off the would-be killers about Norquist's plans?'

'Yes.'

'Because?'

'We believed Loz knew or guessed that Norquist had been talking to us and had betrayed details of his dealings. Norquist was disposable.'

'I see. But if there's a connection between the switch and Norquist's death – and we should remember that was probably caused by a stray British bullet – it means that Loz must have had notice of Norquist's plans far in advance of you. A dozen or more men had to get tickets and time their arrival at Heathrow. That would need several days' preparation. As soon as the operation had begun and all these suspects were in the air bound for London, someone leaked the fact that an American diplomat was about to be topped at Heathrow, on a website they knew was being monitored. Diversion strategy in place.'

'And because his plane was late, it worked even better than they had planned,' she said.

Harland leaned back in his chair and put his hands behind his head. 'That means Sammi Loz is the planner, or at least one of the planners. It's odd that Teckman hadn't sussed all this by now.'

'He couldn't, because he didn't know of the corrupt relationship between Admiral Norquist and Sammi Loz. Only we knew this.'

'Right, but he suspected something, because he asked me to watch Loz.' He paused. 'That's who I have been with.'

'With Loz!' She was shocked. 'Our people are looking for him all over. Where is he? You must tell me.'

'I can't.'

'You have to.'

'I can't, because you will wade in and others may be killed.'

'But he's in British hands?'

'Sort of.'

'I will have to tell my people that immediately. For God's sake, why didn't you say this before?'

'Operational security,' he said, grinning.

'Bullshit.'

'I needn't have told you at all, Eva.'

'But don't you see, we are working on this together now. There are things that only we can put together.'

'Naturally that idea pleases me, but forgive me if I have a jaundiced view of your motives, Eva. I know where your loyalties lie – with your mother and Mossad. I come pretty well down the list after those two.'

She lit a cigarette and blew a stream of smoke. 'I can't deny you're right. But this isn't a question of loyalty. This is about collaboration for a mutual benefit.'

'That sounds like a phrase from the communist era. Anyway, I'm out of this. I will tell Teckman what I've learned from you, but then I'm going to join the Secretary-General and go back to my work.'

'Talking to Hamas?'

'No, acting as a special adviser to Jaidi.'

'Who is another patient of Dr Loz's,' she said tartly. 'Does he receive home visits like Norquist did?'

'You *are* well informed,' said Harland. Then he told her about his own back problem and Sammi Loz's skills, neither of which seemed to interest her much.

'Will he be tried in Britain?' she asked suddenly.

'Probably.'

'But there is information that he has been arrested. Do the Americans know? They are looking for him too.'

'That's a rather sensitive point. I don't think anyone knows we've got him.'

She looked puzzled. 'How come?'

'He's not under formal arrest.'

'You mean you don't have him?'

'I'm not completely up to speed with the situation,' said Harland.

She pulled a cell phone from her shoulder bag and got up. 'I have to report on this. I am sorry, it is too important to wait.'

She went a little distance off into the sand and made her call. Harland's eyes flicked between her back and two men who had sat down in the shadows between the pool and the rear of the hotel's lobby. As he watched her he decided he still loved her, or rather needed her, but outweighing this was her propensity to hurt him, cut him out of her life. She had done it twice before and even if she came back when her mother passed on, there was no question in his mind that she would do it again. She was pathologically elusive.

When she returned he said, 'Were they pleased? Was it worth the trip?'

She nodded. 'Yes. Thank you for this, Bobby.'

'Well, at least you didn't have to sleep with me to get the information.'

'That's beneath you.'

Harland felt a guilty satisfaction that he could still hurt her. 'That's the old game, isn't it? That's what you were doing when we first met in Rome. The beautiful swallow from the East ensnaring all those tired officials and politicians.'

She gazed at him with the familiar look of defiance. 'Fuck you, Bobby.'

'Okay, okay. I'm sorry. But you should know how much I've missed you. Really, you should know that. I realise it's over but you bloody well could have told me why you were leaving, helped me understand.'

She lowered her eyes and drew a circle in the sand with her shoe. 'You're right. It was cruel of me. But I thought it was the best way.'

He glanced back to the hotel. 'You see we have company here. I saw them at the airport – Syrian or Lebanese footpads.'

'No, they're with me.'

'You travel with a bodyguard?'

'In Lebanon, yes. It's still a dangerous place. People go missing.'

'So you're not staying here?'

'No, I have to return. It is not easy to travel from here to Israel. I want to be back as early as I can for my mother's sake.'

'Right,' he said, getting up. 'So it's goodbye?'

'Yes.' She handed him a card. 'You may need to call me. This number will reach me wherever I am. I think we will need to be talking about this again.' Her flawless English was suddenly tinged with the Czech accent he once loved to hear.

'I'm not working that beat any more. I'm out of this business.'

'If you say so.' She held out her hand.

He took it, drew her to him and kissed her on the cheek. 'That's it then,' he said.

'We will talk. Sooner than you think.'

He let her go and she walked away towards the three men.

Harland took out his own cell phone and dialled the number on the card she had just given him. He saw her answer. 'You didn't take my mobile number,' he said, and gave it to her.

When she had disappeared into the hotel he made his own call – to Sir Robin Teckman.

CHAPTER TWENTY-FIVE

Herrick arrived back in London from Africa with Philip Sarre and Joe Lapping three days after the attack. On the night the missiles struck, Sarre and Lapping took her to a desert airstrip about seventy miles from the island. Five hours later they were picked up by a Cessna Titan and flown to Khartoum, where Herrick was treated for her cuts and bruises. They remained there for nearly three days while their passports were equipped with registration stamps and visas to make it seem that they had been in Sudan for over a week. Then they took a flight to Frankfurt and finally one to Heathrow, landing at midday on Sunday. Herrick was never so pleased to see the orderly patchwork of Surrey and Kent appear through the plane window.

At home she listened to her messages, then took a pile of newspapers into the tiny south-facing garden with a jug of lime juice and returned calls to her father, Harland and Dolph. Munroe was overjoyed to hear she was back. He knew better than to ask what had happened after he left Cairo, and instead pressed her to make plans for a trip to the west of Scotland in late July. Neither Dolph nor Harland answered their phones. There was one other call, from a Dr Leonard Jay. She didn't recognise his name or the number he'd left, but called the cell phone anyway and left a message.

She browsed through the Sundays, trying to keep a sense of failure and deflation at bay. It was difficult. Karim Khan was dead. Sarre had seen a body in the burning ruins of the villa which was almost certainly Khan's. The body was quite cold and rigor mortis had already set in, which made them suspect that he had not been killed by the missile but had been dead for some time before the strike. There was only one conclusion. Sammi Loz had ended the life of his friend, either by suffocation or with an injection of a lethal combination of drugs from the medical kit.

Khan's death shocked Herrick, because she had calculated that one thing she could rely on was Loz's love for Khan. However vain and ruthless he appeared to her, this had seemed to be a constant in his life. But plainly he had decided to leave the island, and knew that he could neither take Khan with him nor risk leaving him to be questioned further.

But had Loz died after killing Khan? Sarre and Lapping spent as long as they dared in the ruins of the bath-house trying to see if anyone was still trapped below the rubble. Sarre emerged and offered the theory that only the rock-solid bath had saved Isis, and unless Loz had been in it with her he would certainly have perished beneath the tons of rubble. Herrick could not remember the slightest sound or movement to indicate that he had survived.

And the attack, coming out of the night with such demonic force. Why? The motives still baffled her, although she knew after receiving an oblique call from the Chief on Sarre's cell phone in Khartoum, that it had probably been her fault. The satellite phone she'd left plugged into the computer up in the turret had for some reason kept dialling out, dropping the connection and then dialling again. It seemed likely that the Americans, already monitoring the communications coming from the island, had picked up the endlessly repeated signal and used it as a homing device for the first missile. This meant the CIA was aware that Khan and Loz were on the island, which in turn meant that they had been decoding the traffic both ways. They must also have known that a British intelligence officer was responsible for sending those signals, but that consideration had been overridden by the need to eliminate Khan and maybe Loz too. At the back of her mind she wondered if the CIA station in Djibouti, which would have controlled the Predator, was in possession of entirely accurate information.

She lay dozing in the sun, running through it all and trying to focus on what was left in the ruins of the attack. Khan was gone. Loz was probably dead. However, she was still certain that a third person existed, a man whom both Khan and Loz had met in Bosnia and then subsequently in Afghanistan.

She picked up her cell phone and called Dolph again, who answered on the first ring.

'Welcome back, Isis,' he said, on hearing her voice. 'By Christ, we were all relieved when we heard you were okay.'

'Thanks,' she said. 'Look, I need to ask you something. A couple of weeks back you mentioned some photographs from Bosnia. You had an idea that there was a photographer on the front line where Loz and Khan were serving. Am I imagining it or did you actually say that? I was half-expecting you to send me some material by email.'

'That's right, but I never got hold of him.'

'Can you trace him and see if he is willing to empty his archives for us? Photographers keep everything, and he might just have what I'm looking for.'

'Sure.'

'And there was a French journalist who covered the siege of Sarajevo – I think you said she now works for Nato. Can you get hold of her too? It's important.'

'I thought you were retired from this inquiry.'

'Not that I've heard.'

'Yeh, I can't imagine that Vigo and Spelling missed out on the full story of what happened. I mean, it doesn't look good for the people who went on the pyramids package tour.'

'Thanks for the encouragement. I was acting on the Chief's orders throughout. You know that.'

'The *former* Chief's orders. He's been airbrushed from the official history. He left on Friday, although he's not actually due to leave until Wednesday of this week.'

'Christ!'

'But I'll stand by you all the way.'

'Somehow that doesn't reassure me in the way it's meant to.'

'Seriously, Isis, you have my support, if it counts for anything. Look, I'd better go before you give me something else to do. We'll speak tomorrow when I know about the photographer and the French hackette.'

'Thanks Dolph, you're a good friend.'

The moment she hung up her phone rang again, and she answered to Harland, who asked, 'Can you do dinner tomorrow? I'll be at Brown's Hotel, Albermarle Street. We'll speak then.'

She managed to say yes before he hung up.

Monday morning came early with a summons from Vauxhall Cross. Spelling wanted to see her in the Chief's office no later than eight-thirty.

She took a cab into London. It was again a beautiful day, and as they drove through Kensington Gardens she suddenly felt a calm resignation about what was going to happen. If she was to be expelled from the Service under a cloud, so what? A summer in Scotland beckoned and then she'd find a job in the autumn and begin to lead a normal life, without having to allow for the possibility that every call she made was being listened to. There was nothing Vigo or Spelling or any of the other whey-faced bureaucrats could do to her, and she felt good about that.

As the taxi crept through the rush-hour traffic down Vauxhall Bridge Road towards SIS headquarters, her phone rang again.

'Hello, it's Leonard Jay.'

'Hello,' she said doubtfully.

'Dr Jay from Oxford!'

'Oh yes. Do you have any results for me?'

'Yes, that's what I'm ringing about,' he said huffily. 'I was concerned to get them to you as soon as possible since you did sign up for the priority service and we have already received payment. I would have sent them by post, but you specifically instructed us to convey the results of the analysis to you personally by phone.'

'Absolutely right. What are the results?'

'Well, it was difficult with the first sample because while there was a preponderance of material from one individual – ninety per cent of the scales of skin and the hairs came from that person – there were traces of other people too. So we made the assumption that it was this person who interested you and obtained a clear picture of his genetic profile.' He drew breath. 'Now the second sample, which reached us about ten days ago, was from one person. There was no contamination to contend with and we had—'

'And?' she said impatiently.

'To answer the question in your letter, these two samples are from different people.'

'Are you certain about that?'

'As certain as I can be about anything. We do a lot of forensic work, Ms Herrick, and we applied the same rigorous standards to your samples as we do to evidence for a criminal case. These are two different people. I am absolutely sure of it. I had a slight worry that sample B, that is the second one you sent me, might be matched against some of the minority material in the first sample. But we found B did not match any of the traces in A. There is no doubt about this.'

Herrick pressed a finger in her ear as the cab roared forward to make the lights on Vauxhall Bridge, and asked if the results could be couriered to London.

Dr Jay said that would be no problem.

'Is there anything else you can tell from either sample?' she asked.

'As a matter of fact there is. Both are male and both come from Mediterranean stock.'

'You can say that for certain?'

'Yes, recent advances mean we can show that on the Y chromosome of both men there is a common mutation present that originally appeared in the peoples of the Middle East. Indeed this marker has been very useful in the study of ancient migration patterns. There is still a distinction to be found in the character of the Y chromosome between the men of northern and southern Europe.'

'So you can assert that neither sample comes from, say Anglo-Saxon or Indian men.'

'Well, not categorically, but you might conclude that the two were from roughly similar genetic stock.'

'You might be able to say they were Arabs, for instance?'

'Yes, you could certainly argue that.'

The cab pulled up a little distance from the main entrance of SIS and Herrick asked the cab driver to wait while she finished her conversation.

'But to be sure,' she said, 'you would have to do the test again with new samples, is that right?'

'Oh, I don't think there's much point. As long as you are not proposing to take this to a court of law, I think we're on pretty safe ground.'

She gave him an address in central London used by SIS as a letter-box and then hung up.

The Chief's office had clearly suffered an unceremonious exorcism. Propped against the wall outside were Sir Robin Teckman's library of books about the Soviet Union and the Middle East, his family photographs and his collection of landscapes by Cavendish Morton. On the other side of the entrance was some rugby memorabilia that she recognised from Spelling's office, and a new widescreen TV.

After a few minutes in the corridor, Spelling's assistant told her to go in. Vigo and Spelling were sitting on one side of the maple veneer conference table that had also migrated from Spelling's office over the weekend. Vigo indicated that she should take a chair opposite them. Spelling did not look her way, but it was already plain to her that the battlefield general was glorying in his new power and the bold decisiveness that was expected of him.

'We haven't long,' he said, removing his glasses. 'I must be at Downing Street for a meeting of COBRA within the hour. Walter, where are the others?'

Herrick reflected that Teckman would never have announced he was going to Downing Street. She found herself idly wondering why COBRA – the Prime Minister's emergency committee, named after Cabinet Office Briefing Room A – had been convened.

'I believe they are on their way,' said Vigo. His eyes appeared more hooded than usual and the pallor and puffiness of his skin betrayed his long hours in the Bunker.

The others, it turned out, were the new head of Security and Public Affairs, Keith Manners, who had returned from the Joint Intelligence Committee, a man named Leppard, who was responsible for the 'deep background' briefings of the media, and a polished, dapper little fellow from the legal department, named Bishop. Finally came Harry Cecil, who had risen over the weekend on the thermals of sycophancy.

Isis was left with several seats empty either side of her, while the six men were ranged opposite, a seating plan eloquent of the trouble she was in. She noted too that she was unperturbed, crossed her legs and leaned back in the chair.

Spelling cleared his throat. 'Following a break-in at 119 Forsythe

Street on the night of May twenty-four you were formally warned by Walter Vigo that your behaviour was not only illegal but a serious security risk. At that time Mr Vigo took pains to explain to you that anything which allowed Mrs Rahe to believe her husband was dead might in turn alert the suspects that we were aware of the Heathrow switch. Is this so?'

'I'm not sure what you're saying,' said Herrick coolly. 'If you're asking me whether I agree that it jeopardised security the answer is no. If you're asking whether Walter spoke to me, yes.'

'Don't play the dumb bunny with me, Ms Herrick,' said Spelling nastily.

'Okay, I agree that Walter did talk to me in the company of Nathan Lyne. But since Mr Lyne is not a member of this Service and nor was Mr Vigo at the time, I do not think that it can be classed as an official warning, not in the terms of current employment legislation at any rate.'

'It is not for you to question Mr Vigo's position with this office,' said Spelling.

'But I am right,' she said, 'and any lawyer would certainly back me on that, unless you can prove that Walter was re-employed by that date.'

Bishop from the legal department looked unsettled.

'Ten days ago,' continued Spelling, 'you were among a number of people from this office who became involved in an illegal operation in Cairo, during which you seized a known terrorist suspect by force from the custody of the Egyptian security services. By the extent of this operation and the measure of violence offered to the Egyptians, this action can only be classed as a very grave offence indeed. It was certainly an illegal one, both in terms of the remit granted to the Secret Intelligence Service by Parliament and in the context of Egyptian law.'

Herrick felt her temper rising and she cut in. 'Is that the same legal context that allows the Americans to export suspects to countries where torture is routine? Are the "extraordinary renditions" that emerge from these sessions part of the legal framework you refer to?'

'Torture is irrelevant to your behaviour,' said Spelling.

'As a matter of fact it is entirely relevant. Karim Khan produced a great deal more valuable intelligence when he was free of duress than he did when he was being threatened by the Albanian Intelligence Service and the CIA and then subsequently electrocuted, burned and hung from the ceiling by the Egyptians. That intelligence is still live and useful, particularly in regard to his association with Dr Sammi Loz.'

'Sammi Loz was a minor player,' said Vigo, shifting in his chair, 'and certainly not worth the grave risk you exposed this Service to both in Cairo and on the island.'

'So you were aware of the location,' said Herrick sharply. Vigo did not have time to reply before she set off again. 'Actually, Sammi Loz is, or was, a critical part of a network we are only just beginning to understand. The Americans have long appreciated this, even if their focus on Khan concealed that fact. I assume that my communications from the island were intercepted by them and that they are in possession of everything I got from my questioning of Loz and Khan. If Loz was worthless, why on earth would they aim two Hellfire missiles at the place they knew him to be staying? If they believed he was just a bit player, why would they have mounted a surveillance operation on his apartment and offices in New York?'

Spelling leaned forward over the desk. 'It is not for us to answer to you, Miss Herrick. And it's not for you to lecture us on spurious terrorist networks. It is simply our concern to process the disciplinary procedure against you as fast as possible. Believe me, you are in serious trouble.'

Harry Cecil, who had been making a note of the exchanges, licked his lips in anticipation of the kill.

'Really? I don't see that at all,' said Herrick. 'I was asked by the Chief to take part in an intelligence operation overseas. In case it escaped your notice, that is the job of this Service.'

'I will not have you tell me what our job is,' snapped Spelling.

'Nevertheless, I *am* going to tell you about this operation, the sole purpose of which was to wrest a valuable suspect from certain death, to say nothing of torture. It must be clear to you by now that the Chief's plan entailed reuniting two suspects in circumstances likely to induce them to betray their past and the associations they had in Bosnia and Afghanistan. This was beginning to work. It was an ingenious and thoroughly legitimate plan, and I am certain that anyone in the media would agree with that.'

'Let me just make this utterly clear,' said Spelling. 'You have signed the Official Secrets Act. Any notion you have of leaking the events of the last week will meet with the gravest possible response from this office.'

'I am sure of that, but you cannot deny that for me to have refused the Chief would have placed me in breach of both my contract of employment and my moral obligation to this country.'

'Nonsense,' said Vigo. 'You must have been aware that this was the desperate act of a man who wished to cling on to power in this office. In these circumstances, you would have been quite within your rights to refuse to join this adventure, at the very least to seek advice as to its wisdom.'

'Presumably you would have made yourself available for such a consultation?' she said, turning on Vigo. 'But with your record you can hardly blame me for not speaking to you.'

'That's enough!' said Spelling.

'Your relations with the arms dealer Viktor Lipnik,' she continued, 'and the circumstances of the attack on a plane carrying Robert Harland into Sarajevo are all well known in this Service. That's why you were forced out. And you're suggesting that I ask *you* about the *morality*, the *advisability* of an operation!'

Spelling had risen to his feet and placed both hands on the table. Cecil stopped writing and gaped at Herrick. 'The fact of the matter, Miss Herrick,' said Spelling, 'is that we no longer have need of your services. You will leave this building and hand in all your passes...'

'But I haven't finished,' she said. 'You see, I don't think you have the slightest idea what this lowlife has been up to.'

'Perhaps it would be better if I left,' growled Vigo.

Spelling shook his head irritably.

'You can stay or go,' said Herrick, relishing the dissolution of the panel facing her. 'But nothing will stop me saying what I know.'

Spelling cast around, then said, 'To put it in plain language, you are fired and you will remove yourself from this office forthwith. Do you understand that?'

'I will go once I have told you about Walter Vigo, the man in whom you place such misguided trust,' she said without a trace of emotion. 'In collaboration with the CIA station in Tirana and the head of the local intelligence service, Marenglen, Walter Vigo conspired to mislead me and this Service about the fate of Karim Khan when he was first held in Albania. His death was faked on a mountainside so I would not pursue what was a crucial inquiry about his connections in Bosnia and Afghanistan. Further to that, he arranged for my house to be broken into and searched while he believed me to be at RAPTOR's command centre in Northolt. Happily, the two Albanian criminals who were supplied by Marenglen did not find what they were looking for, which means I am now in a position to reveal the critical – some would say criminal – misjudgements made by Vigo in the course of Operation RAPTOR, which I emphasise came from my work at Heathrow during May.'

All six men were now standing. Spelling's face had drained. Harry Cecil and Leppard had moved round the table to take hold of her.

'Since you are no longer a member of this Service,' said Spelling, 'what you have to say is of no interest to us. You will now be escorted from the premises. Formal notice of termination will follow this day. In the meantime, I would remind you again of the very tough sanctions of the Official Secrets Act. If you choose to ignore them in the smallest way, we will come down on you so that you will live to regret it. That means certain prosecution and a custodial sentence. I trust I make myself clear. Now I have to leave.' With this, he stalked from the room. Vigo followed at a studiously sedate pace.

Cecil and Leppard waited for a few moments while the others filed out and then without speaking, steered her to the elevator bank. 'It's okay,' she said. 'I can find my own way out.' Nonetheless they went with her to the front desk and waited until she had retrieved her cell phone. As the security guard handed it to her it began to ring. She answered to Robin Teckman.

'They've just bloody well fired me,' she said. 'I'm being escorted from the building by that little twerp Cecil and Leppard.'

The Chief laughed. 'Really? Well, it happens to us all at some time or other. Now, pop yourself in a cab and come round to the Cabinet Offices. You'll find the entrance door a little way up from Downing Street. Present yourself there in forty-five minutes. There's a meeting I want you to be in on. Your name's on the door. Don't be early and don't be late.'

Herrick put the phone in her bag and with a broad grin said, 'Cecil, I wonder if you would be so kind as to get me a cab… for Whitehall.'

CHAPTER TWENTY-SIX

Herrick presented the ID tag that Cecil and Leppard had failed to take from her and passed through the security gate of the Cabinet Office. She was met by a brisk young civil servant who introduced himself as Entwistle and asked whether it was her first time in COBRA. Only then did she understand she was to attend the same meeting as Spelling and Vigo.

'The Prime Minister is running a little late,' said Entwistle, 'so Sir Robin suggested we put you on ice for fifteen minutes or so in a room next door. Is that all right?'

'What's this about?' she asked.

'I think you're in a better position to say than I am,' he replied, pushing at a door and gesturing towards a stairway. He dropped her off in a small, windowless basement cell where there were old magazines and brochures issued by departments of state. He returned with some coffee brimming in a utility china cup. Herrick settled down to idle her way through the property ads in *Country Life* and briefly entertained a life in some distant shire with a couple of dogs and an undemanding man who cooked.

Forty minutes later Entwistle breezed in. 'Rightyho, you're on. When we go in, I will point out the seat you should take. The Prime Minister is opening the meeting with a brief preamble. If you're not sure what to do or say, just follow Sir Robin's lead. Okay?'

She shrugged hopelessly, unable to hazard what events had brought her from being fired an hour before to a meeting presided over by the Prime Minister. They moved along a carpeted corridor and came across a huddle of men and women, all in their early thirties, who Entwistle said were the staff of the Civil Contingencies Secretariat who would be swinging into action once the COBRA meeting was over. He reached a pair of doors, looked round and said, 'Okay?' again. She nodded.

He opened one of the two doors and she found herself propelled into a large white room with a low ceiling and somewhat harsh lighting. There were no pictures or other adornments. Seated at the centre of a long table was the Prime Minister with his shirt-sleeves rolled up, displaying a weekend tan. On his right was the Foreign Secretary, hunched over a pile of papers; on his left was the Home Secretary, who was the only one of the three to notice her entrance. Enwistle pointed to a seat two away from Sir Robin Teckman, four places from Richard Spelling and Walter Vigo, neither of whom acknowledged her. The remaining chairs were taken by the Director of the Security Services, Barbara Markham, members of the Joint Intelligence Committee and Ian Frayne, Intelligence Coordinator in the Cabinet Office, who had originally been head of Security and Public Affairs at Vauxhall Cross when Herrick was a trainee. He flashed her a welcoming nod.

'So I stress,' said the Prime Minister, 'I have not convened the Civil Emergencies Committee lightly. Overnight I have been given information which cast Operation RAPTOR in a very different light, and makes me doubt the value of the way it was set out in the wake of the assassination of Vice-Admiral Norquist. Clearly these faults must be rectified before I speak to the President this afternoon. I hesitate to call it a misjudgement until the internal inquiry has reported, but I do emphasise at the outset this morning that I am concerned that RAPTOR is being run without full recognition of the risks and dangers that we face at every hour of the day. We may have to consider that it is flawed in its very concept.'

There was a slight murmur around the room, a shuffling of papers, the almost perceptible adjustment of each person's position.

'Now, this committee's brief is not to take over the business of our Secret Intelligence Service, but I do intend to get to the bottom of what is happening and make my dispositions accordingly. I wonder if I could begin with you, Richard, as the Chief of SIS designate?'

Everyone noticed the stress on the last word. 'Well, Prime Minister.' Spelling's eyes swept confidently around the room, rallying support

294

which, in the downward glances and blank expressions, was evidently less forthcoming than he had expected. 'I first of all want to draw the attention of the committee to the immensely detailed understanding we now have of the men who passed through Heathrow on May fourteen. There has never been an operation like this. This is the cutting edge of surveillance and both the United States and UK governments have benefited hugely from our ability to watch these men and monitor every move they make, at the same time as studying their backgrounds, psychological profiles, associates, support systems and financial backing. It is a triumph of modern intelligence gathering and it has greatly increased our knowledge of Islamist groups. Besides this, the risks of this *in vitro* experiment are minimal, because each man is covered by a squad of no less than six highly trained and armed personnel. The suspects are already virtually handcuffed.'

'That's very reassuring, Richard,' said the Prime Minister, with a slightly pained expression, 'but I've heard all this before. It seems to me and my two Cabinet colleagues that Sir Robin's new information does call RAPTOR into question, particularly the value of what one paper I have received from the Joint Intelligence Committee notes as its "unyielding and exclusive focus".'

'Yes,' he replied, 'but Prime Minister, these were the terms that our American partners insisted upon.'

The Prime Minister's gaze traversed the table and alighted on Teckman. 'Sir Robin, perhaps you would like to go over the material you brought to me on Friday evening?'

Teckman began to speak quietly, so that the people at the furthest extremes of the room had to lean forward to catch what he was saying. Herrick smiled to herself. This was always his method of drawing people towards his argument.

'While I don't want in any way to undervalue the efforts made by the men and women of RAPTOR, over the last forty-eight hours we have made certain discoveries about the nature of the terrorist threat to the West, the possibility of which has largely been neglected.' He stopped and glanced in Herrick's direction. 'Few of you will be aware that a key figure in this has been my colleague, Isis Herrick. She was first responsible for establishing what happened at Heathrow on May fourteen and subsequently worked with RAPTOR. Now she has brought crucial intelligence from Egypt. Even she is unaware of what she conveyed to us by satellite phone late last week.'

The faces around the table, including the Prime Minister's, began to examine her with interest. She acknowledged his compliment with a nod, inwardly wondering what on earth was in the recording that she had overlooked, then remembered that she had only managed to listen to a small portion of it. After that she had been fighting off Loz in the bath-house.

'The part I am going to play you was of exceptionally poor quality and has been rescued by extensive work by GCHQ technicians.' He placed a briefcase on the table and unzipped it. Inside was a large tape player. 'Here we go,' he said, pressing the play button with the uncertainty of someone unused to electrical equipment.

There was a rustling noise, which Herrick recognised as coming from the dead leaves on a vine outside the window in Khan's room, followed by silence. You could hear a pin drop in the bomb-proof underground chamber, as the eyes of each person came to rest on the spools of the tape recorder.

Then came a voice – a whisper floating on the breeze that had now audibly taken hold of a cloth hung in front of the window, though only Herrick could possibly have seen this in her mind.

'She is a devil that girl – no?'

'That is Dr Sammi Loz,' said the Chief. 'The important part is coming up now.' He turned up the volume control.

'She thinks she is clever. And she is. She is catching us out all the time. You Karim, she plays with you. But we play with her also. We wait. And we let her think she is so fucking smart. Eleven days. That's all we have to wait for. *Inshallah.*'

There was silence, then a sigh from the bed. 'What are you doing, Sammi? What do you plan?'

'This is not for your ears, old friend. But it's good, very good. Months of planning and we have fooled them like children. *Al kufr milatun wahidun* – right, Karim?'

Teckman stopped the tape. 'That is an Arabic phrase which translates as "unbelief is one nation". It's a well-known Hadith among Islamist groups, and expresses the view that all non-Muslims are the enemy of Islam. They both knew this phrase. I understand from the

Director of the CIA whom I spoke to last night, that one of the post-cards sent by Khan to Sammi Loz at the Empire State building contains a crude rendering of the same phrase in code. However, I should stress that we do not believe Karim Khan knew of Loz's intentions and that the presence of this code is not significant. However, he did represent a considerable danger to Loz, which is why we believe Loz eventually had to kill him – hours before the strike. The clue to the nature of the threat comes now. Khan is speaking.'

He pressed the play button again and turned up the volume. The room was filled with a buzz of static and then the single word 'Yahya' was spoken by Khan.

It came again. 'Yah–ya.' Slow and deliberate.

Loz told Khan to be quiet. 'Not here,' he said sharply.

But Khan persisted. 'You follow Yahya too much, Sammi. Yahya is a bad person.'

'Please, old friend, I do not want to hear that name. Forget you ever knew it. If you don't, it will fall from your lips when you are with that woman and then we will be both be in trouble. She is communicating everything we say to her colleagues in London. Things move at lightning speed these days. You have forgotten because you have been away from the world for so long.'

Khan seemed to misunderstand him and asked groggily, 'Yahya in London? Is The Poet in London?'

'Forget The Poet,' said Loz. 'Forget Yahya. Forget these names. Okay?'

Teckman switched off the machine and put it away. Then the Prime Minister asked if there were any questions.

After a pause, Vigo coughed and said, 'I wonder if I might ask Sir Robin what relevance this has to RAPTOR. The recording is very impressive in its own way, but it does nothing to dissuade me of the value of our current operations.'

Teckman looked down the table and dispatched a parched smile in Vigo's direction. 'That's a very good question, Walter. Intelligence from Beirut over the weekend, provided by friends of ours, confirms that Sammi Loz, instead of being a peripheral interest, is right at the centre of this affair. There is a link between Loz and the suspects that you have under surveillance. Loz was connected to Vice-Admiral

Norquist as a patient and a business partner. I am afraid to say that the latter association allowed the Admiral to be exploited by Loz and then subsequently by Mossad, who were aware of his dealings. I won't go into the whole story now. Suffice to say that Loz was in a position to know about the timing of Norquist's trip here and put into place a scheme to kill him. We have long been puzzled by the poor calibre of the men hired to kill Norquist. We know the bullet is likely to have come from one of our own people and not from the two tearaways who were killed on the motorway, but the fact remains that these men were tasked to kill him, or at least cause a substantial redeployment of security personnel in and around Heathrow.

'I have no doubt that Sammi Loz wanted Norquist dead. He must have known by then that Norquist was working for Mossad, and that information about Hizbollah was going straight to Tel Aviv. But I maintain that the primary objective was to create a strategic diversion. Incidentally, I note with interest that in the minutes of a meeting held five weeks ago at Vauxhall Cross, this was the exact phrase offered by Mr Vigo.'

He glanced at Vigo, who nodded vigorously.

'So what we have,' he continued, 'is a line which traces between Khan, Loz, Norquist and therefore the RAPTOR suspects. This clearly establishes the value of Isis Herrick's outstanding work in Albania and Cairo, and underscores the necessity of removing Karim Khan from the custody of the Egyptian Intelligence Service. Without taking Khan, we would not have been able to make these connections.'

Spelling leaned forward and caught the eye of the Prime Minister. 'But look these men are all dead. Norquist, Khan and Loz are all dead. What we are left with are the RAPTOR suspects.'

'I agree that Khan is probably dead,' said the Chief. 'One of our men saw him, or a body on his bed. As to Loz, we cannot say. The ruins of the villa have now been searched thoroughly. We had very precise information from Isis about the location of Loz at the moment of impact and no body has been found there. So I am bound to conclude that one very cunning, wealthy and determined terrorist is on the loose. Maybe two, if we include the individual referred to as Yahya whom Loz is so obviously desperate to protect. For the record, I happen to think we have a problem, and that we have five days to find them.'

'But the evidence is so slight,' said Vigo.

'I am unpersuaded of that,' said the Prime Minister. 'How much of this do the Americans know?'

'A certain amount,' said Teckman, 'though I felt it wise to be circumspect about Norquist. There is no reason to trouble his family or his good memory.'

'Quite right,' said the Prime Minister. He looked around the table. 'Clearly radical adjustments are needed in the scope and direction of RAPTOR. What do your soundings in Washington recommend, Sir Robin?'

'Exactly what you suggest. I think it's fair to say that we have taken the Anglo-American experiment as far as we can. I don't doubt its usefulness in academic terms, but we now face a distinctly practical problem which I think must necessarily involve the BND in Germany, Mossad, and the Direction Générale de la Securité Extérieure, and the DST in France. Clearly the Italians, Spanish and Nordic services should also be involved.'

'But this means they will have the benefit of our knowledge,' said Spelling. The room noted the plangent tone in his voice and to a man and woman decided that he was not up to the job at this or any other time. 'We have to consider the history of security lapses in Europe,' he said.

'We *are* in Europe,' said the Prime Minister, and turned back to Teckman. 'Sir Robin, I should make it clear now that I want you to stay on at SIS at least until this operation is satisfactorily completed. I am very grateful for the efforts you and Miss Herrick have put into making sense of this over the last few weeks. Will you also convey my personal thanks to anyone else who was involved.' Teckman gave an oblique, patrician nod.

At this point, several things began to fall into place in Herrick's mind and without knowing what she was going to say, she began to speak. 'I'm sorry... but it just occurred to me who Yahya might be, sir. I mean, it's a long shot but, well, I think it's worth considering.'

The Prime Minister nodded. 'Yes...?'

Her hand reached for a biscuit from the tray in the centre of the table, and she began to nibble unselfconsciously. 'I had some tests done... kind of out of hours, if you see what I mean. I took some material from the keyboard of a computer used by a man named Youssef Rahe. Rahe was involved in the switch, though he was our man – a contact made by Walter Vigo. Then Rahe disappeared in Lebanon and a body was found in a car – unrecognisable and badly burnt. I got a friend to obtain a sample from the corpse to see if the DNA matched the material that had fallen into the keyboard habitually used by Rahe – keyboards collect a lot of hair and skin, as you perhaps all know.' She paused, aware that most of her audience didn't know whether to be embarrassed or intrigued. 'I got the results this morning. There is no match between the two samples, which means that Rahe was not killed. Instead, I believe his place was taken by another man who we spotted passing through Terminal Three. He was tortured, executed and disguised as Rahe so that we would think our man had been discovered.' She stopped and nibbled some more. 'Sorry, am I making any sense?'

'Not to me,' said the Prime Minister, 'but please go on. I'm sure everyone else understands the significance of what you're saying.'

'Well, it just struck me that there was a connection between the eleven suspects and Rahe after his supposed death. When one of the men died – the Stuttgart suspect – all the telephone calls from the local group of helpers were monitored. There was one significant call and that went to Beirut, informing an unknown party that the man was dead. You see, a very strong argument can be made that Rahe was in on this from the beginning and was manipulating us. Would you mind if I asked Mr Vigo a question?'

Vigo's head turned to her and he blinked. 'I should remind you,' he said, 'that it was I who ordered those calls monitored from Stuttgart.'

'I know, but we all should have been thinking about Beirut. It should have set off some kind of alarm that Rahe had been taken from a hotel there. My question is this: where did we first learn about the website carrying the messages about future attacks? Was it through Youssef Rahe?'

'Yes, it was,' cut in Spelling, clearly having decided to jettison the co-architect of RAPTOR.

'So we have basically been sold a dummy by Rahe and Loz. I believe that we know who Yahya is. Yahya is Youssef Yamin Rahe. I have to ask you how you came in touch with him, because I believe he has been using his connection with us all the way along.'

Vigo shook his head. 'This is all guesswork. I am not going to answer these questions until there is some kind of evidence.'

'I think we shall have all the evidence you require,' she said. 'I just need that answer.'

'For God's sake answer her, Mr Vigo,' barked the Prime Minister.

'I met him through my book-dealing business.' He spoke as though drugged. 'Then I went to his shop in Bayswater. We talked and it was clear he might be able to help us.'

The room went silent again as Vigo slumped back in his chair, then in a lifeless voice asked the Prime Minister's permission to leave. The Prime Minister nodded. Vigo rose stiffly and limped from the room.

'Have you any more surprises for us, Miss Herrick?' the Prime Minister asked.

She shook her head.

'Sir Robin, does all this seem likely to you?' he asked.

'Yes,' he replied.

'Then it is clear that you must trace Youssef Rahe and Sammi Loz wherever they are, as a matter of urgency. You will, of course, have the complete backing of the Security Services, the police and the diplomatic service. What else do you propose?'

'The first thing is to get the eleven remaining suspects off the streets as fast as possible. I believe the BND and the French service may have already been alerted to some kind of operation. It was hopeless to expect us to be able to carry out this type of surveillance on their territory without them getting wind of it. We should make them party to everything we have learned, apologise and urge that these men be arrested.'

The Foreign Secretary stirred. 'On what charges?'

'Initially, on violation of immigration controls. We have the evidence on film that each man was carrying false passports. More serious charges may follow, but at least we'll know the Heathrow team is under lock and key.'

The Prime Minister whispered to the Foreign Secretary. Herrick could not help lip-reading what he said. 'Get that tosser of an ambassador in. Tell him the game's up and that I'll be speaking to the President this afternoon. Keep Norquist out of your talk. I'm going to

301

need that as ammunition with the President. I'll want a note about that from Teckman.'

The Foreign Secretary got up and left. 'Right,' said the Prime Minister, also rising. 'The Civil Contingencies Committee will meet three times a day and liaise with the JIC staff. I expect constant progress updates for the next five days. Needless to say, there will be a media blackout on this. And that will last until I say otherwise. That's it. Let's get on with it.'

Only Herrick did not get up as she left. Instead, her hand darted forward to retrieve another biscuit.

CHAPTER TWENTY-SEVEN

The seascapes by Cavendish Morton, the photographs and the small bronze of a man fly-fishing were back in the Chief's office by lunchtime that Monday. Also returned to his complete control was the British end of RAPTOR, which took rather less time to effect than the hanging of his pictures. As he moved round his office, trying new positions for the canvasses, he dictated a memorandum that instructed RAPTOR to focus its efforts on preparing the foreign agencies for the arrest and charge of the suspects. The teams in the Bunker were instructed to concentrate their resources on predicting the exact location of every suspect over the next forty-eight hours, so that decisions could be taken about a coordinated action across Europe. At the same time, RAPTOR was tasked to provide evidence against the helper cells, the men and women who had smoothed the way for the suspects to merge into the life of cities all over Europe. Preliminary estimates suggested that in each case at least ten people might be arrested and charged with aiding and abetting a terrorist plot, although there was some doubt as to whether the evidence was strong enough to meet the requirements of more liberal regimes in Scandinavia. All governments were to be urged to use the Al Capone option: to seek convictions and custodial sentences for ordinary criminal matters such as theft, fraud and forgery, rather than for terrorism.

As British diplomats began to sound out and brief governments, they insisted that a news blackout was required until at least the end of the week, by which time the date mentioned by Loz in the recording would have been reached. In several conference calls, the Chief acknowledged that there were likely to be check-in systems designed to alert a central control figure of an arrest. The failure of one suspect to make regular contact might be enough to tip off the entire network. The reaction of most security services was still to press for arrest at the earliest possible date. The Chief also told them about Mohammed bin Khidir, the man apprehended in Stuttgart who had died when he bit into a cyanide capsule. The other suspects were likely to have been equipped with suicide pills in their teeth, so drugging them, perhaps by dart, would be a necessity rather than an option.

Herrick was present for most of these conversations and noticed once or twice a distinct lack of surprise in the voices of the various intelligence chiefs, especially from the French and Italians. Between calls she remarked as much to Teckman.

The Chief gave her an injured look and said, 'After the work you have done for us, you can pretty much write your own ticket, Isis, but I do urge you not to give voice to these unworthy suspicions.'

Of course, she thought, the crafty old buzzard had found a way of keeping his main European allies in the picture. For a moment she marvelled at the ferocious will that lay beneath the Chief's cheerful, gregarious presence.

One thing that remained held tightly to the chest of the British Secret Intelligence Service was the identity of Sammi Loz and Youssef Rahe, now in Teckman's mind established as Yahya or The Poet. The Chief considered issuing descriptions and backgrounds, but then decided not to risk either of the men hearing that they were still regarded as live threats. He saw to it that Sammi Loz's name lost the prominent place it had occupied on the FBI watch list for the last few weeks. Agents monitoring the empty consulting rooms in the Empire State withdrew.

In a gap between the Chief's calls and discussions, Herrick phoned Dolph on his mobile.

'Where are you, Dolphy?' she said.

'In the sticks, having coffee with Britain's premier war photographer. He's just agreed to download his entire Bosnian archive into my computer.'

'You should be here. Things are moving fast.'

'Yeah. I heard from Nathan Lyne. Look, I may have hit the jackpot with this stuff. I'm bringing it back.'

'Come to the office. There have been changes.'

'Yeah, Nathan told me that, too.'

'You don't seem surprised.'

'I'm not. They shouldn't have messed with you. Though I have to say I didn't fancy your chances yesterday.'

'You were right: they fired me.'

'Tossers. Now look, I'm kind of busy here. Why don't you call Hélène Guignal. She's the bird who was in Sarajevo. I think she's good. Really, I've got a feeling about her.'

She dialled Nato headquarters in Brussels five times before getting through to a colleague of Guignal's in the Press Office who said Hélène was on vacation. Pretending to be a spokesman from the Ministry of Defence who needed Guignal urgently, Herrick managed to extract a mobile number that would raise her on the island of Skiathos. She tried this, but the phone was turned off.

She returned to the Chief's office. Teckman looked distracted for a second, then leapt from his desk. 'Come with me.'

A Jaguar with outriders took them to Battersea Heliport, where Guthrie was already waiting with Barbara Markham and her deputy. The helicopter took less than ten minutes to touch down at Northolt, near to the Bunker's entrance.

'Do you know, I've never seen this operation,' he murmured to Herrick as they descended in the lift.

'You didn't need to,' she said.

'Perhaps if I had come here I would have seen what made you so annoyed,' he smiled.

When they had reached the Bunker, Teckman strode into the main space and nodded to the people he recognised. Nathan Lyne rose from his desk and came over to Herrick. 'So, Isis. I see no Vigo. I see Richard Spelling twisting slowly in the wind. And here you are with all the great panjandrums of the British security establishment. What the hell have you been up to?'

'Not much.'

He grinned. 'Just in case you're feeling bad about Walter…'

'I wasn't.'

'He knew you were on that island with those two men. Your communications traffic made that clear.'

'Did you know about it, Nathan?'

'Of course not. I had no idea where you were. Even Andy Dolph wouldn't tell me. But you're safe – that's what matters – and your stock's risen. Things have turned out well for you.'

'But we lost one of the suspects. This wasn't just any old suspect. He was really important. And we don't have much time.' She noticed that the Chief had sat down in front of one of the larger screens. 'Come and talk him through it all,' she said. 'He's going to need you over the next few days.'

The Chief shook his hand without rising. 'I've heard about you. I gather you were responsible for sending Isis to Albania, Mr Lyne. That was a very good decision. Now tell me what I'm looking at.'

Lyne pulled up a chair and went through the screens devoted to the nine remaining suspects. Most were live feeds from inside and around the apartments where they were living. Ramzi Zaman, the Moroccan, could be seen passing through the field of the camera, preparing a meal in his little kitchen in Toulouse. Lasenne Hadaya, the edgy Algerian, was seated on a couch, aimlessly throwing a ball into the air and catching it. In Budapest, Hadi Dahhak, a diminutive Yemeni with a hooked nose, was seen arguing with two men over a newspaper. Lyne said that all they ever talked about was football. He ran a piece of recent film which showed the Syrian suspect, Hafiz al Bakr, strolling in a park with one of his helpers. The story was the same with the Saudis in Rome and Sarajevo, the Pakistani in Bradford, and the Egyptian in Stockholm. Each man was aimlessly frittering away his days. There were no breaks in the routine, no sense of imminent action, no sign of preparation. Lyne took the Chief through some of the background research but Herrick could tell he was losing interest, and he suddenly left Lyne's side and bounded up the stairs to the glass box where Spelling, Jim Collins and Colonel Plume of the National Security Agency were talking. A few minutes later he called for all the staff to assemble at the bottom of the stairs.

'We have a problem of interpretation, ladies and gentlemen, and I need your help on it. The men you have been watching over these last few weeks will in all probability be under lock and key within a very short time. We have other intelligence to indicate that there may be some kind of action by the end of the week, so obviously we can't allow these characters to be on the loose any longer. Before this happens, I want you to consider what their plan is. Why have they been put in place with such elaborate care? What is the meaning of it? I don't want proof, I want your thoughts, the wildest ideas that may have occurred to you over the last few weeks.'

Herrick looked around and saw a number of anxious expressions. This was something new to RAPTOR personnel.

'We are pursuing certain lines,' continued the Chief, 'which take the investigation further, but I do think we should try to work out what this is all about, don't you?'

There was an embarrassed silence and then Joe Lapping put up his arm.

'Yes, Mr Lapping,' said the Chief.

'Maybe it's about nothing,' said Lapping. Collins and Spelling looked up into the great black space above them.

'Perhaps you'd care to develop that idea,' said the Chief.

'I don't mean to take anything from Isis Herrick's achievement in spotting what was going on at Heathrow. I was there, and it was a really good piece of work. But maybe – just maybe – we were meant to see it. After all, we were led there by one of the suspects who hung around outside Terminal Three in a most public fashion. It was almost as if he was making sure we didn't miss him.'

Herrick realised he could be right. It was unlikely that Lapping would have heard about her testing Rahe's DNA against the corpse in Lebanon, so he wasn't falling behind the latest theory.

'But you are aware,' said the Chief, 'that the orthodox view on the events of that day portrays the assassination attempt on Vice-Admiral Norquist as a strategic diversion. What would be the point of such a strategy if the suspects were all part of some kind of hoax?'

Lapping cleared his throat. 'I haven't been involved much in the operations down here, but always at the back of my mind it seemed that these men were acting like the Stepford Wives. They just drink coffee, read the papers, sleep, cook, do the shopping, watch TV, play soccer. They don't look as if they're going to do anything.'

'He may be right, sir,' Lyne chipped in. 'A double deception to draw our attention away from another action, or simply waste all our resources, is not out of the question. Al-Qaeda has vast resources, by our estimates three- to five-hundred-million-dollar revenues each year, mainly from Saudi princes and businessmen. A tiny fraction of this goes into terrorist actions. About ninety per cent is used in setting up networks and infrastructure. They could afford to string us along on an operation without having any material end in sight.'

'*The Subtle Ruse*,' said Lapping.

'And what's that?' asked the Chief. Every face turned to Lapping, who despite his confidence in matters of scholarship, was unused to public performance. Herrick saw his Adam's apple move up and down before he spoke.

'A book written a hundred years before Machiavelli by an anonymous Arab author – probably an Egyptian living in the time of the Grand Emir Sa'd al-Din Sunbul. It uses examples from Arab literature and seeks to edify the reader with stories of ruses, stratagems, guile and deceptions taken from different walks of life. In essence, it instructs you how to outwit your opponent and in turn be alert to his ploys.'

'I see. You're not suggesting this was directly taken from the book,' said the Chief, ' but you are saying…'

'That a man who had studied ancient Arab literature would know the book and have learned some of its lessons.'

Herrick remembered that Joe Lapping had been asked to research a man with a literary background who might have fought for the Bosniaks in the civil war. And Rahe, of course, spent most of his days in a bookshop. Certainly it was a suggestion that stood up to examination, but the more important idea was that Rahe had led them to Heathrow and hung about in front of various security cameras. She was appalled that she had not thought of it herself.

The Chief was nodding. 'That's an interesting theory. Anyone have any other ideas?'

There were a number of tentative suggestions which he dismissed politely, then in his most solicitous manner he told the assembled intelligence workers they'd done a fine job which would undoubtedly make the arrest of the men a lot simpler. When they began to disperse to their desks, still looking mystified, he told Lapping he would be required at Vauxhall Cross that afternoon and asked Lyne to be there on the following day. 'I'm sure you can be let off school this once,' he said with a wink to Lyne. 'You do speak Arabic, don't you?'

Lyne said yes, he did.

They arrived back at SIS headquarters just past 2 p.m. Herrick went straight to her desk and called the mobile number for Hélène Guignal. Mademoiselle Guignal answered drowsily. In the background Herrick heard the unmistakable sound of waves breaking and water running up a beach. She explained what she wanted, but Guignal said she was inclined to postpone the conversation until she was back at her desk in Brussels.

'Fine,' said Herrick. 'We can put a request through the Secretary-General of Nato for a formal interview on these matters by Nato security personnel. This is important and the United Kingdom *does* require your help.'

'Who are you?'

'It's enough that you know I am investigating an international terrorist cell and that I believe you hold information which may be useful, in fact, critical to my inquiries.'

The woman suddenly became cooperative.

'One of my colleagues says you knew some of the foreign Muslims who defended Sarajevo during the siege?'

'Yes, I lived with one. How can I help?'

'We're interested in two men, Sammi Loz and Karim Khan.'

'Ah yes, I knew them both, but not well. They were the medics, no? The ones that came out with supplies then stayed. Those guys?'

'Yes,' said Herrick. 'Would you mind telling me the name of the man who you lived with?'

'Hasan Simic. He was of mixed parentage but was brought up as a Muslim. He liaised with the foreign Muslims – the *jihadistes*. It was a tough job. They always wanted to do what they wanted to do. They kept themselves apart. They were not like the Bosnian Muslims.'

'Can I talk to Mr Simic?'

'He's dead. He died in ninety-five.'

'I'm sorry.'

'Don't apologise. He was born to die young. A very beautiful man but *un sauvage* – you know? If he had not been killed, he would have been taken to the Hague for war crimes.'

'How much did you see Khan and Loz?'

'I met them about four or five times. A few of the men used to come to our apartment when there were breaks in the fighting. I had food, you see. Not much, but more than they had. We made big pasta dinners. Karim was a favourite of mine. *Très charmant ... très sympathique.*'

'What about Loz?'

'*Un peu plus masqué, comprenez vous? Dissimulé.*'

'And you were working for press agencies then?'

'*Oui, l'Agence France Presse.*'

'The other men – the friends of Hassan. What were their names?'

There was a pause.

'Do you remember Yahya?' asked Herrick.

'Yahya? No, I do not remember this man. Who was Yahya? What did he look like?'

'He would have been in his late twenties, early thirties. A short man, of Algerian origin. We believe he was a very private man. Inconspicuous. He may have been some kind of scholar before he went to Bosnia. Perhaps he even studied in Sarajevo before the Islamic Institute was shelled. We are not sure.'

'And it is this man you are really interested in?'

'Yes, it is possible that he used the name Youssef. Karim and Sammi used to call him The Poet. That was their nickname for him before he became a friend of theirs.'

'Maybe ... *Ah oui, oui, oui!* I know the man you mean, but his name is not Yahya. The man I think of was called Yaqub.'

'Yaqub?' said Herrick doubtfully. 'Are you sure?'

'*Oui, un autre prophète.*'

'How do you mean?'

'So, we have three names for this man and they are all the Arab names for prophets in the Bible.' Her tone was of someone being forced to talk to an idiot. 'Youssef – or Joseph, is the son of the Prophet Yaqub – or Jacob! And you mentioned Yahya, who is the Prophet John, son of the Prophet Zachariah. This is obvious. He is using *nommes de guerre* from the Bible. One day he must use the name Zachariah. That is logical. No?' Herrick made a rapid note of this.

'And you know he was Algerian?'

'Yes, he comes from Oran. I know this because my father served in Algeria. I have been to Oran.'

'And this man was bookish and withdrawn, somebody who kept to himself?'

'He came to the apartment once with Hassan – never the others. He was a mystery to them. But he was polite and well-mannered. There is little else that I remember about him.'

Herrick hung up, thinking that it was a pity Hélène Guignal was not at her desk in Brussels to receive an emailed file of one of the images of Rahe at Heathrow. That way Herrick would be sure of an instant no or yes in her attempt to tie Rahe with Yahya or Yaqub. She got a picture out of the files nevertheless and put it in plain white envelope, thinking it was bound to be useful over the next few days. Then, with her notes of the Guignal conversation, she went to find Dolph, who she heard had arrived back from Hertfordshire.

He was with Lapping and Sarre in one of the conference rooms near the Chief's office with his laptop fixed to a projector. They were sprawled about the room watching the photographer's archive of the Bosnian civil war; frame after frame of haggard faces staring from fox-holes and ruined buildings. There were men pleading for mercy, women dashing across the street, barefoot children wandering snowy craters and Serb gunners coolly observing their targets below.

'This is all stuff from ninety-three and ninety-four,' said Dolph, after he had given Isis a brief kiss and welcomed her back. 'He's organised it by date rather than subject. He spent the early winter of ninety-three on one of two fronts manned by the Mujahideen Brigade. So we should be nearly there.'

Herrick reminded herself that none of them knew Rahe was now a prime suspect. Lapping had got near the truth of the matter with his observations about Rahe's behaviour at the airport, but he hadn't gone the extra few yards to the logical conclusion. More important, they did not know there was now some urgency to find Yahya and Loz. The Chief had been most specific that she should not talk about this.

After forty-five minutes fruitlessly peering at all the group shots from the front, they came to the end of the relevant part of the archive.

'This photographer,' said Herrick, 'did he remember anyone like Khan or Loz?'

Dolph shook his head.

'Or anyone else significant?'

Dolph shook his head. 'I could do with a pint. What you say we treat ourselves over the river, lads?'

Herrick asked if they had seen any groups of soldiers before she came into the room.

'A few.'

'I'd like to go back over those pictures.'

'Why?' asked Dolph a little truculently.

'Because *you* don't know what we're looking for.'

'We're looking for Khan and this guy Sammi Loz.'

'But none of you has seen them in the flesh and there may be someone else important in the photographs. This man was taking pictures throughout the crucial period.'

Dolph peered into his screen to locate the relevant files while Lapping went to get them all coffee.

At length Dolph found the photographs from mid-November 1993 showing a group of about a dozen men moving a burnt-out truck. The ground was covered with a light dusting of snow and the sky above was bright. Ice sparkled in the trees. Their faces were turned to the ground and in profile as they put their weight behind the truck. With the shadows playing across the snow, the energy expressed in the men's bodies and the interesting form of the wrecked vehicle, it was easy to see why the photographer's eye had been attracted to the scene, and why he'd kept his finger on the shutter button through eight frames. Dolph sped through the images, almost animating the sequence. At Herrick's insistence they went back over them again slowly. At the fourth image, she shouted. 'Stop there.' She went to the wall and pointed to a man's head which had lifted into the light and faced the camera. 'Can you enlarge it? Here, the area at the front of the car.'

Dolph highlighted the area with his mouse and made a couple of keystrokes. 'Who the fuck is that?' he asked as the picture sprang onto the wall.

'That,' she said, withrawing the photograph from her envelope and slapping it against the wall, 'is Youssef Rahe, otherwise known as Yahya or Yaqub. Take a look for yourselves.'

Dolph got up and peered at the two pictures. It took him a few seconds to understand the significance of the match. 'Isis, you're a bloody marvel. He's the main man.' He thought for a moment. 'Everything that's happened this morning with Spelling and Vigo is because you knew that already. You were expecting to find Rahe here – or at least you were looking for him.'

She nodded.

'Fuck my Aunt Ethel's goat.'

They all approached the wall and made comparisons between the two pictures. 'And look here,' she said. 'The scrawny one with the beard. I'm pretty sure that's Sammi Loz.'

'If you say so,' said Dolph. ' Is Khan there too?'

She examined each face in turn. 'No.'

Dolph's shrewd eyes sought hers again. 'How did you find out about Rahe?'

'The bookstore,' said Sarre. 'You got something that night, didn't you?'

'Christ, you're a piece of work.' said Dolph. 'How long have you known?'

'Since this morning we have known that Rahe was not killed in Lebanon. The body belonged to someone else.' She explained about the samples she'd sent to the laboratory and the recording of Sammi Loz talking to Khan which gave her the name of Yahya.

'So all the crucial connections took place in Bosnia,' said Lapping.

'Yes, which is why we need to work out who these people are.' She jabbed her finger on the faces of the other men. 'We should get all the shots blown up, each face digitally enhanced.'

'But I can tell you now,' said Sarre, 'that none of these men came through Heathrow that day. I know their faces off by heart.'

'And that is rather the point,' said Lapping.

'Behold, ladies and gentleman,' said Dolph, 'the viscous matter that passes for Joe Lapping's brain is at last on stream.'

'But you didn't get there Dolphy,' returned Lapping. 'Isis left you in a cloud of dust.'

'Fuck you Joe, just because every hooker in Sarajevo tried on Mummy's Christmas pyjamas.'

'I hate to be a dampener,' said Herrick, unable to laugh, 'but we don't have time for this. We have to find out who these people are. If necessary, bring the photographer to London and fly that woman Guignal from Skiathos. We need all the help we can get. Anyone who was there – journalists, aid workers, soldiers. Get the Security Services to pull them in and give them a slide show. And we will need to compare these men with all the photographs we have on file.'

'What's the ticking clock?' asked Dolph.

'We don't know,' she said.

The three men exchanged looks, unnerved by the urgency in her voice and the undisguised command in her manner.

CHAPTER TWENTY EIGHT

The operation to arrest the nine suspects would begin in the early hours of Wednesday morning, giving the security forces across Europe about thirty hours to prepare themselves. Vast amounts of surveillance detail, much of it merely proving minor crimes and association, was already hurtling from the Bunker to intelligence services in Paris, Rome, Copenhagen, Stockholm, Budapest and Sarajevo. With this went the names, addresses and photographs of the members of the helper cells. In its final hours, everything RAPTOR had hoarded and secreted was unloaded with abandon.

By the time Herrick went with Colin Guthrie to the Chief's office late on Monday afternoon, ninety-four people, including twenty-three female helpers, were on the arrest list. The Chief informed them that local agencies were gradually taking over the job of monitoring the suspects, though in some cases it was clear they were already familiar with the routines of the suspects as well as their Anglo-American watchers. The surveillance equipment installed by Collection and SIS was kept running so that each country could tap into the live feeds still flickering twenty-four hours a day deep underground at Northolt.

The US President and the British Prime Minister had been seized by an unusual spirit of international cooperation. RAPTOR would now be presented as an initial inquiry into what one diplomat termed the 'morphology of terrorist cells', an exercise whose purpose was to benefit all Western allies. To disguise the unwavering focus on the men who had passed through Heathrow, it was decided, principally by the French, British and American governments, that the dragnet should also include suspects who were not members of the Heathrow group. For this reason the Dutch, Belgian and Spanish governments were brought into the operation and asked to arrest people they had been observing independently of RAPTOR. The Spanish government which, with the French, had in the past mounted among the most successful operations against al-Qaeda and associated North African groups, said it would arrest three men living in La Rioja; the French opted for a man in Marseilles; the Dutch and Belgians had any number of suspects who could be hauled in for questioning, if not actual arrest.

All hope of a publicity blackout had quickly been dropped. The number of people was far too large to contain the news, so it was decided they should make the most of the situation by issuing a joint statement by the Americans and major European governments about the unprecedented cooperation between intelligence services. The Russians were informed on the grounds that the Syrian suspect in Copenhagen, Hafiz al Bakr, had served in Chechnya and was connected with a group who had planned an attack against a Russian embassy.

'It's interesting how these things turn out,' said the Chief. 'You know, it's my firm belief that the idea of keeping this to ourselves was just as much ours as the Americans. A bit of sucking up.'

'Walter's bid to get back in the saddle,' said Guthrie.

'I suppose,' the Chief mused, without sign of malice. 'I must say he made a bit of a fool of himself with Youssef Rahe, given that he never acquired much from the man. Of course we'll need to debrief Vigo as soon as possible. Before we move on the bookshop.'

'You're going to search Rahe's shop?' asked Herrick.

'Yes, before the other arrests, sometime tomorrow evening. But I don't want the scene fouled up by a lot of heavy-handed Special Branch. I've arranged that you will go through the place the moment the police move in. But first I want you to see Vigo.'

'What about the photographs from Bosnia?'

'We'll hold off on that until tomorrow morning. For the moment it's enough that you've established Rahe was in Bosnia. We're ninety-nine per cent sure he is the man referred to as Yahya and you've got a picture of him from the period. That's not a bad day's work, Isis.'

She nodded, aware that the energy was suddenly draining from her.

The Chief noticed the expression in her eyes. 'I know you've had a time of it, but I need you for at least the next six days. Try to get some sleep before tomorrow. Don't spend more than an hour with Vigo.' He handed her an address in Holland Park. 'Take Harland with you. He knows how to handle the bugger.'

'Harland?'

'Yes, he should be at Brown's by now and I've asked him to help out.'

'Harland?' she said stupidly again. 'What's he doing here? I thought he was in the Middle East.'

'No, he's here.' The pale eyes narrowed slightly. 'You're not there to parry with Vigo. Just tell him we need a complete account of his relations with Rahe. If he proves difficult, mention that one way or another we will press for a prosecution.'

Normally Herrick would have relished the return match, but she left Vauxhall Cross without much enthusiasm and only when she found Harland in a jaunty mood in the hotel bar did her spirits lift slightly. It had been a matter of days since she'd seen him climb into the little boat on the Nile, but it seemed like weeks, particularly as Harland appeared so different. She asked why he was looking so pleased with himself.

'I'm not,' he said, 'It's just that life seems suddenly full of possibility.'

'I know you were on the road to Damascus. Did you get God or something? What happened?'

'Nothing I'm going to tell you about, and you needn't look so bloody sour, Isis. Let's have a drink. You're looking a bit part-worn.'

He turned and ordered two Soho Cosmopolitans and just in case the man needed reminding, rattled through the ingredients. 'One measure of citron vodka, one measure of Stolichnaya oranj vodka, cointreau, cranberry juice, fresh lime juice and a twist of lemon. Plus two very cold glasses.'

They drank the cocktails with ceremony. When they'd finished, Harland said, 'And now for bloody Vigo.'

They took the Tube to Holland Park with perspiring office workers and walked up Holland Park Avenue. The evening was warm. Harland removed his jacket and hooked it over his shoulder with one finger. Herrick noticed how young he was looking, even though his hair seemed more grey than brown in the early evening sunlight.

They approached the impressive entrance to Vigo's double-fronted house. Harland pressed the bell for several seconds. The buzzer sounded and they were let in to find a nervous but perfectly attired middle-aged woman in the hallway.

'Davina, this is Isis Herrick,' said Harland. 'We've come to see Walter.'

'He's expecting you,' said Davina Vigo. 'He thought you might like drinks in the garden.'

Vigo was sitting in a slice of sunlight underneath the boughs of a spreading chestnut tree. He regarded them with a baleful look and limply gestured them to chairs. Herrick noticed that Davina remained standing in the French windows with her arms folded apprehensively. He offered them a Pimms cup which they both declined.

'Isis is here to ask you some questions.'

'And you Bobby, why are you here?'

'Because I am.'

'But…?'

'But nothing, Walter. As far as I'm concerned, you should be in jail. If you'd been prosecuted for the last business, none of this would have happened. You're within an inch of being arrested now, so…'

'On what grounds?'

'Aiding and abetting a burglary of Isis's house, for one thing. But that's only a start. They want your blood, Walter. What we need are straight answers to our questions and, more than that, we need you to volunteer everything in your mind, every tiny scrap of information, every faint suspicion that you possess about Youssef Rahe, also known as Yahya.'

Again the slow-motion blink. 'Yes, of course,' said Vigo. 'Where do you want to start?'

'How did you meet him?' asked Herrick.

'At a sale of early Arab manuscripts. Rahe was there to look at them before they went into private hands. I saw him at the preview. We talked.'

'Who made the first move?' asked Herrick.

'I forget.'

'In the light of what you know now, do you think you were targeted?' asked Herrick.

'Well, obviously,' he said disagreeably. 'But at the time I thought he might be useful in understanding the GIA – the Groupe Islamique Armé. The Islamists had taken their fight to France. We felt we were looking at the Islamic equivalent of the Cambodian massacre. He seemed to know quite a few people involved.'

'Sure he did,' said Herrick. 'He'd been in Bosnia with all of them.'

Vigo sighed. 'It's easy with hindsight to say that, but our job does involve taking calculated risks about people.'

'And as you got closer, he began to open up,' said Herrick, brushing the remark aside. 'Did he give you anything worthwhile?'

'Yes, there were names – names that were useful in the round-ups after September eleven.'

'And you plugged in and heard about the people passing through his shop, people asking for help in London. That sort of thing?'

'Yes, the information was always accurate.'

'How much checking of his background went on?'

'As much as was necessary. The story about his upbringing, his job, where he lived in Algiers, all that seemed to tally.' Vigo's manner was now markedly less cowed.

'And you got his brother and family out?' said Herrick. 'Where are they?'

'In England. They were granted asylum.'

'Did you meet the brother? Can you describe him? Where does he live?'

'In Bristol, under the name of Jamil Rahe. He's younger than his brother. Tall, a little overweight, an engineer by training.'

Herrick took out the envelope from a bag and dropped a selection of shots of Rahe and Sammi Loz in Bosnia into his lap. 'Is the man you know as Youssef Rahe here?' Harland looked at the picture but said nothing as he registered Sammi Loz.

Vigo pulled a pair of reading glasses from his shirt pocket and examined the picture a little wearily. 'Yes... I see Rahe.'

'Anyone else?' said Herrick briskly.

He looked through the pictures and then handed them back,

tapping the top image. 'That's the man I know as his brother – Jamil Rahe.'

Herrick glanced at the figure in a balaclava, pulled out her mobile and phoned Dolph, who said Jamil Rahe would be added to the arrest list.

'Let's wait,' she said. 'This may concern a murder charge, as well. He's important.'

She snapped the phone shut. 'A man of very similar appearance coordinated the switch at Heathrow, having come to an arrangement with a washroom attendant in Terminal Three named Ahmad Ahktar. Ahktar and his family died in a fire after the switch. The point is that we have witnesses who saw him watch the planes that day. Also, he appears to have shown interest when Norquist's escort left the airport.'

Vigo said nothing.

'About Youssef Rahe,' she said. 'In the last twelve months, what kind of information was he passing to you?'

'Much the same as before. Things he heard from the Arab community in Bayswater and Edgware Road areas. Useful material about mosques – who worshipped where, the financial support of certain charities, here and abroad. It all helped. Then he was approached by a group, mostly Saudi and Yemeni in origin.'

'And you encouraged him to be recruited?'

'Naturally. It seemed a very good opportunity.'

'When was this?'

'Summer of 2001.'

'And he told you about the website, the screensavers that contain a daily message?'

Vigo nodded. 'That's what you were looking at in the shop, I assume.'

'It would help if you'd just answer my questions,' she said. Vigo stared back at her and she became aware of something stir in the shadows of his personality.

'I wouldn't take that tone with me, if I were you.'

Harland got up and crouched by Vigo's chair. 'Walter, you should know that I'm here on the off-chance that I get to beat the living shit out of you. Otherwise I would not waste my time. Now, answer Isis's question, or by this time tomorrow you'll find yourself on remand in Wandsworth Prison.'

'The screensaver,' she said. 'You were monitoring the messages coming in each day?'

'You forget, I was no longer part of the Service by then.'

'So who was?'

'GCHQ and the Security Services.'

'But there was something different about the information on Norquist's travel arrangements?'

'I gather it was in a double encryption,' replied Vigo.

'We know the Israelis had access to this particular service,' said Harland. 'How long had it been going?'

Herrick wondered how the hell he knew that, but let Vigo answer.

'Two years or so. I'm not sure. You have to remember that once I had handed over Rahe to SIS, I had very little contact, although I did see him on the book-dealing circuit.'

'When the tip about Norquist came in, you were asked to check it?'

He nodded. 'Yes, I called him and he phoned me back on the day of the switch. Before he left for the airport.'

'Tell me about him,' said Herrick. 'What kind of man is Youssef Rahe?'

'Very able,' Vigo replied. 'A true scholar in his own field. A good father and husband too, I would guess. He has none of the obvious appearance of a fundamentalist. He goes to the mosque infrequently, doesn't pray five times a day, is relaxed and liberal in his attitudes.'

'Where do you think he went?' she asked.

'Beyond Beirut? Naturally, I have no idea.'

She sat back and laid her phone on the table deliberately. 'I'd like that drink now,' she said.

Vigo poured the Pimms, holding back the mint leaves and fruit in the jug with a silver spoon.

'What would you do if you were in our position?' she asked quietly. 'We have two or three main suspects who are rich and mobile. They plan months, maybe years ahead and have a very sophisticated understanding of the way we work. What would you do? Where would you go?'

'There are two options, clearly. You can make it very difficult for them to move by releasing their photographs and all the information you have on them. But that may not deter anything planned to happen this week. So I would be inclined to risk revealing nothing whatsoever and hope to trace them. Sammi Loz probably thinks we believe him dead, and neither Youssef or Jamil Rahe know you're onto them. So I would use that slight advantage.'

'How?'

He breathed deeply and looked away to a column of gnats dancing in the sunlight. A blackbird sang out some way off. 'Well, there's no obvious way. But if Youssef is unaware that we're onto him, Jamil also thinks he's safe. You say you believe Jamil is a major figure in the Heathrow plot. I suggest you find him and start by monitoring his phone. If an attack of some kind is expected, then Jamil will be part of it. From what you say, he's murdered before – his own people. Then there is the mosque. You say Jamil made contact with this attendant from Heathrow at the mosque. I take it you're referring to the Cable Road mosque in Belsize Park, the one attended by Youssef Rahe and which is now believed to be under the influence of Sheik Abu Muhsana?'

Herrick nodded.

Vigo talked on, unaffected by Harland's hostility, and began to adopt the professorial manner he had used with Southern Group Three back in the Bunker. At length, even Harland was listening with grudging nods. They discussed ways of prodding Jamil to make contact. He added that this should all happen before the raids on the continent, so that it appeared to come out of the blue, but would be sufficiently menacing for Jamil to break cover. 'These men are not without fear,' he said. 'As Seneca said, "Fear always recoils on those who seek to inspire it; no one who is feared is unafraid himself". '

'Let's keep to the point,' said Harland.

'I find Seneca is always to the point. It's a consolation that we experience nothing in the way of anger, failure, disappointment and sheer bad luck that has not been explored two thousand years ago.'

'I can see why you're reading him,' said Harland. 'I think it's highly unlikely the Chief will want anything more to do with you, other than arranging for you to be tried.'

'We shall see,' he said, studying Isis. 'After all, we've all been duped and made to look fools, have we not? Now, I know Bobby that you and I have never seen eye to eye; that we have a history, as my wife says. But I would suggest that we are the best people to be working on this. I know Youssef and Jamil Rahe, and you two both know Sammi Loz. We're the natural front line – the only front line. And with your contacts in Mossad, we should make an admirable team.'

Harland flinched enough for Herrick to notice. 'I agree with Harland,' she said. 'It's not going to happen.'

'Well, give it some thought overnight. If I don't hear from you or the Chief tomorrow I will understand.'

Herrick and Harland rose.

'And please, no more threats. You know as well as I do they can't put me on trial. Any more talk of this nature and I will make life extremely difficult for this government and several past governments. Tell Teckman that. He knows I mean it.'

'I suppose that's how you wrapped your coils around Spelling,' said Harland.

Vigo got up heavily and made towards a bed of hostas. 'I will expect to hear from you tomorrow.'

'One other thing,' Herrick called after him. 'I want you to admit that you had my house searched by Marenglen's men.'

Vigo stopped in his tracks. 'We wanted to know what you had got, Isis. We knew you weren't just looking at the computer. I think you'll find the Deputy Director was also aware of the need to find out. You could say it was an official operation.'

'What, with armed Albanian pimps?'

'Needs must,' said Vigo, turning back to his hostas.

CHAPTER TWENTY-NINE

They were in Holland Park Avenue again. Herrick snapped the phone shut after talking to one of the Chief's two assistants.

'He's going to call me later,' she said to Harland. 'They don't know when. Look, we don't want to be in a restaurant when he rings. Would you mind if I made dinner at my place? I've got a sort of garden – we can eat outside.'

Harland shrugged pleasantly and they went to a shop nearby to buy wine and some rump steak.

'Vigo is such a complete and utter bastard,' she said as they left the shop. 'I mean, what's his game? What does he want?'

'Influence,' said Harland, flagging down a cab. 'He likes pulling the strings without anyone seeing it's him. He likes the aura of power and he wants acceptance – the clubs, shooting parties, the best stretches on the Tweed; all that bollocks. In one way he's just an unrequited snob, both socially and intellectually.'

'But he is sharp,' she said, as they climbed into the cab.

'Oh yes, very, but somehow that makes him more disappointed. All that superior talent and where is he now? Desperate to have some minor role in the final stages of this operation.'

'You think Teckman will go for it?' she asked.

'Yes, he expected him to make the offer of help. He reads Vigo like a newspaper headline because Vigo wants everything that the Chief has acquired effortlessly. Teckman understands his longings.'

They were silent for the remainder of the journey and watched London slide by, bathed in a soft, crepuscular light.

When they arrived, Herrick went to change and put Harland to work on her terrace, clearing dead leaves and wiping down the chairs and table.

The garden was a triumph of neglect. Where a more careful gardener would have tidied and pruned and scraped away at the ground, Herrick had simply bought a collection of shrubs, vines and climbing roses one afternoon five years before, planted them and left them to their own devices, with the result that the roses had spread over the bushes and reached into two apple trees next door, closing off the garden to inspection from neighbouring houses.

Her attitude to cooking was similarly uncomplicated. As Harland drank a glass of wine outside, he watched her through the kitchen window as she threw together a salad, then briskly dealt with the steak and mushrooms. She had it all ready in under twenty minutes and brought it out to him.

'Have you heard from your father?' he asked.

'Yesterday. We're planning a trip when this is over.' She tore off the end of the baguette and began to work at the steak. 'Actually, I can hardly wait. You know they bloody well fired me this morning. I was pushed out of the building by a creature called Cecil.'

'But you were seen to be right – vindication is rare in your job.'

'I haven't even been officially reinstated yet.'

'How's his wrist?'

'Just sprained. He was lucky. It was his right hand, so he wouldn't have been able to paint and that would have killed him.'

'You're pretty close to the old man,' he said.

She picked up her glass and thought about it. 'Yes and no. Proximate in the sense that we have led our lives together without my mother for so long – yes; intimate in the sense that I know what's going on with him and he with me – no.'

'You rub along.'

She smelled the night air and said, 'God, I'm glad to be back,' then paused. 'These things are so bloody difficult to talk about, you know. People expect love to be one of a number of standard and recognisable varieties, but it isn't like that. The relationship – God, I hate the word – is as individual as the people, and that's all there is to it.'

'But you'll miss him.' He saw the look pass across her face and he wished he hadn't said it.

'Yep,' she said. 'He's exceptional, untrammelled. That's what I'll miss – the idea that there will be no one alive who is quite so independent and, well, strange.'

Harland remembered Eva looking after Hanna Rath in the Tel Aviv apartment, the protectiveness that had made her leave him.

'You want to talk about this personal stuff,' she continued, 'then tell me what happened in the Middle East and why you're so frisky suddenly?'

'I'm not.'

'Well, tell me how you knew the Israelis were deciphering the messages to Rahe from that website – the one that trumpeted Norquist's arrival in London. Who the hell told you about that? I mean, I've only known about Youssef Rahe since this morning, so how did you get onto this so quickly?' She fixed him with an acute look that let Harland know he couldn't be evasive.

He set down his knife and fork and told her about the strained meeting with Eva at the Playlands Hotel. Then about Sammi Loz's relationship with Norquist and Eva's appearance on the Heathrow security film. At one point during his account, Herrick darted to take one of the two remaining steaks and proceeded to consume it at a speed that temporarily put Harland off his stride. He shook his head in disbelief. 'Have the other one,' he said sarcastically. 'You obviously need it.' A very short time afterwards, her hand moved to the dish to take the third steak.

'So the upshot,' he continued, still shaking his head, 'is that Mossad were watching this thing very closely and were not surprised when Norquist was killed. They know about Sammi Loz, but they have no idea about Youssef and Jamil Rahe.'

'Which is the important one – Rahe or Loz?' she asked. 'Who gives the orders?'

'Youssef Rahe – everything points to it,' he said.

'But on the face of it you would say Loz. He's the one with all the money and he's got the better contacts both in New York and the Middle East, to say nothing of the Balkans.'

'So what? Rahe is better hidden. He's been the strategist all along.' He sighed. 'Look, Isis, I don't have the stamina to think about this any more.'

'There's something I don't get,' she said, sitting on the edge of her chair. 'Why are you still working for Teckman on this? Now that RAPTOR is winding up and Teckman has got his job back, we're hardly short of people. Why aren't you floating about with Benjamin Jaidi in the Middle East? I mean, I'm glad you're here and all that, but why? What are you doing?'

'Thanks,' he said, 'but I have to tell you you're becoming remorseless.' He reached over and touched her face, without thinking about it. For a second she looked startled, then let her head collapse into his hand and smiled with a mixture of shyness and devilment.

'What do you think about all this,' she asked. 'The clash of civilisations – Islam versus Christendom?'

'Christ, I don't bloody well know.'

'But don't you want to understand what we're in the middle of? How we got here?' she asked.

'All I know is that there are lunatics, envious of Western technology, resentful of Western wealth, who believe that the solution to humanity's problems is to drag us back into some barbaric state on the lines of the Taleban regime.'

'But you're not anti-Muslim?'

He shook his head. 'No, but I fail to see why Islam hasn't produced proper democracies. If people can begin to participate in democracies in South America there seems no reason why they shouldn't in the Arab countries.'

He noticed she was energised by the prospect of argument. She leaned forward, eyes suddenly glistening. 'And yet a democracy might produce a regime like the Taleban. The fact that people have the vote doesn't guarantee a social democratic system. So you could argue that it is the religion which is at fault, that it is inherently expansionist and intolerant. You could even say that the precepts of Islam are incompatible with democracy and *therefore* human rights, because only democracy can guarantee human rights.'

Harland hadn't seen this side of Isis Herrick before. He liked it, but felt that he was being sluggish. 'Then you make the fact of religious belief the belligerent act and that's very hard for a true democrat to accept.'

She smiled, her mind moving faster than she knew. 'But surely there's no difference between a person who holds doctrinaire political views, like the old style communist, and an Islamic fundamentalist. Their basic positions, whether involving a political creed or a religious one, are anti-democratic and so present a threat which all true democrats must oppose with equal force.'

'That's quite a right-wing stance, Isis. I assumed you were an out-and-out liberal.'

Suddenly the exhilaration in her eyes was tempered. She drank some wine and her gaze swivelled to the dark. 'I am a liberal, but when I was watching Sammi Loz the other night, I saw pure, visceral hatred in his face. He pays a lot of lipservice to Bosnia and the Palestinians, but I somehow didn't think that was his priority. There was an element of savagery which I simply can't contend with.'

He moved to touch her face again.

'In other circumstances, I would say this was rather romantic,' she said.

'Why, what's wrong with the circumstances?' His fingers splayed backwards into her hair.

'I'm sorry, it *is* romantic. Yes it is. To my amazement I find myself very happy to be with you here in my manky little garden. It's taken me by surprise, that's all.'

'Good,' said Harland, not really knowing what he intended. 'Your garden isn't manky, and you are exceptionally attractive – uniquely attractive, in my view – although it's clear you don't feel it.'

She stiffened in his hands. 'Don't say that. That's what Loz said to me.'

'I know… I know about what happened to you. Philip Sarre told the Chief.'

'How odd that he should tell you.'

'He was concerned.' He stopped. ' Anyway, you haven't said what's wrong with the circumstances.'

'It's just that I feel we ought to be doing something to work this thing out. Get Rahe. Find Loz. Look at Dolph's photographs… you know.'

'But you need rest.'

She put her lips to the palm of his hand for a second, then lifted her head. 'Why are you in London? Aren't you meant to be with Jaidi in the Middle East?'

'He's gone back to New York. Things didn't work out in Syria.'

'But that wasn't really my question. Why are you still working on this?'

Harland withdrew his hand, mild exasperation spreading across his face. 'I'm here partly because Teckman asked me to come. He thought he might need help persuading the powers that be that Norquist was in a tangle with Mossad and Loz.' He paused and picked up his glass. 'But the actual reason is that Jaidi and Teckman over-lapped at Cambridge, something I only recently discovered. Teckman took pity on the little man from Zanzibar and introduced him to people, made his life bearable in the cold, damp fens. They have been friends on and off for thirty-five years and were especially close when Teckman was with the British mission to the UN and Jaidi was a minor official. At some stage in the last few months, Jaidi told Teckman about a character named Sammi Loz in New York. Teckman had probably already had him investigated or knew at least that he had shown up on their radar. So, in the wake of Norquist's death, Jaidi gets me an appointment. Then Teckman approaches me the day after-wards. They fixed it between them. Now that we know Loz was working for Hizbollah and has most likely set up a group with Youssef Rahe, clearly Jaidi wants to protect himself and the other well-known patients on Loz's books. You see, Jaidi has been recommending Loz to all manner of folk. Who knows, he may have been responsible for introducing Norquist to Loz and now suffers some kind of remorse. At any rate, you can see that with the Israelis sniffing around, every-one needs to be extremely careful. Information is power when it comes to Israeli foreign policy.' He stopped. 'That's why I'm here to see this thing through. And by the way, that was the reduced version of the story and I don't want to be cross-examined on it.'

'Okay, okay!' She held her hands up in surrender. 'But you have to admit it's interesting that there are so many parallels. These pairings across the Atlantic for instance – Jaidi and Teckman; Loz and Rahe…'

'You and me,' said Harland, grinning.

'That's not what I meant.'

He touched her lightly on her forearm and let his hand rest there.

'The question now is am I going to allow myself to be seduced by you?' She looked at him with an open expression that made him think she was considering it with the same fierce logic that she applied to everything else.

'I'm not necessarily seducing you,' he said. 'I'm more one for synchronised desire.'

'Really? That strikes me as an unworkable strategy. How do you know when you're synchronised?'

Now he was embarrassed. 'Believe me, I'm rather out of practice.'

'Why don't I make some coffee and you can try to remember what to do next.'

She divided the rest of the wine between them, then scooped up the dishes and went inside. He heard a clattering as everything was chucked into the dishwasher, then some music that was very familiar to him. 'What's that?' he called through the window. 'Where have I heard it before?'

Her head appeared in the window. 'It's Sufi music. You heard it on the island. When I was in Sudan I bought this in the market. It's wonderful, but I was worried it would seem silly and out of place in England.'

She reappeared a few minutes later with coffee. 'You know there's one thing I slightly resent about you and the Chief. Leaving me on that island with Khan and Loz. I was very exposed.'

Harland nodded. 'The Chief told me you had backup. By the time I left, Sarre and Lapping were within a few minutes' boat ride.'

'But I didn't know they were there and they couldn't know what was going on. What kind of backup is that?'

'I suppose he felt he had no option, because there were so few people at his disposal. But he was right in one way. You drew them out and got the crucial information about Yahya and the time frame we're working in.'

'Still, it was bloody irresponsible of him, don't you think?'

'Yes, but I'm afraid I was partly to blame. I insisted on leaving. I had to go.'

'Alpha shit,' she said matter-of-factly. 'Still, you pulled a rabbit out of your own hat, though it turns out to be a much smaller one than mine.' She smiled mischievously at him.

They were both aware that they were marking time, but Harland reckoned he had made one move and that it was now her turn. The music slipped into the night to entice the uncomprehending world of a London suburb, and they watched each other. Without warning, she moved from her chair to stand over him, then put her hands down to his jaw, cupped his face and bent down to kiss him.

'We don't have to go to bed,' she said. 'But I thought I'd let you know that we are synchronised.'

'Good,' he murmured as she kissed him again.

'But on the whole, I think I'd like to go to bed very soon – with you.'

'Yes,' said Harland. 'That seems a good idea.'

They left the table and went to her bedroom, which struck him as a remarkably private, perhaps even lonely, place. It was bare but comfortable, and on one side of the bed there was a stack of books and a picture of a small girl and a woman standing in the shade of a tamarisk tree. The woman looked remarkably like Isis, but he knew it must be her dead mother, and that the girl with her face creased with laughter was Isis. He suddenly felt the scale of her loss all those years ago and turned to her and held her, partly because of this flash of understanding, but also because he was desperate now to end his own long, morose isolation, and prove to himself that he could love and listen as well as the next man. She wriggled free to undress, which she did with little fuss, then stood before him without the slightest embarrassment. Harland was aware of his inability to grasp the whole of her in his mind – to resolve the neat white figure in front of him with the turbulent, driven person he'd seen working in the field. She came to him, hung her arms round his neck and told him to take off his clothes. At length they fell to the bed and became lovers. Finally Isis grew silent and went to sleep in his arms. His eyes closed too, but less happily. In his mind were three words – victim, survivor, person; the three stages he had been told the torture victim must go through. Was he yet the person he had once been? Was this thing that had happened to him fourteen years ago in the cellar of the house in Prague still distorting him? He was now certain that was what his bad back had been all about; not Eva's disappearance, or the air crash.

As Sammi Loz had said, the body remembers. Old pain – that's what he had to ditch to become a person again. He looked down at Isis's face and remembered why he had first been drawn to her. It wasn't her looks, which in fact had taken him some time to get used to. It was her conviction that no matter what Khan had done or might be, his torture would be a crime.

Then he closed his eyes.

Some time later they were woken by the phone ringing. Harland heard her answer to the Chief. They were expected in the office at 6.30 a.m. the next day.

CHAPTER THIRTY

Early next morning a group of about thirty people assembled at Thames House. Herrick and the key members of the SIS team arrived shortly before Vigo entered the building. The Chief had evidently spoken with him overnight and agreed that the man Vigo had identified in the Bosnian photographs as Jamil Rahe was the only hope of tracing Youssef Rahe and Sammi Loz. Vigo was once again the architect of a plan, but now he had the support of the entire security establishment and, though looking drawn, somehow managed to present a picture of righteous self-possession.

Jamil Rahe had been traced to a maisonette in a quiet street in Bristol, and a surveillance team was already in place. At 8.15 a.m. a uniformed policeman and a member of the local Special Branch, posing as an immigration official from the Home Office, approached the building and rang the doorbell. The exchange with Jamil Rahe was relayed to Thames House from a microphone in the Special Branch officer's briefcase, and it was agreed that their manner was striking precisely the right balance between suspicion and reassurance. They explained that a form had been overlooked in the processing of Jamil Rahe's application for political asylum and that it must be completed that day to make everything legal. Across the street a cameraman, hidden in the back of a TV repair van, silently recorded the scene. The three men were still talking on the doorstep when the first images arrived through the secure internet server at Thames House. One glance showed that he was the man from the Bosnia photographs. These images were then forwarded by email to a laptop in the possession of Special Branch officers on the roof of Heathrow's Terminal Two.

At length, the big Algerian offered the two officers coffee while he filled in the form. They went in, and within a very short time the plain-clothes policeman had secreted a tiny transmitter in Rahe's home so that the sound coming to Thames House was of much better quality. Jamil said he was familiar with the form they'd brought and insisted that he had already filled in one like it. The officers apologised. While he sat at the table writing, they gently questioned him about the kind of welfare benefits he had been claiming, his prospects of work and his wife's attendance at a language course. Once or twice Rahe's replies seemed rather too considered, particularly when one of the officers mentioned that with his brother Youssef in London things would not be as difficult for him as it was for other new immigrants. The fifteen minutes of talk and coffee passed off very amicably, yet by the time they left, saying that this would certainly be the last he saw of them, Jamil was plainly on his guard.

Five minutes later, the police at Heathrow contacted Thames House. Three plane-spotters had identified the Algerian definitely as the man who stood with them on the observation platform on May 14 and on several occasions before that. Jamil Rahe was now confirmed as a very significant element in the story, and not for the first time the Chief looked towards Herrick and winked his thanks. Now all they had to do was wait for Jamil to make contact with someone.

An hour passed, during which the Chief and Barbara Markham, the Director General of the Security Services, discussed the raid on Youssef Rahe's bookshop in Bayswater. The Security Services wanted to move on the premises immediately, but the Chief argued that they should wait for as long as possible, although plainly it had to be done by the time the arrests started across Europe the following morning. Eventually they compromised on 5.00 p.m. that afternoon, with the agreement that the staff of the Secret Intelligence Service would have the run of the place once it had been secured. The Chief returned to Vauxhall Cross, leaving Dolph and Herrick to watch as a stream of visitors looked over the shots from Bosnia. Journalists, diplomats, army officers and even the odd aid worker had been contacted the previous evening and asked as a matter of urgency to Thames House. They were all on time for the unusual invitation to coffee and croissants, but as each of them pored over the photographs laid out on a table and consulted a map where the photographs had been shot, it became clear that the remaining men would not be so easily identified. 'Well,' said Dolph as the last one left, 'we've still got the Guignal gal. Maybe Lapping should fly out to Skiathos with a disk. He might even lose his virginity.'

'It would be quicker to get her to an internet café and send them by email,' she said.

'You're not worried about security?' he asked.

'Damn security, and anyway we *do* need to speak to her about Jamil Rahe. She may remember him. Why don't you do that?'

Dolph's eyes flared. 'All of a sudden I'm your runner, Isis. Why the fuck don't you do it?'

'Sorry,' she said. 'We'll both talk to her, okay? It will be better.'

Dolph still looked put out. 'You're tired. You need to rest.'

'Yes,' she said, managing a grin. 'I'm sorry.'

'You've had a rough few weeks and sooner or later it's going to tell.'

'Lecture over?'

'I mean it,' he said, looking down at the photographs.

She *was* tired, damned tired. She thought of Harland in her kitchen that morning, sitting as though drugged, over a cup of coffee. They said little, but she had tried to let him know that she didn't regret sleeping with him. He was affectionate but also slightly remote, as though mentally drawing back to grasp the scale of something. Fine, she had thought, she'd wait, and if this turned out to be a one-night stand, all well and good. It had been very pleasant.

'Don't worry,' she had said, brushing her knuckles across the top of his hand as the cab pulled up at Brown's Hotel. 'There're no strings. I'm not like that.'

'I'm not *worried*, just astonished that it happened. More than that, I'm moved and extraordinarily grateful that you would favour my old bones.'

'Grateful is not a word that should ever be used in the context of sex.'

They smiled at each other and it was left at that, but as he reached for the handle of the cab door she noticed the haunted, puzzled look in his eyes. She clutched at his arm and immediately regretted it because it made her seem needy, when in fact she was just concerned for him.

'Are you okay?

He had replied with slight irritation, 'Yes, of course I'm okay.' Then he pulled free and got out of the cab.

It had been a very unsatisfactory parting and she wished she could put it right.

Dolph and Herrick had returned to Vauxhall Cross by 11.00 a.m. but it was not until 1.10 p.m. that they were told that Jamil Rahe had left his house with a sports bag over his shoulder and walked to the end of his road to catch a bus. A feed from Thames House was hooked up and they were able to hear Jamil's progress. The bus took him to the centre of Bristol, where he moved unhurriedly from store to store buying odd items – a pair of socks, a packet of soap and a school exercise book. At length he came to an electronics shop where he browsed through the display and then, as though on impulse, bought a pay-as-you-go cell phone. The phone stayed in the box and the watchers were fairly certain he wouldn't be able to use it straight away because it would require a period of charging. Rahe then whiled away time in a park, briefly visited a library and considered the programme of movies at a multiplex cinema. The consensus was that he had acti-vated a pre-planned routine to make sure he wasn't being followed. Several times he went through 'dry cleaning' channels – an escalator in a shopping mall, an underpass and an alley, each of which allowed him to observe at leisure the people in his wake. The police response was briefly to implement a procedure known as cascade surveillance, which involved filling his path with watchers, like water falling over a boulder. But Rahe moved so slowly through the city centre that it soon became necessary to revert to traditional methods and just hang a little further back.

Herrick realised time was getting on. Even though the raid on the Pan Arab Library had now been put back to 6.00 p.m. she would need to leave Vauxhall Cross by 5.15 and it was now 3.30. She went and found Dolph and they tried for a fifth time to raise Hélène Guignal. She answered on the first ring, and in response to Herrick's question, told them that she had her laptop with her and could pick up her email. The Bosnia photographs were sent to her.

Ten minutes later she called them. Dolph put her on speaker.

'These pictures are *étonnant* – how do you say? Amazing. The whole group is here.'

'Which group? Do you remember their names?'

'The one standing in profile is Hassan, my boyfriend. And you have seen Yaqub and Sammi, yes?'

'That's Youssef Rahe,' Herrick said to Dolph.

'Who else do you see?' he asked impatiently.

'Larry.'

'Larry? Which is Larry?'

'The man in the foreground. He is the American – a convert to Islam. *J'oublie son nomme islamique, mais Les Frères* – the Brothers – they called him Larry.'

'This group referred to themselves as the Brothers?' asked Dolph.

'Yes.'

'Right, the tall man by the tree. This man we now believe to be Algerian, like Yaqub. He is passing himself off as Yaqub's brother?'

'Please, I don't understand.'

'He is pretending to be Yaqub's brother?'

'*Non!* He is not his brother! But he is *Algérien*, yes.'

'His name?'

She hesitated. 'Rafik….no, Rasim. That is it – Rasim.'

Dolph was scribbling a note to Herrick.

'Any other name for him?'

'No.'

'Do you know anyone else?'

'These are the only names. Some of the others I recognise but I did not know them well. I do not know their names.'

Dolph passed Herrick a note which said, 'THEY WERE ALL IN THE HAJ SWITCH.'

She wound up the conversation, saying that she or someone else would call that evening and that Guignal should keep her phone on. She also said Nato headquarters would be made aware of her help in this matter, a way of underlining what she had already told Guignal about not showing the pictures to anyone or speaking about them.

'We'll have to get someone to Guignal,' she said. 'We need to know everything she can remember about the Brothers.'

'There are so many fucking names in this thing,' said Dolph. 'As soon as we've nailed one group, up pops another with a fresh load of backgrounds and connections.'

'But we're peeling the onion.'

'Yeah, and I'm fucking sure that every one of them went to the Haj. Nathan Lyne wanted to keep on it, but Collins and the rest of them said we should focus on the suspects we knew about in Europe. They were going to come back to it. A bad mistake.'

'So what you're saying is that you agree with Lapping's theory about the Heathrow Group being a set of cardboard cut-outs. The Bosnia Group – the Brothers – are the core of the operation?'

'Fuck, I don't know. I guess we'll see tomorrow when they begin questioning the nine suspects. But think about it. Every year people are trampled to death on the pilgrimage. Twelve years ago 1,400 people were crushed in a pedestrian tunnel. The main problem was identifying the bodies because everyone is dressed the same and bits of ID get lost.'

A few minutes later, they went to report the conversation with Guignal to the Chief, and the information was relayed to the Joint Intelligence Committee. Sarre, not Lapping, was dispatched to Greece to interview Guignal and if necessary persuade her to return with him to London. The Chief was extremely keen that the pictures should not fall into the hands of the French DGSE, so the local MI6 in the Athens Embassy was sent on ahead to babysit her until Sarre arrived. Then Nathan Lyne was asked to focus all the resources he could muster at the Bunker on the Haj switch. There would be a joint CIA–SIS meeting at Vauxhall Cross that evening, at a time to be determined later.

In Bristol, Jamil Rahe was still aimlessly traipsing round the city centre. He certainly appeared cool, but a clue to his actual state of mind came when he called into a chemist and bought antacid tablets and a pack of double strength painkillers. Then he went to a coffee bar, took some of these with an espresso and settled by the window to watch the street. It was now believed that he was waiting for a check-in time or the right moment to use a dead-letter drop to make a contact somewhere in Bristol city centre.

By now it was 4.30 p.m. Herrick, Dolph and Lapping separately left

Vauxhall Cross to go to Bayswater. Herrick had made an appointment in the hairdressing salon across the street from the Pan Arab Library, while Dolph and Lapping planned to install themselves in a betting shop fifty yards away. She had been told that Harland would also be there. On the way, he called her mobile to say he was already in position at a café named Paolo's down the street.

As she sat waiting for the hairdresser to finish his previous appointment, Herrick glanced up from her magazine. Everything was as normal. Rahe's disagreeable wife was sitting at the desk serving customers and working at the computer. The assistant whom Herrick had spoken to once could be seen darting between the shelves and a pile of books that had clearly just been delivered. The street itself was relatively free of traffic, though there were quite a few pedestrians about and a gas repair team was examining a hole in the pavement about thirty yards from the bookshop.

She received a hair wash then a head massage, which made her suddenly feel so drowsy that she had to ask the stylist for coffee. While a couple of centimetres were taken off her hair she watched the shop in the mirror. At about 5.30 she noticed the bookshop filling with an unusual number of customers. If these were members of the public it meant the raid might have to be delayed, but then it occurred to her that the book buyers were from the police and MI5. It wasn't beyond either to raid the place early and take any evidence for themselves. Moreover, the Secret Intelligence Service had no rights in this domestic matter and agreements between chiefs tended to be ignored or bypassed by officers on the ground. She sent a text message to Dolph, asking him to have a look at the shop. A reply came. 'Just had 5–1 winner at Windsor.' A minute later she saw him pass the Pan Arab Library with Lapping in tow. Another text arrived – 'Nothing doing yet'. They headed back to the betting shop.

A few people left the bookshop, but one or two remained.

At 5.47 Herrick left the salon and took a stroll up to the café, where she spotted Harland with his head buried in the *Financial Times*. He did not look up, but signalled to her by waggling the fingers at the edge of his newspaper. It was 5.52. She walked back and noticed the gas workers ahead of her replace the manhole cover, pack away their gear into the back of the van and make a beeline for the shop. Then three unmarked police cars pulled up just before the shop. The raid was on.

She phoned Harland and hurried towards the entrance of the bookshop. Dolph and Lapping were already there and pressing their case to be admitted behind the police officers, apparently without success. When Herrick arrived, slightly out of breath, she was told by a thick-set Special Branch officer that he knew of no agreement that would allow SIS people to search the premises before it had been secured.

'Of course it's been secured,' said Herrick, pulling out her phone again. 'There're only a couple of women.' She used the speed-dial to call the Chief's office and walked a few paces away to explain the situation to his assistant. He told her to keep the line open while the problem was sorted out. Herrick went back to the policeman and said, 'Look, you do realise we're working for the Prime Minister's office? It's imperative that we have access to this building now.'

'I don't give a toss who you're working for,' replied the policeman.

Harland was behind her now and also began to argue with him. But at this moment one of the men inside the shop appeared to have been contacted and the policeman barring the door was told to stand aside.

Herrick's first thought on entering was that there were too many people there. Men were already rummaging around the shop, randomly picking books from shelves and searching the drawers of the desk. Rahe's wife and the shop assistant were seated on two chairs at the end of a run of bookshelves. Lamia Rahe, as they now knew her name to be, was looking at the ground, holding her head in her hands. The assistant's eyes oscillated wildly. No one seemed to have any idea what to do with them, and even Herrick didn't know whether they had an arrest warrant for Mrs Rahe. She went up to the officer in charge and was about to suggest clearing the shop when she realised that she was still holding an open line to Vauxhall Cross. She placed the phone to her ear. 'Christ, I'm sorry. Are you still there?'

'I gather you got in,' said the Chief's assistant. 'But while you're on, you might as well know that the man in Bristol appears to be about to make contact. He's just switched the SIM cards from the new phone to one he had in his pocket. We heard a few moments ago.'

Herrick hung up, and was about to ask the officer to stop the search, but at this moment she became aware of an insistent noise coming from the apartment above the shop. She noticed Lamia Rahe's head rise at the sound, but no one else seemed to have noticed. She found herself calling out to the room. 'Can everyone shut up for a moment.' She held up her hands and clapped rapidly. 'Please! Can you shut up!' The shop went silent and they all heard the sound of a mobile phone. Then it went dead.

'Have you searched upstairs yet?' she asked the policeman.

'There's no one there. We've checked.'

'No children?'

He shook his head.

'I'm certain that phone was silenced by someone. Didn't you hear the slight noise before it stopped ringing? And anyway, where the hell are the children? School finished at least two hours ago.'

Of course. There weren't any children. Suddenly she understood that they had been part of a cover.

Herrick was aware of Lamia Rahe's gaze coming to rest on her with an oddly thoughtful expression and knew she had recognised her from the night of the break-in.

She looked away. 'I think you should see who stopped it ringing.'

Then Lamia Rahe erupted from her chair, gesticulating and muttering in Arabic.

'Sit that woman down,' said the officer. But before anyone could take hold of her, she had produced a gun from her shirts and, still screaming, took aim in Herrick's direction. Herrick went blank, then at the precise moment the gun went off, something hit her like a train from behind. Next she was sprawling across a length of rope matting by the desk. Five or six shots were loosed off into the mêlée of men at the front of the shop. One of the policemen pulled a gun and fired a single round. Lamia Rahe sank to the ground, dead.

Herrick whipped her head round. Immediately in front of her was Harland, who had been hit in the back by a bullet meant for her. Beyond him lay Joe Lapping, who was writhing on the floor, clutching his right thigh, and Andy Dolph was on his back with blood all over his chest. For a moment she simply could not absorb what she was seeing. She scrambled over to them. Dolph was white but he grimaced a kind of smile and whispered an oath.

'Get help,' she shouted. 'Get an ambulance here.'

She cast around. The confusion was total. The shop assistant had dropped to the side of her dead boss and was shrieking and hammering on the floorboards with her fists. Two policemen were shouting into their radios and another three had taken off to the back of the shop to climb the stairs to the flat. There was a noise from above, something being moved across the floor, then a sash-cord window being flung upwards, but Herrick was unable to interpret these in any meaningful way. There were more shots, so rapid that it seemed like a machine gun was being fired. Something fell above them.

Somehow she got a grip on herself and, dimly remembering the first aid course she once attended during IONEC training, she began to conduct a hurried triage. Of the three, Harland was the best off. The bullet had sliced across his back like a sword stroke, giving him a gash of six to seven inches long on the left side. Dolph had been hit just below his collar-bone and there was a nasty exit wound in the middle of his shoulder blade. When she saw the massive amount of blood pouring from just below Lapping's groin on his right thigh, she knew she had to act.

'We can't wait,' she shouted. 'Let's get all of them to St Mary's right now. It's only minutes away.' The commanding officer agreed. St Mary's was alerted and two of the unmarked police cars moved to the front of the shop. Dolph was placed in the back seat of the first car, which tore off towards Paddington with a single blue light clamped haphazardly to its roof and a siren wailing. Lapping went in the second car, Harland having elected to wait for the ambulance. To show that he was going to be okay, he insisted on getting to his feet and then bent over so that a policeman could press a field dressing to the wound.

By now, the men who had gone up to the flat were spilling down the stairs. None was hurt, but they were evidently very shocked and couldn't answer Herrick's questions. She got up and physically accosted one of the men.

'What the hell happened?'

'Look for yourself,' said the young officer quietly.

Driven now by an insane need to complete what she had come for, she mounted the stairs to the flat and entered a kitchen. Sunlight streamed through a window. She passed through a living room at the front of the building and then turned left towards a bathroom and bedroom. It was here she found Youssef Rahe lying dead beneath an open window. Net curtains ballooned into the room. Beside him was a gun.

It was obvious what had happened. Having heard the shots from his wife's gun, Rahe had pushed at the door of a secret compartment built behind the headboard of the double bed, causing the bed to shift a few inches across the room. He had then attempted to escape through the window, but hearing the police already in the flat, had turned round to fire on them and been shot himself. There were four or five bullet wounds in his upper body and a number of holes around the walls and furnishings.

Herrick crouched down by the body to make sure it was Rahe. He had lost weight and grown a beard, and in his final expression there was a hardness and strain which was never evident in the film of him from Heathrow, but it was definitely the man she had thought of as a harmless little butterball. Two silver bangles on his left arm caught her attention, and then just beyond them, under the bed, the mobile phone. It must have flown from his pocket as he was hit by the hail of police bullets. She retrieved it and slipped it into her pocket, all the while looking at his face and half praying that his eyes would open and all the knowledge of what he had planned with his group would be restored. Already she understood that his death was a disaster.

She rose, stepped over the corpse and hefted the bed a little further into the room so she could get at the wall-hanging that disguised the entrance to the compartment. She lifted it and felt along the side of the entrance for possible booby traps. Satisfied that the entrance was clear, she reached inside and pulled at the cord switch. A single fluorescent strip flickered. She squeezed through the opening and immediately realised that the compartment had not just been taken from the bedroom, but ran the entire length of the flat, shaving space from three different rooms. At the far end there was another door which opened into the utility cupboard in the kitchen. Judging by the dusty impression of his hands around its edge, this was the preferred way in and out, even though it must have required Rahe to crouch down. She turned round. The compartment was oppressively narrow, measuring only four feet across, and was without natural light or ventilation. There was an air freshener at each end, yet there was still a marked staleness in the air, the odour of tedium and sweat. At the end nearest the street there was an old-fashioned army camp bed propped against the wall. Next to this was a rolled up prayer mat and some lifting weights.

Her eyes moved to a shelf where there was a cloth laid out with half an apple, an open packet of cheese crackers and a bottle of mineral water. Underneath she noticed a small red lightbulb. The wire from the socket ran down the wall and through the floor to the bookshop below. She guessed this was a warning light, operated from the cashier's desk. But there were no other power points – nowhere to plug in a computer or charge a phone.

She moved towards two wire coat hangers on a waste pipe that ran from the flats above. On one of these was an old brown suit jacket with biro stains in the lining. She felt the jacket with a clapping motion, then stopped, delved inside the pocket and withdrew a passport and a wallet. She was about to examine these when a man's voice called out from the bedroom. 'Don't shoot,' she shouted.

She left the foetid atmosphere to find four policemen in the room, two of them wearing body armour and carrying Heckler and Koch machine guns. One of them said, 'You have to leave the building now, Miss.'

'Of course,' she said. 'You know where to find me when you need a statement.'

'You can tell the officer downstairs,' came the reply.

In the event, she slipped away without being challenged and melted into the crowds that had gathered in the street to watch Harland being helped into an ambulance.

CHAPTER THIRTY-ONE

Herrick rushed to St Mary's Hospital but was told she would have to wait for news. After an hour, a woman in her thirties, still dressed for theatre, came to speak to her. Lapping's injury was far more dangerous than Dolph's because the bullet had grazed the femoral artery and he had been on the point of dying from blood loss when he was brought into casualty. He was now very weak, but out of danger. Dolph's injuries would take a lot longer to heal. The collar-bone had been shattered by the impact of the 9 mm bullet and his shoulder blade would need further surgery. It would be three or four months before he was able to work again. Harland was also still under anaesthetic, having had an operation to repair the damage done to the muscle tissue and skin on his back. He wouldn't be fit to see anyone until the following day.

As the doctor spoke, she touched Herrick's shoulder. 'You know, you look pretty drained yourself. If you were involved in the shooting, you may experience some shock.'

She shook her head and said she had better be getting back to work. She left the hospital by the main entrance and walked through the courtyard. As she hit the street she saw a couple hurrying from a cab. They were unmistakably Dolph's parents. The man in his sixties moved with Dolph's heavy, rolling walk while the woman had his alert eyes. They looked modest people and somehow ashamed of the worry. Herrick turned to say something as they passed but suddenly couldn't find the words. She stopped in her tracks, realising she needed to sit down and collect herself, maybe have something to eat. Across the street there was a pub named the The Three Feathers, festooned with hanging baskets of petunias. She entered an almost empty lounge bar, where a barman and the few customers were glued to *Channel Four News*. A distant shot of the Pan Arab Library was being shown: police tape was stretched across the road, forensics were entering the building as plainclothes officers left with boxes.

Herrick ordered a double whisky and a meat pie that was sitting unappetisingly in the display cabinet. She perched on a bar stool while the pie was microwaved and tried to get a hold of herself by concentrating on the pocket of anxiety lodged at the top of her diaphragm.

As the pie was presented to her on a paper plate, she heard a voice from her left. Walter Vigo stood with one hand on the bar. 'A bad business, Isis. Are they all right?' He attempted a sympathetic smile but produced only a leer.

She turned and examined him for a moment. 'No, they're bloody well not all right. Joe Lapping nearly died. What the fuck are you doing here anyway?' She cut into the pie. Vigo looked down at the flow of gravy with acute distaste.

'I was concerned to see how they were and spotted you crossing the road.'

'Right,' said Herrick, grimacing. 'What is it you really want?'

'A word – somewhere more private, perhaps.'

'I've got to go back to the office in a few minutes.'

'This can't wait.' he said.

'Then say it now.'

He waited for the barman to move away. 'I want to know what you found in the bookshop.'

'If I had found anything it would be none of your fucking business.'

Vigo's mouth pursed into a tight little hole. 'I need to know – lives may depend on it.'

She said nothing and continued eating the pie, noticing that the strange throbbing in her left arm had developed into an ache.

'It's important that I know. I gather there have been some useful discoveries in Bristol.'

'Then go to Bristol.'

'Look, Herrick. These are my people, Jamil and Youssef Rahe. They're my contacts. Where would we be if I hadn't made use of them?'

This amazed her. 'Well, three of my friends wouldn't be in hospital for a start. You were suckered. No one is going to see it any other way.'

'I don't care what they think about this. There may have been significant intelligence in that shop that only I am in a position to appreciate.'

She was struck by the plaintive note in his voice, and if she had been feeling less strange she would have thought about it more deeply. 'You forget, Walter, you're on the outside now. I can't talk to you about any of this.' She gestured to the TV set.

'Do you think I would bother to come here and talk to you if it wasn't important?'

Herrick shrugged. 'Frankly, I don't care what your interest is.'

'I am in touch with people who need this information and can make far better use of it than you. You have the opportunity to save lives.'

'Who?'

He shook his head.

She pulled out her phone and pressed the key to redial the Chief's office.

'What're you doing?' he snapped.

'If you want access to what I know, go through the Chief. You can talk to him now.'

Without a word, Vigo turned and made for the door. Herrick gave it a few seconds before hopping off the bar stool and rushing to the window. A new model Jaguar pulled out from the kerb with Vigo at the wheel. Then she put the phone to her ear and was about to speak to the Chief's assistant, but he interrupted her. 'You're needed here. Please return immediately.'

Herrick laid out the phone, wallet and US passport in front of the head of the MI5–MI6 controllerate, Colin Guthrie. He let out a low whistle. 'Where the hell have you been?'

'At the hospital.'

'And after that?'

'I needed some time, so I had a drink. Guess who I bumped into? Vigo. What the hell's he doing? He wanted to know what I had got from the bookshop.'

Guthrie thought for a moment. 'I imagine he's up to something in his capacity as head of Mercator. One always forgets that when Vigo was pushed out last time round he set himself up as a private intelligence agency. We thought it was pretty much dormant but perhaps we were wrong. Anyway, we've got a lot to get through so let's make a start.' He picked up a printout of an email. 'First, Jamil Rahe. He hasn't said a word since he was arrested, but a search of his house and a garage nearby produced a great deal – twenty passports, equipment to forge visas, blank credit cards, the records of 152 different credit cards, acquired by a skimming device, a telescope, airline schedules, a notebook logging arrival and departure times at Heathrow, computer records of payments to foreign banks, a mass of extremist literature and the usual bloody videos of Mujahadin victories in Chechnya et cetera.' His description tailed off as a dozen or so of Herrick's colleagues filed into his office.

He let the paper slip to the desk and gave them a brief update on the condition of the men in hospital, then divided the group into three teams to chase up leads provided by the items Herrick had taken from the bookshop. She was still feeling odd, but the tasks ahead moved the anxiety to the back of her mind and when Nathan Lyne appeared for a meeting on the Haj switch she began to feel better.

The passport she had found was held in the name of David Zachariah, a thirty-eight-year-old jeweller living in White Plains, New York. Herrick had opened it on the way to Vauxhall Cross and silently saluted Hélène Guignal for predicting that the name Zachariah would appear somewhere in Rahe's portfolio of identities. While Rahe's replacement had been tortured and killed, Rahe had crossed the Syrian border. Fourteen days later he travelled as Zachariah to New York, with a stopover at Athens. He had stayed in the US until the previous weekend, then took an overnight flight back to Britain and landed at Gatwick Airport.

The wallet contained impressive confirmation of the existence of Zachariah. There were three different credit cards with billing addresses in White Plains, each of which was settled regularly by an account held at a bank in Manhattan, where all mail was delivered. Adding credibility to Zachariah's life were the business cards, a membership card of the American–Israeli Friendship Society, a US driver's licence, a dry-cleaning ticket in his name and various notes addressed to Zachariah. There was no such place as 1014 Jefferson Drive in White Plains, and no trace of Zachariah in any local records.

As crucial as the record of these recent trips was the evidence of his movements across Europe during the previous winter. Cross-referencing the point-of-entry stamps in its pages with payments made on his credit cards – acquired with his usual authority by Nathan Lyne – they produced dates for the purchases of airline and train tickets in Hungary, Germany, Italy, Denmark and Sweden, and for the payment of hotel bills. It was obvious that Youssef Rahe had used the Zachariah identity as a cover for his meetings with the helper cells all over Europe. This in itself would be useful evidence in subsequent prosecutions of members of the helper cells.

The credit cards had most recently been used in New York – again hotels and restaurants were in evidence. He also drew $8,800 in cash from his account at the Stuyvesant Empire Bank on 5th Avenue, leaving a balance of $22,000.57. Rahe was well-funded, but where from? The bank revealed that payments of $15,000 were made on the third of each month by a company named Grunveldt-Montrea, of Jersey City, New Jersey. No such company existed in the phone directory. Before leaving New York for London, Zachariah hired a car for a period of three days on one of the cards. Lyne put in a request to the FBI to see if any trace of his journey could be picked up by speeding or parking tickets, or even motel registers, because he had evidently not used his cards to buy gas. Herrick made a note, which ended with the word Canada and three question marks.

The cell phone produced less definite information, although it was now established that the call stifled by Youssef Rahe while he was hiding above the bookshop had come from his 'brother', Jamil. Police reported observing Jamil Rahe switch the SIM cards and dial a number at 6.15 p.m., presumably the agreed check-in time. When he failed to get an answer, he was seen to lower the phone and check the display with a look of puzzlement. At this point the police moved in and arrested him.

It was also clear that this particular phone of Youssef Rahe's was only used to receive calls. Several had been made to him in America over the first half of the year, but they weren't identified in the phone's memory and it would take time for the two or three phone companies likely to have handled them to search the records of millions of subscribers. Herrick was sure that elsewhere in the bookshop there would be other phones to investigate, and that in time much would be exhumed from the computer, although it was now being examined by the Security Services, who had proved resistant to suggestions that SIS should have access.

At 11.15 p.m. the Chief came in, looking grave. The news media had, it seemed, been well briefed by Special Branch about the involvement of SIS 'cowboys', to explain why two people were dead and a further three lay in hospital.

'We're bringing the arrests in Europe forward because the coverage may alert the suspects,' he said. 'However, Rahe's use of multiple identities may work to our advantage. It's likely the people he dealt with on the continent knew him only as Zachariah. They may not make the connection when they hear of the raid on the bookshop.'

He stopped and surveyed the drawn faces around the room. 'Look, I don't think there's much more you can do tonight. I'd rather have you all fresh for tomorrow than working through the night. There is very little we can do until these arrests have been made and we can begin to assess the information they produce.'

'There's a ticking bomb,' said Herrick. 'Loz said something would happen eleven days from last Wednesday night. That could be either Friday or Saturday, according to which day he was counting from.'

'We *think* there's a ticking bomb, which is not quite the same thing, is it? Youssef and Jamil Rahe are out of the picture; the nine suspects will be in the bag shortly; and the evidence is leaning towards Loz being killed on the island. We gather from Foyzi that four bodies were found, one very close to the spot where you say Loz was. Even with this unknown – and I am inclined to think that is *not* an unknown – the network you have done so much to expose, Isis, is dead.'

'But there are the other men in the photograph from Bosnia,' she said. 'We haven't got around to matching the faces with names from Dolph's research on the Haj switch.'

'All that's true. But go home now, then return as early as you like in the morning. By then the nine will be detained and we may know more.' He said goodnight and beckoned Herrick out into the corridor.

'Pace yourself, Isis. Get some sleep tonight. I mean it. You look bloody awful.'

She did not go straight home, but instead took a cab to Brown's Hotel, where she explained to an assistant manager what had happened to Robert Harland. After switching on the midnight news and checking with the hospital, he eventually agreed to let her into Harland's room. He watched as she gathered together some dark blue pyjamas, underpants, socks, shirt and a sponge-bag. She noticed a slim black phone book by the telephone and put it together with the clothes in a small overnight bag, then asked whether the manager would mind if she took a bunch of flowers that were on top of a bureau. He shook his head wearily and she wrapped them in a hotel laundry bag. Later, she dropped everything off at the hospital and talked to a nurse about her three friends. She heard that Harland's sister had been in touch and would be flying back from holiday.

It was 6.45 a.m. when she reached her floor next morning. Lyne was at her desk, using her computer. Nearby was Laughland who she assumed had been told to keep an eye on the CIA officer.

'What's going on?' she asked Lyne, dropping the bag.

He looked up. 'So much for *The Subtle Ruse*, Isis. These guys all meant business. Explosives, nerve agents. You name it, they got it.'

She moved to the coffee machine, thinking furiously. 'Do we know when they were going to attack?'

'No, I've only been here five minutes. I know no more than I've told you, but right now there's a briefing.' Laughland was already at the door agitating to leave.

By the time they reached the Chief's office the briefing was underway. There were about thirty people in the room. Herrick noticed several members of the Joint Intelligence Committee and one or two people from the COBRA meeting of two days before. The Chief was sitting in the window holding up his hand against the reflection of the sun, which bounced off a convoy of waste barges on the river below.

Guthrie was speaking. He paused for the three new arrivals to find a place to perch, then continued. 'The pattern was set by Fayzi al Haqq, the Pakistani national in Bradford. Al Haqq was armed, but was also in possession of a belt of Semtex. He was arrested before he could use either and is now in Leeds. He will be transferred to London later today. We believe he acquired these weapons only recently, and they must have been passed to him or were moved into his home right under the gaze of RAPTOR surveillance. Clearly the helper cells also served as armourers and scouts for the operation. The seven individuals that came in contact with al Haqq have all been arrested, together with a further six in London who were associated with the Turkish suspect, Mafouz Esmet. He is still in a coma.'

He drew breath and looked over his glasses. 'I am afraid that the surveillance not only missed the preparation that has been going on this past week, but it gave us no hint of the precise nature of these men's deadly intentions. So far it has been determined that three of them were in possession of nerve agents: Nassir Sharif in Stockholm, Lasenne Hadaya in Paris, and Ramzi Zaman in Toulouse, all had fifty millilitres of one of two different agents. Hadaya was equipped with GB – or Sarin – in an aerosol spray; the other two had VX, which is less volatile, but much more potent and long-lasting. We do not yet know how they intended to deploy these nerve agents, partly because all suspects are still suffering from the effects of the disabling darts or injections used to stop them biting into suicide pills. There is much work to be done on their targets and on the lines of supply. To this end, the helpers are being questioned exhaustively.

'So the theme emerging is one of random and varied suicide attacks. The Pakistani in Bradford was clearly going to blow himself up at some public target, as was Hadi Dahhak, the Yemeni suspect in Budapest. One of his helpers had the belt and another was discovered with a very recent batch of Czech Semtex – as you know, it's chemically dated. At some time in the near future these materials would have been brought together.

'But what of the other four men? What did they plan? All were detained last night, but no weapons or means of attack were found in any of the safe houses in Rome, Sarajevo or the two in Copenhagen. They are being taken apart piece by piece, as are the homes of helpers in each city, but nothing has been found. What we do know is that two of the men were planning to travel this coming Friday. The Saudi from Sarajevo had booked himself on a flight to Vienna and the

Syrian in Copenhagen was due to go to Cologne. But we don't know why.' He paused, and let his gaze skate across the room.

Herrick rose so that Guthrie could see her. 'It's obvious that Sarajevo wouldn't be an ideal place for an attack because the population is Muslim.' She stopped, realising she was speaking too loudly. But then the sentence fled from her. She shook her head and waited as the words slowly came into focus. 'Sorry, it's a bit early for me. And . . . and . . . in Copenhagen they had doubled up. So maybe one was flying out to take the place of the man in Stuttgart who died.'

Guthrie gave her an odd look, and there were one or two concerned glances from around the room. Beside her, Lyne discreetly touched her elbow. Then she realised that the hand holding the empty coffee cup had been seized by a violent tremor. She sat down, placed the cup on the floor and gripped her wrist with her other hand.

The Chief cleared his throat. 'Yes, both those thoughts are probably right,' he said quietly. 'But it means they would have to be armed or equipped at their destinations and that seems to break with the pattern. My impression is that the organiser of this plan, likely to be the man we know as Youssef Rahe, took a view that the best way to achieve his ends was to put his chaps in place, then let the helpers service all their needs, including storage of the explosives and nerve agents. They minded each one, took all the burden until the moment arrived when he was required to kill himself. It's slightly different to the set-up of the earlier al-Qaeda cells where they lived together and each man had a defined role.'

The briefing went on for a further fifteen minutes. At the end, the Chief made a small speech about the success of the operation, again congratulating Herrick, Dolph, Sarre and Lapping for the work they had all done. But far from being triumphant about the arrests, Herrick left the room in a sombre mood, not helped by the return of the heaviness in her chest and the ache in her arm.

An hour later, just as she had recovered a little of herself and was able to focus on what Nathan Lyne was telling her about the Haj switch, she received a call from the Chief's office and was asked to hold. She waited, reading the conclusion of Dolph's brilliantly tight description of the switch, which gave the names of four more people who had not shown up in the Heathrow switch or on any watch list.

The Chief came on. 'Isis, I'm going to be direct about this. You're off the case. I believe you're suffering from exhaustion. Christine Selvey will be down in a few minutes. She is going to see to it that you get to a doctor in Upper Sloane Street.'

'But there's still work to do,' she said feebly.

'Not by you. You're prohibited from entering this building until I am satisfied you are fit for work. I don't expect to hear from you for at least two weeks. Is that understood? You have earned the rest. Now take it.'

Selvey was already at the door of her office as she put the phone down.

CHAPTER THIRTY-TWO

A young doctor at the private practice saw her quickly. He was short, with wiry black hair curling over a receding hairline and red blotches either side of his nose. Within a few minutes of Herrick describing her symptoms, he started nodding.

'You're suffering from an anxiety disorder,' he said. There was a slight hiss on the 's' in disorder.

'You mean panic attacks,' she said aggressively.

'Yes. I don't mean to be rude, but judging by your appearance, they're caused by all-round exhaustion – lack of sleep, poor diet, too many stimulants – and of course general pressure. Do you take any exercise?'

'No time.'

'You should make time, and you should certainly look into your diet and eating habits. Do you bolt your food? Eat irregularly? Sleep poorly?'

She nodded to all three.

'And you have a fair degree of unpredictable stress in your life? Do you ever relax?'

She shook her head. She knew this man was SIS-approved and must have seen the odd case of burnt-out spy before. Although the Service was notoriously bad at helping the casualties of the trade, it reacted quickly to any hint of psychological disrepair.

'So, how long is this going to last? What can you give me for it?' As she talked, the heaviness in her chest began to disappear and she breathed more easily.

'Nothing. As soon as you take some rest the symptoms will leave you but in future you'll have to learn to manage your stress levels. I suggest regular physical activity, maybe some abdominal breathing exercises. Perhaps you should consider yoga?'

'Yoga!' she said contemptuously.

He shrugged. 'Look, it's up to you. I can't give you a pill to affect the choices you make. You have an overactive fight and flight response. This releases your body's hormones to enable you to meet a dangerous situation, or flee from it. You're leading your life at such a pitch that your body is unable to distinguish between what is real danger and what is simply pressure. You're constantly on the alert, boiling over with unspent hormones. This is the first episode and there is very little to concern yourself about. It's an amber light, that's all. If I were you, I'd go home, have a sleep and then take some time off. If you don't accept this advice, you will eventually find yourself with more serious problems – possibly a nervous breakdown, alcohol dependency, that sort of thing. You have to look after yourself, you're getting on.'

'I'm in my early thirties!'

'As I said, getting on.'

'Do you have any advice for the short term?' she said sharply.

'If you experience the hyperventilation again, you can stop it by breathing into a paper bag to slow your intake of oxygen. But it's not ideal. It may not give the right impression.'

'I see that,' she said.

She left the surgery with Christine Selvey, whom she found sitting primly in the waiting room reading the *Economist*.

'Everything all right?' asked Selvey pointedly.

'Iron deficiency,' said Herrick. 'A few supplements and some rest and I'll be fine.'

'Good. Then we'll see you in a couple of weeks or so. I hope you don't mind me saying that the Chief was quite emphatic you take the time off.'

They parted, Selvey giving her a last matronly nod.

'Fuck it,' said Herrick, as she made her way up Sloane Street to find a cab.

When she reached home she had no difficulty in falling asleep. She woke at 2.00 p.m. feeling disorientated and vaguely guilty. How the hell was she meant to turn off just like that? She called her father, but found herself being evasive when he asked why she had so much time to talk. He was busy painting – the light was right, the tempera just mixed – and he would prefer to ring her later on. She read the paper and ate some salad with self-conscious restraint, then phoned St Mary's Hospital. Dolph and Lapping were still too poorly to receive visitors, but Harland was sitting up in his room. She asked them to tell him to expect her.

On the drive there, she stopped at Wild at Heart on Westbourne Grove and chose another bunch of flowers. As she waited for the credit card payment to go through, her eyes drifted to the couples sitting outside the cafés along the north side of the street, and she thought that the doctor was right. She really must find a way of taking more time off, having more fun.

It was 3.25 by the time she found Harland's room. He was sitting by an open window, in the shade of half-drawn curtains that lifted into the room on the breeze. One shoulder was bare, but the rest of his torso was wrapped in bandages. He sat forward so as not to risk his back coming in contact with the chair, and winced a greeting at her.

'What happened?' he snapped. 'Why were you out of the office? I phoned you. They said you were on holiday. What's going on, Isis?'

'I felt a little faint in the meeting this morning and suddenly I'm pegged as a borderline neurotic. I was given two weeks' gardening leave. More important, how are you?'

His eyes turned to the floor. 'Shitty. They won't give me any more painkillers.'

'Did you get the things I brought last night?' She was aware they were talking like a married couple, concern somehow metabolising into briskness and formality.

He nodded.

'Don't you have some painkillers in the sponge bag?'

'You're right.' He gestured to the bedside cabinet.

She gave him the bag and knelt down beside him, determined to end the difficulty. 'I don't know how to say this…'

'You don't have to. She wouldn't have hit you. I just put myself in the line of fire. Bloody stupid of me.'

She shook her head. 'That's not what the police say. They say you pushed me out of the way, and I know that to be the case. Please, I want to thank you... I mean, I *am* thanking you ... I'm just not very good at putting it into words.'

'Isis, this doesn't suit you.' He smiled. 'Please get up and tell me what's going on. There are a few hints on the news, but they must be keeping most of it quiet.'

'They've arrested the lot of them, plus Rahe's associate in Bristol. But it was more serious than anyone suspected – nerve agents, suicide bombers. They still don't know what four of them were planning to do. That's as of this morning, when I was last in the loop.'

There was silence. Harland looked at the window. 'I've just had a call from Eva. She said she needed to see me in New York.'

'So it's back on – you and her?' asked Herrick.

'Don't be bloody stupid, Isis.' He paused. 'She told me there had been some activity on a website that had been dormant these past three weeks. It's an important site and before it went down they were gaining useful information from it.'

'You're talking about the thing on Rahe's computer. The encrypted messages in the screensaver?'

'No, this is something they kept to themselves.'

'By *they*, you mean *Ha Mossad Le Teum*,' she said.

'Yes, the dear old Institute for Coordination in Israel,' he said.

At this moment a nurse walked through the open door with Herrick's flowers in a vase. 'I hope you're telling Mr Harland that he's not allowed to use his mobile phone in here. Just because he's darling of the ward doesn't mean he can break all the rules.' She fussed over the flowers and bent down to look into Harland's face.

'I saw a doctor using one ten minutes ago,' he said.

'If you kept to the odd text message, no one would know.'

'I'll bear that in mind,' he said.

Harland swallowed a couple of pills with a gulp of water, then the nurse left with a friendly wink at Herrick.

'The *Institute* had been watching the activities of Sammi Loz for some while,' he said. 'And I know Eva well enough to be certain that she wouldn't leave her dying mother to go to New York unless it was absolutely essential. Second, if she called me about it, she probably needs help. And I'm not exactly in a position to give that help.'

'You say this website has been down for the last three weeks. You're thinking that was the time Loz was with us?'

He nodded.

'What did you tell her?'

'I said you would go, and that you would meet her in the breakfast room of the Algonquin tomorrow morning. That's why I was trying to call you, to tell you to get on a plane.'

'You said I would go to New York to see your ex-mistress! You must be suffering from shock.'

'Well,' he said, his eyes brimming with mischief, 'I imagined you might have thought you owed me. It was cheap of me, I know.'

'And you think what she's got to say is serious?'

'Yes. And I've been thinking about something else. Loz is utterly obsessed with the Empire State building. He goes on about it like it was his second love.'

'His first love being a contest between Khan and himself?'

'I'm serious, he's got a thing about it, and about the meaning of those tall buildings in New York. He picked up a quote from Benjamin Jaidi. After Loz mentioned it I got a copy of E.B. White's *Here is New York*, where it comes from.'

Herrick looked blank.

Harland turned to the window. '"A single flight of planes no bigger than a wedge of geese can quickly end this island fantasy."'

'Well remembered,' she said.

'There's more. "This race – this race between the destroying planes and the struggling Parliament of Man – it sticks in all heads. The city at last perfectly illustrates the universal dilemma and the general solution; this riddle in steel and stone is at once the perfect target and the demonstration of non-violence, of racial brotherhood; this lofty target scraping the skies and meeting the destroying planes halfway, home of all people and all nations, capital of everything, housing the deliberations by which the planes are to be stayed and their errand forestalled."'

Herrick had sat down on the bed. 'That's some prescience. But surely it's about the United Nations building, not the Empire State?'

'True, but this has some meaning for him in a general sense. Look, I don't know if the little bastard is still alive. But if Eva called me, I know it's important. She's agreed to pass on everything she has to you. I told her you were trustworthy and that you were the most natural talent I'd seen since I met your father. That intrigued her.'

'Thanks. But you're forgetting I'm washed up. Besides, I am not that good. I've made a lot of mistakes over the last month.'

'Self pity doesn't suit you.' His tone softened. 'You're not yourself. Who would be, after finding a pair of armed thugs in their house, being on the end of a brace of missiles and watching their friends being shot up? The Chief is only concerned not to lose you. Let's face it, he took the right decision sending you home.' He paused. 'I think you should go to New York. It would be good for you. You can catch the last flight. It's always half-empty.'

'I've never been to New York.'

'Time to lose your virginity then. Hand me my bag.'

He took out the address book. 'That was very thoughtful of you,' he said, waving it at her. 'Look up the number for Frank Ollins. He's with FBI – an awkward sod, but straight and reliable. He was in charge of the Sammi Loz inquiries.' She found the number and copied it down.

He asked her to get his wallet out of the bedside cabinet and then offered her ten hundred-dollar bills. 'You'll need it, and it will save you time. There's a flight at midnight.'

'I can't take it.'

'Why not? You're working for me now, you're my agent, and you're going to be dealing with Eva. That certainly requires payment of some kind.'

'That reminds me of something in Shakespeare. I forget where it's from. My father made me memorise it for obvious reasons. "Friendship is constant in all other things, save in the office and affairs of love. Therefore all hearts in love use their own tongues. Let every eye negotiate for itself, and trust no agent." ' She took the money and put it in her pocket. 'Don't trust me to say what you should be saying yourself.'

'Okay, okay. Now, go catch that plane. You have my mobile number and here's Eva's.' He pulled a card from his wallet and handed it to her. 'Stay in touch. If there's anything important I'll let the Chief know.'

She bent down, kissed his cheek and let her head hang by his so that she looked myopically into his eyes. 'Thanks,' she said. 'I do owe you.'

360

Then she straightened, a hand still lingering on his forearm. 'I'll call you first thing tomorrow.'

She walked from the room without a backward glance.

CHAPTER THIRTY-THREE

The last plane from Heathrow landed at JFK at 2.30 a.m. Herrick slept most of the way, having been given an upgrade by a kindly man on the check-in desk. By the time the cab dropped her at the Algonquin Hotel on 44th Street she was beginning to feel herself again. She slept a further six hours in her modest single room, then got up and hurried to the Rose Room to meet Eva Rath. She ate breakfast, read the *New York Times* and watched agitated New York professionals pick at bowls of fruit and granola. After forty-five minutes she dialled Harland in hospital.

'Your girlfriend's a no-show.'

'Wait a little longer. She may've been delayed.'

'She *did* know I was coming? I mean, you *are* certain you told her?'

'Have you tried the number I gave you?'

'I will. I hope she bloody well answers. Speak to you later.'

She signed the bill and went upstairs to make the call, and consider what she should do if Eva Rath didn't make an appearance. As she sat by a window looking out on an already steamy Midtown, her cell phone rang.

'Hey, Isis, it's Nathan. How're you doing?'

'Fine, really. Totally recovered. Just got up.'

'The big sleep. It's way past three.'

'How can I help you?' she said tartly.

'We know what the four other suspects were doing, or at least we think we do. A vial of mysterious fluid was found in a fridge in Copenhagen, and an empty one in Sarajevo. We think the four may have infected themselves with some kind of disease. None of them has track marks, so we believe they've inhaled it or simply administered it orally.'

'Has it been analysed?'

'The Danes think it's some kind of cold virus. That set off alarms because genetic engineers have used a modified adenovirus as a vehicle to carry messages into the body.'

'What?'

'Sorry, going too fast for you, Isis? Basically, the cold virus is killed by the immune system, leaving whatever is inside the virus to do its work.'

'Another virus?'

'Who knows? We don't really have a handle on that right now, but if these guys are using it we can assume they're treating it as a suicide bomb. So they're all in isolation until we know what the hell they're carrying.'

'And the people who arrested them, are they in quarantine?'

'Sure, all the members of the relevant helper cells, too. The apartments where they lived have been hosed down with every kind of anti-bacterial and anti-viral agent known to man.'

'Tell me about the Haj switch. How many men have you come up with?'

'It's still five, over and above those accounted for.'

'So how many in the picture from Bosnia?'

'Isis, should I be telling you this?'

'Whose desk are you sitting at, Nathan? I want everything you've got. How many people from Bosnia?'

'The French lady is here with Philip Sarre. I talked to her last night. She's hot stuff…'

'What about the photograph?'

'So, we've got the two Rahes and Sammi Loz. Plus there's the American named Larry. We think his second name is Langer, but we're not certain. There is one other in the photo, a Jordanian named Aziz Khalil. Hélène also remembered another man of unknown origin joined the group later. His name was Ajami, but he's not in the shot. She's given us a lot of general material on the Brothers. We're getting a picture of a very tight little group, a prototypical al-Qaeda cell, though the general feeling here is that we are not dealing with al-Qaeda *per se*, but an earlier formation. As you know, a few of these men trained in Afghanistan, but just as many holed up in the tri-border region in South America. North Africa is important and the crucial thing is that the three big civil wars – Lebanon, Bosnia and Algeria – have all contributed to the Brothers' membership. There's a lot of retributive energy in them. That's a strong theme.'

'Has the attack date let out by Sammi Loz been confirmed?'

'Shit, I was forgetting. Yeah, three of them have said it's tomorrow, beginning early in the morning with a suicide bombing of the conventional kind in Hungary.'

'And ending where? In America, later the same day?'

'No, we don't think so. There's been no indication of that.'

'Let's go back to the photo. We've got three faces – three members of the Brothers unaccounted for in the arrests – Larry Langer, Aziz Khalil and Ajami. Do they match with the Haj switch?'

'We think so. But it's difficult. Dolph did all the work on this. He's still in really poor shape.'

'But he hasn't got worse?'

'No, a lot of pain and some internal bleeding. They have it under control.'

She absorbed this. The image of Rahe's wife screaming like a banshee and Harland, Dolph and Lapping sprawling on the floor of Rahe's bookshop, filled her head.

'So, there are two more people in the Haj switch that we don't have pictures for, but have you got any names?'

'These guys change identities like T-shirts. We've got a couple of Arabic names – Latif Latiah, Abdel Fatah – but they don't show up on any watch list. We don't have a clue who they are, where they come from.'

'Are the Saudis helping?'

'Kind of, but there's a lot of resistance to the idea that the pilgrimage would be used in this way. The Saudi government put in security measures during the last Haj to stop any kind of demonstration by fanatics. They're saying the switch just didn't happen.'

'Right, they watched nearly three million people, all dressed identically in white, for a full five days and can definitely say what each one of them was doing?'

'Yeah, well...'

'There's a really good case for threatening to release Dolph's research on this. Has anyone thought of twisting their arm a bit?'

'We've already threatened. But they're not playing. Look, I've got to go.'

'Hold on, I have a couple more questions.'

At that moment a fire truck, horns blaring, passed along 44th Street under her window. Herrick blocked one ear.

'Holy shit!' said Lyne when the noise had died. 'That kind of proximity to a fire truck means you could only be in Manhattan. What the hell are you doing?'

She reached for the packet of Camels she'd bought at Heathrow and lit up. 'Okay, so I am in New York, but it's where I should be.'

'For chrissake Isis, you should be taking time out. You looked like shit yesterday.'

'Thanks, but to answer the question at the back of your suspicious corporate mind, I am perfectly okay, utterly sane. Besides, you've only to look at the evidence to see this is the place to be. We know Rahe was here as recently as last week; we know he hired a car for three days – what for? – and we know that this entire network has been funded by money made on the New York property market. Rahe had a whole different existence here as Zachariah. Besides these things, there's a website which was dormant during the period Loz was out of New York but has now started up again. What could be clearer?'

'Hold on there, gal. What website? What're you talking about?'

'Harland has a line in on Mossad – Eva, his ex. She was meant to meet me here with information about a site they've been monitoring. I suspect that is where the confirmation came from about the assassination attempt on Norquist, though I don't have any hard evidence.'

'You're losing me.'

'Sorry, *I'm* going too fast for *you*. Look, there were two sources of information on the Norquist hit. One came through the encrypted screensaver that we had access to through Rahe. The other one has never been explained properly, but I'd put money on it that this is where it came from.'

'That's all history. Do you know what the website is?'

'No idea. Bloody Eva didn't make the breakfast meeting.'

'So what are you going to do?'

'Phone her, then start looking into Rahe and Loz's lives here. You can help by getting the Chief to release to me all SIS research on the property dealings.'

'That means I have to tell him where you are.'

'But you were going to do that anyway.'

'Stop being such a ball-breaker. I am trying to help here.'

'Right, get me that stuff and send it to isish1232004 at Yahoo. Don't encrypt it. That's like a flag to the NSA, and anyway I don't have any of the programs on my personal laptop. Just serve it up as it comes.'

'Teckman is likely to want to put your people in New York onto this.'

'That's fine.' She stubbed the cigarette out. 'Now call me whenever you get something.'

She hung up. This was okay, she thought, she could do this. As long as she wasn't expected to go to meetings and watch the hours tick away, there wouldn't be a problem. She flipped open the phone again, dialled Eva's number and got the message service. 'I don't know where the hell you are,' she said. 'But I'm waiting at the Algonquin to meet you.' She left her own number and rang off.

She ordered coffee from room service and then started setting up her Apple laptop, fitting it with a US phone adapter. By the time the coffee arrived she had typed a list of what she needed to do, half-admitting to herself that she was shooting in the dark. The first item simply read Ollins. She dialled the number Harland had given her, and within a couple of rings an alert voice answered. 'Ollins here, please state your business.'

Herrick explained that Harland had told her to call.

'Yeah, I already heard from the sonofabitch. Last time I talked with Harland he was helping a fugitive from justice, as it happens, a man whom we knew to be a terrorist. I don't know how things are in your country, Ms Herrick, but in mine that's not a good place to start when you are asking a favour.'

She waited a moment before replying. 'Did Harland tell you he was in hospital with gunshot wounds? Did he tell you that he was shot by the wife of the suspect Youssef Rahe, Sammi Loz's principal European contact, who was in New York last week using the identity of David

Zachariah?' She had guessed right. All this was new to Ollins. Now she had his attention.

'No, he didn't mention it. You say Youssef Rahe was here?'

'Right. He drew money and he used a rented car. We requested information from the FBI on this yesterday and got nothing. We really need to know where he went.'

She gave him the details of the car rental, then told him there were five other men thought to be part of the network in Europe. She could hear him making notes. 'Your people should know most of this. I know it's being shared.'

He grunted. Evidently it hadn't reached him. 'Okay, Ms Herrick, what do you need from me?'

'Two things. I want to go to the Stuyvesant Empire Bank on 5th Avenue and talk to them about the account David Zachariah used. I need you to be with me because otherwise I won't get access. Second, I want to get into Sammi Loz's rooms in the Empire State building.'

'You know Sammi Loz was one of the men killed in Egypt? There was a definite ID of his remains.'

'I was there, and I can tell you there was no proof.'

This seemed to impress Ollins and he gave another of his grunts. 'Look, about the bank, Ms Herrick. I can't make it until this afternoon. I'll meet you there at three-thirty, quarter of four. I'll call ahead. We'll see about the Empire State later.'

She gave her number and told him she was wearing a dark blue T-shirt and a beige linen jacket.

She left the hotel with a little tourist map and turned right to walk the hundred or so yards to 6th Avenue. On reaching Sixth she became aware of the enormous scale of Midtown, which she hadn't at all appreciated during the cab ride in from the airport during the middle of the night. Then the compressed, thunderstorm heat of Manhattan hit her. She walked south to Bryant Park, where she drew iced tea through a straw and tried Eva again but without success. Then she made her way along 42nd Street to 5th Avenue. Passing the New York Public Library she glanced up at the couples sitting on the steps, fanning themselves in the sluggish air like a theatre audience.

It took nearly an hour of tramping up and down 5th to locate the

Stuyvesant Empire Bank, which turned out to be just half a dozen blocks from 34th Street. Its frontage was so nondescript that she passed it several times. All the while the Empire State building loomed imperious and Germanic in a strange apricot light that escaped from behind the massive cloud formations to the south and west.

Just six blocks away, she thought. Less than ten minutes' walk. Rahe must have visited the Empire State the previous week. This gave her an idea. She called Lyne from the street and asked him to send pictures of Rahe and the suspects in the Bosnia photograph to her email address. She also asked for a picture of Sammi Loz.

She began to retrace her steps to the hotel while going over the details of the pictures. Lyne tried to interrupt several times, eventually saying, 'Isis, you're not listening.'

'Sorry, go ahead.'

'We've got some good information on Larry Langer. He comes from a Connecticut family. They're rich people, originally in the garment industry, who moved out of New York. Langer was a delinquent kid – a real nut. Disappeared to Bosnia for five years and returned briefly to the States in ninety-nine after wandering the globe, saying he was a Muslim. That didn't please his family because they're Jewish. They haven't heard of him since. But they have reasonably fresh pictures, and these are being released worldwide tonight, together with the Bosnia photograph of Aziz Khalil. They didn't want to do it, but now they totally buy the idea that there may be five guys still out there.'

'Send one of Langer to me.'

'You got it.'

'What about Latif Latiah, Abdel Fatah and Ajami?'

'Nothing.'

'And you've circulated all the agencies with the information. What about Mossad?'

'I couldn't tell you about that. But I guess someone has talked to them.'

'So what are you doing now?'

'Nothing much. Waiting, I guess, and working through the night. Oh, I nearly forgot, I had a call from Dolph. He's doing fine now. So's Joe Lapping.'

Seeing the tourist map tucked under her arm, a beggar in ragged shorts and T-shirt had started to bother Herrick, singing her praises in extravagant terms. 'Honey, just let me drink your bathwater,' he shouted.

Herrick spun round. 'Will you fucking well leave me alone you creep.'

'I hear you're getting into the ways of the city,' said Lyne, when she returned the phone to her ear. It was then that her eyes caught sight of a familiar walk way off down 5th. A man holding some ice-cream cones, moving through the crowds just like Foyzi had in Cairo. Then he disappeared from sight.

'Are you there, Isis? What's up?'

'Nothing. I thought I saw someone I recognised.'

'Look, why don't you get a little rest? You're doing everything you can. Oh, one other thing. I told the Chief I heard from you.'

'I knew you would – you're a bloody boy scout…'

'He agreed I could send it, but he's awful sore you're not at home watering the roses, or whatever you English girls do when you're relaxing.'

'Leave it out, Nathan.'

'Well, it's good to have it official, anyway,' he said. 'Besides, you do need to rest. Go lie down for chrissakes, or you'll be thinking you know everyone in New York.'

She hung up and made her way back to the hotel, where she took a shower and lay naked in the cool sanctuary of her room for about an hour, getting up once to try Eva again and download her email.

She arrived at the bank at exactly 3.30 to find a dapper figure dressed in a black lightweight suit marching up and down the sidewalk, talking on his cell. She pulled her passport from her shoulder bag and put it under his nose. He nodded, but continued to speak. At length he hung up and put out his hand.

'Special Agent Ollins, pleased to meet you. Your guy, Youssef Rahe, made a trip up to the Canadian border last Wednesday. We got a payment at a gas station.'

'But we know he didn't use the Zachariah cards.'

'Exactly. He paid in the name of Youssef Rahe. Maybe he made a slip or something. Anyways, we can place him at a gas station outside Concord, New Hampshire, last Wednesday at 11 p.m. That's just eighty-five miles from the border. What you think he was doing there?'

'Picking up someone.'

'Right. That's the only reason he would go up there. The attendant remembers him because of the Arabic name. He says the car was headed north and there was a passenger inside. Who might that be?'

She lifted her shoulders.

Ollins brushed the top of his close-cropped blond hair with the flat of his palm, apparently absorbing Herrick for the first time. 'Okay, let's see these people,' he said, jerking his thumb at the bank.

They were shown into a room, where three bank executives were nervously ranged along a table. Herrick withdrew her laptop from her bag and switched it on. 'Gentlemen,' said Ollins. 'We need your help, and fast. Miss Herrick is from England and she's working with us on a counter-terrorist operation. She has something to say to you and some questions to ask. We would appreciate it if you'd do everything in your power to help her.'

Ignoring the throbbing pain in her arm, Isis began to speak slowly, breathing as calmly as she could. 'You are aware that we've already made inquiries about account 312456787/2, held in the name of David Zachariah. And we're grateful for your service. First of all, I want you to confirm that the picture I am going to show you is of the man you knew as Zachariah.' She spun the laptop round on the table.

The three executives leaned forward, two of them reaching in their pockets for reading glasses. They exchanged looks, then one said, 'That is Mr Zachariah, yes.'

'Now I'm going to show you some of Mr Zachariah's associates.' She turned the laptop back to her and clicked on the icon for the Bosnia picture. 'This is not too clear, but I want you to look at it very carefully and see if you recognise anyone.'

Again they huddled round the laptop and squinted at the image. 'Maybe it would help if you emailed us this picture and we had it enlarged and printed out,' suggested one.

All this took five or six minutes and eventually a secretary appeared with the copies of the Bosnia photograph, as well as the new Langer picture, which Herrick intercepted and placed face down on the table. As they looked again, she ran through the names she had in her notepad – Larry Langer, Aziz Khalil, Ajami, Latif Latiah and Abdel Fatah.

'We believe all these men are still at large. We are particularly interested in Langer.' She turned over the study of Langer, a haunted-looking man in his thirties with sunken eyes and a beard, smiling ruefully at the camera. 'This man appears in the other picture before you.'

'Langer, Langer,' said one of the executives.

'His people were in the rag trade – the garment industry. It's close to here, isn't it?'

'Yes, we have had dealings with the family.' He swivelled to a terminal by the wall and turned it on. For some time he worked through the files. 'Yes,' he said, pushing himself back so the others could see. 'Lawrence Joseph Langer. Date of birth, 1969. He had a checking account with us for twelve years, though it was inactive for long periods.'

'Can you look up Zachariah's records and see if there are any transactions between the accounts?' asked Ollins.

'No problem,' said the man, printing off the file on Langer.

After a few moments he spoke again. 'It seems that Mr Langer was in receipt of money from Zachariah on several occasions. But more significant, perhaps, is that Mr Langer also provided a reference when Mr Zachariah set up his account here in the late nineties.'

Ollins had the printout of the Langer account on the table and was going over it with a pen in his hand. He ringed several items.

'Look at this,' he said, pointing Herrick to a line which read, 'Account holder's address: Room 6410, 350 5th Avenue, New York, NY 10118… Dr Loz's rooms.'

Over the next hour they turned up two more secrets from the records of Stuyvesant Empire. A search of the name Langer-Ajami produced a business account that had remained at the bank for just eighteen months before being transferred to Lebanon. This stirred the memory of one bank official, a solicitous man with silver hair and a gold pin that pinched his shirt collar together under the tie knot. He said he now remembered interviewing Langer about a carpet import business that was going to sell Turkish rugs and matting in outlets along the east coast.

Another suggestion from Herrick unearthed dealings between accounts held at a bank in Bayswater, London, in the name of the Yaqub Furnishing Company and Yaqub Employment Agency. Herrick explained that these were almost certainly Rahe's accounts. It was noted that for a period of two years, money had flowed from a real estate company called Drew Al Mahdi to the Yaqub concerns in England. Herrick pointed out that Al Mahdi roughly translated as 'rightly guided one' and that this was a phrase used by the Shi'ite community. The bankers all shrugged and said they weren't familiar with the different sects of Islam, or for that matter Arabic.

By five, Ollins had heard enough. 'You gentlemen will keep this bank open until we have been over every account here. Is that understood? Because what you have here is nothing less than the funding of a terrorist organisation with your bank at the centre.' He scooped up all the printouts and copies of photographs and asked for an envelope to put them in. Before leaving, Herrick emailed all the pictures to Ollins at his office so he would have them in electronic form when he returned.

Outside, Ollins made his dispositions on his cell phone, ordering three colleagues into the bank immediately and redeploying others in the Bureau's state headquarters down at Federal Plaza.

'You got to understand, this happened on my watch,' he said to Herrick with a pained expression. 'You know, we've been doing every goddam thing in this city – twenty-four-hour monitoring of suspects' phone calls, email and internet usage. We've monitored their credit card spending, their bank accounts. We pay attention to the people they talk to in the street, what newspapers they read, what their neighbours say. I'm telling you, there's nothing we haven't covered in the lives of hundreds of individuals. And then we miss this, for chrissake!'

'We did too,' Herrick managed to say, though she was now very short of breath. 'All the effort was concentrated in Europe.' All she could now think of was the sense of impending panic that had swamped her in the last few minutes of the meeting. 'Could we have a drink somewhere? I'm suffering a little from jet lag and a month or so of this bloody case.'

'I'm sorry, I don't have the time,' said Ollins automatically, then he seemed to notice something was wrong. 'Hey, sure I do. There's a bar a couple of blocks away. We'll get you something to drink. Maybe something to eat, too.' He took her elbow and led her downtown to O'Henry's Tavern on 38th Street. Above them the sky had darkened into a premature dusk and as they walked big drops of rain began to spatter the sidewalk. There was a pause followed by a sudden rattle of hail on car roofs. Herrick glanced up at the Empire State before they left 5th Avenue and saw lights beginning to dot its massive flanks.

In the bar, she put her hands over her mouth, trying to control the intake of oxygen.

Ollins looked at her, now genuinely concerned. 'I know what you got. I had it myself a couple of years back.' She looked at him doubtfully from behind her hands. 'You got a panic attack,' he said. 'You want to know a breathing exercise?' He didn't wait for an answer. 'Close your eyes. Shut off one nostril and breathe in on the count of four, hold it for twelve with both nostrils closed, then let it out on a count of eight through the nostril you closed at the beginning. Okay?'

She began the exercise forlornly while Ollins ordered a scotch and a Diet Coke. When the drinks arrived she opened her eyes.

'Keep going,' he said, smiling. 'Do ten rounds. Then I'll let you talk.'

At length the symptoms began to disappear, although her arms felt weighed down and her legs were still like jelly. She took a sip of the Scotch, shook her head and slapped her cheeks.

'Listen,' said Ollins, 'I know what it's like. Our line of work, you never relax, you don't sleep nights, you eat shit and wind up a friggin' nutcase.'

She nodded as Ollins ran through the connections they had made. At length, she found the energy to press her case on the Empire State.

Ollins hesitated. 'Sure, why the hell not? What is it exactly you want to see? I mean, we've been over the place so many times I lost count, and when we heard Loz had died we sealed the place up.'

'You never know what's to be found. I've learnt that in this last month. Every wall has something behind it.'

The barman gave them an umbrella someone had left and they ran through the rain, hugging the buildings for shelter. The temperature had fallen dramatically and along the way there were still dirty drifts of hailstones. When they got to the Empire State Ollins pushed past the crowd of tourists lining up to ride eighty-six storeys to the observatory. A security guard intoned, 'Electric storm. Observation deck closed. Inside viewing area only!'

Inside the lobby, Ollins shook hands with the guards behind the desk and exchanged some words about a Mets signing that day. Then they took the elevator to the sixty-fourth floor. Ollins brushed his hair and flicked droplets of water from his clothes.

'I gotta tell you,' he said, 'I can only be ten to fifteen minutes maximum. I have to get back to the office for a meeting.'

She murmured her understanding and thanked him. The doors opened. Ollins turned left and hurried along a corridor on the north side of the building, the light fabric of his suit flapping as his legs worked. There was no one about, and she heard not so much as a voice or telephone bell from behind the doors they passed. 'Most of these offices are waiting to be leased,' he said, gesturing left and right with a flick of his hand. 'They're too big or too small or there's not enough light. Things are tight with the downturn. And this building always feels the draught first. You know it was built just after the crash?'

They came to a door with a plate that read Dr Sammi Loz DO FAAO. Ollins took out a pocket-knife from his belt and selected a small pair of pliers. He cut a wire loop that ran from the handle to a stud on the door jamb. From it hung a notice: FBI LINE – DO NOT CROSS. He turned two keys in the door, pushed and ushered her in. Herrick found herself in a cool, spotlessly clean waiting area with a couch, several chairs and a reception desk.

'What happened to his receptionist? Did you interview her?' she asked.

'Yes, but she wasn't any help.'

'Did she know anything about the other part of his life? The deals in Tribeca done by the Twelver Real Estate Corporation, or for that matter Drew Al Mahdi?'

He shook his head. 'We didn't know about any of that when we talked to her, but my guess is she didn't. She's your normal single mother from the Bronx. Good-looking, but no college professor.'

'Can I talk to her?'

'Yeah. Maybe tomorrow.'

Herrick went through to the consulting rooms. She pushed at a bathroom door and changing room, both of which could be accessed from the reception area, and returned to the room where Loz obviously worked. There was an expensive chair and a maple veneer table, a light box, framed diagrams of human anatomy on the wall and plastic models of the different joints lined up on a shelf. A withered plant stood in the window and some bathroom scales nearby were covered in dust, but otherwise the place looked as if Loz had left half an hour before. She took her mobile from her bag and dialled Harland, ignoring the fact that it was past 11 p.m. in London.

'I am standing in Loz's consulting room,' she said without any preliminaries. 'Everything looks normal.'

'Describe it to me,' he said.

She went through everything she could see and ended by saying, 'There's nothing here. And by the way, Eva didn't appear or call.'

Harland cursed, but she couldn't hear him because Ollins was saying he really had to leave. 'Hold on a moment would you? Frank Ollins is here and would like a word.'

Ollins took the phone. 'I hear you got shot up, buddy. That explains why you sent a woman over to do your work. Get better. I want to see those wrists cuffed when you come back to New York.' He handed it back to her.

Harland said. 'The bed! Isis, you didn't mention the treatment bed in his room. There was a really sophisticated adjustable bed. Levers all over the place.'

'Well, there isn't one.'

'That's odd. There has to be.' said Harland. 'What about the Arabic inscription on the wall, the one that says something about a man who is noble doesn't pretend to be noble.'

'There's nothing of that sort, no.'

'This could be important,' said Harland. 'Find out if Ollins has removed anything and call me back.'

Ollins shook his head. 'There was nothing to take, Everything that was here *is* here.'

'What about the treatment bed in the consulting room?'

Ollins shrugged. 'I don't know about that but I can't delay my meeting because a goddam bed's missing.'

'And the computer, is that working? It might be worth going through it.'

'I have to go,' he said.

'But I can stay and bring the keys back to you later? Federal Plaza, right? Look, I have helped you, haven't I? I'm at the Algonquin. You have my number. I'm not going to steal anything.'

He thought for a moment. 'Okay, but have them back to me by morning. And call me on the cell when you leave this evening. I'll tell the guards in the lobby.'

With that he bade her goodbye and hurried through the door, letting it swing shut behind him.

Herrick walked to the window and looked down through the rain at the traffic crawling along 5th, aware of the unearthly solitude and detachment of the building. It rose above things, she thought, literally and metaphorically. She felt the weight of its presence.

Now utterly calm, she turned on the computer and for half an hour or so went through Loz's appointments diary, making notes. She spotted the initials RN, and concluded this was Ralph Norquist because of Loz's visit to RN on May 13. She also found BJ – Benjamin Jaidi.

There was still water in the cooler. She took a cup and wandered round the room gazing absently out of the window again. Her back was to the door when she heard a noise. She whipped round. The handle was moving. Then, improbably, someone knocked, and opened the door.

CHAPTER THIRTY-FOUR

She knew instantly that the woman standing in the doorway was Eva Rath.

'Miss Herrick?'

'Why bother to ask? You know who I am. You've been following me all day.'

The woman gave her a formal smile and approached with her hand outstretched. Herrick declined to take it and instead lit a cigarette.

'Isn't there some kind of no-smoking policy in the building?' said Eva.

Herrick shrugged. 'What do you want? There's nothing to interest Mossad here. The FBI have been over this place a dozen times.'

'Then why are you here?'

Herrick thought for a moment. 'Because I'm interested to see where Loz worked. I want to know what this is about.'

'That is simple. It is about hatred and revenge.'

'Revenge for what, exactly?'

'The failure of the Muslim world – the failure to build a functioning state in Palestine, the failed jihad in Bosnia, the failure to retain Afghanistan, the defeat in Iraq. Take your pick. There's no shortage of causes. They have to assert themselves and terrorism is the only way they can do it.'

Herrick noticed that the trace of Eastern Europe in her voice clashed with her impeccable grasp of English idiom. 'Well, they might have had a better chance in Palestine if you hadn't wiped out all the moderate politicians.'

Eva smiled again. 'And the computer, what are you looking for?'

'The site you told Harland about on the phone. That's why I'm in New York.'

'It will not be on *this* computer,' she said imperiously.

'What exactly is the site? We're surely not still talking about the encrypted screensaver on Youssef Rahe's computer in London?'

'No, no. That was used to deceive you, although we didn't know that at the time either.'

'But it predicted the hit on Norquist?'

'Which was used to distract you.'

'Did the confirmation about the Norquist hit appear on this other site?'

'Yes.'

'Then who told us about it? We had two sources saying he was going to be hit.'

'It's simple. I told Walter Vigo by phone from Heathrow, while waiting for Admiral Norquist to arrive.'

'You *know* Walter Vigo?'

'Yes, I thought Harland must have told you our history. I helped him with a problem in the East some years ago. Vigo was my SIS handler.'

It was another story, an age ago, and anyway Vigo was finally out of the picture. Or was he? That clumsy approach in the bar a couple of days before came to Herrick's mind – the strange, almost plangent appeal, so completely out of character.

'And now he's working for you – right?' she said. 'The Mossad has contact with Vigo's company, Mercator? That's why he tried to get me to give him the stuff from the bookshop in London.' She slapped her forehead. 'Of course, Vigo had me followed from the bookshop and then you trail me around town here. You people are really plugged into this case, aren't you? Did you know about the suspects in Europe all along? Was Vigo keeping you in the loop the whole way through RAPTOR?'

Eva shrugged.

'So one way or another,' Herrick continued, 'it was the old alliance. America, Britain and Israel were working on RAPTOR even though the first two had no idea they were sharing with you people.'

'We don't have time for this,' said Eva.

'Let's get this straight,' Herrick said venomously. 'This is my investigation and I do have time for it.' She paused. 'As I understand it, the significant point about the website you've been monitoring is that it started up again after three weeks of inactivity?'

'Yes. That is true.'

'And you believe it's being run from New York?'

'But not from these rooms,' said Eva. She placed her shoulder bag on the reception desk and swept Herrick with a look of appraisal. 'Harland said you were the most natural talent he'd ever seen.'

Herrick ignored this. 'The site started up again last week when Rahe was here in New York. So he could well have had something to do with it?'

'Maybe,' she said.

'The trouble is that we've never worked out who was running this thing,' said Herrick. 'We thought it was Rahe, but if you look at the money trail it must have been Loz calling the shots.'

'Maybe both,' said Eva. 'Can I have one of your cigarettes?'

Isis handed her the crush-proof packet. Eva coaxed one out by tapping it on her palm and lit it with an oblong gold lighter. Then she walked to the window to look at the lightning illuminating the clouds on the northern horizon.

'Did you know this building is hit five hundred times a year by lightning?'

Herrick couldn't help but admire the woman's self-possession, the absence of the need to explain or to excuse herself. She returned to the computer. 'I guess that's why Loz liked it,' she said.

Eva turned. 'Outside the bank, you looked sick. What was the problem?'

'You were watching me then?'

'Of course.'

'Why? Why didn't you just make yourself known? You could have joined in at the bank.'

'I wanted to see what you would do.' She stopped and tipped her ash into the waste-paper basket. 'I admit... I was also interested in you. Are you Bobby's girlfriend?'

Herrick turned from the screen. 'I don't do this, okay?'

'So you are?'

Herrick shook her head. 'I'm really not going to talk about it.'

'But you were ill. There was something wrong. I saw you.'

'There was nothing wrong. I was tired. I needed to eat. I do now, in fact.'

Eva revolved her bracelet on her wrist. 'What are you doing? Let me see.' She came to stand at Herrick's shoulder. 'Let's look into the computer's history.'

She pulled the keyboard towards her and began to work, eyes flicking from her hands to the screen. Then she straightened and stood back, allowing Herrick to see a list of web addresses. There was almost nothing for the last six months, but in November and December of the previous year someone had visited the official UN website and sites concerned with Palestine, Bosnia, Afghanistan, Iraq and Lebanon. Herrick began to write down the pattern of research on a piece of Sammi Loz's headed notepaper. She scrolled down the list of sites visited in the last three years, noting down about twenty of them.

'Why're you taking these notes?' said Eva.

'Force of habit,' Isis replied. As she said it, her eyes drifted to the address printed at the bottom of the notepaper. She read it several times, then got up and walked to the door. 'This is 6420,' she called out. 'This office is 6420!'

'Yes,' said Eva. 'It's still listed in the lobby as Loz's place.'

'No, you don't understand! In the bank this afternoon there was a document in which the Empire State was given as the address of the account holder – an American named Larry Langer who was a member of the Rahe-Loz group in Bosnia – the Brothers. We assumed he'd given Loz's address for the account records. But he didn't. He gave 6410 – not 6420. That means they could have another space on this floor.'

'Well, let's go and take a look,' said Eva, picking up her bag.

The storm had moved closer and the windows and polished floors flickered with lightning. But in the corridor, as they checked the office numbers, there was only the sound of their footsteps and the feathery exhalation of the air-conditioning. As they rounded a bend into one of the main corridors on the northern side, the lift bell pinged and they heard the doors open. Both instinctively withdrew into the corridor they had just searched. Herrick noticed Eva's eyes, straining to interpret the new presence on the deserted sixty-fourth floor.

They waited. A pair of heavily booted feet were approaching them – the solid, purposeful walk of a man, but a man who didn't know the floor well. They heard him pause three times to look at the door numbers.

Eva peered round the corner. 'It's okay,' she whispered, 'I think he's a messenger looking for an office.' Then she called out. 'Can I help you?'

'No, I'm doing fine,' came the reply. Herrick didn't need to see the man to know who it was. He was just a few paces away now and there was nowhere she could possibly hide. She stepped out to join Eva.

The clothes were the same: a scarf was wound loosely round his neck; the faded khaki shirt looked in need of pressing and the blue jeans were sagging and creased. His only concession to the city was an unstructured dark blue jacket.

'This is Lance Gibbons of the CIA,' Herrick said in answer to an inquiring look in Eva's eyes. 'We met in Albania. Mr Gibbons is a great believer in the value of the "extraordinary renditions" that come from torture victims.'

'Cut the crap, Isis. You know I was right about Khan.'

'It hardly matters now,' snapped Herrick. 'What are you doing here?'

'I'd ask you the same question, but I wouldn't get a straight answer,' said Gibbons.

'We were looking over Dr Loz's offices with the permission of the FBI,' said Eva coolly. 'Are you here for the same purpose?'

'Mam, last time I saw this piece of work,' he said, jabbing his finger an inch away from Herrick's chest, 'a fucking towel-head A-rab was about to stick a needle in my arm, which meant I didn't know shit from sawdust for three days and nights.'

'You deserved it,' said Herrick, moving off in the direction of the lifts. 'You didn't see what your friends had done to Khan. I did. It was disgusting.'

'So what *are* you doing here?' Eva asked Gibbons.

'Looking for someone.'

'Who?'

'None of your goddam business.'

'Maybe we can help each other,' said Eva. 'Which office do you want?'

Gibbons said he didn't have a number.

By now, Herrick was by a small corridor which ran from the main aisle to the south of the building. She looked up and saw a sign pointing to 6410.

'Got it,' she called out. At the far end they found the door. Herrick bent down and put her ear to it. There was no sound. Gibbons moved her aside with the back of his hand and put a card into the crack by the lock but after a minute of working had failed to open the door. He stepped back and hit the door twice with his boot just by the lock. There was still no joy. Then he moved to the other side of the corridor and prepared to launch himself at the door but was stopped in his tracks by a voice coming from the northern aisle.

'Hey, you there! What in hell's name d'you think you're doing?'

The silhouette of a uniformed guard had appeared against the pulses of lightning. Herrick saw the outline of the gun, then the silencer fitted to the end of its barrel. But it was the rolling, lopsided walk of the man approaching in the gloom that made her feel as though she was seeing a ghost, for the second time that day. Before she could see his face the man said, 'Big lorry jump all over little car.'

It was Foyzi.

Herrick struggled to understand what was going on, but Gibbons evidently had no such problem. 'This is the little cocksucker I've been tailing since Egypt.'

Foyzi's rubber-soled boots squeaked the final paces to the light, and his face came into view.

'I saw you in the street buying ice-creams,' she said stupidly.

Foyzi made a little bow to her. 'Tenacious as ever, Miss Herrick.' The New York accent had been dropped in favour of an almost Wodehousian English. 'I always find opening a door is more easily achieved with the appropriate keys, don't you?' He felt in the top pocket of his uniform. 'Here we are,' he said, flourishing them. 'Now, ladies, step aside and I will open the door for us all.' He waved the gun in a small arc in front of them.

'Mr Gibbons, perhaps you would like to lead the way.'

Inside Foyzi hit a switch and fluorescent light flickered behind five or six panels in the ceiling. They walked into an unfurnished, L-shaped space with a reception desk tucked into the angle. Everything but the steel-grey carpet was white. 'Welcome to sixty-four ten,' said Foyzi, prodding Gibbons in the back with the gun. 'If you would move to the furthest door, I'll introduce you to your hosts.' Then he seemed to change his mind. 'But of course, I'm forgetting the convention that CIA people never go anywhere without a gun.' He patted down Gibbons, conjured an automatic from the back of his waistband and put it in his pocket. 'How *did* security allow you into the building with *that*?' he said with distaste. 'And ladies, would you empty your purses over there.'

Herrick's Apple Powerbook slipped noiselessly onto the desk, but not her phone, which remained in her pocket. Foyzi murmured something and set it aside, then began to sift Eva's belongings, first examining her mobile phone, then a US passport and a piece of folded notepaper. He held it up to her.

'It's a medical prescription for my mother. She has cancer – her name is Rath.'

'In Hebrew,' said Foyzi, and placed the note in his top pocket.

He went to the door at the end, opened it and beckoned them to go through. Herrick saw a room mostly lit by candles. There was a smell of incense on the air and a faint sound of music – the Sufi chant Herrick had heard on the island.

Sammi Loz was bent at the centre of the room, working at his treatment. Karim Khan lay on the bed, wearing only a loin cloth.

Loz put his hand to his lips. 'We will speak quietly. Karim is asleep.' His hands returned to Khan's leg. 'We expected you two women, but not this person. Who is this, Foyzi?'

'The man who had Khan tortured,' said Foyzi. 'He followed me here.'

'That is interesting,' said Loz. He let Khan's foot down and stepped away from the bed. 'We found that it was best to travel with Karim sedated. It has certainly helped his recovery, but he will no doubt wake in a short while, and then I think it will be good for him to meet the man responsible for his torture. It will be a pleasing symmetry, for him to see his persecutor killed. Now tell me who this is,' he said, moving to Eva. 'A nice erect posture and a firm, well-exercised figure.'

Eva returned his look with an absolute lack of fear and said nothing. Herrick absorbed Loz. He had started a beard, which gave a pronounced hook to his chin and he seemed to be thinner. The wild look she had seen in his eyes on the island had been replaced with what she thought was a rather self-satisfied calm.

He waved a remote at the CD player to silence the music. 'Isis, who is this woman?'

'I don't know. She was trying to help me find this place. You should let her go. She has nothing to do with this.'

Foyzi handed him the passport and a piece of paper. Loz read out the name Raffaella Klein.

'She's an Israeli,' said Foyzi.

Loz dropped the passport and paper and brushed his hands on his white shift, then adjusted the little white hat that signified he had undertaken the pilgrimage to Mecca during Haj. 'She has everything to do with you, Isis. You see, we watch the comings and goings in my room.' He pointed to a monitor sitting on a pile of telephone directories. The screen was divided between a view of the consulting room and one of the reception desks. They had watched everything for the last hour or so.

'I wish now that I had asked Foyzi to install microphones also. But then we didn't know we'd have such interesting visitors.' He looked at Herrick sharply. 'Why did you come here?'

'How did you get off the island?' she shot back.

Loz placed his palm in the air as if holding a serving plate. 'Foyzi helped us. I hired him on that last night on the island. British Intelligence was paying Mr Foyzi only a little money. I could pay a lot more. It's as simple as that. It was Foyzi who gave me the idea of placing the bodies of the men he lost to suggest that we had all perished in the missile attack. It worked well, did it not? And then we were able to travel to Morocco and to Canada with very little trouble.'

'To be picked up on the Canadian border by Youssef Rahe – the Poet?' said Herrick.

'Yahya. His name was Yahya al-Zaruhn. There was no one his equal. No one! And now he is dead, killed by British spies.'

'Police actually,' said Herrick. 'But let's not forget that Rahe had a

384

man tortured and killed to make it look as though he had died. That's hardly heroic.'

'A traitor,' said Loz. 'A filthy Jewish spy.'

Herrick sensed Eva stiffen and realised that she must have known the man they were talking about. The Mossad had certainly been wired into the Rahe-Loz network from an early stage.

'Sit down,' he shrieked suddenly.

Foyzi waved the gun and they all sank to the floor. Herrick and Eva leaned against the wall while Gibbons sat upright with his legs crossed in front of him. Loz returned to Khan and began to stroke the backs of his legs. He seemed to have resolved to concentrate on the treatment, and for nearly an hour said nothing to them. Herrick let her eyes wander the room. Near the windows there was a bowl filled with candles, the flames shuddering in the draught from the window, and some dirty plates with the remains of a meal. Propped on the table was the Arabic inscription mentioned by Harland. There were also some books, a copy of the Koran and other texts. One, entitled *Hadith Literature and the Sayings of the Prophet*, was lodged in the seat of an elaborate new wheelchair that had evidently been purchased for Khan.

The three of them exchanged glances, but each time anything meaningful seemed to pass between them, Foyzi stirred himself from Herrick's computer and gestured at them with the gun. At length, Loz stretched upwards, cracked his knuckles and moved away from Khan's side towards the windows.

'How long are you going to keep us here?' asked Herrick.

'Not now, please,' he said. He seemed to be entranced by the passage of the storm, which had swept round to the south and was creating an astonishing display over the ocean.

Eventually, Herrick could stand it no longer and started to translate the framed inscription. ' "A man who is noble does not pretend to be noble, any more than an eloquent man feigns eloquence. When a man exaggerates his qualities it is because of something lacking in himself". ' She paused. 'Why does that mean so much to you?'

Loz did not turn round. 'Because they were the first words spoken to me by Yahya, in the middle of a gunfight in Bosnia. Can you imagine that sort of presence of mind? Later, he gave me that to remind me of the friendship that was born in the moment all those years ago.'

'But what about the last part of the quote?' asked Herrick. She turned and read, '"Pride is ugly. It is worse than cruelty, which is the worst of all sins." Hasn't it occurred to you that the action you and Yahya planned in Europe for tomorrow constituted the very worst kind of cruelty – the killing and maiming of innocent men and women. The suffering is almost too great to imagine.'

He got up slowly and straightened his robe. 'We are always like this,' he said to Foyzi, as though explaining an old and cranky friendship.

'Like what?' she said. 'Last time we laid eyes on each other you were trying to rape me. Tell Foyzi what you were doing in that bath-house when the missiles struck. I'm sure he has no idea you were attempting that.'

He moved across the room as quickly as a cat, seized her by the hair and banged her head rapidly against the wall five or six times. 'Dirty white bitch lies,' he said, still holding her hair. Suddenly Herrick was in the police interrogation room in Germany, where she was hurt in exactly the same way during the Intelligence Officers' training course. Later, she had decided that it was being screamed at that she couldn't stand, and so it was now.

Eva placed her hand on her shoulder and Gibbons threw her a look of sympathy. She prayed they realised she was pushing Loz for a reason.

'That hurt,' she said. 'Why do you take such pleasure in hurting women? Is it because you fear them?'

Loz returned to Khan. 'I do not, but sometimes it is necessary.'

'No, the truth is you're a psychopath who thinks that because you heal people you are morally excused when it comes to hurting and killing. I suppose it's a kind of God complex. The great Dr Loz dispensing kindness and random acts of cruelty and slaughter, with all the capricious will of God Almighty. I had heard of doctors playing God before, but I never dreamed I'd live to see one who actually thinks he's God.'

Loz's hands stopped moving and his gaze sought Foyzi's. 'Listen to that woman,' he said despairingly. 'It reminds you of every mother.' Foyzi nodded and opened Isis's Apple.

'Is that your problem?' she said. 'Is that why you're such a fucking psychological freak? A mother problem?'

His head turned to her and he lifted his upper lip to display a row of perfect white teeth, and picked at something in his mouth. 'I have none of those problems. I am merely doing what must be done.'

'But you're not – all the men have been caught. Hadi Dahhak, Nasir Sharif, Ajami, Abdel Fatah, Lasenne Hadaya, Latif Latiah.' She included names of people they knew had been to the Haj but had not been arrested. 'Those men who were going to spread disease, and murder with explosives and poison, they're all in jail.'

'She's clever, no?' Loz said to Foyzi. 'She thinks we do not know which ones are still at liberty. She thinks she can trick us. She is in love with trickery, this girl. But she doesn't know how many soldiers we have in the field. She has no idea, which is why she comes snooping in the Empire State building. She comes to my building and pokes around with her friends.'

Foyzi nodded and walked over to the bed with the open laptop. Herrick caught a glimpse of the Bosnia picture.

'This is very impressive,' said Loz. 'Where did you get this from?'

'A British photographer.'

'Yahya… Larry… myself. The Brothers. I must certainly have a copy.'

'You can get one in the papers tomorrow.'

He nodded, lost in the memory invoked by the photograph. Gibbons glanced at Herrick and raised his eyebrows.

'We all look so young,' continued Loz. 'A decade adds much care to a man's face.' He looked down. Khan had begun to stir. He had moved his feet, and Herrick could see they were still swollen. 'We have visitors, old friend, and they have brought us a gift which reminds us who we really are and what we stand for. Sit up and see what she has found for us. Providence has blessed us at an important moment.'

Khan pushed himself up on one arm. When he saw Isis he showed signs of recognition and, to her astonishment, a hint of a smile played at the corner of his mouth.

At that moment there was a thunderclap right above the building. The lights dimmed, the glass in the windows rattled and Herrick felt a tremor shoot down the wall. The next time it happened she was sure

Gibbons would try to make a move. She had felt him flinch and get ready, but then restrain himself.

Khan lay back on the bed. Loz took the computer to the window and began to read the emails she had received from Nathan Lyne that day. Herrick understood they would delineate exactly what SIS didn't know about the Brothers, and cursed herself for breaking the most basic security rule. When he had finished, he examined the prescription found by Foyzi in Eva's things.

'Again Providence has smiled on us,' Loz said to the room. 'We have an English spy, an American spy and, if I am not mistaken, an Israeli spy at our mercy. Perhaps we should kill each one as a symbolic sacrifice to Islam and put it on the internet. That would be a fine conclusion to the life of the website, a finale to beat. Foyzi, do you think you can find a webcam at this time of night?'

Foyzi nodded obligingly, but Loz's eyes had gone to Khan, who was shaking his head.

'You think that's such a bad idea, Karim? But of course, I didn't tell you who this American is. This is the man who had you tortured. Don't you recognise the American pig?'

Khan raised his head and nodded. 'Yes, he was in Albania. It is the same man. But he also gave me water. And he was not the one to torture me. It was the Arabs.'

Loz shouted and jerked the gun at Gibbons. 'Stand up. I shall kill him now. Or do you want to do it?'

Again Khan demurred.

'Why do you see everything in these terms?' pleaded Herrick. 'Arabs against Jews; Americans against Arabs. Karim just said it. It was Arabs who were prepared to torture a fellow Muslim, and worse, they did it for money.'

The intervention had worked. Loz walked off, and Gibbons let himself down on the floor again. Herrick understood why he took the risk of doing so without asking.

'Look at the United Nations.' Loz was evidently pointing to the UN building over on the East Side, although none of them could see it. 'The people in that building are responsible for the death of Muslims everywhere – in Bosnia, Afghanistan, Palestine and Iraq. That building is the source of the evil because it is run by the Americans, the Jews and the British. You three are the United Nations. Not us. You. So you are our enemy.'

'Does your plan include an attack on the UN?' asked Herrick.

Loz flashed her an appreciative smile. 'You're very smart, Isis. I told you that we were made for each other.'

She nodded. 'I should have guessed why you made so much of your contact with Benjamin Jaidi. You were staring your enemy in the eyes. What's that quote about the riddle of steel and stone?'

Loz held his head back and stared at the rain. 'It goes like this. "This riddle of steel and stone is at once the perfect target and the perfect demonstration of non-violence, of racial brother-hood, this lofty target scraping the skies and meeting the planes halfway, home of all people and all nations, capital of everything, housing the deliberations by which the planes are to be stayed and their errands forestalled." Secretary General Jaidi likes that quotation but *not* for the reason I do. If you think about it, there is not one true statement in that quotation. It is all lies. Racial brotherhood... try being an Arab or an African. Home of all people and all nations... capital of everything... None of it is true. The only time the delibera-tions stopped the planes flying was in Bosnia when Muslims were being killed by Serbs as the West stood by. That's when the United Nations stands back.'

'Actually, I agree with most of what you say,' said Herrick.

'That's because you are an intelligent woman,' said Loz. 'And you understand in your heart that that place cannot go on. Things must be changed from the outside. It is full of corruption. It is owned by you and the Jews and the Americans. You run it as though it is your back yard. How many times do you think the Americans have vetoed Secu-rity Council resolutions against Israel?'

Herrick shrugged and said she didn't know.

'Of course you do not because you do not notice these things. But we Arabs count. The answer is thirty-four times in the last three decades. What chance do the Palestinians have with that record?'

'Are you using planes?' she said calmly.

'We are soldiers, we fight on the ground.'

'So guns and explosives – bombs?'

'No, Isis, I do not tell you. You will see soon enough. You will see everything from here, and you will hear about the other things we plan. Patience, little girl.'

Harland had used up most of his illicit supply of painkillers and was now feeling distinctly seedy. His sister Harriet was keeping him company through his sleepless nights by reading to him from the diary of Samuel Pepys, which she insisted had the right combination of titillation and longueurs. She'd told him she would leave as soon as he dropped off, but that didn't look like happening soon because Harland couldn't get used to the sensation of sleeping on his front, especially now the painkillers had upset his stomach.

'Hold on one moment,' he said to Harriet.

She smiled radiantly. 'What, darling?'

'I think I should check on someone. Haven't heard from her since this afternoon.' He eased himself from the bed, swung his legs to the floor, then groped for the phone secreted in his sponge-bag. He dialled Herrick and waited. The phone rang ten times before she answered.

'How are you?' he asked.

'Fine,' she replied.

'What are you doing?'

'Staring at the rain. There's a big storm here.'

'Are you okay?'

'Sure. I had a nice glass of wine with Ollins in the bar. He's a real charmer. Now I'm back in the hotel room with a bottle of red and a book. It's great. I couldn't be happier, nor more relaxed.'

'Isis, are you all right?'

'Sure, I'm just a bit sleepy. Early start tomorrow. Got to hang up now.'

'Isis? Isis?'

She had gone.

'Something's wrong,' he said, looking at Harriet. 'I mean, this is a woman who makes you look straight-laced and dowdy. She is utterly driven. Doesn't sleep until she's attacked a problem a thousand different ways. I've never seen anyone like her before – not in my former line of work, anyway.'

'You sound smitten,' said Harriet.

390

Harland brushed this aside. 'The point is that everything she said was untrue. For instance, she said she had been to a bar with Ollins. She said he was charming. Whatever his merits, Special Agent Ollins is not charming. In the circumstances, it is utterly unlike her to curl up with a book and a bottle of red wine. So it follows that when she said she couldn't be happier or more relaxed she meant she was exactly the opposite. She has to be in some kind of trouble.'

Harriet saw he was serious. 'What're you going to do?'

'I'll phone Teckman, then try Ollins.'

Standing in the centre of the room, Herrick lowered the phone and deliberately pressed the button to end the call that Loz, with some pleasure, had insisted she take while he pressed Foyzi's gun to her neck.

'That was good, Isis. You're quite the actress.' Loz laid an arm across her shoulder and gave the gun back to Foyzi. 'Another time and another place, we would have been a sublime match. As the Prophet said, "to taste each other's little honey." '

She looked into his eyes and saw an oscillation in his pupils and what she decided was a profound and insane puzzlement. 'Do you know what you're doing? I mean, do you have any real understanding of other people's pain?'

'Of course I do. Look at Karim. I have done everything that a man could do for his friend. I have cleaned and mended his body, lavished my skill on his injuries. That is an understanding of pain and it is proof of the debt I owed him.'

'What makes Karim different from the people you're going to kill tomorrow? When Langer explodes his bomb or Ajami spreads the poison that infects the bodies of children and pregnant women, or Aziz Khalil coughs out his germs, they will in all probability kill people who have a much greater capacity for good than you, Karim or I have. Why is Karim to be saved and those people destroyed?'

Loz looked mildly unsettled. 'I do not have to answer to you.'

'But you do,' she said vehemently, chopping the air with one hand. The other slipped the open phone into her pocket. 'I was the one who saved Karim Khan, not you. I risked my career to stop this man being tortured. If you don't believe me, ask Gibbons. He knows what I did.

He knows I risked my father's life to free Khan and place him in your hands.' Her hand went to her pocket and pressed a button at the right-hand corner of the keypad. 'You owe me an explanation and you have a duty to yourself to reconcile these things in your head – hatred and love of humanity. Because the love you profess for Karim and Yahya is mere egotism unless you recognise that the part of them you love is the human part, the thing we all have in common.'

Loz wagged his finger. 'If I spent any time with you I would go mad from these arguments of yours.'

'It is not me that drives you mad,' she said sadly, 'it is reason.' She stopped and, raising her voice, asked, 'What good do you think will come of blowing up the UN building tomorrow? What do Langer and Khalil and Ajami and Latiah and Fatah think they're doing? Sure, they're going to kill an awful lot of people at the UN, but what good will that do? The world will look at Islam and say Muslims cannot be trusted. You will achieve nothing but the exclusion and revilement of your own people.'

Foyzi had moved round Herrick as she was speaking. Without warning, his hand dived into her pocket and pulled out the cell phone. He showed it to Loz and pointed at the number displayed on the screen. Loz looked at her furiously, took the phone and threw it against the floor, where Foyzi crushed it under his boot. Then Loz whistled round and caught her on the side of her face with the flat of his hand. Again and again he hit her until she crumpled to the floor. Finally he took the automatic from Foyzi and beat the back of her head and neck with it.

Harland had picked up the phone on the first ring and immediately signalled to Harriet to give him a pen and paper. Then, as he listened, he wrote the number of a direct line in Vauxhall Cross and frantically whirled his index finger in the air to tell her to dial it on the hospital phone.

Harriet's call was answered and she nodded to her brother. Cupping his hand over his phone, he hissed, 'Tell them Herrick is with Loz in New York. Tell them he's alive. She's left the phone on so I can hear.'

Instead of relaying this information immediately, Harriet said to the operator, 'Put me through to Sir Robin Teckman and tell him to hold for a very important call from Robert Harland. Say those exact words to him. Mr Harland will be with you shortly. This is a matter of national security.'

Harland's hand moved across the paper and he managed to write 'UN – tomorrow – bomb (?) Langer, Khalil, Ajami, Latiah.' He missed the last name and waited. But suddenly the line seemed to be over-whelmed by static, and then she was gone. He gave the cell phone to Harriet and took the hospital phone from her lap. 'See if you can hear any more… Hello? Hello?'

'Yes,' said the duty officer at Vauxhall Cross.

'I need to speak to the Chief.'

'I'm afraid that's not possible.'

'This is a national security emergency. Get me Sir Robin. Tell him it's Robert Harland.' He gave an old identification code that he remembered from fourteen years before.

'Just putting you through.'

After a couple of minutes the Chief came on the line. 'Bobby, what can I do for you?'

'Herrick's in New York. She's with Loz. He's alive. She kept her phone on and I heard a conversation that seemed to suggest they're going to blow up the UN tomorrow.'

'Where is she exactly?'

'I've no idea. But I just had a very odd, coded conversation with her when I called her a few minutes ago. I believe she saw a friend of mine from the FBI named Ollins, who was investigating the Loz case. She had a drink with him, so I would imagine he knows where she was going after that.'

'Then get on to your friend.'

'I tried after talking to her. His phone is off and I don't have his home number.'

'Then ring the bloody FBI in New York.'

'Yes.'

'I'll send someone round to St Mary's to be with you in case you get another call. Let me know what Ollins says and I'll start cranking up things our end. If you need to call me again, tell the operator you're ringing on a Code Orange matter. They won't mess about if you say that.' He hung up.

Harland called international directory inquiries on Harriet's cell phone, got the number of the FBI in Manhattan, and found an equally unhelpful operator on the other side of the Atlantic. 'This is very important,' he said. 'My name is Robert Harland. I am ringing from Secret Intelligence Service headquarters in London and I need you to trace Special Agent Ollins and get him to the phone. Do you understand?'

'I am sorry, sir,' said the woman at the other end. 'I cannot do that at this time.'

'What's your name?'

'I am not at liberty to tell you, sir.'

'Let me just say this to you then. Ollins is in possession of information that may avert a terrorist attack in New York tomorrow. He may not know what he has. If you wish to keep your job beyond tomorrow afternoon, I suggest you get the Special Agent to the phone. I'll wait here until you do that.'

The line went dead for what seemed a period of endless deliberation. Eventually a man's voice came on the phone. 'With whom am I speaking?' he asked.

Harland gave his name. 'I need to speak to Special Agent Ollins on a very important matter. The British government will be in touch with the US government in the next hour, but if you get Ollins for me we might just be able to short-circuit the system and avert disaster. It's up to you. I hope for everyone's sake you make the right decision.'

From the floor, Herrick could see Eva's face, but not Gibbons'. She briefly wondered why neither had attempted to help her, but then reflected that they were both professionals and were likely to be playing a longer game, keeping themselves in reserve.

She raised her head slowly, giving the impression that she was more stunned than she actually was, and indicated to Foyzi that she would like to return to her place against the wall. Foyzi waved the gun with irritation. She crawled towards Eva and Gibbons and pushed herself up alongside them. Eva darted her a look that said, 'wait'; Gibbons stared unblinkingly ahead.

Something had come to pass while she had been collapsed on the floor, too shocked and beaten to have taken much in. Loz had wheeled the bed next to the window, and was engaged in a heated exchange with Khan, although none of them could hear what was being said. Each time Khan spoke he lifted his head from the bed, the muscles in his neck strained, and his wiry legs twitched towards the floor. He was trying to get up to confront Loz on equal terms, but Loz wouldn't let him, and interrupted by pressing down on his chest, leaning into his face to rebuke him.

Herrick slid down the wall a fraction so she could see Khan's mouth under Loz's elbow. When his head popped up again she had no difficulty in lip-reading what he said. 'I don't question your judgement, Sammi. But it was wrong to hit her. You have too much violence in you and I...'

He was again forced down, and this time Loz's hand moved nearer his neck.

Eva spoke very quietly to Foyzi. 'My people know of you. You're a freelance. You're not committed to this madness. My government will pay you five times what he has given you.'

He shook his head. 'A deal is a deal.'

'It wasn't on the island,' Herrick snapped.

Loz turned with one hand still restraining Khan. 'Shoot them if they talk. Shoot them...'

The rest of the sentence was obliterated by a crack of lightning overhead. The Empire State was tapping the storm and drawing its power to earth. The lights flickered again and then went out completely. Gibbons hurled himself at Foyzi. Eva went to the right, rolling and springing to her feet like a gymnast to deliver several ferocious kicks to Foyzi's upper body, just as he loosed off three rapid close-range shots at Gibbons. The gun dropped from his hand with the final kick. Herrick dived for it and came to her feet, aiming at Loz, who had not moved from his position near the window. She glanced left and right. Gibbons was hit; Foyzi lay dead from stab wounds from a knife still in Gibbons' hand.

Nathan Lyne ran panting to Harland's room after being driven across London in an unmarked Special Branch police car that topped 100 mph on the flat of Park Lane.

Harland had put the phone down on Ollins a few minutes before.

'She's in the Empire State,' he said, turning to his address book. 'The FBI man left her in Loz's old office. She's there by herself. I'm calling a friend who was due to meet her.'

Nathan took the hospital phone and spoke on the open line to Vauxhall Cross. 'You got all that?' he said. 'What floor?'

'Sixty-fourth,' said Harland, hearing the first rings on Eva's phone.

Eva heard her phone ringing out in reception and prayed it would be her headquarters in Tel Aviv. She ran out and picked it up, together with the gun that Foyzi had taken from Gibbons.

'Yes?' she barked, turning back to the room.

'It's Bobby. Where are you?'

'The Empire State.'

'Isis kept her phone on. We heard something. Is Loz alive? What the hell's happening?'

Eva went back into the room, where Herrick was on one knee beside Gibbons. 'It's okay,' she said between breaths, 'we disarmed them. Your friend is here. She's got Loz and Khan covered.'

Harland began to speak, but Eva lowered the phone because Gibbons was saying something. His voice was a whisper. 'If you say where we are, every fucking jackass cop will be here. We don't have time for that. We don't know what these men have planned. We can't let them be arrested.'

'You're losing blood,' said Herrick. 'You need to get to a hospital.'

'Forget that,' said Gibbons. 'Just get these bastards talking.'

Harland told Lyne what he'd just heard on Eva's phone. 'They're with another man – an American. They seemed to have overpowered Loz. This man has been hit, I think. He's insisting they don't get help until they've found out what Loz was planning.'

Lyne frowned. 'What the heck are they doing?' He stopped and met Harland's eyes, then spoke to Vauxhall Cross. 'The situation is under control. Tell the FBI to hold off. This is very important.'

Eva put her phone on the table, went over to Loz and placed Gibbons's gun at his temple. At the same moment, Herrick seized the end of the bed and wheeled it away from them.

The two women said nothing to each other. The situation was beyond words.

Herrick looked down into Khan's eyes and murmured, 'I'm sorry. I have to do this.' Without thinking any more, she raised Foyzi's gun, and brought the silencer and barrel down on Khan's still-bloated right foot. He shrieked. She looked up at Loz. 'Tell us the plan. Tell us where your men are. How many of them?'

Loz shook his head in disbelief. 'You cannot do this.'

'Hurt him again,' said Gibbons from the floor.

Herrick aimed and struck again. Although she pulled the blow at the last moment, the scream lasted much longer and died only when Khan had run out of breath. She paused. Her hand slipped to Khan's side and momentarily snatched at his hand and squeezed it. The pressure was returned.

Now Eva worked on Loz. 'We've only just started. We will cause your friend unimaginable pain. Are there five men or more? Where are they? Stop his suffering.'

Loz hung his head and then shook it.

Eva nodded at Herrick, who hit Khan again.

Gibbons had dragged himself from the floor. Holding his stomach with both hands, he lurched to where the food and the candles were by the window, picked up a plastic bag, then made his way to Herrick and handed it to her. Then he threw himself across Khan's body, pinning him to the bed. Herrick looked down at Khan and wrapped the bag over his head.

'No!' shouted Loz. 'I will tell you.'

Eva stepped back and reached for the phone. 'Can you hear this, Bobby?'

Harland told her he could.

'Tell us what the plan is. Then we'll let your friend breathe.'

'There are six,' mumbled Loz. 'Three in New York. Two in London. One in Holland.'

Eva repeated this to the phone.

Khan's legs were trembling and jerking in the air, as though he was suffering a seizure.

'Let him breathe,' pleaded Loz.

'What's your plan?' Eva screamed. 'What's your goddam plan?' She hit him on the ear with the gun.

He shook his head again.

Herrick was now aware of Gibbons whispering to her. He was pointing to the TV monitor on the floor. 'The cops are in the other room,' he hissed. She glanced down and saw the figures darting across both halves of the split screen. She held the bag tighter round Khan's head. His right hand weakly tore at Gibbons's back. The other flailed in the air near Herrick. His legs stopped moving.

Eva stepped back from Loz. 'Tell us and you'll save him.'

'They are martyrs. Martyrs with explosive. You understand! Martyrs! You cannot stop martyrs who give their lives to the struggle!'

'Suicide bombers with Semtex, men spreading disease and toxic agents?'

He did nothing and she repeated the question, screaming in his ear. He nodded. 'Yes.'

'When're they going to attack?'

'They have passes for two o'clock.'

'American or European time?'

Khan had now stopped moving completely.

'Please! Let him breathe!' Eva signalled to Herrick, who pulled the bag from Khan's head.

'American time – after the other attacks.'

'There aren't going to be any other attacks. Who are these men?'

'You know some of their names,' said Loz. 'I will tell you everything if you let Khan live.'

He gave them the names, haltingly, as if he couldn't quite remember, but soon they had six names, only three of which Herrick recognised. He repeated them slowly again while Eva held the phone to his mouth. Langer, Khalil, Al-Ayssid, Ajami Hossein, Mahmud Buktar and Iliyas Shar. One American, three Arabs and two Pakistanis. He told them the men's details. Their phone numbers and addresses were on a laptop by the table, which none of them had noticed before. Everything was there, including his last message to the martyrs.

Herrick looked down at her victim and nodded to him. Only she and Khan knew that she'd punctured the bag with her fingernails before wrapping it around his head. Despite the ferocious assault on his feet, he had gone along with her and play-acted his suffocation. She bent down, stroked his hair and kissed him on the forehead. Her other hand went to Gibbons's shoulder.

Loz saw all this. He looked perplexed for a moment, then seemed to understand. 'The goddess Isis used the essence of Ra to defeat him,' he said. 'That is what you did to me. You used my essence – my love for Karim – to defeat me.'

Herrick heard this but was too concerned about Gibbons' condition to reply. She tore to the reception area and bellowed into the corridor. Within seconds, the place filled with members of the SWAT team they'd seen on the CCTV. They pressed field dressings to Gibbons' wounds and then four of them picked him up and rushed to the elevator bank. Ollins, who had come in behind the men, crouched down by Loz.

'How much information have you got from him?' he asked Eva quietly.

'He's told us there are six men, three to attack the UN building here, two in London and one in Holland.'

'Where in London? The UN offices?'

Loz's eyes had come to rest on the patterned rug a few feet away. 'This has been my prayer mat since I was a small boy. It has been with me all these years.' He smiled to himself. 'It's the only thing I have left.'

'Forget the self-pitying shit,' said Ollins. He took hold of Loz's jaw and banged his head upwards against the wall. 'Where in London? Where in Holland? How are they going to make these attacks at the United Nations?'

'He can't speak if you're going to hold him like that,' said Eva.

Ollins let go and Herrick took over. 'You've got men at the Hague. Is that right? The War Crimes court, the Chemical Weapons Inspectorate – which part of the UN in Holland?'

'You will not find these men.' Loz worked his jaw from side to side as though recovering from Ollins' assault, paused and turned to Herrick, his eyes locking onto hers with the strange, wild look she had seen on the island. He bit into something, winced and opened his mouth to reveal foaming saliva. Herrick grabbed his shoulders, more out of desperation than any hope of saving him. Then, with only the smallest convulsion, the cyanide capsule silently took his life. His head lolled sideways and a little stream of dribble ran from his mouth onto his chest.

Ollins swore and thumped the floor. Herrick sat back, shocked.

'Is he gone?' They turned to see Khan, his head raised from the bed. 'Is he dead?'

'Yes,' said Eva.

Khan's head sank back.

'He killed himself because of the failure,' said Eva. 'He killed himself because he'd told us everything.'

'What makes you so damned certain?' asked Ollins.

'Because this man lived to outwit people. Once he knew he was beaten there was no point in living. If anything was still going to happen, he surely would have waited until at least the end of tomorrow to see the realisation of his plans.'

Herrick stood up and looked over to Khan. 'Are there any more surprises for us, Karim?'

'Yes,' he said at length. 'The man called Langer.'

'Larry Langer?'

'Yes. Langer is waiting to kill the Secretary General. Jaidi got him a job at Sammi's request six months ago. He has a pass that allows him anywhere in the building. He is waiting there now for Jaidi to meet the Israeli Ambassador to the United Nations for breakfast in his office.' He stopped and looked up at Herrick. 'If you bring me that computer, I will show you the other plans.' His hand flopped out towards the laptop. 'You see, Sammi told me everything because he trusted me. But you saved me, Isis Herrick, and now I will help you.'

Twenty-one days after that night in the Empire State building, Isis sat down for dinner with her father and Harland – effectively three generations of British Intelligence officers, as Munroe pointed out – at a pub in the Western Highlands. There were still several hours of daylight left, but they'd been forced to abandon fishing on the loch nearby because clouds of midges had risen when the wind dropped, making it impossible for them to concentrate. She glanced at Harland's face, already covered with tiny red blotches from midge bites, but he still looked jubilant. An hour before, he had caught his first sea trout from the old wooden rowing boat they were using. It was a big specimen, weighing just under five pounds, which had snatched at the fly as he dragged it across a ripple on the water, then fought for its life for a full twenty minutes before being landed.

They had said little to each other during the day and now there was silence between them. Without warning, her father rose to his feet in the empty dining room and held his tumbler of whisky up to her and then to Harland.

'This is to you two,' he said. 'And to the most remarkable intelligence operation of the last two decades.'

Harland smiled and, when Munroe sat down, raised his own glass to Isis. 'It was your success.'

She couldn't agree with them. She shook her head and stared down at the table mat.

'What is it?' her father asked. 'Come along, spit it out.'

'I hurt Khan… real pain… deliberately inflicted to get the information. That's torture, whichever way you look at it.'

'Yes, but even Khan understood why you had to do it,' Harland told her. 'Without it, those men would have caused havoc with their bombs and poisons and diseases. It was an operational necessity. You took the only course open to you in the circumstances. I know. I heard it all through Eva's phone.'

'Yes, but I did it without thinking. That's how these things happen – you slip into them without realising the threshold you've crossed. I'm no different from The Doctor, or Gibbons for that matter.'

'That's the world we live in,' said Munroe gently.

'But it shouldn't be,' she replied, turning to her father. 'If we are to stand for anything, we have to preserve our standards and morals whatever the price. The only way we can argue for our system and beliefs is if we are utterly rigorous with ourselves as well as other people. We have to make sacrifices not to become like the other side.'

Her father looked at Harland, who spoke. 'It's a matter of weighing the lesser of two evils. You were there and you had to make a decision. Besides, Khan went along with it. As a result he will soon be a free man, and can rebuild his life. That's all you need to take from this.'

'The question is, would I have done it anyway – without his

cooperation?' She paused and put her hand up to her father who was about to interrupt. 'And the answer is yes, I would.'

Munroe tapped his daughter on the hand. 'Enough of this,' he said. 'Now, let's think about what we're going to order so we can get back on the water as soon as possible. The conditions are perfect and there's a bit of a breeze coming up.'

Herrick looked out over the slate grey loch but her mind was still in the Empire State.